Hazard doesn't try to kick the gambling habit. He feeds it. By seeking out any escapade that takes him across the grain of society. By becoming a free-lance intelligence agent. By using his extraordinary gift of near-total recall. He even gambles with his life when he begins a personal vendetta against his brother's killers.

Hazard has his own unorthodox weapons: the prize of his armoury is Keven, his gorgeous mistress. Together they are engaged in a top-secret government-sponsored telepathy experiment, and Hazard can transmit key messages to Keven through sheer mental power—but Keven gets more from Hazard than just long-distance *mental* thrusts . . .

Crammed with tension, sexual intrigue, action and menace, this explosive thriller includes a classic chase from Connecticut to London, from the Riviera to the Great Pyramid, as Hazard and Keven are drawn into the lethal nerve centre of a global, vicious plot by Arab extremists who plan to annihilate Israel in a 'six-hour war'.

Gerald Browne

Hazard

Panther

Granada Publishing Limited
Published in 1976 by Panther Books Ltd
Frogmore, St Albans, Herts AL2 2NF

First published in Great Britain by Hart-Davis,
MacGibbon Ltd 1974
Copyright © 1973 by Pulse Productions Inc
Lines from 'It Was a Good Time' (Rosy's Theme)
from the MGM film *Ryan's Daughter* reprinted
by permission of Leo Feist Inc
Made and printed in Great Britain by
Richard Clay (The Chaucer Press) Ltd
Bungay, Suffolk
Set in Monotype Times

1

THE TRAIN.

Its starting point was ten miles northeast of Denver, a base known as the Rocky Mountain Arsenal. From there it headed east.

It was eleven cars. Eight flatbeds followed by two sleepers and a messcar. The rear sleeper was for the officers. A colonel, a captain, a first lieutenant, and two second lieutenants. Only five, so the officers had room to spare. Thirty-eight enlisted men were cramped into the other sleeper, and the mess car was also for them. The officers' meals were carried back to their private compartments.

None of the men or officers wore shoulder flashes or any sort of insignias, making it impossible to know what unit or branch of the army they represented. All such identification had been ordered removed. The train itself was just as anonymous. It was, however, obviously an army train, recently painted the official olive drab right down to its wheels. Even the elongated diesel engine, a General Motors DD–40 with six thousand horsepower, had all its serial numbers painted over.

The enlisted men especially had looked forward to the duty the train involved. The danger of it, according to their way of thinking, was offset by the relieving change it offered; a trip east with the reward of a short leave at destination. But soon after they were underway the men became irritated by the perpetual noise and motion. The close quarters irritated them. They felt trapped and they griped about not getting enough consecutive hours of sleep because they had to do watches of four-on, four-off. Orders were that two men be posted at all times on each of the flatbeds, one man forward and another aft of each section of the cargo. The forward posts were better because the men positioned there had partial protection from the wind and could stand with their backs to it.

This circumstance provided the duty sergeant with something to hold over the men. It wasn't much but over the miles it became significant, and some of the men who weren't already in the sergeant's favour played up to him, hoping to be assigned one of those forward posts. The sergeant wasn't fair about it but no one expected him to be.

Four-on, four-off, day and night the men stood their duty with automatic rifles slung over their shoulders and their heads scrunched down into their windbreakers, thinking as little as possible about the cargo they were guarding and helping deliver. Frequently they cursed it just for being there.

The cargo was concealed completely by heavy black plastic tarpaulins well secured all around. The long humpish shapes of it, identical on every flatbed, offered no meaningful suggestion of content, shape, form. To hold the cargo steady in place, steel cables were looped tightly over the tarpaulins and attached on both sides to the bodies of the flatbeds. Steel uprights prevented the cargo from shifting. It had taken six days to load the train after four months' planning and making the special fittings. There could be no mishap.

Making certain of that, the train was preceded by an advance unit. Another DD–40 engine ran exactly three miles ahead. It was equipped with an electronic device that scanned the tracks for any discrepancy. The advance engine also gauged the curves electronically and by remote control regulated the speed of the main train, keeping it well under the safe limit. If an accident was unavoidable, it would happen only to the advance engine. The main train would stop automatically.

But for no reason other than an emergency would the train stop. It had first priority, absolute right of way. No waiting for switches to be pulled, no slowing to accommodate other rail traffic. The route the train took was not as direct as it could have been. It circumvented cities such as Wichita, Tulsa, Little Rock, Birmingham, Atlanta. At times it was headed north and at other times south as it made its way eastward.

Those people along the route who happened to notice the train paid it some special attention only because it was an army train. No reason, however, to feel any apprehension about it. Actually, many who saw it from small-town station platforms or at crossings or from the rear windows of houses silently appreciated the reassurance it represented. It momentarily reminded them that they were not so abstractly protected. No one thought much more than that about it.

Except a man in Oakley, Kansas.

And a man in Lonake, Arkansas.

Another in Heflin, Alabama.

And another in Blackville, North Carolina.

Each of these four men observed the train passing with the same intense interest. Each, like the train, was apparently just passing through. But it was not coincidence that all four, though hundreds of miles apart, were much alike in appearance. Hair black, complexions swarthy, eyes dark. Each appraised the train coolly, watched it until it was out of sight, then went to the nearest public telephone and placed a long-distance call to the same number. Area code 212, number 249–4131. No hellos and they didn't identify themselves. Each spoke only five words. The same cryptic five.

'*Ana fi el tariq*' – I am on the way.

An hour after dawn on the third day of its journey the train approached the outskirts of Charleston, South Carolina. Again it avoided the city proper. Through a series of complicated switchings from one track to another it was routed around to the United States Naval Depot.

Inside the depot it rolled on to pier 4, where it stopped alongside a navy cargo ship, AKA 35. Immediately a contingent of marines formed a guarding line around the train. They were deployed no more than a dozen feet apart. The army men who had accompanied the train still had to stand their positions on the flatbeds while the specialists began on the cargo.

They worked on one section at a time, unbolting the steel cables, pulling them off, over, and away. They did it methodically, were not at all careless about it. Then the heavy black tarpaulins were removed.

The cargo appeared to be nothing more than rectangular blocks of concrete about twenty feet long by four feet wide. Each block of concrete had a serial number stencilled on it in red. For example: USAAC—RMA–3–72–1783–OD–5. Also, each block was bound by a pair of one-inch-thick steel bands. On the top surface beneath each steel band the concrete was recessed. For handling.

A one-hundred-ton crane would do the job. Its special dual cable was lowered to the first of the cargo. Specialists hooked

11

and locked the ends of the cables to the steel bands of a concrete block. The connections were checked and rechecked. Then a powerful green light flashed to the crane operator. There would be no trusting hand or verbal signals.

The crane gradually put tension on its cables. Slowly the concrete block was raised free of the flatbed. It was hoisted up a hundred and fifty feet and swung smoothly over the side of the AKA. Every man's eyes followed it as it was lowered to disappear into the hold of the ship.

The transferring of the entire cargo took two and a half days, working in shifts nonstop. The men bitched a lot to take the edge off and there were the usual volleys of competitive obscenities between the sailors, soldiers, and marines.

The task could have been done in less time, had the cargo been something more predictable and not so dangerous, such as nuclear warheads.

2

HAZARD HELD the shot glass of Stolikvaya vodka four or so inches above his glass of draught beer. He'd already downed a third of the beer so it wouldn't overflow. The vodka was properly ice cold. Hazard dropped it into the beer, shot glass and all. It was a minor ritual that he enjoyed, partly because such an unorthodox combination and this unusual way of mixing it made most people cringe.

'That's my excuse,' said Hazard, watching the disturbed beer foam up.

'He worries,' said Carl.

'He'll do that anyway,' said Hazard. 'My going up there won't make any difference.'

'You ever call him?'

'Sometimes,' lied Hazard.

'Wouldn't hurt you to call.'

'That's your opinion.'

They were at the bar in the Sign of the Dove. The front windows of the place were propped open because it was April and the start of nice weather. Hazard could see out to Third Avenue, five-thirty traffic and people passing. His view was limited by the window that cut the people off from the neck up and the thighs down, so he was watching only torsos. His imagination invented pretty faces and good legs for the girls when their bodies appeared deserving.

Carl told him: 'Disliking that town isn't a viable excuse.'

'That's this year's word, isn't it? Viable. Who sets the style for the way you guys talk? Kissinger?'

Carl had to smile and it wasn't easy because he was very tired. 'It's not a bad little town,' he continued. 'Not really.'

'It's the ass end of the world.'

'I know how much he'd like to see us.'

'Not me. You go.'

Carl tried to brighten. 'How about next weekend? We'll drive up together and surprise him.'

13

'I've got something going next weekend.'

'A horse?'

'A sure thing,' said Hazard. He lifted his beer to the late-afternoon light and examined the smaller glass captured in it. He could see that most of the vodka had remained undiluted, which was the purpose of that way of mixing. A Siberian depth charge is what Hazard called it. He took a gulp and got some of the vodka's one-hundred proof power along with the beer. If he'd been alone he'd have grimaced. When his throat and mouth felt normal again he told Carl, 'I thought of going up to see him last Christmas but I was feeling too good and didn't want to waste it.'

'You're a sentimental soul,' said Carl.

'He started it,' said Hazard.

A concurring grunt from Carl. Then a long silence that said the subject was closed unless Hazard wanted to keep on it.

He definitely didn't. He got his mind off it by attributing some imaginary ideal heads and legs to a couple of good bodies that were passing by. Then he brought his attention to Carl via the mirror behind the bar. 'You look whipped,' he said.

Carl lowered his eyes, then his head, not wanting to realize how tired he was. He'd just flown in from Vienna with a stop-over in Washington to deliver personally some dispatches he knew weren't really that urgent or important. The dispatches could have been sent in the regular pouch but he'd been re-quested to deliver them, wasn't in a position to refuse. Not that he was lower echelon. That was the trouble, actually. He was middle echelon, which in the hierarchy of the State De-partment is the worst possible classification. The middle is where they put those who might not go any higher but could still be of use. Carl realized that but wouldn't quit because for the time being he liked the assignment he was on.

Carl had originally wanted and especially prepared himself for a foreign service career. He'd started as a junior officer at the embassy in Lisbon. After two years there, he got a jump up to Cairo, where he was second assistant liaison to the chargé d'affaires. Carl's intellectual qualifications were ack-nowledged. However, according to the periodic reviews sub-mitted confidentially to Washington by his various seniors, Carl's political attitudes weren't exactly on target. What that

14

really meant was that Carl was too idealistic, not flexible enough in his beliefs to make the necessary compromises between what might be right and what was strategically best. Moreover, he often wasn't even diplomatic about how he felt, came right out and said, for example, that he believed some of his own country's power plays were degrees of war.

Thus Cairo was, in State's opinion, much too delicate a spot for Carl. It upped his foreign-service grade a notch and transferred him to Saigon. For duty with a section of the pacification programme known as C.O.R.D.S., short for Civil Operation and Revolutionary Development Support. As one of the many Foreign Service junior officers assigned to CORDS, Carl's function was to advise the South Vietnamese civilian and military administration on ways to gain acceptance by the people of that country.

Perhaps at that point State hadn't entirely given up on Carl. Perhaps it hoped such duty might help conform him. However, being in the proximity of a long-term war and witnessing personally its devastation only set him off, activated his convictions.

In the course of his duties in Vietnam various atrocities came to Carl's attention. He investigated them on his own and wrote extensive reports. Over the months he accumulated a thick file, which all together made My Lai seem comparatively mild. When his reports received no official action, Carl pressed the matter. Shortly thereafter he was recalled.

State would have preferred to dismiss him but it decided not to risk focusing attention on him and his incriminating file. Smarter to keep him in, give things time to fade.

Carl was reassigned. For the past year and a half he'd been an assistant representative to the Strategic Arms Limitation Talks. Not really getting to do any of the talking but at least he was part of an effort that seemed to suit his ideals and he worked hard and hopefully at it.

Now Hazard told him, 'There's nothing I'd give that much of myself to.'

'You might.'

'Never.'

'What's more important?'

Hazard drank more of his depth charge and thought about what he believed. It came out bitter. 'Peace is another of

15

those abstractions that don't really exist.'

'There have been peaceful times.'

'Just intermissions. Time out to get ready for another go at it.'

'If I was susceptible you could depress me.'

'Be good for you.' Hazard smiled. He realized once again how much he cared for his brother, and how ridiculous it was for them to be discussing such impersonal things considering that they hadn't seen one another in over six months and only briefly three times in the past two years. Better, thought Hazard, they should have stayed on the subject of their faraway, flag-waving father, whose disposition was worse now with the realization that neither of his boys would ever attain the public importance his displaced ambition had aimed them toward.

'What do you hear from Catherine?' Hazard asked for the sake of change.

'She's in town.'

'Staying with you?'

'At the Pierre.'

That told Hazard enough, but Carl didn't let it go at that. Carl gave his wife the benefit of an excuse, perhaps because he needed it. 'She's only in to do some shopping,' he said. 'Wanted to be close to Bendel's and Bergdorf's.'

Just coincidentally Catherine happened to be in the same city, Hazard thought, and was grateful for his own less-complicated, unmarried status. 'Think you'll get together, you and Catherine?'

'I'll be seeing her while she's here.'

'I mean really back together.'

'There's a chance.'

'Try kicking her in the ass a couple of times,' advised Hazard.

'Is that what you'd do?'

'Maybe. Anyway, that's what she's been asking for.'

'She kicks herself,' said Carl.

'Not hard enough.'

'I think she's serious about a divorce this time.' There was regret in the way Carl said it.

'What's different about this time?'

'Just the impression I get.'

16

'Catherine's never been serious about anything,' said Hazard and wished immediately that he hadn't because it included Carl. He tried for quick repair. 'I mean she's different, a very unusual person.'

'You should have been the diplomat.'

'I'm a lousy liar.'

'You always were.'

'At least I always tried,' said Hazard, meaning it as a reverse compliment. 'Not like you.'

That negative phrase seemed to hang in the air between them, as though hyphenating them.

There was only a year's difference in their ages, but Carl at thirty-five appeared considerably older. One would have guessed he was in his mid-forties. His face was lined for that many years. Also, much of his dark hair was already lost and he was about fifteen pounds overweight. What Carl chose to wear only added to the older impression. A dark, square-cut suit, white shirt with a short collar too snug, black regular-width tie knotted small and tight, and the sort of black shoes usually preferred by older businessmen.

Conversely, Hazard looked younger than thirty-four. Closer to thirty. His hair helped. It was light brown, full and thick, and slightly long. He was taller than Carl by about four inches and he was lean, had the sort of body that said activity. The way Hazard dressed conveyed confidence and defiance. Brown velour trousers cut like jeans, antelope suede jacket broken in enough to qualify as his comfortable favourite, fitted shirt soft as its creamy colour looked, good leather boots. No tie. Hazard hadn't worn a tie in ten years. He considered a tie an insidious accessory, a restricting loop around the neck symbolic of hang-ups. He owned only one tie now. A gift from a girl who thought she'd gotten to know him. He kept it. On a hook on the back of a closet door. He used it to buff his boots.

The contrast between the two brothers was more than superficial. So much so that it seemed incredible they were from the same parents. Carl had always been the intense one, introverted and generally sober. Even during his younger years he seldom indulged in any of the flamboyant vanities that would have been normal. It seemed no distraction was ever compelling enough to bring Carl out of his serious

17

self. Whenever he attempted to be outgoing it was too obviously forced, and it was said and accepted that he lacked a sense of humour.

Hazard went to the other extreme and was better liked for it by nearly everyone. He sought out any escapade that took him across the grain of society. Even before he was old enough he was greatly preoccupied with girls, developed a way with them that resulted in his usually getting his way with them.

Of course, this was when grass was still something to be kept off of and pills were only for those who were physically ill and acid was a symptom of indigestion. It was when dancing was still a moving embrace and Elvis was up there twanging and twitching and Brando set the phlegmatic style and the local police didn't realize how easy they had it protecting the peace that was disturbed by dual straight mufflers on cars that had to roar to a certain illegal standard, cars that were shaved clean and leaded smooth, stripped nearly beyond recognition of their superfluous Detroit ornamentation and souped up so they could drag competitively at two in the morning on some residential street. It was the infancy of revolution, merely the rather naïve stirrings of it, and Hazard was into it. He was a good-time rebel, seemingly immune to any discipline or punishment his father gave out. Hazard did what he wanted, stoically paid whatever price his father put on it, and went right back to doing what he wanted.

Not like Carl.

Carl was the sort of student who had to work hard for good grades. Hazard could look once briefly at a page and recite it verbatim. He was a mnemonist, one of those rare beings endowed with the ability to recall at will whatever his senses experienced. During his early years he was so frequently called on to perform this feat that he got to be self-conscious about it, considered some sort of cerebral anomaly. As a result, he didn't use his special mental gift to best advantage. Studies were too easy for him, boring because they mostly involved memorizing. To please his father he followed Carl into Dartmouth and then, to please himself, he didn't finish. No matter that his grades were high among the highest. That only verified his opinion that the entire system was false-bottomed. Hell, he thought then, he could get more of an education just browsing in a good bookstore or library.

18

In need of challenge Hazard went searching for it. After two years of transcontinental bumming, going nowhere, everywhere, he found what appealed to him most was uncertainty, chance, contesting his destiny rather than merely accepting it.

He became a professional gambler.

With his unusual mental faculties he should have been very successful at it. However, too often he chose not to stick to the professional's logic, allowed his emotions to influence his choice, ignored the creed: *cowards love favourites but an underdog is a fool's worst friend.* Perhaps Hazard felt he deserved such a handicap or, more likely, he was not immune to the gambler's unconscious need to lose sometimes as well as win. Winning was a letdown from the excitement of the idea of winning, like the chase being more enjoyable than the kill. Whenever Hazard won big he was only temporarily elated; a depression would soon set in and the only way to counter it was to spend fast and bet back in big chunks. Anyway, he managed to lose enough so he never got substantially ahead, and to win enough to nearly support his better than average life style.

Hazard, the day-by-day plunger.

Carl, the pacifist, the plugger.

But perhaps the difference between the brothers who now stood together at the bar of the Sign of the Dove was best summarized by something they had in common. They were both named Hazard. It was their family name. Carl, however, had always been just Carl, while hardly anyone ever thought of Hazard as Norman.

Now Hazard had finished his depth charge and was trying for the bartender's attention to order another. He told Carl, 'I know what you need.'

'Sleep,' said Carl.

'Forget about everything. Go some place and just forget.'

Carl hadn't had a real vacation in years. It was his own fault. He just kept going.

'There's a guy I know who owns a place in Barbados,' said Hazard. 'Right on the beach. Never uses it. I can give him a call.'

To avoid committing himself, Carl asked, 'How's your money situation?'

19

'Way ahead,' lied Hazard. At that moment all he had was in his pocket. Nine hundred and some odd dollars. But his bookie was paid up and what he owed Diner's and American Express wouldn't come due for a couple of weeks. Not exactly financial security but it was normal for him and no reason to panic.

'I can let you have some,' said Carl.

Hazard disregarded the offer. 'I've got a friend who'd go down there with you and help you relax.'

Carl seemed to be considering it.

'A blonde,' said Hazard, and grinned. 'At least she was last time I saw her.' He tried quickly to think of someone he could persuade to go along with Carl for nothing but the trip. A few possibilities came to mind, but no one for sure. It would mean he'd have to ask a special favour and he didn't like having that kind of debt.

'Sounds inviting,' said Carl, not really enthused.

'It's what you need. Two, three weeks of that.'

'Maybe. I'll let you know.'

It was Carl's way of saying no, which Hazard knew from times before, when he'd tried to get Carl away from his dry government routine. He ordered another beer.

And vodka? The bartender wanted to know.

Hazard hesitated, half closed his eyes as though concentrating, and then decided no on the vodka. The bartender placed the benign glass of draught in front of Hazard.

Within a few seconds a dark-haired girl appeared in the archway entrance to the bar. She had on a full-length Paris policeman's cape and held a miniature Yorkshire terrier in the fold of her arm. Her eyes found Hazard and she went to him. She gave him a kiss that said possession with its brevity. Hazard introduced her to Carl. First name only. 'This is Keven,' he said.

'Souping it up again?' she said to Hazard with a smile that didn't camouflage her disapproval.

'Just beer, plain beer,' said Hazard.

Keven eyed his glass then, giving way to suspicion, took a close look and even sniffed above its head. 'You're a good boy,' she said, while her fingers soothed the Yorkshire between its ears.

Hazard told himself she meant him, not the dog, which

20

didn't even belong to her. She borrowed it sometimes from a neighbour. He put his arm around her, inside the cape.

She asked Carl, 'Are you going with us to the track to-night?'

'I'm afraid not,' said Carl. 'But thanks anyway.'

'There'll be other times,' promised Keven, not just being polite.

Hazard liked her for that. He quickly downed half the beer and called for the check. He wouldn't let Carl get it. He charged it on his Diner's.

When they were outside Carl wanted to take a taxi. His apartment was on 49th, downtown, about twenty blocks out of the way, but Hazard insisted on driving him. They walked to Hazard's car, which was parked in a yellow zone on 61st. Stuck under one of the windshield wipers was a parking ticket.

'Another invitation,' remarked Keven.

Hazard dropped the ticket into a nearby mailbox and got into the car. Keven refused to let Carl ride alone in the back seat. There was plenty of room for three in the front. The car was a 1938 Packard sedan in nearly mint condition. Original black paint without a scratch, interior upholstery authentically re-done. Hazard had won the car playing gin the same January afternoon two years ago when he'd lost heavily on Miami in the Super Bowl. It was claimed that the Packard had once belonged to a gangster and was bulletproof. It was solid and heavy enough but Hazard doubted that any gangster would be suicidal enough to settle for such a getaway. The best the Packard could do was zero to sixty in forty-five seconds, which didn't even beat an old Volkswagen.

When Hazard explained this to Keven, she said, 'That's probably why they made it bulletproof.' She preferred to be-lieve the car had seen plenty of gangland action. Another thing she especially liked about it was being able to ride high above all the lower-slung newer cars, a superior vantage from which she could discreetly observe the various indiscretions of people in cars alongside. She thought she now knew why, really, there were so many accidents.

They dropped Carl off in front of his apartment building. Hazard promised to phone Carl the next day and Keven ad-vised Carl to relax in a warm bath with a cupful of soda bicarb mixed in to make the water feel soft. Soft as love, she said. They watched Carl go in, his walk stiff-weary, as though the entire weight of his body had gone to his legs.

Hazard headed the Packard up Third Avenue and it wasn't until they were stopped for a traffic light at 64th that Keven discovered Carl had forgotten his attaché case. Hazard's first thought was to keep the case until tomorrow. Surely Carl wouldn't be needing it until then. But Keven reminded him that they were expected up in Connecticut in the morning, so Hazard cut over to Second Avenue and drove back downtown.

When they turned on to 49th, that one-way street was backed up with cars, barely moving because a delivery van was double-parked, causing a tight squeeze for the cars wanting to get by. Carl's building was halfway down the block. When they were almost to it they saw Carl come out. He was flanked by two men in black suits. Dark-haired with swarthy complexions.

Carl and the two men entered a waiting limousine. Another man of similar appearance was in the front seat next to the driver, who had on a visored chauffeur's cap.

Hazard thought it best to wait until he was alongside the limousine; then it would be simply a matter of getting Carl's attention. But the limousine at once started away from the kerb, aggressively using its left fender to pull out into the line of traffic. It was three cars ahead of the Packard, and Hazard could only watch it proceed around the double-parked van and increase its speed to the corner, where it turned right against the light and was gone.

Hazard remembered how tired Carl had been. What was more important than the rest Carl needed so badly? Hazard didn't want to believe Carl was allowing himself to be used to the breaking point by the damned government. Some extreme emergency must have come up, something important that truly demanded Carl's attention.

Hazard considered leaving the attaché case with the doorman of Carl's building but decided that would be too casual. He'd call Carl the next morning. If Carl needed the case, Hazard would make a special trip down from Connecticut the following night.

He replaced thoughts of Carl with the expectation of picking some winners at the track that night. Also, he anticipated having a couple, or maybe three, hot dogs. He was hungry and no hot dogs ever tasted as good as the ones sold at the track. His stomach concurred with a grumble.

At that moment Keven told him, 'I'm hungry too.'

Hazard wished for some sure way to keep his thoughts to himself. She was incredible.

She insisted that he stop at a health-food store on upper Madison. While she went in to shop, Hazard read the racing form. He didn't have to study it. No straining to assimilate the crowded lists of rather hieroglyphic abbreviations and numerals. He merely scanned each page once, using his eyes like a camera to record all the information. In less than two minutes he had it all in mind. He folded the paper and dropped it to the floor of the car. The Yorkshire immediately began tearing at it as though it were a helpless enemy.

Hazard slouched down and started handicapping, mentally reviewing and comparing the past performances, workouts, best times, distances, and all other possibly meaningful statistics of the horses that would be running that night. By the time Keven came from the store he'd made his selections in four races.

He drove while she fed.

Into his mouth she stuffed prunes and dried apricots, raw almonds, cashews, pumpkin and sunflower seeds. Deaf to his complaint that he wasn't a goddamn bird, she kept on feeding him: little mealy apples and sections of anaemic stunted oranges not half as tasty as the ordinary but twice as expensive because they were guaranteed to have been organically grown. She topped a carton of natural cultured yogurt with a generous sprinkle of raw wheat germ and shoved spoonfuls at him. He opened his mouth and took it rather than have it slop all over him. She encouraged him with remarks of how much better all these things were for his well-being, and although he was grateful for her caring for him, he had to say the flavour and consistency of the yogurt resembled coagulated milk of magnesia. For a final test Keven unwrapped a pressed-fig-and-sesame bar that didn't taste bad but not good enough really to qualify as dessert in Hazard's opinion. All the while Keven blithely munched away, making appreciating sounds as though everything tasted marvellous. But Hazard noticed she

23

didn't finish the yogurt, gave it to the Yorkshire on the premiss that the dog required something more nourishing than a racing form.

They arrived at Yonkers Raceway too late to bet on the third race. A horse named Skippa Skoo took it by a head.

'I had him picked,' said Hazard, irritated.

'He only paid three forty,' said Keven. She detested favourites, ignored them, never bet on anything less than four to one.

Hazard shrugged off what he considered an avoidable loss and looked to the next race, an Exacta. That is, it offered a try at picking the horses that would come in first and second. The payoff was, of course, proportionately greater, frequently as much as a hundred to one. Hazard's system for playing the Exacta was to key on one horse, the one that he thought had the best chance of winning. He combined that choice with two or three other horses, a couple of second favourites and the most promising long shot, covering every possible order of finish. The whole thing depended on the key horse. If it ran out, all was lost.

Which is what happened.

The horse Hazard keyed on got boxed in on the final turn, had plenty left, but couldn't make its move. Right off, Hazard was out three hundred. Keven, on the other hand, had disregarded the Exacta and placed a straight five-dollar bet on the fourteen-to-one winner. That put her seventy-some dollars ahead. She managed to be not too elated and knew better than to boast about it. She left Hazard bitching to himself while she went to collect.

Hazard wandered around trying to lose the loser feeling. His seeing the various cliques of heavy players didn't help. They were regulars, pros. There was nothing slick about them. No fifty-dollar hats and hundred-dollar shoes. They were mostly paunchy types in baggy, pleated trousers and wash-and-wear shirts, talking through their teeth that clamped half-smoked unlit cigars. An altogether separate caste, elite in this element. They let that be known by exposing their thick folds of hundreds, which they counted and recounted, over and over as though disbelieving how much they were up or down. No show of emotion, ever. Certainly not a smile among them. It was serious business. They seldom watched a race. Usually

24

they stayed inside the grandstand area, indifferent to the excited, urging crowd. Above such behaviour. They might as well have been waiting for a bus instead of a race result on which they had thousands riding. At times, when they had inside information that was particularly solid, they bought their tickets, went directly to the win windows and stood there without a doubt, ready to cash in.

Hazard recognized several of these heavy players from other times, other tracks. He knew them well enough to exchange nods. It occurred to Hazard that maybe they had something good going tonight. Perhaps he could get in on it. But it would mean he'd have to talk his way in with them, and they'd consider it a handout. He vetoed the idea. It wasn't his style. They weren't his style.

Instead, he bought a hot dog, squirted it with mustard and ate it quickly. It would have tasted better, he thought, if Keven hadn't stuffed him with all that garbage.

He went back to where he'd said he'd meet her. He found her intent on the tote board, oblivious to the two silk-suited Seventh Avenue types who were on the offensive, had her in a verbal crossfire.

Hazard wasn't worried, but he cut in, claimed Keven with an arm around and took her out of range. She didn't act glad to see him but that wasn't unusual. Whenever he came back to her she just picked up where they'd left off, as though they hadn't been apart. Not that she was cold. Rather, she preferred getting to and staying with the heart of things. In many respects her eccentricities were equal to Hazard's, and no doubt that was one of his reasons for liking her.

She called his attention to the number-three entry on the tote board. 'Could be an overlay,' she said.

'Could be,' he said.

The number-three horse had been a two-to-one favourite on the morning line but was now ten to one. The odds were being affected by an unexpected amount bet on a couple of other horses in the race. Keven was very excited about it. To her it was like finding a fantastic bargain at Bloomingdales. A favourite going at a good price.

Hazard concentrated for a few moments and again mentally handicapped the race. His conclusion was that the number-three horse had a definite edge. That meant someone

25

was purposely manipulating the odds and would, at the last possible moment, chunk down on number three. An overlay.

'If only the price stays up,' hoped Keven.

Hazard grunted.

Then she looked at him and changed. He could feel her pull away before she did.

'You're a cheat,' she said.

'What the hell did I do?'

'I'm not going to care anymore. You just go ahead and do whatever you want. Ruin yourself, I don't care.'

He suspected she meant the hot dog but he wasn't ready to admit it. 'I didn't do anything.'

'You don't have to lie.'

'I'm not. I don't know what the hell you're talking about.'

'Eating that horrible stuff.'

'What horrible stuff?'

'They're full of sodium nitrate and other toxic things,' she said with distaste.

He knew she knew. He couldn't get away with anything, the way she was tapped in on his mind.

'You've got mustard on your mouth,' she told him.

He was relieved to hear that. Caught but relieved because at least it was something tangible that had given him away. He rubbed his mouth while his eyes were on the pari-mutuels. 'It definitely looks like an overlay,' he said, to change the subject.

She remained cool, dug into her purse for some raw almonds and ate them. An intentional object lesson. He could hear her teeth crunching on them.

'I'm going to bet,' he said, and started away.

'I want to leave.'

His look told her she'd better not.

She went with him, and during the wait in the long line at the seller's window Hazard tried to make small talk but couldn't get a word from her. He believed the punishment exceeded the crime.

After that race Hazard was ready and happy to leave. The number-three horse won and paid eighteen-fifty. Hazard had two hundred on it so for the night he was ahead by fifteen hundred. And Keven was two hundred fifty richer. It called for some laughs but during the ride back to the city she only

26

talked to the Yorkshire, who seemed to agree when she said how stupid most people are, the way they mistreat themselves. However, when they were going down Lexington Avenue she turned to Hazard and with a contrite smile asked, 'Baskin-Robbins?'

He was happy to hear it.

That chain of ice-cream stores had a branch in the next block and he double parked while she went in to get a double cone for him and a pint for herself.

Now it was time for laughs, as he drove and licked fast to keep pistachio from dripping, and she eagerly spooned cocoa bean revel, her favourite, straight from the carton. The only excuse she offered for this total lapse in her health-food convictions was an immodest reference to herself as an uncontrollable ice-cream freak. She was such a regular Baskin-Robbins customer that she deserved having at least one of their thirty-one flavours named after her. Keven Krisp Caramel, for example. Anyway, she was the only girl Hazard knew who could devour a whole pint alone, with ease.

The Packard pulled up at the entrance to her apartment building. 'My tongue is frozen,' she complained between spoonfuls.

Hazard said nothing. His fingers were sticky from the ice cream. He wondered if this was one of the nights when she wanted him to take the initiative. She didn't usually. Usually she liked to make the decision, at least pretend to be making it. Above all, Hazard could never assume that she'd be staying the night or weekend at his place. He always had to stop at her place, giving her the option. Sometimes she let him know immediately by asking, 'What are we stopping here for?' Other times she kept silent for a long while, as though thinking herself into it and finally projecting her feelings. 'You'll be lonely if I don't stay with you tonight, won't you?'

It had become routine by now. However, it was not a matter of conscience with her. It couldn't possibly be, considering she was the one who'd set the terms of their relationship at the very start, telling him, 'Let's keep this on a purely physical basis.'

This night she got out immediately and went in to return the Yorkshire to its owner. That she came back out was a promising sign but not to be taken as a commitment. She sat

27

there in the Packard eating her ice cream. 'I've got a good one for you.'

'What?'

'Who was the world's fastest psychiatrist?'

'Fastest?'

She nodded, believing she had him stumped.

After only a moment's thought, Hazard told her, 'Dr Albert Weiner of Erlton, New Jersey. He treated as many as fifty patients a day, using simultaneously four or five consultation rooms. His principal methods were narcoanalysis, muscle relaxants, and electroshock. So many of his patients died from his using unsterile needles that he was tried on twelve counts of manslaughter and convicted of same in 1961, December twelfth, to be exact.'

Keven didn't know if that was fact or fiction. She'd invented the question because the idea of a fast psychiatrist had seemed funny and impossible. She hadn't expected a serious response. It was a sort of perpetual game with them, her testing his reservoir of knowledge. At any moment she'd just ask him something, usually something trivial but not infrequently something important. And almost always he'd just reach into his extraordinary mind and recite the answer. At first, Keven was awed by Hazard's ability to do this and, even now, after hundreds of times, she was impressed. To satisfy her suspicion that he might be bluffing, she went to the library and checked up on some of his answers. She found he was right, practically verbatim right.

She decided to try another, a piece of trivia she'd read and made a point of remembering especially for this purpose.

'What English king had the most legitimate children?'

He hardly hesitated. 'Edward the First. Had sixteen children by his two queens, Eleanor of Castile and Margaret of France. Eddie died in the year 1307 at the age of thirty-five.'

Keven nodded that he was right.

'Want illegitimate?' he asked.

'Okay, smart ass. Who?'

'Henry the First sired, as they say, twenty-two illegitimate children, ten sons and twelve daughters by six mistresses. And he lived,' added Hazard with appropriate emphasis, 'to be sixty-seven, a ripe old age for those days.'

'Let's go to your place,' she said.

It was only five blocks away on Park Avenue in the seventies, one of those older, better-preserved buildings. Hazard's apartment wasn't large, wasn't expensive, and actually wasn't his. It was three rooms that had been sectioned off from a once-spacious fourteen-room flat. It was a cooperative, with a monthly maintenance charge of four hundred and twenty dollars. And the owner had temporarily lost it by having confidence in three queens while Hazard was looking down his opponent's throat with a club flush. Hazard still had another two years of the three coming to him. The only things in the apartment that belonged to Hazard were his clothes and personal items, a Marc Chagall signed lithograph, a stereo cartridge player, and a twenty-three-inch remote-control colour television. Keven had some things there, kept neatly in an old, clean, compartmentalized steamer trunk that stood open on its end in the corner of the bedroom. Nothing of hers hung in the closets. Not to crowd him, was her excuse. Of course, the trunk could be shut, locked, ready to be hauled out at any moment.

As soon as they arrived at the apartment Keven went to the trunk and changed into a floor-length silk jersey at-home gown that nicely declared her lines. Hazard wasn't subtle about watching her change. Nor was she shy although she did take his point of view into consideration. Sometimes she enjoyed having him undress her and at times turnabout was more than fair play, but usually they enjoyed this arrangement – intimate act and very appreciative audience of one.

Hazard went to her, held her full length against him. After a brief kiss they kissed another longer one. And after it, when their mouths were still almost touching, she told him, 'My tongue is thawed now.'

She broke gently from him then, got some things from a drawer of the trunk, and went into the bathroom. Hazard could still feel the impression her body had made on his. He was always a bit amazed that she had such a lasting effect on him. He was more accustomed to turning abruptly on and off.

Before Keven, less than a year ago, the women in and out of Hazard's life had mostly been models from the agencies, from Ford's or Stewart or Wilhelmena. Those taller than average, hungry-looking girls who carried their identities around in folios of photographs. They seemed to be always
29

hurrying from booking to booking, from go-see to go-see and bed to bed. Taking off from Kennedy to work a week, a month, or to do the collections somewhere for so much. Without more than a good-bye phone call, and usually that only when a flight was delayed, they impetuously quit New York for Rome or London or Paris. They seemed addicted to change, needing constantly to alter where they were and how they looked according to fashion's superseding phases. The most consistent thing about them was their transientness.

Here now, soon gone. In love today, out tomorrow, or surely the day after. Hazard, at the time, found them and their ways attractive and congenial.

When he met Keven he thought at first sight that she was another of those pretty models. Just another. She was certainly pretty enough, with long dark hair and eyes like children's blue marbles with slivers of silver flaws in them. Also, she had the height for a model, though she wasn't too thin, didn't have that starved-for-the-sake-of-fashion sort of body. Hers was a less angular sort of leanness, more feminine. Where Hazard first saw her she seemed out of place. Standing her turn in line at one of the windows of the off-track betting parlour on East 58th Street. On a summer Saturday morning.

His approach was direct because he was sure of the type he thought she was. Would she have lunch with him?

She ignored the invitation.

How about dinner that night?

Her eyes told him to fall through the floor.

What was she doing tomorrow?

She told him she was taking her children to the park.

The several rings on her left hand, Hazard noted, were antique, not a legal ceremony among them. But by then she'd reached the window and made her bet. She walked away and he didn't follow for another try because her walk didn't ask for it and there had been that mention of her children. Anyway, she was just another, he told himself.

But the next afternoon he rented a bike, which was unusual for him, and pedalled through the park, not really believing he'd see her but holding to a small hope he would. The park was crowded with people trying to escape temporarily from concrete and, after about an hour of it, Hazard had had enough. He started to leave via 72nd Street, and that was where he saw her. On the corner at an ice-cream vendor's.

Any doubts he'd had about recognizing her were immediately gone. She was outstanding. With her were two small black children, both girls, about four or five years old, hanging on as though their lives depended on her. That set Hazard back a bit. Her children she'd said. It was possible.

Nevertheless, he went over to her, expecting more of the brush-off he'd gotten the day before, so he was surprised when she smiled at meeting him again. She asked amiably if he'd won his bet. He lied yes and she laughed that she'd lost. He tried to think of some tactful way to ask about the children, decided he didn't have to the way she was mothering them. He pushed the bike along to walk with them up the park side of Fifth Avenue. She let him believe whatever for a while and then told him the children were from the New York Foundling Hospital. She was officially treating them to a day out, a voluntary once-a-week duty on her part.

He helped by carrying the two little girls on his shoulders while Keven pushed the bike. He bought balloons that wanted to get away. And more ice cream.

That was the start of them.

He learned right off that Keven wasn't a model and didn't want to be one. She couldn't handle the day-by-day possibility of rejection, she admitted. She'd been on her own for eight years, nearly nine, since she was sixteen.

When she told Hazard that, he immediately imagined her running away from an adequate home and love to make a lot of young mistakes, a girl this pretty. But then, without a trace of self-pity or bitterness, she explained with a smile that she'd been what was called an unwanted child. Her grandmother had come over from Ireland to be someone's maid in San Francisco. Her mother was somewhere, she said vaguely, not noticeably resentful.

Hazard couldn't see how she could ever have been unwanted.

Especially now as she came from his bathroom with the ends of her hair wet, the robe loosely tied, and her remarkable eyes looking forward to pleasure. She brought him a glass of water and a handful of vitamins and minerals.

'What's the little yellow one?' he asked.

'Take it.' She was standing above him. She smelled of fresh

31

tangerines, a natural extract she used instead of perfume. Unexpectedly arousing.

'I only want to know what it is,' he told her.

'Folic acid.'

It sounded ominous. He took all the others.

'Folic acid helps your body utilize —'

'You think I need help?'

'Come on.' She exaggerated her impatience.

'You don't like the way I utilize?'

His hands were on the backs of her legs, moving slowly over the silk, feeling through, knowing her skin, the same fine texture all over.

'Please take it,' she said.

'I will,' he promised.

And a moment later she tossed the little yellow pill anywhere to free both her hands.

After lovemaking they held together for a long while in the lingering float of what they'd felt, a natural sedation that should have taken them easily to sleep. But it was only one thirty.

Hazard reached under his side of the bed for the remote-control switch while Keven got the television schedule from under her side. He clicked the set on. She consulted the listing and announced, *The Barkleys of Broadway, I Am a Fugitive,* or *The Mummy's Hand.'*

'You pick.'

She took a moment to decide she was more in the mood for Astaire than Paul Muni in chains or Dick Foran in a pith helmet.

Hazard clicked to Channel 2 and there was Ginger in her chiffon prime and the suave Fred creating centrifugal force on a surface so shiny and perfect that they seemed to be dancing on still, black water.

It was only the second or maybe third time Hazard and Keven had seen this particular movie, so it was comparatively fresh, considering they'd seen most of the late-night films many times over. They knew some practically scene by scene. So well, in fact, that they could cut the sound and do the dialogue themselves. Keven did a fair Joan Crawford and Olivia DeHaviland. Hazard was best at Bogart. Sometimes, just for the hell of it they'd switch roles. Every time Hazard did Bette

32

Davis, Keven laughed so much her belly hurt and her eyes cried.

By the time Astaire and Rogers got all wrapped up in a happy ending it was nearly 3 A.M.

Hazard clicked the television off.

Keven began brushing her hair, long soothing strokes.

'How about some breeze in the trees tonight?' he suggested. 'Do you feel like breeze in the trees?'

They also had small children at play, waterfalls with intermittent rippling brook, horses gambolling, rain on a roof, country birds, tinkling Himalayan bells, sea breakers, and a blizzard.

She preferred country birds, she said.

In Hazard's opinion country birds was the least tranquillizing, all those birds nervously chirping and trilling. However, he inserted that long-playing cartridge into the tape unit.

'How about a game?' he asked.

'Just relax.'

She stopped brushing and from the night table on her side she removed her black sleeping shade.

He asked her if she was sleepy and, when she told him no, he was again silently grateful. He thought back to how different and not nearly as good it had been for him before with the models, who could go unconscious in a minute, leaving him with nothing to do but envy them and all the other easy sleepers in the world. Like most insomniacs he felt deprived, victimized by some personal but abstract dysfunction, terribly insular. Also, insomnia wasn't something one readily admitted to, as though in a competitive world it revealed a weakness, a handicap, like putting extra weight on a horse that had to run.

He considered it a blessing that Keven was as chronic an insomniac as he was. She was certainly glad that he didn't sleep well.

Sharing the problem actually made it less of a problem. Now, while the rest of the world seemed to be sound asleep, they didn't have to feel so singularly damned. Now each had someone to not get sleep with. It helped make them all the more compatible. It took them to obscure all-night Chinese restaurants, to deserted Wall Street canyons, for a practically private voyage on the Staten Island Ferry. Adventures together replaced their individual bitching.

'Want some warm milk and honey?' she asked, still believing in such sleep-inducing remedies that had never really worked.

'I don't think so.'

'I'll do your feet,' She smiled.

'We could play cribbage or something.'

'I'll do your feet.'

She got a jar of vitamin E ointment from her trunk and sat cross-legged on the end of the bed with a pillow on her lap. She covered the pillow with a towel and he placed his bare feet on it.

Included in Keven's personal orthodoxy regarding the benefits to be derived from natural things and natural ways was her belief in Reflexology – a method of therapeutic massage applied to the soles of the feet. Purportedly, areas of the feet contained nerve centres that related to various other parts of the body. By massaging the feet, nervous tensions affecting those other parts could be relieved. For example, the little toe corresponded in some remote way with the sinuses, the inner edge of the arch with the spine, the centre of the heel with the sex glands.

Keven dipped her fingers into the amber-coloured ointment and began where Hazard's big toe joined the under part of his foot.

She told him, 'This will relax the back of your neck.'

Perhaps he was vulnerable to suggestion but after a minute or so damned if it didn't seem that his neck muscles were letting go, losing a tightness that he hadn't even realized was there. His head was propped up slightly and his eyes caught on Carl's attaché case on a chair across the room. He hoped that his brother was getting a really good long sleep. He glanced at the travel clock on the night stand. It said 3 : 10 A.M. and was ticking the night away. The fragment of old insomniac bitterness that came to him was immediately dissolved by the comforting attention of Keven's hands. Her being there. He closed his eyes to pretend, putting the illusive singing birds in some nice friendly trees and himself and Keven in the soft dip of a country meadow. Lazy, fat clouds hardly moving above pacifying smells in the air and there was nothing he could possibly do but sleep.

34

3

CARL WAS in a corner.

On the floor of the small, bare room with his knees drawn up and his head down, pressing the sockets of his eyes to his kneecaps. The position put an extreme strain on his back and he couldn't hold it very long. His hands were bound behind, making it all the more difficult.

He was trying to escape the light. The maddening light. Five thousand watts centred above, out of reach. There was a large silvery reflector around the light, mulitplying its intensity, and all the surfaces of the room were glaring white.

Carl thought he knew why they had chosen this way. The light was their substitute for the sun, and the room was a desert. If those natural elements had been readily available, no doubt they would have staked him face up. This was bad enough.

He didn't believe he could take much more. The air had become overheated, stifling, but it was his eyes that bothered him most. His eyes burned as though they had soap in them and his lids were protesting. No matter how tightly he clenched his lids they wouldn't stop twitching. He felt he was on the edge of a full-out scream, still hanging on but about to let go. He didn't want to do that.

He'd been locked in the room and under that persecuting light for five hours. Every half hour or so they came in and asked him. The same question. When they first left him alone he'd used his suit jacket to shield his eyes. They found him doing that and stripped him of everything but his shoes and socks. He was embarrassed to be nude in front of them and he understood the remarks they made in Arabic. Around midnight he'd thrown one of his shoes up at the bulb. On his second try he smashed out the light. They came immediately, replaced the bulb with another that seemed even brighter and took away his shoes. That was when they'd bound his hands.

The entire matter didn't seem to make much sense.

He'd already told them what they wanted to know.

The location.

At first he'd refused but after thinking about it he saw no harm in it. For one thing he recalled the Disarmament Committee hearings he'd attended last year. Certain ecologically minded senators had objected to the Government's use of that area as a dumping ground. The Government took the position that in all the world there was no better place to discard that stuff because there it would surely be out of everyone's reach. Expert testimony had supported the Government's claim that it was safe and inaccessible there.

Accordingly Carl now believed that the piece of information these men wanted was useless. As a matter of fact, his revealing the location, thought Carl, would, if anything, discourage any subversive plans. If what they'd wanted had been something he considered vital to national security, they'd never have gotten it from him.

But, then, why would they go to such extremes to get him to disclose this information? Surely not out of ignorance.

Carl suspected there was more to it. Very possibly these men were not what they appeared to be. Although they seemed authentically foreign they might be IRB men, members of the State Department's Intelligence and Research Bureau. He had heard of such incidents: government officials being tested in this manner, being purposely subjected to under-fire conditions in order to measure their loyalty and breaking points. But why him? He didn't warrant that kind of attention.

Unless, of course, someone had an ulterior motive. Could it be that someone at State was out deliberately to prove him disloyal? There was only one reason anyone would want to do that. His Vietnam file. Discredit him and thereby discredit his file.

As much as Carl detested that possibility, as much as it offended and disillusioned him, there was, he realized, a practical advantage to it. At least under those circumstances it was doubtful that he was in any real physical danger. No, State wouldn't go to the extent of actually harming him. Intimidation and that relentless light would be their limit. Anyway, Carl decided, if this was a sample of their underhandedness, he didn't want any more to do with them. He was

36

through. He might as well make it easy for them.

Now he heard them coming again. All four. Their steps on the landing. The door being unbolted. He remained in his strange, corner position, to protect his eyes from the light that much longer.

They pulled him up, brought him to the centre of the room where the light was brightest.

His eyelids twitched in spasms.

He was told to open his eyes.

He refused by just not doing it.

The question was asked. Again only that same question.

Carl answered it correctly as he had so many times before.

There was a long moment of silence. He sensed their closeness and reviewed what they looked like. He'd heard and remembered their first names.

Mustafa. Apparently the leader of the group. A man of extraordinary size, close to three hundred pounds, and none of it overweight. Bald except for a sparse, wreathlike growth. Scalp that shined as though polished.

Badr. Gaunt, with a bushy black growth connected all the way across the pronounced ridge of his brows.

Hatum. The one with the extreme nose that began nearly out of his forehead and hooked big.

Saad. Paunchy, shorter than the others. Black hair slicked back, a dab of moustache over a little bow mouth.

They all smelled of the same black tobacco and too much of sweet aftershave colognes. They wore identical dark suits; lightweight, synthetic, white drip-dry nylon shirts; cheap ties; and cheap shoes.

It was Badr who said. '*Yemken mayoukounsh gheir gabn*' – 'He could be merely a coward.'

'*Aou kazaab shater,*' Hatum said – 'Or a very brave liar.'

Mustafa put that same question to Carl again.

Carl decided that as long as they didn't believe the truth he might as well try a lie. He gave his answer but this time he transposed the first two numbers of the second part.

Calmly Mustafa requested Carl repeat the answer.

Carl again transposed the numbers.

At once a thumb and finger were on Carl's jaws, pincering hard, forcing his mouth open. In practically the same motion something metallic was inserted into his mouth.

The muzzle of a revolver.

Carl had to open his eyes now. He saw it close up, the dull grey noses of the bullets in the chamber, the hammer cocked back. But his mouth wasn't the only place. From behind another revolver muzzle was shoved between his buttocks. After what seemed a lifetime, the revolver muzzle was withdrawn from his mouth.

Carl closed his eyes, gave the correct answer and explained quickly why he'd contradicted himself. Because the truth hadn't been good enough for them.

The light was turned off.

The end of the play, thought Carl, although his eyes felt as though the light were still on.

They went out of the room, leaving the door open. Carl's clothes were returned to him. He dressed and went out to the hallway where they waited.

'*Sein douret el mayah?*' he asked – 'Where is the bathroom?' Carl said it in perfect Arabic, letting them know he'd understood every word they'd said. If it surprised or alarmed them they didn't show it. Badr merely gestured toward a door at the end of the landing and Carl went to it, alone. That was their attitude toward him now, Carl thought. Whatever it was about, it was now over and everyone could relax.

In the bathroom he opened the cabinet above the sink on the chance that it might contain something to soothe his eyes. A dirty glass shelf held an old rusty can of Dr Lyon's toothpowder and a scattering of used double-edged razor blades. Carl turned on the cold water. It ran rusty for a while but finally cleared enough for him to splash his face with double handfuls, keeping his eyes open. It wasn't soothing as he'd expected. It made his eyes sting even more. When he got home, he thought, he'd treat his eyes with a boric acid solution and maybe, if he could manage to keep awake long enough he'd take that soak in the tub that Hazard's girl Keven had suggested.

There was nothing to dry with, so he left the bathroom with his hands wet and his face dripping. The four men were waiting for him. He went with them down the stairs and out to the limousine. Carl paused to get a good look at the house and the area. They realized what he was doing but didn't try to prevent it. Finally Carl got into the limousine, sat between

38

Mustafa and Badr in the back. Hatum rode up front with Saad, who had put on his chauffeur's cap.

Within a few minutes the limousine was doing the limit on the New York Thruway. It turned off on to the Palisades Interstate Parkway and headed south.

Carl noticed signs saying they were on the way to New York City. He'd be home in an hour, he estimated. The luminous hands of his watch told him it was twenty-five after three. He scrunched down to relax. He closed his eyes, clenched them because his lids were still twitching. He knew he should be angry at having been put through this ridiculous episode, but at the moment he was too tired to feel much of anything.

Mustafa nudged him and asked, 'Are you sure these are the coordinates?'

Carl opened his eyes to read what was printed on the slip of paper Mustafa held up to him.

33:7w27:5N.

'Exactly,' said Carl, hoping to God that was the last time he'd be asked.

During the ride the men smoked a lot. The enclosed air became thick with a pungent aroma that Carl related to experiences in Cairo. Mustafa remained silent, but Badr, Saad, and especially Hatum talked crudely about women. Carl had some thoughts of Catherine, but only nice ones. He recalled a day on a remote Algerian beach when she had been unusually happy with him, holding on as though she considered him valuable, content that they were isolated there together. It was a day she'd given and could never take back, he thought, remembering the spontaneous lovemaking that had seemed like a melt in the sun.

A change of speed.

The limousine was approaching the George Washington Bridge. There it was with all its lights strung high, as though celebrating itself.

Saad steered to an exact-change lane, tossed the right amount of coins into the receptacle, and kept going.

There was almost no traffic at this early morning hour. Only a few cars travelling far apart. Saad got the limousine into the extreme right lane. He paid attention to the mileage indicator on the dash. When they'd gone four-tenths of a mile, about halfway across, Saad pulled the limousine over and stopped close to the outer barrier. He released the hood latch, got out and propped up the hood.

Carl wondered what was wrong. Engine trouble? God, wouldn't this night ever end?

A car went by. They waited until it was well past and all the lanes coming and going were vacant as far as they could see. Then Badr opened the rear door. Badr and Hatum pulled Carl from the back seat. Carl struggled, but he was no match for the two of them. They forced him over the barrier and across the walk to the railing. They lifted him. He felt the edge of the rail hard against his middle. He grabbed at its grit-covered metallic surface. They shoved and got him jack-knifed over it, so that for a fraction of a second he was head down.

It was about a three-hundred-foot drop. Equivalent to a fall from a twenty-story building. And at that height hitting the water would be like hitting concrete.

When he went over they didn't even bother to look down.

4

THE SUN came up at 5:58 that morning.

At 6:15 Hazard and Keven arrived at the installation in Fairfield, Connecticut. Keven opened the imposing iron gate with her little finger, by activating the tiny transistorized remote-control unit that Dr Kersh had issued to her. She enjoyed doing that. It always gave her a sense of invisible power.

The high hedges bordering the double-laned drive were badly in need of trimming. The drive, about a quarter of a mile long, had several easy curves to break the monotony.

After a final bend there was the main house, set on a wide slope above Long Island Sound. The house was three stories, about forty rooms and not as old as it appeared. The original owner, whose fortune was made from mass distribution of canned soups, had so much admired an eighteenth-century house in Surrey, England, that he'd had it duplicated here line for line and room for room. It was in the Georgian style, brick, with may large chimneys and high, symmetrical eaves. About half of the abundant ivy vines that clung around and high up on the structure were dead. Typical of the prevailing condition throughout the twenty-five private acres. The grounds were not entirely neglected but considerably overgrown, as if the effort required to keep nature in hand was being put to better use. Actually this slightly degenerated status gave the place an attractive quality. The expanse of lawn that sloped down to the Sound was somehow prettier for not being meticulously manicured. The grass tufted high where it could, or cared to, sharing with weeds that weren't really ugly and a nice scatter of wild yellow daisies.

Hazard parked the Packard on the far side of the house. At this early hour everything was still. Except for the dog that belonged to Dr Kersh, a grey-and-white English sheepdog that came wagging and bounding eagerly. Hazard took time to give the fluffy animal some attention, pushing the long hair

41

back from its face to see its black, happy eyes.

Meanwhile Keven hurried ahead down the path through the adjacent woods. She was well on her way before Hazard remembered she had his shoes in her canvas carryall. He'd been driving in his stocking feet as he often did.

To shout this early would have been disturbing, so he cursed to himself and proceeded down the path, not able to avoid stepping on some fallen acorns and stones. When he got to the beach house Keven had already been inside and was now leaning against the porch railing. She was obviously irked.

'I've been robbed,' she said.

'We've been robbed?'

'Not you, just me.'

They went in and she showed him that all the clothes and personal things she kept there were missing. Nothing of his was gone, only all of hers.

'There must be some explanation,' said Hazard, trying to think of one.

'Yeah, a thieving transvestite.'

'Nothing we can do about it now,' he told her.

'I can't even brush my teeth,' she complained, 'and what am I going to do for underwear?' She went around looking for *something* that was hers. She was relieved to find her health-food books were among those stacked against the wall. She touched several to verify them.

Hazard removed his socks, which were dirty from the walk down to the beach house. 'I'm going to try for a nap,' he said, and went into his bedroom.

Keven had insisted from the start that she have her own room and, although the beach house consisted only of two main rooms, she'd converted a small dressing area into a separate place for herself. The single bed and unpainted dresser she installed there took up all but a foot or two of the space, but Keven was adamant about the arrangement. Hazard couldn't be absolutely sure in what bed she would spend the night.

Now from the neutral territory of the centre room she watched him undress. 'Want some Granola?' she asked.

'No.'

She fixed two bowls anyway, poured whole milk over the

mélange of rolled oats, soy oil, wheat germ. coconut, sesame seed, sea salt, and natural brown sugar. She took it in to him.

He realized it was her excuse and held back telling her it was foolish that she still needed one. Besides, he didn't mind Granola as much as a lot of the other things she forced on him.

Between spoonfuls she took off her clothes and finished eating while sitting up in bed next to him. Then she snuggled down and turned on her side wanting him to fit himself against her. He knew and did.

Three hours later Hazard was brought to semiconsciousness by the distant sound of Dr Kersh's motorcycle. There was no mistaking the guttural roar of the big old Harley-Davidson. Hazard tried to sink back but soon knocks and calls got him up.

Hazard put on his trousers and went out. He found Kersh sitting on the porch steps, intent on the changing white triangle of a lone sailboat far out on the Sound.

'Glad you got here early,' Kersh said with a genuine smile

He was in his fifties, a chunky man, too thick chested and wide shouldered for his height. He had salt-and-pepper hair, a fine undisciplined mass of it, in need of a trimming. His sideburns were particularly wild. Except for his hair he might have been taken for a construction or dock worker. Scientist would have been anyone's last guess. He had on blue jeans that were frayed at the bottoms and a grey sweatshirt stencilled *New York Knicks*. Evidently he wasn't yet dressed for his workday. He didn't get up for Hazard or offer his hand. Their friendship had gone beyond such ritual.

The most Hazard could manage through his usual early half-awake depression was a sort of moaning grunt. A smile would have been a strain and not sincere. He went by Kersh and down the steps to the beach sand that felt hotter than he'd expected to his bare feet. He dug his feet in and found it too cool underneath.

'Can you be ready in a couple of hours?' Kersh asked.

Hazard shook his head sharply, meaning no and trying to clear.

'You've got to today,' Kersh told him.

'Why?'

'Visitors' day.'

'Oh shit.'

Kersh agreed. He'd brought a mug of coffee down with him from the main house. He sipped and made a face as though he found either it or his thoughts distasteful. 'Can't be helped,' he said. 'I assume Keven is with you.'

'Who's going to be here?'

'Richland. And some other Washington snoop.'

'For how long?'

'Just the day. We'll be doing an exercise for them. Nothing too unusual.'

Hazard squatted. He noticed the beach needed raking and thought he'd rather do that than anything else. 'What if we hadn't shown up today?'

'Never occurred to me.'

'Would you have been officially pissed?'

'More like personally disappointed,' Kersh said, looking away to the rocky shore line so Hazard couldn't read his eyes. 'By the way,' Kersh told him, 'your violence report came in the other day.'

'How'd I do?'

'You must have enjoyed it this time.'

'I hated it.'

'Maybe that's why you did so well.'

'I won't have to go again. will I?'

'Not for another six months.'

Kersh extended his mug of coffee. Hazard was about to reach for it when Keven came out.

She had on one of Hazard's shirts and was carrying two steaming cups. 'For openers,' she said brightly, handing a cup down to Hazard. It was rose hips tea. She sat beside Kersh, gave him a cheek kiss and glanced disapprovingly at his mug of coffee. 'That stuff slows down the sex drive.'

'Last time you said it was bad for the stomach,' Kersh said.

She shrugged. 'One thing bothers another.'

Kersh ceremoniously poured out what coffee remained in his mug, as though it were poison.

Hazard turned away and did the same with his cup of rose hips tea. Got away with it, he thought.

But not really. Keven merely chose not to say anything about it. This time. She told Kersh, 'I suppose you've heard I was robbed.'

'I had your things moved up to the main house,' said Kersh.

That set her back. 'You didn't.'

'Had to.'

'Why?'

'A matter of morals.'

Hazard heard Keven's teeth on the rim of her cup. She seemed irritated enough to take a bite.

Kersh was amused by her reaction. He let her fume awhile longer before explaining that the move was only temporary, to accommodate the two official visitors from Washington, who would be around that day inspecting.

Keven almost concealed her relief.

'They'd never accept love as an explanation for such behaviour,' said Kersh.

Keven jumped on the word. 'Love?'

'Is that such an overstatement?'

'Over,' said Keven.

'Way over,' Hazard put in.

Kersh didn't believe it. At every opportunity over the past six months he'd been obliquely promoting love between them, hoping they'd oblige by falling hard and deep. His motive was partly scientific. It would help substantiate a theory related to his current project. 'Anyway,' he told Keven, 'I'll have your things brought back down as soon as our visitors leave.'

'No hurry,' said Keven, blasé about it now.

'All right,' said Kersh, 'maybe in a day or two.'

'By bedtime tonight,' she said quickly.

At noon Hazard and Keven went up to the main house. Parked in the front drive was a new Chrysler with a federal eagle emblem bolted to its rear bumper. Hazard thought he should get such an emblem to beat the parking tickets. Merely out of curiosity he glanced into the car. There was a half roll of Certs breath mints on the front seat and two Schlitz empties on the floor.

Keven had gone ahead into the house. Hazard caught up to her in the foyer, a large oval-shaped area with a brown-and-white marble floor and extensive boiserie on the walls and doors. The foyer was unfurnished except for a grey metal office desk, an incongruity that stood as an example of how the once elegant residence had given way to prosaic use. The place reminded Hazard of those British war movies in which an imposing estate was taken over to serve as division headquarters, but not once during the past two years had Hazard ever seen anyone actually seated behind that reception desk. He suspected it was there merely for show. A strategically placed desk, even an empty one, might be reassuring to the sort of people who worked for the government, thought Hazard.

Such as the two men who now were following Kersh down the wide stairs.

Introductions and handshakes.

Mr Richland and Mr Whitley.

Hazard sensed their disapproval of his hair and casual clothes. Smile, he told himself, be good for Kersh's sake.

Richland was a district director for the agency. A top man who reported to higher-ups. Whitley was a Southerner who'd been rewarded his spoils in the form of a prominent spot on a federal-appropriations committee.

Hazard could see right off that both men were drinkers. Their complexions were the giveaway, especially the backs of their necks – blotchy red, as though the capillaries had exploded under alcoholic pressure. And the nearly ochre cast of their eyes was the sum of too many straight bourbons. They'd tied one on the night before, thought Hazard. Evidence was the morning beers to get them going and the breath mints to cover up.

Kersh had just given them a tour of the place and was glad they'd hurried through it. Neither Richland nor Whitley was really interested and, realizing that, Kersh hadn't bothered to explain the purpose of most of what he'd shown them. The special computer system, for example, located in a sealed subterranean area. It deserved more than indifferent glances and nods from Richland and Whitley. These computers were an accomplishment in electronic architecture, had actually been designed by other computers. Though extremely compact, they were insatiable. Their microprogramming allowed simultaneous feeding of unrelated information and rapid digestion to a simple, single response. This computer setup was not only analogous to a brain but to an entire nervous system. It had taken some of the best computer specialists several months to adapt it to the complex requirements of Kersh's research.

Impressive also was the experimental equipment Kersh had

46

assembled for photography in a high-frequency field. The field was formed by two vertical, facing copper plates seven feet square. The plates were placed six feet apart, precisely parallel, and their rear edges were connected by an electrical Tesla coil. Initially Kersh's high-frequency-field experiments had been limited to still photographs, using a positive-type sheet film with a unique emulsion. However, not satisfied with mere stills, Kersh had successfully incorporated a means of electronically recording movement in the field. It fed into the computer system and back to various monitors. It was not an insignificant breakthrough.

In another laboratory area was the equipment used for X-ray crystallography, the photographing of defraction patterns on the micromolecular level. It was an XR–7 Polaroid system more advanced and less complicated than similar equipment used by Maurice Wilkens at Kings College, London, in his work that helped Crick and Watson come up with the double helix answer for DNA and RNA.

On seeing the XR–7 Whitley asked, 'What's this contraption?' and walked on before Kersh could answer.

Kersh was actually grateful for their indifference. Interest, he realized, might lead to involvement and involvement would undoubtedly bring some degree of interference. Kersh didn't want that. Besides, having to patronize those who control the purse strings was something Kersh had learned early in his career when he'd applied to a private foundation for his first research grant. The fact that big money held such a vital rein on science rubbed Kersh the wrong way, but by now he was pretty much resigned to it.

He led Richland and Whitley into his office. Hazard and Keven followed along.

In former times it had served as a formal reception room. Now it resembled a badly managed bookstore. Every inch of wall was shelved and that still didn't provide enough space to hold all Kersh's books. Heavy technical volumes were everywhere, many just stacked in the middle of the room, creating something of a maze.

Lunch was laid out on a low glass table. Sliced chicken sandwiches and coffee prepared by Kersh's young wife, Julie, who was seven months pregnant. When Kersh introduced her,

Hazard detected a trace of smirk behind Richland's and Whitley's politeness.

Julie was a pretty, serious girl. Only three years before she'd been active in protest marches and Central Park demonstration. Then she'd found Kersh. She loved him devotedly, the way an honest searcher loves a discovery. In her present condition, a product of that love, she transmitted the serene confidence of a woman being fulfilled. Julie sat with them at the table only long enough to be courteous. Then she invented an excuse to leave, kissing Kersh a good-bye on his mouth.

By then Richland and Whitley were on their second sandwiches.

'Julie baked that bread,' Kersh told them proudly.

'Delicious,' Whitley said with his mouth full.

'Is there anything else I can get you?' Kersh asked.

Richland and Whitley exchanged uncertain glances before saying no.

Kersh got a fifth of Old Granddad from his desk drawer. He put it on the table along with some white styrofoam disposable cups. 'I'll get some ice,' he offered.

'Not for me,' Whitley said. He uncorked the bottle with one hand and poured half a cup. Equivalent to a double.

'This'll do fine,' Richland said, helping himself.

Keven cringed as she watched the two men toss down the bourbon. Then, because she didn't particularly like them, she decided they deserved the toxic consequences.

'What are those supposed to be?' Richland asked, pointing at two photo enlargements that were scotchtaped to the edge of a shelf above Kersh's desk. They were contrasting prints, nearly all black, except for an uneven luminescent outline around an indistinguishable shape, like a negative reproduction of greatly magnified skin and hairs backlighted and slightly out of focus.

Keven told him, 'The one on the left is my big toe. The other is the tip of my nose.' Then, working her eyelashes some, she added, 'I think.'

A grunt from Whitley.

Kersh smiled. He decided not to explain that the two enlargements were high-frequency-field photographs and that the one on the right was not Keven's nose but rather the tip of one of her breasts. Instead, Kersh started explaining the exercise that was planned for that afternoon.

Richland got up to use the phone.

Whitley obviously wasn't listening. He took a yellow legal pad from his briefcase and used a ballpoint to make some notations. He interrupted Kersh. 'How many have you got on staff?'

'Twelve.'

'Permanent?'

'Two part time.'

Whitley lefted the top sheet of the pad, evidently referring to something he'd written on the second sheet. 'Going over your expenditures,' he said, sounding like a prosecutor, 'I noticed a couple of items that seem out of line. One in particular is a trip to California last February. Somebody stayed at the Beverly Hills Hotel for three days and really lived it up.'

'That was a long-distance exercise,' Kersh said.

'I'm expected to accept all this as a valid expense?'

'Yes.'

'Over a hundred fifty dollars for room service in one day?'

Keven condemned Hazard with a look. They were his expenses. At Kersh's request he'd made that trip alone, but evidently, thought Keven, he'd enjoyed some expensive company. 'Seems rather extravagant to me,' she said.

Hazard knew what she was thinking. He was tempted to come right out with the truth, tell them he'd hosted a crap game in his hotel room that day. Considering the number of Polo Lounge types that had been in and out of the game all day long, that room-service tab was low. To hell with it. He turned to Richland, who was still on the phone and having some trouble with whomever was on the other end. Hazard could hear only bits of Richland's covered conversation, but he gathered he was talking to a woman, trying to arrange something for that night. 'I realize your time is worth money,' was one bit Hazard overheard. With no sympathy, Hazard thought that would be the best Richland and Whitley could do – a couple of hurry-up hookers.

Meanwhile, Whitley was still proving he had a mean eye for unnecessary or excessive spending. Now he was suggesting that Kersh cut back some on all operations' costs. Kersh didn't give in on that, and Hazard noticed Whitley didn't press the point, just poured himself another double bourbon and folded.

As soon as Richland was off the phone, Hazard took it over. First he dialled Carl's number direct and got a busy signal. At least Carl was home. He dialled another number. After the third ring he heard it pick up. As usual the person on the other end said nothing. Hazard said his code letters. T–R–A–K, which alphabetically corresponded with the last four digits of his own New York number reversed. Deliberately loud enough to be heard by Richland and Whitley, he asked what the line was on the Mets that night at Shea. He listened and then said, 'I'll take the Mets for a nickel.' Betting five hundred, despite his better judgment that Gibson of the Cardinals would have the underdog Met batters striking, grounding, and popping out all night.

After that he gave Carl's number another try. Still busy.

For the exercise it was decided that Richland would stay at the installation with Keven and Kersh. Whitley would go along with Hazard and Kersh's first assistant, a young Ph.D. named Lowery. Lowery's primary responsibility would be to see that certain controls were maintained. Also he would keep an exact chronological record of each image that was chosen. For this purpose he had an oversized clipboard holding a pad of special, printed forms. Attached to the upper part of the clipboard was a special, very accurate watch with a green signal light set in the centre of its face. Lowery also would be in charge of the images, which were in a metal box. About a thousand of them.

Hazard, Whitley, and Lowery went out and down the slope to the private landing and a twenty-metre power ketch that Kersh had hired for the day. The owner and his son had sailed the boat over from Westport.

The three men went aboard, the mooring lines were unhitched, and immediately the idling gurgle of the ketch's engine changed to a louder boil, getting under way.

They headed straight out. It was a bright, nearly cloudless day. The wind was cool, but Hazard took off his sweater anyway to get the sun. For some protection he sat on the deck leeward of the rear cabin house.

Hazard looked forward and noticed how out of place Whitley seemed there in his suit and tie, having trouble keeping his balance against the ship's pitches and rolls. He watched Whitley take out a cigar and try to light it in the wind. Whitley didn't give up, used almost a whole book of matches, and must have inhaled plenty of sulphur before he finally got the cigar going. He puffed hard and some of the tobacco's aroma was carried backed to Hazard. Hazard wasn't a cigar smoker but he knew an authentic Havana when he smelled one. Probably gets them via Canada, Hazard thought, suspecting that Whitley's political hypocrisy wasn't limited to such minor transgressions.

At the installation, Keven was being made ready. She was seated in a contour chair in the centre of a windowless room. The walls she faced, those on both sides and the ceiling, were blank and black, not painted but covered entirely with a felt fabric so that the black was softer and unmarred. Behind her was a partition of special, dark glass, something like a two-way mirror with reflection. It allowed unobtrusive observation from the adjoining laboratory area.

Keven knew what to expect, having been through these procedures numerous times before, but it usually took her a while to get used to the room. The feeling of being enclosed alone caused an uneasiness that she called 'the clausties'. She usually got over that soon enough, but then there were all the wires and terminals. Kersh had explained the purpose of each and reassured her that there was no danger. Still, she couldn't help but feel edgy about them. Also, the possibility that she might not do well, might fail completely and disappoint Kersh and everyone was another source of her apprehension.

It was expected that everything would come to her and, through her, be fed into the computers just below. The computers would record, process, and relay immediately whatever came to the monitors in the laboratory.

In Keven's opinion it was awfully complicated. With the confidence she'd acquired over the past six months, she was sure she could do just as well without being all wired and connected up like some living instrument. She told Kersh that and he agreed with her. But, he explained, personal experience, no matter how valid it might be, was not scientifically acceptable. That was especially true, he said, in researching this subject, which was already handicapped by countless personal experiences over hundreds of years.

Thirty-six electrodes were attached to Keven's scalp.

Kersh placed them himself and was very exact about it.

In several ways the procedures differed from the usual electroencephalograph. Interpreting the results of a regular EEG always required guesswork because of the electrical activity between various areas of the brain. It was like trying to analyse the recording of a thousand-piece symphony orchestra, hoping to isolate a single instrument from the whole. For this very reason, neuroscientists had eagerly taken any opportunity to implant terminals deep within the brain itself.

However, the electrodes being used by Kersh overcame the old EEG problem without having to resort to delicate surgery. They probed the brain with the same precision as implanted terminals but did so electronically. Each electrode was preset to record at a certain fixed depth. Those voltages, for example, that originated in the occipital lobe would be recorded independently from those that came from the adjacent cerebellum. The electrodes were colour-keyed and numbered according to where they would be positioned on the scalp. Also, the electrodes themselves were much more efficient than those usually used. They were made up of an alloy of platinum and element 44, ruthenium, a very scarce and extremely hard metal more sensitive to electricity than any other known substance. Capable of picking up charges well beyond fifty millionths of a volt, the average potential of the human brain, which is actually much less than the electrostatic charges that occur when a person combs his hair.

Methodically, precise to the centimetre, Kersh applied the tiny, silvery-white discs to Keven's head. The contact surface of each electrode held three points that penetrated the skin. However, they were so sharp and fine that Keven hardly felt them go in. Anyway, she was brave about it, said it didn't hurt nearly as much as the pain she inflicted on herself whenever she plucked her eyebrows.

When the depth electrodes were all securely in place, more electrodes of a different type were attached to various other parts of Keven's body, to measure her heart and metabolic rate, breathing, blood pressure, body temperature, and muscle reactions. Two final attachments were made to the outer corners of her eyelids.

She remained seated upright, eyes open, facing the soft blackness of the wall. Nothing else in sight, but her mind was racing, changing, presenting a hodgepodge of unrelated images. Nothing definite. She again was worried about failure.

A keyboard of numbers and letters was swung automatically into position, so that it was easily within her reach. Also an electronic apparatus that looked like a slanted easel.

In the adjacent laboratory one of Kersh's assistants determined that all systems were functioning properly.

Kersh was in the laboratory now. He quickly looked over the bank of monitors that were presenting a computerized translation of Keven's physical and mental processes at that moment. Kersh saw that everything was within normal range. There was the expected alternating between alpha and beta brain waves, with more betas coming through because Keven was acclimating herself to the surroundings and circumstances.

From where Richland was seated in the lab, he also had a good view of all the monitors. To emphasize his official presence, he asked about the brain waves, the alphas and betas he'd heard Kersh mention.

'Alphas are the primary waves that occur when the mind and body are at rest,' Kersh told him.

'Everyone has them?'

'The average brain transmits eight to thirteen alphas a second at a range of two to fifteen millionths of a volt. Each alpha pulsation lasts about ninety thousandths of a second.'

Richland nodded as though he understood. 'So where do the betas come in?'

Kersh doubted that Richland was genuinely interested, but he also couldn't just ignore the man. Unfortunately. 'An abrupt change in the brain-wave pattern takes place each time a person experiences any sensory stimulus or is required to make a mental effort of any sort. What happens is the alphas cease entirely and the betas take over.'

'How do you know one from the other?'

'Betas are obviously different. They're lower in voltage, have longer duration, and come at a faster rate, normally from eighteen to thirty per second. As soon as the brain accepts the stimulus or becomes used to it, the betas disappear and the alpha pattern returns.'

'You mean we're always going back and forth like that?'

'Yes.'

'Why?'

'No one knows for certain. There have been various theories but as yet no definite explanation.'

'Shows how little anybody knows.'

'About the brain, yes,' Kersh admitted.

That verified Richland's opinion. He wasn't the only one there who didn't know what was going on.

Kersh waited until he saw alphas now coming more consistently from Keven. Then, satisfied that she was settled enough, he spoke to her via the intercom. 'Test the keyboard.'

Keven had learned the keyboard by touch. She hit three of the keys.

On a monitor screen in the lab appeared the letters Y–O–U. Also, predictably, the beta monitor showed temporary activity. Twenty-three cycles per second, normal voltage, average duration.

'Now try the graph.'

Keven's fingers found and took up a thin, metal stylus. It felt cold to her touch, and she realized that her hands were moist from tension. She used the stylus like a pencil on the slightly grainy surface of the easel, careful that only the very tip of the stylus made contact. She drew the shape of a heart. No image appeared on the easel but its pressure-sensitized surface electronically relayed a clear outline of the image to a corresponding monitor in the lab.

Richland saw the heart shape appear, scoffed to himself, and shifted impatiently.

'We're ready,' Kersh said. He pressed a square button on the console, which caused the remote signal on Lowery's clipboard to light green. By then the ketch was about four miles out on the sound. It came about sharply, reduced speed, and ran parallel with the Connecticut coast. The wind had picked up considerably and the tide was running strong. The ridges of the swells were white and spraying.

Lowery motioned for Hazard to join him at midship. Lowery also tried for Whitley's attention, but had to go forward to get him. Hazard noticed Whitley's face and even his neck had lost colour. The man appeared cold, but there was perspiration on his forehead and above his lips.

With the wind and sea as they were, Lowery nearly had to

shout when explaining to Whitley the controlled conditions under which the exercise would be conducted. Whitley merely gave a single emphatic nod every once in a while. Not really listening. His cigar had gone out but he still held it tight between his lips. Hazard imagined the end of the cigar soaking in Whitley's mouth.

Lowery opened the box of images to show Whitley how the four-by-five cards were always concealed. He demonstrated how the battery-powered box rotated the cards on a spindle, how it automatically selected and presented one card at random out of more than a thousand. The face of each card was entirely covered with an opaque adhesive paper that Hazard would peel off. No one but Hazard would get a look at an image until after it had been transmitted. That way they'd be absolutely sure only Hazard was doing the sending, explained Lowery.

A final approving nod from Whitley. He gazed longingly at the far-off horizontal strip of grey that was land. Wishing he were back on it, he pulled the knot of his tie down, unbuttoned his collar and breathed deeply through his nose.

Hazard's look told Lowery he was ready.

Lowery activated the box. The spindle rotated the cards for several seconds and then pushed up a single card.

Hazard took it. He carefully peeled off the opaque adhesive and glanced at the image. An easy one, he thought.

It was an ordinary circle with a much smaller circle at its centre.

Hazard immediately fixed his mind on that image. He had to force his senses to detach, ignore everything else – Lowery, Whitley, the sea, the wind. It wasn't easy. It never was. Because success depended on more than simple concentration. It required that he focus his thoughts not only on the image as he saw it but also as Keven would see it. That meant concentrating sumultaneously on two related but separate things. Not easy. Ordinarily impossible.

Circle containing a smaller circle.

I see it, thought Hazard, and I see it as she sees it.

He visualized Keven's eyes, their special blue colour with slivers of silver in them. Her eyes set on the circle containing a smaller circle. Her eyes delivering that image to her brain.

He felt a spray of cold sea water on his face, distracting. He was momentarily aware of Lowery and Whitley nearby, a peripheral impression of them. But he used the sea, its repetitive chopped-up mass, to bring his mind back to nothing but the circle containing a smaller circle.

There it was again, isolated in his mind's eye.

And then, there in his mind was Keven seeing it.

The image.

As he saw it.

As he saw her seeing it.

The two still consecutive.

For several minutes his mind shifted its intense concentration alternately between those two impressions. Back and forth, more and more quickly. Until the image became a constant and his mental view of it and his mental view of Keven seeing it superimposed one on the other for no more than the duration of an ordinary fragment of thought.

He couldn't hold the composite, didn't try. The impressions became consecutive again, individual thoughts in order, and he felt he might lose them altogether and have to start over. He knew he'd lose them if he tried too hard. So he released the intensity of his concentration slightly, just enough, and that kept the impressions there. Then he pulled the separate thoughts back together to form the necessary composite again. I see it and see it as she sees it. The image. He held it for as long as he could and then let it go.

There was the choppy sea, the sun and the wind that had been hitting him. He handed the card to Lowery.

During all that time Kersh's attention never left the laboratory monitors. He anticipated what might come through, so he was less surprised than pleased by what the computers picked up from Keven, swiftly processed and relayed.

Kersh recognized it as the same extraordinary sequence that had occurred in previous, similar exercises. Beginning with a regular, steady alpha-wave rhythm and then an abrupt block of all alphas as the beta waves took over. Indicating that Keven was responding to a sensory stimulus. Perfectly normal.

However, at this point came the first significant variation from the normal pattern. For no apparent reason, the beta waves continued, and quickly their cycles per second increased from twenty-three to fifty-four. There was also a sharp increase in beta amplitude to sixty millivolts, and the beta impulses more than doubled in duration to eighty-five thousandths of a second.

Obviously Keven's brain was very hard at work. Relaxed as she was, and alone in that silent room, it was doubtful that she was responding to any external sensory stimulation. At least not to this extent.

Kersh noted the auxiliary channel that corresponded with the electrodes attached to the corners of Keven's eyelids. Indications of very rapid eye movement. Her eyes were shifting erratically, as though she were being bombarded by myriad visual attractions. Despite the fact that she was looking at nothing but a blank black wall.

All the while, the beta waves kept coming from her. Within less than a minute they had doubled again in frequency, voltage and length; were peaking up to a hundred and ten cycles; one hundred twenty-five millivolts, one hundred seventy thousandths of a second.

Kersh tried to identify with what Keven was experiencing at that moment. By comparative standards her brain was electrocuting itself. Yet she felt no pain.

The betas went on and up to one hundred thirty cycles, one hundred fifty millivolts, two hundred thousandths of a second. And then, abruptly —

The betas stopped.

As though someone had pulled the plug or severed the wires, the monitor that had been registering the beta rhythm indicated no beta response at all. Strange enough, but all the more so because the expected didn't happen – there was no reversion to an alpha-wave rhythm. The monitor that registered alphas showed no sign of activity. And the eye movement, so prominent before, had suddenly stopped.

Incredible as it seemed, every monitor relating to Keven's brain was now presenting nothing. Blank. It appeared that her entire cerebral cortex had shut down. For one, two, three, four, five seconds.

Then, while all other channels stayed void, there came a distinct pulsating wave of a different sort. It didn't begin low and build up – it came through full at once. Eleven cycles per second with a very high amplitude of two hundred fifty millivolts. Each wave was extremely short, a mere ten thousandths

57

of a second. Graphically, the pattern being recorded was one of long, sharp, individual spikes, like a symmetrical line of identical inverted icicles.

It was relatively easy for Kersh to determine from which part of Keven's brain these waves were coming. He only needed to see which of the keyed depth electrodes on Keven's scalp was picking up this isolated electrical activity.

The old brain. That was the point of origin. Deep down past the new bark, inside the old bark where the three earliest brain vesicals had evolved. Just anterior of the brain stem, those three known as the rhombencephalon, metencephalon, and thalamencephalon, also called the hind, mid, and fore sections of the old brain. In the evolution of the human thinking and sensory mechanisms, these three had been the first to develop. However, most of their earlier functions had since been taken over by newer brain parts.

Kersh suspected that the waves originating in the old brain were possibly the so-called lambda waves that neuroscientists had detected infrequently on the EEGS of certain subjects. It seemed that lambdas showed up with some subjects and didn't with others. Kersh wasn't sure they were that unpredictable and generally ignored lambdas, so he arbitrarily called them something else. Psi waves.

Now, as abruptly as they'd begun, the psi waves coming from Keven cut off. Leaving once again that inexplicable, contrary one, two, three, four, five seconds of blank. Then in proper reversion sequence the recognizable beta waves returned as strong as before. Gradually they subsided to normal range.

Kersh focused on the monitor that corresponded with the graph, the easel-like electronic apparatus on which, earlier, Keven had drawn a heart.

Within seconds, there, on the silvery face of that monitor, appeared the image she had chosen to draw this time.

A circle containing a much smaller circle.

Kersh didn't know, of course, whether or not that image had been telepathically received by Keven, whether it was a hit or a miss. He wouldn't know until the rest of the exercise was done and the score added up with Lowery.

'Know what that looks like to me?' said Richland from the rear of the lab. He'd gone for the bottle of bourbon and had

58

missed most of what had happened. He wouldn't have understood it anyway. Now he gulped from a styrofoam cup and said, 'It looks like a tit.'

Kersh didn't turn to Richland, thought it better not to in order to control his flare of anger. He kept himself in check by once more reminding himself that his affiliation with Richland and all the others like Richland had been his own choosing. Out of necessity, yes, but he'd known pretty well beforehand how it would be.

In 1950 at the Cavendish Laboratory of Cambridge University Kersh was one of a small group of biologists working on the possible genetic importance of protein molecules. While at Cavendish, it became apparent to Kersh that the protein theory, then supported by so many scientists, was not going to prove itself the answer to genetic structure. He preferred to believe that the solution lay in the area of nucleic acids rather than the proteins.

To research that field he left Cavendish in 1952 and established himself at Harvard. He was close to the nucleic acid answer when, in 1953, Crick and Watson proved he was right by beating him to it. A disappointment, but Kersh drew valuable self-confidence from knowing he'd been on the right track. That fact also brought him a certain amount of recognition.

Crick's and Watson's double helix discovery was a huge jump ahead. Kersh wisely jumped ahead with it. He stayed at Harvard, refocused his efforts, and over the years made numerous valuable contributions. His reputation grew within the scientific community and reached its height in 1968 when he was awarded a top international prize – just this side of the Nobel – for his work on the replication of DNA and RNA.

By then he was in his fifties, and late one Saturday night at his desk, having worked straight through without dinner, more or less out of habit, he paused for a moment, glanced at his plastic-protected prize certificate and realized how much he really hadn't lived, how much of his time he'd given to his work. Most of his best. It was a feeling that had been coming on for quite a while. He decided he wouldn't rest on his laurels, stay in the rut. There was still time, and possibly he could make the best of it.

Soon afterward he took a leave of absence. Went to warm

59

foreign places and tried not to think of such things as crystalline A-form DNA fibres. Within six months he had met Julie, loved her, married her, returned to Harvard, and found he couldn't pick up where he'd left off. Changed that much.

It was during his prolonged sabbatical that he'd developed an interest in extrasensory perception, particularly telepathy. Julie's influence had much to do with that. Her belief in it was emphatic and she enjoyed discussing it with Kersh. She related telepathy to something spiritual, a psychic phenomenon. Without belittling her theories, he naturally took a scientific position. If telepathy did exist, he said, there was a scientific explanation for it.

Did he believe there was such a thing as telepathy?

Possibly.

'Then why,' asked Julie, 'hasn't science given it more important attention?'

He wasn't sure. Perhaps the most inhibiting factor was the religious belief that God, not man, works in strange and wondrous ways. Geneticists were getting some of the same treatment for their discoveries that chromosomatic arrangements could be manipulated to predetermine human characteristics.

Julie didn't believe that was a good enough excuse.

Kersh agreed, and told her, 'As much as they deny it, scientists also want acceptance outside their own special community. That's what often holds them back more than anything else.'

Julie put the question to him again. 'Do you believe in telepathy? Yes or no?'

'There must be something to it,' he conceded.

There was an impressive amount of evidence in favour of humans having such an ability. But little of it scientifically acceptable. Except for the work of J. B. Rhine at Duke and a few others, all of whom had gone at it rather defensively, attempting to prove the existence of telepathy rather than assuming it did exist and concentrating their energies determining how and why.

The new challenge of it appealed to Kersh. Also, for him, a not unimportant consideration was Julie's enthusiastic interest. Work was better when there was love in it.

He outlined a research programme and submitted an official request to the appropriate board of grants at Harvard. The board, though taken aback by Kersh's proposal to research telepathy did not turn him down. They just politely tried to dissuade him, urged him to continue with his brilliant work in molecular biology.

Kersh stood fast. The board stalled, suggested he take another sabbatical.

Kersh insisted.

Harvard lost him.

But where to get financing for the research of telepathy? One of the private foundations? Too controversial a field for them, Kersh decided. He looked to a more likely money source.

The letter he wrote to Washington was purposely vague, but it received a prompt reply and a week later Kersh flew the shuttle down to Washington for a meeting. As he was escorted down one of the wide upper corridors of the Pentagon, past offices with doors displaying gold-leaved eagles and stars and other emblems, he felt sure he'd come to the right place.

His timing was perfect. There were just six weeks left in the fiscal year and every federal agency was concerned with its dollars; not pinching to make do, rather trying to spend what remained of that year's appropriation. The worst thing would be to have money left over, which might cause next year's appropriation to be reduced. A federal agency could lose its standing if it were too conscientiously frugal. It was the season to be prodigal, and Kersh sensed the spirit of waste in the air.

He was led to and through double doors to his appointment with an Assistant Deputy Director of Plans. Kersh wasn't kept waiting, was shown right in to an office that had much the same durable character as the corridors, the most noticeable difference being underfoot – wall-to-wall grey carpeting. In one corner a stanchion held a drooping Stars and Stripes fringed cheaply in gold. On a wall were framed photographs in proper nonpartisan sequence. FDR, Harry, Ike, Jack, LBJ, and Dick. Signed but probably not really by them. The only thing on the desk was a grey manila folder, not thick, not labelled. A dossier on Kersh.

The Assistant Deputy Director's name was James W.

Mumford. So said a propped-up plastic strip. Mumford was in his late forties. He'd recently taken off twenty-five pounds and looked the worse for it, drawn and sallow. His grey suit hung on him, and his shirt collar, at least a size and a half too loose, was forced into gathers by the shoved-up knot of his tie.

Mumford did his best imitation of a warm smile. He began with some flattery and then got abruptly to the point. He let Kersh do most of the talking. Within fifteen minutes the proposition was laid out.

'Rumour had it that we tried telepathy with the submarine *Nautilus*,' Mumford said.

Kersh remembered hearing about that. Surface to underwater telepathic communication. A futile attempt at best, never verified.

'Not true, of course,' said Mumford. 'We think the CIA started the story just to make us look foolish.'

Rivalry between the various intelligence agencies. That was something Kersh was counting on. There were ten separate agencies sharing an annual six-billion-dollar budget. Among them were the FBI, the AEC, the Treasury Department, and the State Department's Intelligence and Research Bureau. None of these got a very big slice. At least not compared to the National Security Agency, the CIA, and the DIA. The last had the intelligence divisions of the Army, Navy, and Air Force under its authority making it the biggest spender.

Since the Bay of Pigs fiasco the CIA had recouped its losses and apparently was the intelligence agency most favoured by the present administration. That left the DIA a poor second. Not poor in money but starving for prestige.

The CIA had come to be synonymous with U.S. intelligence. Few persons even knew the DIA existed. The Defense Intelligence Agency had been formed in 1961 by Secretary of Defense McNamara. The idea was to consolidate the intelligence units of the various military services. The move gave the DIA a big edge in personnel under command. The DIA was big, so big in fact that it got caught up in its own bureaucracy. It operated like a giant vacuum cleaner, sweeping up raw data gleaned by DIA agents over the world, but DIA suffered a glut of facts and a poverty of analysis.

Meanwhile, it was the CIA that predicted the Soviet invasion of Czechoslovakia and Israel's blitz victory in the Six-Day War. It was the CIA that engineered the putschs and coups like the one in Iran that put the Shah back in power and kept the Russians from getting control of the Iranian oil fields. It was the CIA that did the things behind the things that made the headlines. The smaller, trimmer CIA used clever footwork, beat its rival agencies to the punch, and had made itself the lightweight champion of the smart-ass, know-it-all division.

That being the case, Kersh believed that not the CIA but the DIA was his best prospect. He figured the DIA had more money to get rid of and would also be more receptive because of its secondary position.

However, after twenty minutes with this DIA man, Mumford, Kersh doubted his own strategy. Mumford showed no sign one way or the other; merely sat there riding his swivel chair, noncommittal.

Kersh went to his reserve ammunition.

He let Mumford know he'd only accidentally chosen to come *first* to the DIA with this proposition. Implying that his next stop would be CIA headquarters across the river at Langley.

That got nothing from Mumford, not even a blink.

Kersh brought in the Russians. He'd boned up on what they were reportedly doing in the field of ESP. A surprising amount of information was available in such ethical publications as the *Foreign Science Bulletin*. And Kersh had access to papers written by Russian scientists, extracts of symposiums held at the geophysics department of Moscow University, the Leningrad Academy of Science, and the Kazah State University. Among those involved was Dr Leonid Vasilev, whom Kersh knew to be a top Soviet scientist. He was holder of the Lenin Prize, a member of the Soviet Academy of Medicine, and chairman of physiology at the University of Leningrad. Excellent credentials. Also participating was Dr Ya Terletsky, the noted physicist, a chairman at Moscow University, and Dr M. Bongard of the Biophysics Institute of the Soviet Academy of Sciences in Moscow.

From what was reported, Kersh gathered that, unlike the United States, the Soviet Union had been seriously experimenting with ESP for the past twenty years. In 1966 the Russians conducted the first long-distance-telepathy exercise. A receiver-subject in Moscow successfully received several simple-image messages telepathically transmitted by a sender-subject in another city more than a thousand miles away. The exercise was performed under fairly controlled conditions. Since then, more complicated, highly controlled experiments had been conducted in Moscow, Leningrad, Prague, at various state universities, and most recently in Academgorodok, where the elite of Russia's scientists were stationed. Most impressive was the fact that the experiments were supervised by men of Vasilev's calibre. That indicated a priority interest by the state and meant, of course, that the military was also in on it. Evidently the Soviets, not deterred by any religious or other prejudices, had accepted the fact that ESP was possible and had gone full speed ahead to develop an understanding of it. In 1969 a centre for the preliminary training of telepathic subjects was established at the University of Leningrad. Just a year later another for advanced training was put into operation at the State University in Moscow. Of course there was no way of knowing really how far the Soviets had progressed, but the advantages in using telepathy for security and espionage purposes were obvious.

Mumford acted as though this was last year's news. He told Kersh, 'If, as you imply, they've got it, why aren't they using it?'

'Perhaps they are.'

Finally a reaction from Mumford. A thoughtful grin. It occurred to Kersh that possibly Mumford was enjoying a mental picture of someone putting one over on the CIA, even the Russians.

'How much money are we talking about?' asked Mumford.

Kersh presented a written estimate of costs. To his way of thinking, it was plenty.

Mumford studied the estimate for several minutes and then told Kersh that he thought the bottom-line figure was inadequate. Too low. His tone had the ring of objective criticism more than interest. He also mentioned that nowhere on the estimate did he see a provision for Kersh's personal salary.

That wasn't an oversight on Kersh's part. It just wasn't of first importance, so he'd left it out of this first presentation.

Mumford insisted that Kersh quote a salary figure.

Kersh thought first of a relatively modest amount but then

remembered to triple it, hopefully catering to Mumford's need to spend.

Mumford ended with the vague promise that Kersh might be hearing from him or someone else in a month or two. Along with good-bye he shook Kersh's hand as though he didn't consider it an act of touching another person.

Kersh returned from Washington feeling that he'd failed. Ten days later there was a call from Mumford informing Kersh that the DIA had approved his proposal. It had accepted Kersh's original estimate and voluntarily added on thirty per cent for contingencies. That extra thirty, Mumford explained, would avoid having to reapply for additional funds later on. It was good to have a little slush, he said. There were some DIA stipulations of a minor nature that Kersh would have to agree to, but the important thing, the project itself, had been given the go-ahead and would also be provided for in the DIA's budget for the next year.

Kersh got right to it. He acquired the big house in Fairfield and began installing the equipment he'd need. Within six months he was conducting experiments with various DIA agents as subjects. That was one of the DIA's so-called minor stipulations. Kersh had to use DIA personnel exclusively for his experiments. Perhaps the intention was to keep the CIA from knowing about the project, but more likely it was just that the DIA self-consciously didn't want *anyone* to know it was involved with ESP.

Anyway, those initial experiments were not encouraging. At that time Kersh was just getting his own thoughts organized into workable theory. However, he believed the subjects the DIA assigned to him didn't help matters. They lacked, for example, the necessary positive attitude.

Kersh complained to Mumford several times, and was finally so adamant that the DIA decided to compromise. Kersh could experiment with subjects of his own choosing, but, first, each had to be cleared and enlisted into the DIA. Kersh agreed. At least it was an improvement over what he'd had to put up with.

Shortly thereafter, Kersh met socially with a long-time acquaintance and colleague named Albert Benson. He happened to mention to Benson that he was having difficulty finding qualified subjects for his research. Benson, who had been on the faculty at Dartmouth for many years, tried to be helpful. He gave it some thought and recalled a young man who had once attended Dartmouth – a young man with a remarkable mind, an amazing memory, actually a mnemonist. Offhand, Benson didn't remember the young man's name but he found it in the college records and phoned Kersh to tell him it was Hazard.

From a call made to Hazard's father, Kersh got Hazard's current New York City address. But the two letters Kersh wrote to that address received no reply. It was just a long shot anyway and Kersh gave up on it. But then one day while in the city for a meeting with Richland, Kersh had some time and decided to hell with form, he'd look up this Hazard.

He found him in a bathrobe, not yet shaved, hair mussed, sleepy looking and not very hospitable. It was nearly noon. With unconcealed reluctance, Hazard invited Kersh in and as long as he was making himself a cup of instant coffee Kersh might as well have one. Kersh sat in the living room of Hazard's apartment and felt all the more an intruder when his glance into the bedroom caught on part of a bed and the bare legs of a girl, apparently still sleeping. As an afterthought Hazard closed the bedroom door, not quietly.

Kersh told Hazard why he was there. Hazard became interested when Kersh said what Hazard would get out of it. Five hundred a week for putting in only a couple of days a week; some weeks nothing would be expected of him, but he'd still get paid.

Hazard thought there had to be a catch and said so.

Kersh told him the DIA requirement of having to enlist.

That cooled Hazard. He wasn't about to be recruited into any branch of the government.

Kersh didn't try to convert Hazard, saw that would be futile. But his instinct told him he'd found a good subject and he didn't want to lose him on a technicality that he also considered absurd. He decided it was the right time to make an exception. He wouldn't flagrantly break the DIA rule, couldn't get away with that, but it was worth the risk to bend a little. He suggested Hazard give it a try, say for two or three weeks, just to see how things went. No real commitment to the DIA or Kersh.

Hazard didn't jump at the offer, didn't much like the idea

66

of promising any of his time to anyone. Although the five hundred a week sounded like easy enough money.

Kersh waited a while before making a different sort of appeal. 'I need your help,' he said.

Don't be a sucker for sincerity, Hazard warned himself. But less than five minutes later he heard himself agreeing, 'Five hundred.'

The following Thursday Hazard went up to the Fairfield installation and Kersh ran him through some preliminary tests to measure potential. To put Hazard at ease, Kersh used a deck of ordinary playing cards instead of the usual ESP symbol series. He extracted two cards from the deck so Hazard would be working with an even fifty. The cards were pre-shuffled and put face down into a small box that was placed on a table. Hazard's job was to try to identify the cards in consecutive order according to suit. Top card first and then down through the entire stack.

Hazard acted blasé about it and really was only slightly intrigued by the challenge. As he called out the heart, diamond, spade, or club that came to mind, Kersh tabulated each call in sequence on a score sheet.

On the first run Hazard had eleven hits. Only one above the average score that could be expected through mere chance. Hazard was disappointed but didn't show it. The second run he hit eight, and on the third run, nine. Discouraged and self-conscious about not doing well, he wanted to quit, but Kersh urged him to continue.

After fifteen more runs with less than a little more than average chance results, Kersh suggested a break. They went out and walked the grounds to the upper edge of the woods. Neither man was very talkative, but they were learning one another. They went down to the shore and along to the beach house that was shuttered tight and aging too quickly from neglect. Hazard felt sorry for the place which needed opening and care.

When they got back to the main house Hazard didn't want to undergo any more tests. He was supposed to stay over but he made the excuse that he had a long standing important engagement back in the city. Kersh didn't insist. Hazard left believing the whole episode had been a travesty. You'll never see me again, he thought.

But the next Thursday, there he was.

Kersh didn't seem surprised to see him, nor did he reveal how pleased he was. He liked Hazard.

More tests with the playing cards.

The first run, Hazard hit twenty-two out of the fifty. The second run, twenty-eight.

They did, altogether, a hundred runs, with Hazard repeatedly scoring in the twenty to thirty range. For the last dozen runs, Kersh asked him to try for the exact designation of each card: ace of diamonds, king of clubs, and so on.

Hazard's first attempt at that resulted in twenty-five hits. Of the other twenty-five, he got the correct value of ten cards and the correct suit of twelve. He only completely missed three out of fifty. Remarkable. And he went on to do as well and frequently even better on the following runs. The odds against such consistently high scores were in the area of five billion to one.

Kersh praised him.

Hazard felt good, like a winner.

But what had brought about the drastic improvement over scores from the week before? The difference had to be in Hazard. All week long his pride and competitive nature had picked at him because he'd failed and so quickly retreated. There was that. And then there was Kersh. Hazard found he liked the older man. That was exceptional because normally Hazard was as much a loner when it came to men as he was the opposite with women. Another motivation for Hazard was a practical one – the five hundred a week. Hazard needed it.

The three-week trial period they'd agreed on passed quickly. During that time they had six day-long sessions. Kersh accelerated the tests and exercises, made them increasingly more complex and demanding. Hazard seemed to develop right along with them. The greater the challenge the more determined he was to keep his scores above the probability level. Really bucking the odds.

Kersh didn't bring up the DIA requirement. He was afraid Hazard would quit and he doubted he'd ever again find such a prime subject, surely not one so likeable. But then it got to be four weeks, five, and one afternoon during a break when they were sitting out on the terrace Kersh put it to him.

It brought the usual bitter response from Hazard about the government. But no mention of quitting. Hazard's convictions hadn't weakened, but now there were other considerations. He was hooked. On admiration for Kersh, interest in the project, and surely the weekly five hundred. In the precarious balancing of his winnings and losses Hazard had come to count on that five hundred. He referred to it as his *fuck-you money*.

He asked Kersh, 'Who would I have to answer to?'

'Only me.'

'No Washington shit?'

'No Washington shit.'

'I could quit any time?'

Kersh nodded.

The decision was so contrary to his style that Hazard couldn't be direct. He looked down the slope in the direction of the beach house. 'Maybe I could fix that place up and use it,' he said. 'Would that be okay with you?'

'Fine.'

And so Hazard committed himself to enlistment in the DIA, although his motives for becoming an intelligence agent were something less – and more – than patriotic.

He opened the beach house, cleaned, and painted it. He slept there whenever he came up for his scheduled exercises and he also spent some of his other time there. More often than not he brought a friend along. Models, hardly ever the same one twice. Hazard liked being able to invite them to what he called his beach place up in Connecticut. He didn't ask Kersh's permission to have guests, but Kersh didn't mind. Sure it was a Government installation and undoubtedly the DIA would consider such conduct out of line. However, it wasn't unpleasant for Kersh to glance down to the beach and see a lovely young creature topless and sometimes also bottomless. That was the extent of Kersh's interest in any of the girls Hazard brought.

Until Keven.

She was different from the start. She didn't just lie on the beach or roam around the grounds as though the world were an eye aimed at her. Keven was actively curious about the project. She often intruded on the exercises. She kept asking Kersh to test her, claiming she wanted to know herself better.

Kersh believed she was merely being competitive and he wasn't entirely wrong about that.

By then Hazard had made amazing progress. He enjoyed being number one. No one else was even a close second. An analysis of all tests and exercises showed, however, that he was a much better sender than receiver. As a matter of fact he was comparatively poor at reception. It would have been ideal had he been equally proficient at both sending and receiving, and perhaps the latter could be developed over the long run. But for efficiency, Kersh decided to place total emphasis on expanding Hazard's strength as a sender.

That left Kersh looking for a receiver of equivalent ability. He found and tested several candidates, a few of whom showed potential. But they all lacked the required consistency. He even tested Julie, whose talents didn't approach her enthusiasm for the subject. It was a crucial problem for Kersh. To take his research to a higher level it was imperative that he have a sender–receiver team.

When he tested Keven he didn't even have any high hopes. Mostly he did it only to accommodate her. But when he tallied up her scores and saw how consistently she hit high above the probability-of-chance level, he realized that it was Keven who was accommodating him. She was a natural. Kersh wondered, unscientifically, if such inclinations had been passed down by her superstitious Irish ancestors.

Did she mind enlisting in the DIA?

She didn't know what it was.

Kersh explained.

She told him she hated uniforms. As long as she didn't have to wear a uniform, okay. What she didn't tell him was that it saved her from having to look for another awful, steady job.

So Kersh now had his telepathy team. And a new problem: To make the team work and hold it together.

Much of his success or failure with that problem would be clear at the end of this present demonstration for the DIA men, Richland and Whitley. Ignoring Richland, Kersh again pressed the square button on the laboratory console, signalling to Lowery out on the ketch.

The exercise continued.

Lowery activated the box containing the images. The

spindle rotated, moved up another card at random. Hazard took it and began peeling off its adhesive covering.

At that moment Keven felt a little itch in the centre of her back. Unreachable. It was most distracting, could ruin everything, she thought. She tried willing it away and then resorted to flexing and rubbing against the cushion behind her. But the itch was in that difficult-to-reach concave spot right between her shoulder blades. Damn! She was about to call in to Kersh to have him come give her back a scratch when luckily the itch subsided on its own.

Reminded by this how delicate the line was between the success and failure of what was expected of her, she quickly brought her attention to the soft, black, felt-covered wall before her. She thought about what she was thinking and remembered something she'd once heard Kersh say – that the most amazing thing about the human brain was its ability to reflect on itself, and that was why man felt special enough to have what he called a soul. But it also brought on a lot of suffering, from a punishing conscience to neurosis to total insanity.

Keven tried to feel herself thinking and it seemed she could, although it was a neutral, nondescript, continuous sensation.

Clear your mind, she told herself, and again used the soft black confronting her to try to direct her mind into believing it was receptive.

Suddenly a profusion of images came to her, one after another, just bits and pieces not apparently related, as though her mind's eye were sighting through a rapidly rotating kaleidoscope. She wasn't aware that she was no longer aware of the soft black wall. Nor was she aware that those bits and pieces were increasing steadily in number, that she was presenting them to herself more and more rapidly, too rapidly for premeditation. It was actually a pleasant sort of confusion; so much for her mind's eye to see. Delightful! More and more. There didn't seem to be any limit, and then ...

Change.

It was as though a vertical seam inside her abruptly parted and folded neatly back to reveal an emptiness inside. A void. Not black, but a white, substantial nothingness, clean and still as new milk.

A dormant region.

There on the white, as though projected, all of it, all at once, isolated in unmistakable contrast, was a picture of words. It remained only long enough to register before disappearing. Leaving a void as undisturbed as before. Then, as though reversing experience, a layer of impressions unfolded to envelop and join, replacing the nothing with enjoyable, entertaining, rapid-fire confusion.

Gradually that diminished.

To the point where Keven again thought about what she was thinking and again realized her eyes were open on the soft, black, felt-covered wall.

After a moment she extended her right hand to the electronic keyboard. She had to resist her present thoughts, keep them from distracting her. It was difficult. Her mind seemed to resent her concentration. It protested by offering various impressions, some divertingly erotic.

She nearly giggled, wasn't sure that she hadn't.

Her first finger pecked at the keyboard.

On the corresponding monitor in the laboratory appeared:

BIGBIRDDETAIL715SECTION2VERIFIEDLRBM

Keven had no idea what that meant, didn't know BIG BIRD was the SR-71, the Air Force's new 2,000-mph, high-altitude surveillance plane, DETAIL 715 the code number of certain photographs taken by that plane during a particular flight, SECTION 2 an area in China one hundred fifty miles north of Peking, and VERIFIED LRBM that the plane's cameras had caught a long-range ballistic missile.

Out on the Sound aboard the ketch, Lowery was about to record the card that Hazard had just handed over. He read the message that was printed on it and shook his head. The box had selected a toughie, he thought, and doubted they'd scored a hit on that one. On his exercise report sheet he noted the exact times of transmission and then in the allotted space he wrote:

BIG BIRD DETAIL 715 SECTION 2 VERIFIED LRBM

The exercise called for a run of eight images. The fifth image chosen at random was one designed to test incidental accuracy. A drawing of an oddly spotted, one-eared, three-legged dog.

72

When Hazard finished sending that one they were through for the day. Also, Whitley was belly down on the deck, head over the side, retching up Old Granddad and sandwiches. To multiply the displeasure, he was doing it against the wind.

Hazard, feeling no pity, observed Whitley's anguish for a while and then went below to get out of range.

Less than an hour later they were all gathered again in Kersh's office to review the results. Lowery's record of images sent by Hazard was compared with what the computers had registered via Keven. Out of the run of five they'd scored three perfect hits, a partial hit and an apparent miss.

Kersh congratulated his team.

Keven beamed like a superstar. At that moment she was so high on herself that Hazard couldn't resist bringing her down. He blamed her for the miss.

'It wasn't my fault,' she said, above reproach.

'Had to be.'

'You didn't send it strong enough.'

'Hell I didn't. Anybody could have gotten that one.'

'Not true.'

'You choked on it.'

Actually the missed image was graphically the simplest of all they'd attempted that day. An inverted arrow without a tail. What Keven had gotten was a shape that resembled the flame of a candle.

'That's exactly what came to me,' she said.

A scoff from Hazard.

'No doubt you had something else on your mind.'

He thought she meant her. 'Like what?'

'Yourself. You hardly ever get past that.'

Hazard had intended only a little chaffing, harmless enough, but it was getting out of proportion.

'Admit it was your fault,' she said.

He almost did just to get it over with, but stayed on top by nonchalantly pouring himself a cup of leftover coffee. It was cold and bitter, nevertheless he gulped it down and to the empty cup said, 'Slows down the sex drive.' Her words that morning.

Her Irish went up a few more degrees. 'That's for *sure*,' she promised, and left the room, walking as though she were going a long way.

Kersh had an idea about what possibly had caused the miss. Hazard had sent the inverted arrow; Keven had received it. But at the moment it came to her, Keven's unconscious had interfered, changed the impression to another it considered more acceptable. This wasn't the first time her unconscious had resorted to such guile. But why this time? Kersh felt there was a connection between the two images. Vertical arrow could suggest penetration, aggression. Keven's unconscious had perhaps associated it with masculine dominance and defiantly opposed it, vetoed it, replaced it with an image that was more feminine. Kersh would have suggested all this to Keven if Richland and Whitley hadn't been there.

Richland was half drunk and Whitley was only half recovered. Richland kept saying, 'Impressive, very impressive.' And Whitley mumbled on about what a hell of a good sailor he'd always been, claiming something he'd eaten hadn't agreed with him.

They were anxious to leave. Kersh accompanied them out to their car. Handshakes and good-byes.

From behind the steering wheel Richland told Kersh, 'Goddamn impressive.' The motor was already running but he turned the ignition key again to cause a painful, grinding screech.

The Chrysler pulled away. Whitley lighted up a Havana and took two puffs before his stomach made him throw it out. 'What a day,' he moaned. 'You didn't fall for all that crap, did you?'

'Hell no.'

'It was rigged; they had it rigged.'

'Yeah,' Richland said.

'Some kind of hook-up from that guy what's his name.'

'Hubbard.'

'From him to the girl. A radio or something.'

'That's what I figure.'

'Bunch of real phonies.'

A questioning glance from Richland.

Whitley got it. 'Don't worry your ass, Fred. As far as I'm concerned, the project's full-ahead. I'd even say it's priority.' Besides, it's only a spit in the bucket, he assured himself.

'You're one decent guy, Whit.'

Whitley nodded. 'Reminds me, at the last convention down

74

in Miami I saw this guy in a nightclub. He was blindfolded and could tell you everything you had in your pockets. Now, he was something. He could guess the number on your social security card, driver's licence, everything. No shit. Damndest thing I ever saw.'

5

USUALLY KEVEN didn't stay angry long.

Hazard thought she'd get over it, surely by bedtime.

But night came and she kept to herself in one of the upper bedrooms of the main house. Her things hadn't been moved back down to the beach house, which Hazard didn't find encouraging. He told himself it didn't matter and read some Camus, *Notebooks 1942–1951*. For a while he forced himself to read word for word, line for line, like everyone else, but he soon reverted to taking it in an entire page at a glance.

Around eleven he got up and went down to the beach, from where he could see Keven's lighted window. He imagined her up there munching on sunflower seeds and dried apricots, probably hating her stubbornness, and trying to think of a face-saving way out of it. He thought about giving in, going up to get her, but decided if he did that this time she'd expect it the next. He returned to Camus and finished him.

A half hour later he heard the radio tell him he'd made his bookie five hundred richer because Gibson had blanked the Mets. Feeling like a loser, Hazard went out to try to shake it off and have another look at Keven's window. The light was out. He doubted she was sleeping but the chance that she might be riled him. He started up the slope to the main house, still ambivalent about giving her the impression he needed her that much. Hell, he didn't need anyone. He continued on up.

When he approached the house he saw her light come on. That could mean she'd had enough of being alone. She'd probably be heading for the beach house any minute now. What if he wasn't there? He imagined her panic, pictured her good, loving relief when, timing it perfectly, he finally showed up.

With that rewarding possibility in mind he entered the main house, went into Kersh's office. He remembered that he hadn't reached Carl. He dialled Carl's number direct and got the busy signal. Maybe he'd misdialled. Another try with more care. Same thing, busy. He dialled Operator to have her try and then was put through to another operator who somehow determined the number was out of service.

Irritated, Hazard asked, 'What's that mean, he didn't pay his bill?'

'I didn't say the number is no longer in service. I said it was out of service.' The operator was insolent-polite, typical. 'There is a difference,' she said.

'Up your public booth,' Hazard told her before she could click off.

He waited five minutes more before going out. Keven's room was dark again. He went down to the beach house. He'd be quiet, peek in on her waiting for him.

She wasn't there.

Hazard undressed and went to bed. Just before turning off the light he noticed it was only twenty after twelve. He lay there in the dark thinking he shouldn't have drunk that cup of coffee seven hours back. It kept him awake until nearly four.

Next thing he knew it was eight and he was wide awake. No use trying for more. He got up and went bare out to the beach. No one but him up that early. It was an overcast day, which made the water seem colder. He swam some, feeling strong because he was pissed at everything. After the swim he didn't shower, didn't shave, just dried and dressed fast and went up to the Packard, which started on the first try.

Hardly any traffic. He made it to Carl's apartment building in an hour. He parked in the yellow, got Carl's attaché case out of the trunk and went in. He and Carl would have breakfast somewhere and talk. A big unhealthy ham and eggs, lots of toast and plenty of coffee breakfast. To hell with Granola.

The doorman told him.

The police had been there earlier.

Hurrying wasn't going to help, but Hazard floored the Packard and went through lights all the way down to 30th Street and First Avenue.

Into the place.

Out of reality.

Down a municipal green corridor to where he had to prove who he was to a desk cop. The desk cop told him not to ask because he couldn't answer.

Told to wait.

A cop in white like a doctor. A badge numbered 918 pinned on him. 'Hazard?'

'Yes.'

'This way.'

A stairway down and around. Long-lasting metal on the edge of every step. A smell like the air was sprayed with bug killer. Cop 918 put on blue rubber gloves and unlocked a thick solid door that had 'DO NOT ENTER' on it. Into a long room, cool, concrete floor painted white and slightly slanted, punctuated with a drain.

Everything clean.

A wall of stainless steel, three-by-two hinged compartments.

Second from the bottom, sixth from the left. Opened by Cop 918 and pulled out, sliding easy like an official file. But seven feet of it.

Cop 918 lifted the sheet and folded it down part way for Hazard to see another Hazard.

It's not you. It doesn't look enough like you.

'Being in the water does that,' Cop 918 said.

A long look at the face of Carl, seeing all the times not taken, all the care not shown, things unsaid. Oh brother, never now.

Everything too late.

Cop 918 asked, 'Do you identify him?'

'Yes.'

Cop 918 started to cover with the sheet but was stopped by Hazard. 'I want to see all of him.'

The sheet off then to reveal the entire position of death. Carl's hands, with swollen fingers flexed unevenly, as though to grab anything. A tag on to the right big toe.

'Okay?' Cop 918 asked.

'No,' Hazard said, and walked out.

All Hazard could learn from a sergeant cop was that Carl had been gaffed out of the river just after dawn that morning. Near the 96th Street yacht basin. A pretty good guess based on the condition of the body was that death had occurred sometime Friday night. The medical examiner would take a look tomorrow, not on Sunday. The sergeant's own opinion, and he'd seen a lot of them, was suicide. Before leaving, Hazard signed a city form confirming positive identification and assuming responsibility for the body. I'm responsible for you now, Carl.

Outside he got a lot of change and found a pay phone. After the clanging of quarters came his father's voice. Hazard told him straight out and shared the silence that followed.

His father said, 'Send him home.'

'I'll bring him.'

Hazard had thought there were others he should call but now he realized there was no one else but Catherine. Keven and Kersh; he'd call them later. Catherine was only thirty blocks away.

He seemed out of place at the Pierre. His unshaved face was sceptically noted by the desk clerk when he asked for Mrs Catherine Hazard.

No one was registered by that name.

'How about Miss Leigh-Minter?'

She was there. Under her socially advantageous hyphenated maiden name.

Hazard resented that. All the way up in the elevator to the thirty-fifth floor.

35-A was a two bedroom suite overlooking the park for two hundred a day. A DO NOT DISTURB card was hung on the knob. Hazard knocked before noticing a bell button inset in the door frame. He rang and the door was opened by a young man.

'Yes?' the young man said. He had straight dark hair to his shoulders, was short and bony thin – an adolescent impression contradicted only by eyes on their way to being old too soon. Obviously he valued his boyish build, emphasized it by wearing a black ciré shirt and matching flared trousers cut like a shiny second skin. A tiny platinum spoon hung from a chain around his neck.

Hazard brushed past him and into the living room of the suite.

'I'm Peter,' the young man said as though that should mean something. Then stretching his British accent he added, 'Miss Leigh-Minter's personal secretary.'

Personal, thought Hazard, noticing Peter's platform, stacked-heeled, black-and-beige suede shoes.

'Miss Leigh-Minter is sleeping,' said Peter. He minced even

when no part of him was moving.

'Get her up.'

'I'll do no such thing.'

'Get her.'

Peter retreated behind the closed double doors of one of the bedrooms.

Waiting, Hazard noticed remnants of the night before. Two bottles of Dom Perignon, both half full but gone flat in warm ice buckets. Among the stubs of cigarettes in ashtrays were several marijuana roaches. An elaborate gold-wire roach holder was on a side table along with a plastic vial containing yellow-and-blue capsules, a prescription: TAKE AS NEEDED. There were smudged hotel glasses around. One was placed carelessly on a fifty-dollar bill that had someone named Felicia's telephone number written on it just below 'In God We Trust.' The windows were open wide but it would take more than that to refresh the air.

Five minutes passed.

Hazard was tempted to leave but sat and got up again.

Catherine came out. 'Haz! I thought it was Carl.' The way she said it she wasn't disappointed. She was wearing a full-length robe by Valentino, baby blue, ample silk that swished as she came over to give Hazard cheek kisses, left and right. She had, Hazard noticed, a subtle, attractive fragrance about her, cleaner somehow than dabbed perfume and more effective.

Catherine lit a Turkish oval and inhaled as though she needed it all the way down. 'We're going over to the Bethesda Fountain this afternoon to see the local freaks,' she said.

Hazard hadn't said a word yet, was putting it off until he thought she was ready for it. She sat on the sofa. The blue silk parted to expose her excellent legs nearly all the way up. She disregarded it. That was like her. She was a very beautiful twenty-seven. She knew it and she let you know it. English beauty, fine, well-bred features, healthy blonde hair. She snapped her head to make her hair comfortable, and she was smiling when Hazard told her: 'Carl is dead.'

Her smile stayed on, only because she'd forgotten it. Her eyes held disbelief as she listened to Hazard's words that ended with, 'They think it's suicide.'

80

She didn't speak, got up abruptly and went into the bedroom.

A quarter hour later she returned, dressed now in white silk sharkskin trousers and a pale yellow, sheer blouse. Barefoot, her hair gathered back. Hazard didn't think her eyes looked as though they'd cried any. She sat where she'd sat before, but with her legs drawn up under her. She looked at Hazard and then past him, a covered gaze, not really seeing anything outside herself. Then she closed her eyes and said, 'The fuck of it all is I was the one who wanted to die.'

By late the next day, Monday, the medical examiner's office filed its report. It referred to Carl as a victim, saying he'd suffered fractures of vertebrae, ribs, and there were multiple internal injuries. However, the cause of death was drowning.

He had either jumped or fallen into the river from a high place. Time death occurred was approximately 4:00 A.M., Saturday, April 20th. Summary opinion: perhaps accidental death but more likely suicide. Autopsy not recommended.

Accordingly, the police investigation was swift and routine. It disclosed that Carl was under severe strain from his work and also having marital difficulties. Conclusion: suicide. No further investigation necessary.

On Wednesday afternoon in the small New England town of Winsted, Carl was buried beside his mother and his name was newly chiselled beneath hers on the large granite family marker.

After all the ritual and standard Episcopal implorations to God on behalf of Carl's soul, Hazard remained at the grave site. Stood alone above the mound of funeral flowers. He had never felt so helpless. Futile now to say the unsaid: I love you, brother. No way to show it. How insignificant now the embarrassment of being so direct, saying love, showing love, compared to suffering this total inability.

I would kiss you now, my brother, and hold you and to hell with all ridiculous conventions. I would show you I love you by giving you my time.

A truck came up the cemetery road and stopped a respectful distance away. It was the cemetery groundkeepers come with their shovels, impatient to get their work done. They stayed in the cab of the truck, waiting for Hazard's departure.

Their presence brought Hazard the full impact of finality; his grief increased to such an extent that it was no longer grief. All the energy of his sorrow was suddenly transformed into anger. A fury so deep and intense and unlimited that he didn't believe he could possibly hold it.

Is this all that I can give you, now, brother?

I have to *answer* for you.

Hazard turned from the grave, walked past the truck and out of the cemetery. Through streets of the town he'd never liked. And when he turned the last corner to home he saw his father. Mowing the front lawn.

They didn't say hello again.

Hazard went into the house and wandered around, restless. A glance into his father's study; the bound regiments of various law books. Nothing much changed. Into the kitchen to get an ice cube to suck on. Something he used to do. Back to the front room for a look out at his father still mowing. His father's face was set and unreadable. But Hazard suspected he was probably thinking he'd lost the better of his two boys.

Hazard had intended to stay a few days. Hadn't said he would, just intended. However, he went upstairs and repacked.

When he came out and down the front steps with his bag, his father was turned from him, mowing away. His father reached the far edge of the lawn, pivoted the mower, and began cutting toward Hazard.

Hazard went to him and wasn't sure his father would stop until he did stop. No need for Hazard to say he was leaving. That was apparent. And his father didn't urge him to stay. Hazard thought about just saying good-bye but overcame that and gave in to an embrace. Arms around tight, a long hold with encouraging slaps on one another's backs.

6

'WHO,' ASKED Keven, 'holds the all-time record for the longest kiss?'

'The what?'

'Longest kiss.'

'I don't know.'

'Would you care to hazard a guess?' She grinned at the old pun.

He didn't.

She imitated the way he usually answered, fast and sure.

'A blue-movie star from San Francisco named Sally Beaver and a Hell's Angel from Fresno known only as Big J, for some famous reason.' She shrugged contritely. Hazard still wasn't amused. 'On a beach in Monterey in 1971, August 12th and 13th to be exact, they kept their mouths in continuous contact for thirty-six hours and twenty-one minutes. During that time neither participant ate or drank but somehow both managed to smoke. A lot.' She inhaled, an exaggerated marijuana inhale, and held it so her next words came grunting out from the back of her throat. 'Although the kiss, among other things, was performed entirely in a prone position, the couple finished five miles north of their starting point, impeded by a large boulder at high tide. They could have continued but the chrome studs on Big J's leather jacket were painfully incompatible with Sally's recent silicone injections.'

'You and your Irish imagination.'

'It's true,' she said with a straight face, then conceded with a grin. 'Anyway, it might be.'

He had to laugh, a little.

That was what she was after. She went to him, tilted his head up and kissed him, short but sweet. 'Not the longest but the best,' she declared.

Hazard was grateful for her attempt to lift his spirits. He

smiled a good smile for her, gave her behind a playful swat and told her, 'Back to work.'

They were at Carl's apartment. One of those furnished short-lease places designed for minimum comfort and maximum indestructibility. Every possible surface was burn, scratch and stain proof. Wall to wall synthetic carpet, a beige that could take city dirt. Framed paintings were screwed permanently to the walls, Paris street scenes ordered done by the dozen.

Keven was there to pack Carl's clothes into cardboard cartons that the Good Will people would come to pick up.

Hazard was sitting on a cocktail table in the living room. He'd emptied every drawer, cabinet, and shelf, literally picked the place clean of every scrap of paper. He'd dumped it all on the sofa and was now going through it, systematically item by item.

He found government pamphlets having to do with United States armament policies. Transcripts of Congressional and Senate committee hearings. Verbatim testimony by generals and high officials of the Defense Department arguing the need for an unsurpassed arsenal. For and against, mostly for, such things as SAMs, missile launching subs, and chemical-bacteriological weapons. *As a retaliatory measure* was a phrase that appeared repeatedly. One general, apparently pushed to exasperation by his dove inquisitors, said: 'No damned reason why we should get wiped out with our pants down.' The pamphlets were not secret. They were part of the public record and available from the Government Printing Office on request.

Hazard also found reproductions of the entire file Carl had assembled on war atrocities in Vietnam. Photographs, sworn statements, first-hand accounts by witnesses. There were copies of letters Carl had written to the State Department, bringing the atrocities to State's attention, calling for action, expressing indignation when nothing was done. Copies. Where, Hazard wondered, were the originals?

It would have taken an average person two days or longer to read everything Carl left behind. Hazard did it in under four hours, including the fine print of three $50,000 insurance policies. Each stipulated in legalese they wouldn't pay anything for suicide. Not fair, thought Hazard; death was death

84

no matter how. But then he noticed the beneficiary named on all three policies was Catherine. She didn't need it, so forget it. He tossed the policies into the throw-away box.

Carl's attaché case. Hazard saved that for last. It was locked and rather than search around for the key he used a screwdriver to break open its clasps. Inside was Carl's pass-port, a soiled shirt, the latest issue of *Time*, an ounce bottle of Fragonard perfume gift-wrapped for Catherine, and a blue folder containing some Disarmament Committee memos – routine correspondence.

Nothing. Nothing in all of it.

Keven came from the other room, struggling with a large carton she'd packed. She was trying to pull it along to the entrance hall. Hazard picked it up and carried it there, stacked it on top of another carton near the door.

Keven asked was he hungry.

'No.'

'You must be.'

He hadn't eaten since breakfast and then not much. It was now after six.

'I'm going out,' he told her.

'To eat?'

'No.'

'Without me?'

He nodded and thought she'd protest but she didn't. She smiled. 'Wait a minute,' she said. 'No more than three, I prom-ise.' She hurried to the kitchen.

Out of mindless habit he went to the phone. He hadn't bet on anything in nearly a week, hadn't settled his last loss. He called his bookie, put another nickel on the Mets, didn't know who they were playing. He almost made it a dime.

Keven returned with two tall glasses containing a thick, un-healthy-looking mixture, bilious coloured.

'This will hold you.'

He took large gulps to get it down.

She was glad he didn't ask what it was, that she didn't have to tell him it was brewer's yeast, lecithin, fertilized egg yolks, over-ripe bananas, yogurt, fresh orange juice, a squeeze of lemon, and a dash of sea kelp. She knew his drinking it so fast would probably cause gas but she didn't say anything. At least it was going down and would do him a lot of good.

Hazard didn't complain about the taste or even bother to make a face. He told her, 'See you later.'

'Take care,' she said brightly.

But her eyes, Hazard noticed, were intense, and he left with the feeling that she knew what he had in mind.

He drove to the 17th Precinct station house on East 51st Street. He parked right in front as though he were official. He went in and told the cop on desk duty that he wanted to see someone.

The someone he got to see was a detective sergeant named Binzer. Not a shirt-sleeve, loose-tie, hat-on-the-back-of-the-head stereotype by any means. Binzer had on a dark brown suit, wide, geometrical-figured tie, and an embroidered striped shirt. Everything he was wearing looked new, not in keeping with his face, which creased deep and lined especially around the mouth and eyes, old early from fifteen years of dealing with everything from self-cremating protesters at the United Nations to afternoon sidewalk homicide in Times Square.

What could he do for Hazard?

For a moment Hazard was tempted to tell Binzer what he felt about Carl's death – what he suspected and what he had to go on. However, he realized he'd only come off sounding like a dead man's hurt and angry brother. Besides, the police had it wrapped up and most likely would be inclined to keep it that way. So then and there Hazard decided he was on his own. He told Binzer, 'I want to know who's the registered owner of a particular car.'

Binzer didn't change noticeably. He was too experienced for that. He merely pushed back from his desk a way. He calmly lighted an extra long without taking his eyes off Hazard. Hazard didn't look like some nut off the street but Binzer knew most nuts don't look like nuts. 'Who are you?' he asked.

Instead of saying, Hazard showed him. It was the first time Hazard had ever used his DIA identification card. He'd never thought he would.

Binzer examined it and handed it back. 'Never met one of you guys before.'

'We're around,' said Hazard, trying to act the part.

'What are you into?' Binzer asked.

'Probably nothing, just a lead.'

'Okay, what's the licence number?'

Hazard remembered easily. The episode, brief as it had been and not of particular importance at the time, came back to him now. Not just a vague, general impression but total recall of every detail. The two men who'd come out of the apartment building with Carl. The two others who'd waited in the limousine. Their faces, features. He'd seen the car and the men only for a few moments, which was enough. He told Binzer: 'A dark blue seventy-two Cadillac Fleetwood limousine, New York licence plate number 973–DPL.'

'A DPL plate?'

'Yeah.'

Binzer said that meant the car was registered to a foreign embassy or UN mission. They were the only ones who got DPL plates. DPL for diplomat. 'It lets them get away with murder,' Binzer said.

'Really?'

'Sure. The bastards can park anywhere. They can be stoned and doing a hundred up Madison and give us the finger. They've got immunity. Anyway, if you're after a DPL, that's easy. What was the number?'

'Nine seven three.'

Binzer didn't have to call the motor-vehicles section to get the information. The United Nations was in the 17th Precinct, so it was convenient to have a list of all DPL registrations. In a small bound book that Binzer took from the lower drawer of his desk, he quickly found 973–DPL and told Hazard: 'Registered to the Consul General of Lebanon, 9 East 76th.'

'Thanks.'

'Nothing.'

'Do me one more favour.'

'What?'

'I never asked.'

'You couldn't have,' said Binzer, 'you were never here.'

The Lebanese consulate was in a private, four-story building halfway down on the north side between Fifth and Madison. A nice, expensive neighbourhood. Hazard circled the block a few times looking for the dark blue limo. Lots of limos but not that one. Finally he pulled into a hydrant zone on the corner of 76th. To wait and see. From there he had a good view of the building, could even make out the small national emblem of Lebanon over the entrance way; red-and-white diagonally striped shield with a green fir tree centred.

Hazard stayed in the car. An hour passed. It seemed longer than that to him with nothing to do but just sit there and watch and think about how he was going to handle it if he got the chance.

He had doubts.

Possibly he was way off on an emotional tangent, just grasping in anger. Possibly those four men were coincidental, innocent. No matter, he had to find out. One thing he felt for sure, whether suicide or murder, somehow, directly or as an indirect consequence, Carl had been killed by the fucking government.

At half past seven the dark blue Cadillac limo bearing licence plate 973–DPL turned into the street. It pulled up in the DPL zone in front of the consulate. The driver got out. It wasn't anyone Hazard had seen before. The man entered the building.

Ten minutes later two older men and a woman came out. They were dressed for the evening. At that same moment, as though on cue, a driver came up the exterior steps from the floor below street level. A different driver. It was Saad. Hazard, of course didn't know that name but he recognized the driver as one of the men he'd seen with Carl, the last time he'd seen Carl alive. Saad hurried to open the limo's rear door for his passengers. Then he got in front behind the wheel and drove away.

Hazard followed. It wasn't easy because what Binzer had said about abusing the privilege of diplomatic immunity was certainly being demonstrated by the way Saad cut in and out of traffic, no regard for lights that had just turned red, leaping getaways. Hazard almost lost the limo twice but managed to keep sight of it all the way to Lincoln Center, where it pulled in to the special-access road and discharged its passengers. They were going to the ballet. But not Saad. He steered the limo out to Columbus Avenue and headed downtown.

Hazard went after him, tried to keep up, but Saad really put his foot to the limo, as though the busy avenue were the Pennsylvania Turnpike. The Packard just didn't have enough horses, and those it did have were too old. Hazard felt as

88

though he were on the wrong end of a rubber band as he helplessly watched the limo stretch its lead. Somewhere in the West Thirties Hazard lost it completely. He cursed and took out some of his anger on the Packard's gear shift. He circled around and went uptown, back to Lincoln Center. His stomach was bothering him. It felt bloated and he had sharp gas pains. Tension, he assumed.

The ballet was over at eleven.

Saad timed it just right, got there with the limo as soon as the audience started coming out. He picked up his passengers and again headed downtown.

Hazard managed to get the Packard directly behind the limo. It turned at Columbus Circle and went crosstown on Central Park South. For some reason not so fast now, and Hazard had no trouble staying with it.

The limo's destination turned out to be the Sherry-Netherland at 59th and Fifth Avenue. It pulled up in front; the passengers got out and entered the hotel. They were going to Raffles, the private club for supper and dancing located downstairs at the Sherry. Saad apparently would wait. He manoeuvred the limo into place among the numerous other chauffeured cars standing by there. Cadillacs, Mercedes-Benzes, Rolls-Royces, double and triple parked.

Hazard drove past and around the block. He parked on 61st in a hydrant zone. He walked to Fifth, crossed over and down to the southeast corner of Central Park. Directly opposite the Sherry-Netherland's entrance. He sat on a public bench, from which he could observe without being noticed. He saw Saad was out of the limo, standing talking with a couple of other drivers.

After a few minutes Hazard got up and walked across the square to the Plaza Hotel. Inside the Plaza he went to the lobby news-stand, bought a roll of spearmint Life Savers and, as an afterthought, a ten-cent-sized Almond Joy that cost a quarter because he was buying it there. He ate the Almond Joy on his way out and back across the square to the bench. He saw Saad was still talking with the other drivers.

Don't just stand there, you fat little prick. A moment later, as though directed by Hazard's unspoken instructions, Saad left the group and got into the limo. He turned on the interior light and began reading a magazine.

Hazard had been waiting for that. But now he wasn't so sure. He had to reassure himself that he'd once seen Cagney get away with it in a movie. He shoved his hand into his left jacket pocket, felt the roll of Life Savers there, and started across the street.

Saad was enjoying the magazine. The girls exposed in it had no less than 42-D. He was so involved with trying to make the photographs come to life that he was taken unaware when Hazard opened the limo's right front door and slid across the seat. Hand in pocket, Hazard shoved the hard round end of the roll of Life Savers into Saad's side.

'Don't say anything,' Hazard told Saad, 'just drive.'

Even through his fat Saad could feel the hard pointing pressure of what had to be a gun. He glanced at Hazard's face, saw the set of it matched the threat. He did as he was told, dropped the magazine into his lap, started the limo, and steered away from the Sherry.

Down Fifth Avenue.

'I don't have any money,' said Saad. 'All I have is ten, maybe twelve, dollars.' He hoped his shirt cuff was hiding his watch.

Hazard let up some on the pressure he was applying with the roll of Life Savers. Only so that he could poke it again even harder into Saad's side. With his free hand Hazard reached into his other jacket pocket and brought out a photograph of Carl. When the limo had to stop at an intersection, Hazard held the photograph in front of Saad's eyes.

'You know him?' Hazard asked.

It was a head-on photo of Carl, a good likeness, unmistakable.

'No.'

'Never seen him?'

'Never.'

'How about last Friday night?'

'I was sick. In bed all Friday and Saturday last week.'

The back of Hazard's neck flushed as he heard the incriminating lie. He told Saad: 'His name *was* Hazard. My name *is* Hazard.'

Saad couldn't hide what he felt then. His mouth stayed the same but he started to sweat and his eyes began moving as though looking for a way out. He now knew he was in trouble more serious than a holdup.

On down Fifth Avenue.

'Tell me all of it, and maybe I won't kill you.'

'I don't know anything.'

'Don't shit me.'

'I don't. I just drive.'

'Okay. You just drive and I'll tell you where.'

Hazard let silence work on Saad. At 23rd Street all he said was, 'Hang at left here,' and when they came to FDR Drive he told Saad, 'Downtown.'

'I just *drive*,' Saad kept repeating.

Nothing from Hazard except directions. Off at the Battery Park exit. North on West Street a few blocks and then beneath the West Side elevated highway. Cobblestone pavement, the tyres tattooing, a maze of red-and-white wooden barriers with yellow, blinking reflectors. Then about a half-mile stretch of wire mesh fence. The area beyond the fence had been river but was now being filled in for more city living space. Someone would get richer from it.

A wide opening in the fence. A sign that said AUTHORIZED VEHICLES ONLY was disregarded as the limo turned in on to a dirt road, a way created by the daily going and coming of heavy trucks. No one there now. Bulldozers, graders, earth shovels stood around like grotesque, catatonic beasts. The fill wasn't clean, rather the dumpings of every sort of rubble and junk. Crushed, twisted, mangled, rusted chunks, mounds, slabs, splinters – everything from the skeletons of car bodies to rotting baby-crib mattresses, toilet bowls, and beer cans by the millions. The solid waste of consumers, a massive defecation of instalment-plan buying. All this would be pounded down, pressed, and finally topped off with a few feet of good earth on which would be built structures that would be rooms full of future junk, future rubble.

A short way in, the limo's headlights hit upon a temporary shack with the words ONE MAN ONE JOB crudely hand-painted on it. Along with a poster urging SUPPORT THE PRESIDENT TO END THE WAR.

The limo continued to the end of that bad road, to the river's edge. From there, a clear view of the Statue of Liberty out in the harbour, green giant lady on her private island. In the opposite direction was the money skyline of Wall Street and left of that, closer, just across the highway, the twin towers of the Trade Center, tallest in the world, now lighted up – so high at this close range they gave the impression they were leaning and about to fall over.

Hazard cut the motor, pocketed the key and just sat there, keeping the pressure on Saad. He could sense Saad's spiralling panic, was waiting, hoping it would come out.

Saad, meanwhile, was not encouraged by his surroundings. The place was clearly right for a killing. He reminded himself that he'd always been a coward and living for a cause was different, easier than dying for one. Saad felt that if all was written as claimed, then his own lack of bravery had been and was meant to be. But he had sworn, hadn't he? What about honour? His fear had a ready answer. Honour was important only when there are witnesses.

For nearly a half hour Saad argued with his conscience. It was a one-sided argument.

Hazard kept his pocketed hand and the roll of Life Savers aimed at Saad and every so often he'd move it, thrust it purposely to build Saad's anxiety.

Saad wet his lips, ran his tongue over the bristles of his dab of a moustache and said, 'I must have your word.'

'Sure.'

'You won't kill me.'

'Not unless you lie.'

'The truth is I only did the driving.'

'Where?'

Saad told him about the house that was near Nyack, the interrogation, the George Washington Bridge. He didn't go into detail and he lied about one part, said with a trace of admiration that Carl had held out, that they hadn't been successful in getting the information they'd wanted from him. Saad figured the lie was in his favour because it was something Hazard would want to hear.

Hazard believed it.

'It wasn't anything personal.' Saad was more confident now. 'It could have been any one of a dozen people. It happened, unfortunately, to be him.'

Hazard doubted that. 'What was the information you wanted?'

'I don't know. They never told me. And when they decided

to kill him I pleaded with them not to do such a horrible thing, but I was nothing, only the driver.'

Hazard asked who *they* were.

'Black September.'

'I mean who were the other three?'

Saad told him the full names of Badr, Hatum, and Mustafa. After naming them he felt relieved, as though the blame was no longer focused on him.

'Where are they now?'

'They left the following day.'

'Out of the country?'

'I do not know.'

'You drove them to the airport.' Hazard was guessing but sounded as though he knew.

Saad decided he'd better admit that.

'You took them to the international terminal.'

'I was happy to see them go.'

Hazard nodded thoughtfully.

Saad interpreted it as agreement. He smiled and asked if it was all right if he had a cigarette, started to reach.

Hazard told him no. 'Get out.'

'You gave your word,' reminded Saad, but realized it was useless. Reverting suddenly, he said with hatred, *'Weld l-ihudi-gahba!'* (son of a Jew whore). He opened the door and got out. The moment his feet touched the ground he started to run.

Hazard hadn't anticipated that. Should have, but hadn't. He got out quickly and by the light of the Trade Mart towers saw Saad running up the road as fast as his stubby legs could go under the handicap of sixty overweight pounds. Hazard sprinted after him.

Saad expected any moment to hear shots at him, to feel the sting of a bullet entering his back. He knew he'd never make it all the way out to the street. He cut abruptly to his right, stumbled, almost fell, and got off the road, clawed and clambered up a pile of rubble and down to where it was darker. He made his way over the debris and through the maze of junk and, finally, with his lungs aching, flopped down behind the overturned hulk of a discarded refrigerator. He pressed tight against it, closed his eyes, and tried not to breathe so loudly. He heard Hazard coming, the rubble crunching under Hazard's steps. Hazard paused only a few feet away on the opposite side of the refrigerator. Saad silently begged to God to be merciful and, a few moments later, Hazard moved on, searching.

Saad remained where he was for several minutes, listening, estimating Hazard's movements, now further and further away. Then slowly, careful to make as little noise as possible, he crawled away from the refrigerator and up a small rise to peek over. He saw the limousine not more than a hundred feet away. He thought he'd run farther than that. He looked in the direction of the street and saw how far he'd have to go to reach there. Too far. He decided on the car. Took a deep breath and made a dash for it.

Hazard heard the limo's door slam. It occurred to him that Saad might have a spare ignition key. He ran for the limo and when he got to it saw Saad in the front seat. Saad had the limo's telephone up, calling for help.

Hazard rushed to the rear of the car where the telephone aerial projected up from the centre surface of the luggage compartment. He grabbed the aerial and yanked. It gave some but was still intact. He bent it down, put his entire weight on it and it finally snapped off at its base.

Saad knew the phone was dead when crackling static replaced the voice of the operator who'd been late in answering the remote-service signal. Saad hadn't had time to say a word.

But Hazard couldn't know that. It was possible Saad had got through to someone. He went to the left front door of the limo. Saad moved immediately to the opposite side, hunched down to make himself into as difficult a target as possible, still believing Hazard had a gun. Hazard got the key from his pocket and inserted it into the door lock. Before he could turn the key Saad, risking everything, was across the seat and pressing down the locking button from the inside. Saad had the advantage. Hazard's fingers could not get enough leverage to turn the key.

There was Saad's face, less than a reach away but protected by the rolled-up window.

Hazard gave up on the door.

Saad found it incredible that Hazard hadn't just shot him point blank through the glass.

Hazard hurried around to the other front door. Shoved the

94

key into its lock. But Saad beat him to it, held down its inside locking button.

Impasse.

Hazard backed off to decide what to do. No time to waste, however. Saad's help might be on the way.

Keeping an eye on the limo Hazard searched around among the debris until he found a suitable hunk of metal, a short I-shaped piece of rusted steel. He went to the driver side of the car, reared back, and let go. He expected the glass to smash and fly but instead it merely turned frosty opaque with a cobweb pattern of cracks, and remained intact except for an irregular four-inch hole at the point of impact.

Shatter-proof.

It took a half dozen full-force blows for Hazard to break enough of the window out. He looked in. Saad was against the opposite side. Hazard opened the door. He saw then that Saad had a knife extended directly at him, a five-inch blade. It was more than a match for the gun Hazard didn't have. Considerably more formidable than a roll of Life Savers. But Hazard shoved his hand into his jacket pocket, still pretending to have a weapon. Cautiously, Hazard reached around to unlock the rear door. He took one careful step up and in.

Over the seat Saad cut the air with the knife; short, slashing jabs. It was a weapon he knew how to handle, had known since he was a boy.

Hazard decided he had to make his move. He waited a moment and then made it all at once. Into the back seat, the fingers of his left hand curled slightly but tensed, his wrist stiffened as he'd been taught by the DIA instructors. His left hand by-passed the knife and the fleshy heel of his hand chopped at Saad's forearm, sending it aside, away. Hazard's right hand was already made into the most powerful of all karate fists – the *oyayiuhi ipponken*: four fingers folded in tight and solid, thumb bent with its tip pressed hard down on the second knuckle of the forefinger, a fist strictly forbidden in karate matches because of its lethalness.

In continuous motion with his left, Hazard brought his right hand around and even remembered to rotate it at the last possible moment for a snap of maximum power. Perfect strike. It caught Saad flush on the left temple, sending him against the steering wheel and instrument panel. He slumped down, his dead weight settling.

Hazard pulled Saad back to the seat, shoved him over, and propped him up and put the chauffeur's cap on him. He looked asleep but Hazard was fairly sure he was dead. Blood was coming out of Saad's left ear.

Hazard picked up Saad's knife, got out, and threw it into the river. A harbour police boat was coming downstream at that moment, a short way out, patrolling. Hazard's plan for Saad had been the river but now with the boat and possible phone call, he decided to get away from there.

He drove out and turned north to Jay Street, went up the ramp and, when he was on the West Side elevated highway, felt very exposed. Cars coming. Cars passing. The city to his right looking as lighted and awake as always. The power of the limo felt unfamiliar and he had to restrain his foot not to use it, kept exactly on the fifty limit. He switched on the radio. Music. A piece of soul. He dialled away from it, got some bad news. The Mets had lost in the ninth on a wild pitch.

He glanced over at the body of Saad and thought of Carl. And again when the lights of the George Washington Bridge came into view. He turned off at the 125th Street exit and headed downtown on Riverside Drive, thinking about how to dispose of his passenger. Maybe just leave him in the car somewhere. But remembering Binzer and the DPL licence-plate inquiry made Hazard cancel that idea. He couldn't rely on Binzer to keep that quiet. No, he had to put the body some place where it wouldn't be found for a long while, or never. Where?

The limo was stopped for a light at 102nd Street when Hazard heard it. He thought he'd merely imagined it but then he heard it again, definitely.

A short moan from Saad. He wasn't dead. Almost, but not dead.

Hazard's first thought was to hit Saad again. He pulled over. All it would take was a single blow in the same spot. He took off Saad's cap and made his own right hand into that lethal fist.

But then he couldn't do it.

Saad was just a lump of a man, too helpless.

Hazard tried to call up enough hate. He told himself he had

96

to. He told himself it was an act of mercy. He reminded himself of the consequences, the danger, if, by some remarkable means, Saad recovered.

Three, four times, Hazard was about to deliver the final blow but he just couldn't do it.

By then it was ten to three.

Hazard drove around awhile, avoided the major avenues and was headed east on 98th Street near Amsterdam when he saw the lettering on the truck:

SANTIANO & SONS

Brooklyn, N. Y.

The dark green garbage truck was collecting along that street. Two men were feeding garbage into its wide rear opening. No neat tied-up plastic bags in this area. Plain old classical cans, overflowing.

Hazard took special notice of how the men worked, hoisted the heavy cans up and emptied them in. And when the rear of the truck was full enough one or the other of the men banged loudly on the side, a signal for the driver to activate the device that scooped the load into the huge body of the vehicle.

Hazard drove by. A tight squeeze. He had to go slow and he got a long, closer look. He circled the block and kept a discreet distance behind the truck, matching its stops and starts to the end of that crosstown block. He used the time to empty Saad's pockets. A half pack of Egyptian cigarettes, a ballpoint pen, ring of house keys, and, from Saad's back trousers pocket, a worn, much-sat-upon wallet containing, among other things, sixty-four dollars.

Halfway down the next block the truck stopped at an alley that ran deep between two larger buildings. The alley was half below street level. The two garbage men disappeared down into it.

Hazard decided this was his chance. He pulled the limo up so it was in position with the rear of the truck but out of view of the driver. Quickly, Hazard got out, went around and opened the limo's other front door. He turned and squatted to get his shoulders under Saad. A fireman's carry. Hazard's legs nearly buckled when he straightened up with all that extra weight. Four steps to the rear of the truck. The edge was waist high. He dropped Saad in and saw now that this section of the truck was cylindrical, shaped like a huge horizontal drum partially cut away.

The sour smell of garbage.

Hazard banged twice on the side of the truck.

At once the compressing mechanism went into motion with a grinding sound as its line of thick steel teeth came curving over and down to the inside edge, like a monster closing its mouth, scraping its food back into its belly and with a hydraulic hiss digesting it with fifty thousand pounds of pressure per square inch.

No more Saad.

Garbage.

The dull clanging of pails warned Hazard that the two men were coming back from the alley. He got into the limo, drove by and away.

He left the limo right on Madison Avenue, where it was sure to be towed away. Immunity? No, the limo was anonymous, susceptible after Hazard stripped it of its DPL plates.

Hazard didn't tell Keven what he'd done.

When he arrived home he found her on his bedroom floor, using the door for a headboard. She had ocean breakers on the cartridge player.

'What are you doing down there?'

'I wanted to make sure you woke me when you came in.'

'Were you asleep?'

'Just half.'

She tried to kiss him hello and he wanted that very much, but he avoided her and went into the bathroom.

He took a long shower, lathered thick all over, and rinsed, lathered and rinsed again. While he was drying in front of the mirror he thought he didn't look the same.

He brushed his teeth extra hard and used the Water Pic.

He expected by then that Keven would be trying to sleep, but she was waiting for him on the bed. He detected the fragrance of tangerines in the air. Clean. Welcome. Her arms were extended as though to guide him to her and he went between them to be drawn against her.

The love they made included something they hadn't experienced together before – a desperation, a greed, like a verification of life.

No need to tell her what he'd done, thought Hazard.

She knew.

7

LATE IN the afternoon of that same day Hazard and Keven went up to the installation. They weren't scheduled. Hazard wanted to see Kersh.

He got alone with Kersh and told him right out that he now was sure Carl had been murdered, and that one of the men who did it was dead.

Of all possible questions, Kersh chose to ask, 'How do you feel?'

It made Hazard more certain than ever that his affection for Kersh was not misplaced. 'I'm okay.'

'Try not to let it cut deeper than it already has.'

It's already to the bone, Hazard thought.

'Maybe you need some distraction. Go somewhere for a while, do whatever you like.'

'Can't.'

'Why not?'

'There are three more.' Meaning Badr, Hatum, and Mustafa.

Kersh wanted to dissuade him, but sensed it would be futile, probably even resented. 'How can I help?' he asked.

'I need an advance.'

In the past Hazard had frequently asked for and received advances on his weekly five hundred. Sometimes he was as much as two or three weeks behind. At the moment it just happened he was even.

'And some time on my own.'

'How much?'

'Five thousand, and maybe two months.'

Kersh didn't agree immediately. Not that he had any thoughts of refusing. A better idea had occurred to him, one that would cover what Hazard wanted and possibly include some extra advantages. What he had in mind was a transAtlantic exercise, an ultimate test of telepathic communication. It was well within his power to authorize such an exercise and, if in so doing he was stepping on anyone's toes, hell, they could scream later. He suggested it to Hazard, pointing out that it would put Hazard over there in more of an official capacity. Also, Hazard would be on expenses and the exercise part of it wouldn't require much of his time.

'What about the five-thousand advance?'

Kersh smiled agreeably and that settled it.

Except for one final request by Hazard. He asked that Kersh arrange for him to attend an accelerated violence course, what the DIA called an 'intensive'. Hazard had previously ridiculed the DIA mandate that all active personnel had to attend its special courses every year. A week a year was minimum. Some agents took more for their own good, but not Hazard. He'd gone for karate instruction twice, and then only after having tried every possible way to get out of it.

However, now he was asking to go. If there was one thing he'd learned from killing Saad it was that he didn't know how to kill. He'd really hacked it, been lucky, and knew it.

Kersh promised to arrange for the intensive immediately. He was especially glad to do it because it indicated Hazard wasn't being totally impulsive.

All that was left then was to let Keven know what was planned. She resented not being included in the first place and she said so. As for Hazard going abroad, she didn't like that at all. She was afraid for him, but rather than add to the anxiety of the moment, she kept that to herself. For everyone's sake, especially her own, she acted indifferent, almost blasé about it. 'Senders get to go places and have all the fun,' she complained.

Hazard going alone to take intensive training was something else. Keven suggested, then insisted she go along. She demanded her equal rights, contending that an aptitude for violence was by no means exclusively male.

It was critical to Hazard that he get the most out of the DIA training in the shortest possible time. Keven might be a distraction, he thought. 'It's no place for you,' he told her.

'I'm as much of a damn agent as you are.'

'So?'

'Maybe you're afraid I'll learn some dirty tricks...'

'It's not that.'

'...and use them on you.'

Hazard imagined lethal abilities added to her Irish temper. She had a point.

'Besides,' she went on, 'there's always the big threat.'

'Of what?'

She narrowed her eyes dramatically and extended the initial sound of the word. 'Rrrrape.'

Hazard held back a laugh.

'There were sixty thousand rapes last year and that's only counting this country. One every seven seconds. Don't you want me to be able to take care of myself?'

'That the only reason you want to go?'

'What else?'

She only wanted, of course, to be with Hazard as much as possible before he left. She would have preferred spending the time together some place away and peaceful, but, no matter, she'd take what she could get.

They sparred on the issue a while longer and then looked to Kersh. He already had his mind made up in case he was asked. He pretended to give it some deliberation, finally shrugged, and said, 'If Keven wants to go I can hardly prevent it. After all, it *is* a requirement.'

So Hazard and Keven spent the next three weeks in Frederick, Maryland, at what the DIA people called 'the farm'. It was a large old house and outbuildings set on extensive grounds walled high all around. Once it had been a horse farm and to keep that appearance, as well as the appropriate aroma to the place, there were still a number of horses around, lazy and fortunate.

Taking the 'intensive' meant fourteen hours of instruction each day, and some days as many as sixteen. They received individual instruction with emphasis on judo and karate, which were prerequisites, but they could choose from a wide range of electives – knife throwing, for example, or the relatively benign techniques of poisoning.

Hazard's qualms about Keven, that she might consider the entire thing a lark and be a distraction were quickly erased. From the first day she went at it with a seriousness matching Hazard's own grim attitude. Sooner than anyone expected she was tossing her two-hundred-pound judo instructor around as though he were no more than a despicable loaf of white

102

bread. She seemed to enjoy every hostile minute of it and got so she could execute all the various karate fist and elbow strikes. She became particularly adept at delivering the *kingeri*, also known as the groin kick.

Weapons.

Keven worked out with a nine-millimetre Smith and Wesson double-action automatic, which could put a man down with a hit just about anywhere. The comparatively thin grip of that gun suited her and its shorter trigger reach felt comfortable, allowed her more easily to master the correct squeeze, soft yet deliberate. The gun that was first issued and registered personally to her had been previously used. She politely requested a brand new one and got it. She cared for that S & W lovingly, disassembled and cleaned it even when it didn't need it. Her baby.

Hazard, for his primary weapon, first tried a Colt .357 Magnum, perhaps the most powerful handgun in the world. He didn't like it. Despite its reassuring deadliness, it was too heavy, bulky, and obvious. He settled instead on a 32-calibre Llama automatic, just six and a quarter inches overall length and only twenty ounces. Made in Spain by the Gabilondo firm, it looked like a junior version of the famous .45 Colt service automatic.

Having sacrificed power for convenience, Hazard had to go for accuracy. The Llama was built for rimfire, giving it a velocity of about two thousand feet per second. That helped, but beyond the range of sixty feet it wasn't reliable, especially with soft-nosed ammunition – the kind that was slower but would spread on impact and more likely kill than merely penetrate. To fire the Llama with consistent accuracy took a lot of practice and concentration. When Hazard managed seven hits out of a clip of nine on an inch-and-a-half circle at fifty feet, his weapons instructor congratulated him. But Hazard wasn't satisfied. Not until he was getting nine out of nine, regularly.

Hazard's and Keven's guns were both custom-fitted with a new type of silencer. Compared to the more commonly used and longer type, this silencer was much more discreet. Only about three-quarters of an inch in length and diameter. It screwed on and could be left on.

How to fight with a knife.

103

Considering his adversaries, Hazard believed that was something he'd damn well better learn. He was surprised to find how much dancelike agility it required, and such delicate touch. It wasn't just a matter of stabbing someone. Rely on the sharpness of the blade, he was told. Hazard finally became quite efficient at it, so good, in fact, that his instructor gave him a special kind of knife. On first examination it appeared to be ordinary, with a snap on its handle that shot its five-inch blade straight out. Its exceptional feature was what happened to the blade when it penetrated; when it went into flesh the pressure of resistance activated a mechanism inside its handle that made the blade revolve at high speed in a coring motion. Gruesome. Hazard accepted it with thanks.

During those intensive three weeks at the farm (twenty-one consecutive days, with not even a Sunday off) it wasn't easy for Hazard and Keven to find time and place for being alone. Keven was assigned a room on the top floor of the east wing, rather isolated. Hazard's room was on the same floor but way over on the other side of the building. Fortunately there was never much traffic in the corridor after midnight and they nearly got caught only twice.

Hazard found that having to sneak from room to room added a desirable spice to their activities. Keven admitted to that added effect, although sneaking around for such a natural purpose was against her values, made her also feel unduly guilty, she said.

They compromised. One night he'd sneak; the next night it was her turn.

Keven also complained about having to be so quiet when they were together. Several times she almost suffocated herself with a pillow.

8

ON MAY 18th, shortly before sundown, a clean, white ship entered the harbour of Alexandria, Egypt.

It was a two-thousand tonner with blue lettering on its hull that identified it as the *Sea Finder* out of Washington, D.C. From stem to stern just above the waterline it had a painted red stripe, although that graphic attempt to give the ship sleekness was defeated by the upright structure that stood at midship – a 110-foot framework tower that resembled an oil derrick. It made the vessel appear awkward, top-heavy.

There was no other ship in the world like the *Sea Finder*. It had been specially planned and built by a large, diversified corporation for an admirable scientific purpose. Underwater search and recovery.

Even the ship's propulsion system was designed to better fulfil that purpose. Instead of the usual horizontal churning propellers, it was driven by vertical bladed units that extended down beneath the ship, one forward and another aft. The *Sea Finder* could, for example, rotate a full three hundred and sixty degrees in place as though revolving on an axis. And it could maintain an exact position, hover over any chosen spot of the ocean's floor with the precise control of a helicopter, even in heavy seas.

Neatly stacked and secured on its foredeck were sections of four-and-a-half-inch pipe in sixty-foot lengths. Four hundred of these. Directly below the derrick, a bottom portion of the ship's hull was omitted to form an open well twelve by thirty-six. Using the derrick, the sections of pipe could be fitted together and lowered down through the well into the sea to a depth of twenty-four thousand feet. Attached to the business end of the pipe, a special assembly of underwater lights, television cameras, and sonar devices could scan the ocean floor along a search path twenty-four hundred feet wide and five hundred feet ahead. The accuracy of this sensor assembly was such that at a distance of a thousand feet it could distinguish

105

between two objects no more than three feet apart.

Once an objective was located, the huge tongs fixed to the extreme end of the pipe could be put to work. The heavy-duty tines of the tongs would spread apart and then close around the object like a giant claw. Then it would be only a matter of bringing the pipe up in the same section-by-section manner it had been lowered. And, of course, the recovered object would finally come up with it.

The beauty of it was that all these underwater functions could be controlled with ease from above in the ship's recovery-operations room. A complex electronic system was involved, but its operation had been reduced to push-button simplicity.

The *Sea Finder* was indeed one of a kind. Unfortunately it had not been in service when the submarine *Thresher* went down in 1963 and when an H-bomb was lost in 1968 off Polomares, Spain. It would have been perfect for those jobs. In any case, until another such emergency occurred, the ship was a marine archaeologist's dream come true.

It had proved itself on its maiden voyage by recovering from a depth of three thousand feet what remained of a Portuguese galleon that had sunk in 1682 off the coast of Colombia. From that initial effort, the corporation that owned the *Sea Finder* had already recouped a good share of its seven-million-dollar investment. The galleon gave up seven hundred thousand old pesos, each containing one and a half ounces of pure silver. Other objects recovered, such as weapons, tools, cooking utensils, and porcelain (of mere historic value), were donated to the various institutions represented by the archaeologists voluntarily along on that expedition.

With that profitable first success to its credit, the *Sea Finder* was ready for the even greater rewards promised by the Mediterranean. It was estimated that for the thousand years before Christ and the thousand years after, more than twenty thousand ships went to the bottom of that sea. The Mediterranean, comparatively deep and cold, was especially conducive to underwater preservation. Also the small amount of sediment there, only about six inches every thousand years, meant it was possible that many ships that went down in ancient times were still intact.

To the *Sea Finder*'s crew of thirty and the twelve marine

archaeologists and other scientists aboard, it was an inspiring theory, particularly so considering the numerous Roman ships that had sailed from Alexandria and never reached Rome. Many were laden with tributes and taxes, vast amounts of gold.

So for the *Sea Finder*, with its advanced recovery system, the Mediterranean would be relatively easy pickings.

To guide the ship into Alexandria, an Egyptian harbour official had come aboard. Under his direction it made for pier 2, the mooring station nearest the harbour entrance. Pier 2 was remote and isolated from the rest of the busy port. It was a restricted area, where the *Sea Finder* would attract the least attention. The ship's captain, a man named Copeland, saw the practical side of that. It made good sense not to flaunt the United States flag in those not particularly amiable waters.

By the time all the ship's lines were secure and its engines cut it was dark. In the distance across the way the lights of Alexandria shone and pulsed invitingly, but no one on the *Sea Finder* would be allowed to go ashore that night. An official order. Everyone, including the captain, was to remain aboard until papers had been inspected. And radio silence was to be maintained. Just a formality, the harbour official said.

Captain Copeland did not protest but he firmly reminded the harbour official that he and his ship and men were there with the sanction of the Egyptian Government by arrangements made through the Arab Republic's cultural attaché in Washington. The Ministry of Culture had agreed to allow the American archaeologists and oceanographers to examine certain old documents and charts kept in the archives in Alexandria. The harbour official politely assured Captain Copeland that he saw no reason why everything should not be put straight by the next day at the latest. It was only a normal matter of clearance. Meanwhile, would the Captain please co-operate and be sure no one went ashore under any circumstances?

Captain Copeland gave his word on that.

To make certain his word was kept, three Arab soldiers with automatic rifles stood guard on the otherwise deserted pier.

The crew and scientists aboard the *Sea Finder* had been looking forward to going ashore. They'd been at sea for fifteen days and now they couldn't even go for a walk on the pier. They grumbled about it until Captain Copeland explained the situation. They then became more or less resigned to waiting until the next day to experience the publicized romantic mystique of the ancient city.

The ship settled down for the night.

By midnight everyone was asleep, except one of the crew assigned to gangway watch.

At half past twelve a pair of canvas-covered troop carriers came down the pier and stopped at the ship. The man standing gangway watch thought little of it; he assumed it was only the three guards on the pier being relieved. He didn't become alarmed until one of the guards came up the short gangway and pushed an automatic rifle point blank into his chest. He was told in bad English to be quiet.

Out of the troop carriers came fifteen uniformed, armed men. They quickly went aboard the *Sea Finder* and within minutes had the ship's entire complement assembled on the rear deck. No one resisted. Everyone was frightened by the guns and the serious attitude of the troops who pointed them.

Captain Copeland demanded an explanation.

An Arab wearing the rank of major was in charge. He ignored Copeland's demand, informed the assembled group they were to be escorted off the ship for clearance purposes. No harm would come to them as long as they cooperated.

Several of the crew who had on only their skivvies asked to get dressed.

Request denied.

Captain Copeland thought it best to comply. He advised his men to do the same and he rather courageously promised the Arab major ample retribution when the proper Government officials learned of this outrageous treatment.

The major nodded.

Copeland and his men filed off the ship, climbed up into the troop carriers, and were taken away.

Immediately two other troop carriers came, bringing thirty men, civilians this time. They boarded the *Sea Finder* and spent the next four hours getting acquainted with the unique ship. They already knew it comparatively well from weeks of studying the schematic and systems plans that had been purchased by a sympathizer in the United States and sent over.

That hadn't been difficult; it was not a military ship, but a private one.

The men had been chosen for this assignment because of their various special abilities. Some were recent graduates of the Oceanographic Institute of Alexandria. Others were engineers and communications experts out of the science department of Cairo University. Several of the men had worked for years in the Saudi and Libyan oil fields. What all thirty had in common was impatience with politics and a fervent belief in militancy.

At 3:30 A.M. the ship's diesel-electric engines were started and set at idle. A half hour later the mooring lines were taken in, and the ship pulled away from the pier. The same harbour pilot who had guided the ship into the port now guided her out. With running lights dimmed. Hardly anyone, surely no one of consequence, had witnessed the *Sea Finder*'s arrival – and the isolation of pier 2 had served its purpose. Now no one saw her go. It was as though the ship had never ever been there.

By sun-up it was well beyond sight of Alexandria, headed west at full speed. The following day just north of Darnah it keet rendezvous with a Libyan tanker to take on fuel, and four days later it was at Gibraltar. A friendly hello signal flashed from the rock. The *Sea Finder* returned the greeting, passed through the strait to the Atlantic, and altered its heading to southwest. An automatic dead-reckoning analyser kept it steady on course.

Each day along the way, the Arab crew practised using the search and recovery equipment. Each man concentrated on his own special task. The Arabs had difficulty doing that. Their habit, inclination, was to pay more attention to what the other fellow was doing and tell him how to do it better. They were collectively good at giving advice but individually resented taking it. Despite the confusion this caused, they did manage to get organized and were working together fairly smoothly by the time they neared their destination.

Where they were going was not a port but an area of the ocean known as the Canary Basin – one of the deeper parts of the Atlantic, situated just east of the Mid-Atlantic ridge. They were after a specific position, and the *Sea Finder*'s inertial-navigation system would help pinpoint it.

A reading indicated the ship's position to be 33 degrees 7

minutes west, 27 degrees 5 minutes north. They continued on until the reading showed precisely 34 degrees 5 minutes west, 26 degrees 2 minutes north. They were there. Now they could only hope the information they'd received was correct.

The ship's special engines were adjusted to hold position and the crew went to work. First the gantry was used to lift the leader section of pipe from the foredeck and deposit it on to the narrow, gutter-like runway that ran down the centre of the deck. Automatically the leader pipe was pushed to the derrick, where a huge vice-like block clamped on to its end and hoisted it full length upright within the derrick. Then the pipe was lowered through a surrounding device that snugly guided it down to the well deck just below. There the sensor assembly – with its television cameras, lights, and sonar – was fitted on to the pipe, and the large recovery tongs were secured just below that on the very end.

Upon signal the pipe was sent down into the water of the open well. Stop, so that a second section of pipe could be joined to the first. This second section had already been lifted into position within the derrick above and now it was swiftly connected by a flush collar tightened by a powerful electric wrench. This same procedure was methodically repeated. Section after section of pipe was strung together and lowered into the ocean.

At the average rate of twenty-five sections per hour it took a little over twelve hours working nonstop to send down eighteen thousand feet of pipe. Then, according to sonar measurements, they were less than two hundred feet from the bottom.

It was time to take a look.

The television cameras and lights were functioning perfectly. The monitors in the recovery-operations room were receiving clear pictures. The ocean floor at that depth resembled a desert, void of any growth or life. Nothing at all moved and no irregular shapes – only what appeared to be a sandy, level plain.

But the sonar was picking up something to starboard.

The *Sea Finder* rotated in position, slowly so the fixed cameras on the sensor assembly presented a view all around. Turning slowly. Nothing ... nothing ... and then, there was what they were looking for. No more than six hundred feet away.

In that barren setting with no comparison to help determine size, the long rectangular blocks of concrete looked like tombstones in a disturbed, forgotten graveyard. Or the ruins of an ancient temple. Some of the rectangular blocks lay on their sides, supporting others that projected nearly straight up. Others were scattered around. Just as they'd happened to land after plunging down through three miles of water, dropped over the side by various United States naval vessels.

The *Sea Finder* was manoeuvred for a closer look. Close enough to make out the stencilled serial numbers on some of the concrete blocks. Such as USACC–RMA–3–72–1783–OD–5 and USACC–FD–12–70–B2046–ABV–10. How accommodating that the blocks were labelled so clearly, thought the Arabs. Thank you, United States.

They were even more grateful to their version of God. That they had been allowed to learn this precise location out of the thousands of square miles of ocean proved that He favoured them and sanctioned their cause. He was showing them the way.

33 degrees 7 minutes west, 27 degrees 5 minutes north.

33 : 7w 27 : 5n

It was number for number, letter for letter the information they had extracted from Carl, that Carl had believed safe to reveal because the ocean depths seemed an impossible obstacle.

The Arab crew aboard the *Sea Finder* set about to prove Carl wrong.

The sonar system fixed on one of the concrete blocks isolated from the pile. In the recovery-operations room the objective appeared on a monitor that contained an arrangement of concentric circles, like a target with vertical and horizontal crosshairs. At the moment the bright dot representing the object was on the perimeter right and slightly below the third inner circle. The ship manoeuvred until the dot matched the intersection of the crosshairs. Then the *Sea Finder* was precisely over its target.

Three more sections of pipe were sent down, and then a final section was lowered more slowly, a foot at a time and then inches. There was no guesswork to it. With the sonar and television cameras it was more like retrieving something from a shallow aquarium rather than from three miles deep.

The huge, wide-spread tongs closed in around the middle of a concrete block. And locked.

The pipe was brought up section by section, dismantled as it came.

Twelve hours later the concrete block emerged from the water in the ship's open well, the red of its stencilled serial numbers standing out, darker wet. It was secured, released from the tongs, and put down on the well deck.

The entire crew assembled there for a triumphant look at it. They congratulated one another, exuberantly, and felt important. In celebration bottles of *ariki* were passed around. But what each man tasted more was the promise of greater victory to come, a time soon when he would be one of the heroes celebrated throughout a fully restored Arab kingdom.

As for now, the men had been working twenty-four hours straight. They took eight hours' rest and put in another twenty-four. After recovering a second of those concrete blocks they headed home.

In Alexandria, time had reduced Captain Copeland to silent exasperation. He'd been furious, demanded his rights as an American citizen; he'd threatened and fumed indignantly, exhibited more of his temper and even attempted to reason. All to no effect. Either the guards did not respond or they only told him to be patient.

Copeland tried to make sense out of it. But it didn't make sense. There was no reasonable explanation for their being detained. Unless maybe a war was on that they didn't know about.

Incongruous was the way they were being treated. Not at all badly. They were provided with excellent food, and were comfortably quartered, no more than two men to a room. When some of the crew complained about the lack of female company – they'd counted on that free night in Alexandria – even that accommodation had been offered. Copeland quickly vetoed that. There'd be none of that.

All things considered, if it hadn't been for the Arab soldiers guarding them they might have been guests at someone's

112

large, slightly run-down but still luxurious home. That's what it was, obviously, a private house. No doubt it was government property, Copeland thought, confiscated and used for such instances as this when they wanted to keep someone incommunicado. They were allowed into the spacious courtyard during the day, but the solid, two-story-high wall prevented them from going anywhere or seeing what was beyond it.

Copeland had, at first, feared that some of the more restless and impetuous of his crew might get fed up with being confined and attempt something. However, he was not entirely pleased when they all settled down and apparently enjoyed having nothing to do but laze around and play poker or blackjack. The scientists also seemed more relaxed than distressed, as though they welcomed the interlude. They sipped tall, cool drinks and took the sun, and at night they sat around and theorized. Copeland felt alone with his concern. He just couldn't be patient, as his Arab keepers advised.

At one o'clock on the morning of the eighteenth day everyone was pulled up from sleep. They were taken out and loaded into two troop carriers. After a half-hour ride they were deposited on the waterfront. The armed escort and troop carriers quickly departed, just left Copeland and his men standing there. It seemed unreal to them, as though the entire episode hadn't happened. There they were on the very same pier as before, number 2, it was the same sort of night with Alexandria twinkling across the way and there was *Sea Finder* moored exactly where they'd last seen her.

They went aboard and found nothing missing, nothing disturbed. If anything, the ship appeared tidier than she had been. All the bunks were made up fresh and clean, the galley was spotless, and so was the wardroom. Also, someone had been thoughtful enough to put on a full supply of water and fuel.

At once Copeland placed a radio call to the corporation's top executive in Washington, a man named Nelson. Nelson was close to the Government, had high connections in all the important branches. He'd proved that by successfully lobbying for the interests of the corporation on several occasions. Nelson, if anyone, should know how to handle this situation.

Nelson came on.

Copeland gave him a complete rundown.

Nelson expressed proper concern and said to rest assured, he'd see that something was done. Copeland was right, Nelson said. An explanation was damn well due. Copeland was to call him again in an hour.

Competent man, Copeland thought, he'd get to the bottom of this thing by taking it to the top.

As agreed, Copeland called Nelson again in an hour.

Nelson sounded different. 'Is the ship damaged in any way?'

'No, not that I can see.'

'Is anyone harmed?'

'No.'

'Thank God for that.'

'We were held prisoner for eighteen days,' Copeland reminded him.

'We're filing a formal protest.'

'What should I do on this end?'

'Nothing.'

'But surely —'

'We'll take care of everything,' Nelson said.

'They ought to be made to pay some sort of reparation. Some —'

'Let us worry about that. But remember, Copeland, the bottom line is no harm done. Meanwhile, your orders are to get on with the expedition.'

What Nelson didn't say was that his friends at State weren't inclined to press beyond a mild protest. Things were touchy enough in the Middle East. It wasn't easy to keep balance on the fine line between certain minority votes at home and all that Arab oil over there.

Copeland believed the least he had coming was an official apology, but he finally decided to go along with Nelson. Disgruntled, he said to hell with the archives. They'd search and recover on their own.

The *Sea Finder* put its stern to Alexandria that morning.

9

WHENEVER ANYONE asked Hazard to recommend a hotel in London he always said Dukes.

He'd never stayed there, had only heard Dukes favourably mentioned by various amateur poker players – the bored wealthy kind whose known fortunes made them unbelievable when they tried to buy a pot.

That Hazard should be asked anything about London seemed plausible. He gave the impression that he'd been to and knew places, and though he didn't go out of his way to promote the lie, he also didn't deny it. The truth was he'd been to London only once and even that time didn't really count. It was in 1968 when he'd hit a twelve-thousand-dollar superfecta at Roosevelt Raceway and taken a chartered gambling junket to London. All he'd seen of the city was on the ride from and to Heathrow Airport. The forty-eight hours in between he'd spent indoors, losing. Actually that was the first and last time he'd been out of the States, except for Canada and Mexico.

But now he was in London and staying at Dukes. He found that hotel to be everything he'd always heard and said it was. Situated in a quiet cul-de-sac with a grand iron gate and a cobblestone courtyard, it offered elegant comfort without being stiff about it. Hazard arrived without a reservation, dressed casually, and, as usual, tieless. He would surely have been turned away at Claridges or the Connaught. But at Dukes he was so amiably received he didn't doubt when told the hotel's only vacancy was an expensive top floor suite made available by a last-minute cancellation. He signed in, surrendered his passport to the desk, and went up, to be surprised when the floor waiter and chambermaid greeted him by name. They had future tips in their eyes but also promises of immediate good service. Inside the suite he was welcomed by fresh cut flowers, a salver of fruit and that day's *Times*. It was altogether the way to go, Hazard thought. On expenses.

115

He settled right in, showered, and enjoyed one of the terry-cloth robes provided by the house. Then he ordered a double scotch, specifying Dewars and smiling at the idea of pronouncing it correctly. It was quickly brought, along with his passport, returned to him from the desk. He sat in a soft chair near one of the windows and looked out over Green Park, which was really green. The weather was misting, just lightly, typically. He sipped the drink and reminded himself what he was there for. Not a holiday.

From his single piece of luggage, new, bought for the trip, he removed his Llama automatic, special knife, and two other passports. One of the passports was authentically his, another was his under the name George Beech, and the one he'd used to register identified him as Edmund Stevens. Obtaining the false passports had been routine for the DIA, though there'd been some resistance to his getting two.

The Llama. He slipped it from its holster, a lightweight shoulder holster that held the automatic inverted for an easier, faster draw. He checked out the Llama, reassured himself it contained a full clip of 32 soft noses, ready to go. Two spare clips were snapped on to the holster's underarm strap. He took up the knife and pressed its release button to make the blade shoot out. He thumbed both edges of the blade, carefully, because they were honed so sharp. He didn't like thinking he'd have to use the knife.

What time was it? The clock in his head didn't agree with his watch, which showed quarter after two London time. Maybe he'd feel better if he took a nap. He lay on the bed and tried, but after a half hour he gave up, got up, and used the phone.

He had one lead. It had brought him to London. He'd got it from a cheap, frayed little address book he'd found in Saad's wallet. The book had about twenty telephone numbers, New York numbers for the first names such as Vicky, Shawn, Monika, Tammy. Working girls. Except for one name and number that stood out.

Badr Al Nabua, London, KNI–7894.

Hazard asked the Dukes' operator to get that number for him. It rang a couple of times before a female voice answered with, 'Knightsbridge seven eight nine four.'

Hazard was uncertain about whether he should ask for Al

116

Nabua or omit the Al. 'Mr Nabua, please.'

'Who is calling?'

Good, thought Hazard; his man was probably there. 'Mr Howard,' he said.

'Your number, Mr Howard?'

'I want to speak to Mr Nabua.'

'Please give me your number and Mr Nabua will call you.'

'I'll call back. When do you expect him?'

'This is only a message service, sir. Now if you'll kindly give me —'

'Where are you located?'

'That's irrelevant, sir.'

'All right, what's the name of your service?'

'Why?'

'I need someone to take messages for me.'

That prospect changed her. More amicably now, she told him, 'We're the Wickersham Exchange.'

Hazard thanked her and hung up. He consulted the telephone directory and found the address of the Wickersham Exchange. From the desk drawer he got a letter-sized envelope into which he put several sheets of blank paper to make it look fat and important. He sealed the envelope and printed Mr Badr Al Nabua large on its face. Then he got dressed, harnessed on the Llama under his jacket, slipped the knife in his boot, and went out.

Three ten Argyll Road was a private house converted to commerce. It was occupied by half a dozen small businesses. Wickersham Exchange was on the second floor. There was no name on the door, merely a business card thumbtacked to the door frame. No bell. Hazard went into a narrow anteroom, a short hallway, really, furnished with one abused folding chair. He heard telephone-answering voices coming from the next room and went farther in to find two overweight women seated in front of an outdated switchboard. Their glances made Hazard feel intrusive. He asked to see the manager.

One of the women finished taking a message, took off her headset, got up, and tugged at her dress as she came to him. She had punished, mousy hair, an overpowered face, and a large mouth. 'I'm Mrs Elliott,' she said as though that meant something.

Hazard retreated a few steps to the anteroom. Mrs Elliott

117

followed cautiously as far as the connecting doorway. Hazard took out the envelope from his jacket pocket. 'I'm from the Chase Manhattan Bank,' he said, 'London branch.'

'Oh?'

'It's urgent that I locate a Mr...' Hazard glanced at the envelope for effect. '... a Mr Nabua.' He made sure Mrs Elliott saw the face of the envelope but his fingers covered the embossed Dukes insignia in the upper left corner.

'You have something for Mr Nabua?'

Hazard nodded.

She held out her hand. 'I'll see that he gets it.'

'My instructions are to deliver it personally to Mr Nabua.'

'Then I'm afraid I can't help you.'

'It's a money matter,' Hazard said, and slapped the envelope against the palm of his other hand to let her see how fat it was. 'I'll need Mr Nabua's signature on my receipt.'

'We're not supposed to give out our clients' addresses.'

'Mr Nabua will be glad you did in this case.' The envelope again.

She told him, 'Just a minute,' and disappeared into the switchboard room. Within a few moments she returned with a four-by-five index card. 'I don't seem to have an address for Mr Nabua. He paid cash in advance January last for a year's service. Never gave us an address. We prefer that our clients do so, but he did pay cash in advance.'

'Do you have any idea where I might find Mr Nabua?'

'Not an inkling. As a matter of fact, we haven't heard from him for several weeks now. He used to call in for his messages quite frequently. Perhaps he's out of town. I'm very sorry.'

Hazard's thoughts exactly. 'Well, it's his loss.'

He went back to his hotel suite, got undressed again, and ordered up two more double scotches. In the fading light he lay on the bed with a tumbler of whisky resting on his abdomen. Thinking about what to do next. He'd counted on Badr's phone number.

It had been the right track but it stopped short. End of the line.

On the positive side he at least knew Badr had been in London as recently as a few weeks back, had for some reason been there long enough to hire a telephone-message service, might still be around, might call in any time to get messages.

Hazard thought maybe he could leave some irresistible message with Badr's exchange and maybe Badr would call in and get it and might return the call and maybe on some pretext he might be able to talk Badr into meeting him.

Too many maybes and mights, Hazard decided, and got off that to wonder where the Arab community was in this city. He could find out. But even then it would be like looking for a particular German in New York's Yorkville section of twenty-five square blocks around East 86th. Little chance.

Hazard felt suddenly drained, tired. It was either genuine tiredness or depression or both. His eyes wanted to close but he sat up on the edge of the bed and snapped on a light. He hadn't eaten since the lousy food on the plane and figured that might account for his feeling so empty. Sure. He ordered some dinner.

Waiting for it he got his mind off Badr by reviewing the material he was expected to use for the long-distance exercises Kersh had set up. A small carton containing a hundred opaque, sealed envelopes. Inside each envelope was a printed image. He was to select at random and act as his own control, sending one image every other night at exactly midnight his time. After each transmission he was to record the date on the reverse side of the image, along with any other information he thought pertinent – comments, for example, on his attitude or influencing conditions at that particular time. After every third exercise he was to mail the images to Kersh for evaluation. The schedule called for him to start sending Saturday, May 15th, which was the next night.

Examining the exercise box and its contents Hazard thought about Keven. Where she might be and what she might be doing. He wished she were there with him. She was nearly always good for him when he was down.

Dinner arrived. He ate fast and afterward still felt empty. It was only eight o'clock. He clicked off the light and sat slouched in a chair with his eyes closed.

When he opened his eyes he didn't immediately realize where he was. In London. Sprawled across the bed. He didn't remember having moved from the chair. He must have dozed off for a moment. It wasn't like him to do that. He got up for the bathroom and noticed his watch said four-thirty. Incredible. He'd slept eight hours straight. Not a trivial accomplish-

119

ment for an insomniac. It made Hazard brighten, suddenly feel good, strong, replenished.

He took his time shaving and returned to the bedroom. He glanced out to see dawn just starting. It looked as though it were going to be a nice day. He decided he'd go out and meet it.

Within ten minutes he was headed down St James's. The street was deserted except for a solitary guard at the gate of St James's Palace. Bright red jacket and tall, ridiculous furry hat as advertised. Inhumanly motionless. Stupid, thought Hazard, and continued on to Stable Yard Road, which allowed him to cut through the palace area. Crossing the Mall he recognized Buckingham Palace off to the right, but he rejected it for the park directly ahead.

No one but himself there at this early hour. It was, he decided, a good chance to run. He took off his jacket, shirt, boots, and socks, left them concealed in a clump of shrubs. With his trousers rolled up to just below the knees, he alternated running and walking a hundred along a path that bordered a calm pond. He left the path for grass, softer and wet. All the way around the park was almost a mile and he did the last four hundred full out. He sat on a bench until his breathing was back to normal, then got dressed and wanted breakfast.

He finally found a restaurant open near Trafalgar Square – cheap, greasy, narrow place, but his appetite was worked up enough not to care. The sausage and three eggs and two coffees tasted really good. Just for the hell of it he asked the counterman if by chance he knew any Arabs. The counterman laughed it off and went about his work.

By then most of London was up and around. On the major streets was the hurry of people who had to work Saturdays or at least had somewhere to go. They brought on an outcast feeling in Hazard. He was going nowhere, had nothing to do, unless, of course, he somehow got a new line on Badr. At the moment that seemed unlikely. Badr probably wasn't even in London, could be anywhere, and that went for the other two – Hatum and Mustafa – as well. There were millions of Arabs in the world – anywhere in the world. That was, he thought, a discouraging but realistic appraisal of the situation.

He wandered aimlessly around Piccadilly, window-shopping stores not yet open. After a while he found himself on Jermyn Street, where he came on to Asser and Turnbull and was that establishment's first customer for the day. He bought four silk-jersey shirts.

(No, the gentleman would not be in London long enough to have some shirts made to measure.) He went back to his hotel.

What to do? There was gambling, of course, but he wished he knew someone in London. Not being alone might help. Then it occurred to him he did know someone. Catherine, Carl's widow. He'd once had her telephone number, two numbers actually. He easily remembered them now, but he hesitated, had second thoughts about her, wasn't really all that anxious to call. He almost decided against it but was glad he hadn't when he heard how pleased she seemed to hear from him.

'Are you over on business?' she asked.

'Not really.'

'Pleasure then.'

'Sort of.'

'I want to see you. Are you here with someone?'

'No. Alone.'

'What about today? What are you doing today?'

'I'm loose.'

'Marvellous. I planned a picnic. Does that appeal to you?'

A picnic didn't seem her style, but maybe he was wrong. The idea of a spread of cloth, sandwiches, cold drinks, beer maybe, someplace quiet, just Catherine and himself, unpressured, trading talk about things for the first time, getting to know her and maybe not dislike her. It appealed to him. He told her it did.

She sounded pleased.

'Where shall we meet?'

'I'm in the country.'

'Okay, I'll get a car and drive out. Just tell me where. I'll find it.'

'No. I'll send a boat in for you.'

'A boat?'

'Take a taxi to Lambeth Pier. Be there in an hour.' As an afterthought, just before she rang off, she told him, 'Better bring whatever you need in case you decide to stay over.'

Hazard had no intention of staying over. Still, he didn't

121

think it prudent to leave his weapons in the room. To wear the Llama to a picnic didn't seem right, either, so he shoved it into his bag and took everything along.

Lambeth Pier is on the river directly in front of Lambeth Palace, where the Archbishop of Canterbury resides. Hazard had no sooner arrived on the pier when a powerful Riva speedboat executed a swift, sharp circle, abruptly reversed its engines, and came alongside where he stood. The driver of the Riva shouted his name like a question. Hazard nodded and got aboard. At once the Riva was throttled; its bow bent up and it left the pier with an insolent roar.

The driver steered standing up. He had on a T-shirt, navy blue with white horizontal stripes, and a pair of white shorts. He was very tanned. Apparently speedboating was his profession, and anything less than full speed was a waste of time.

Hazard relaxed and observed London as they went up the Thames under the bridges, passing barges with a racy superiority. After a while they were skimming by Fulham, Putney, and Hammersmith. The outskirts of London, not so many large factories and warehouses. Past such places as Kew, Twickenham, Teddington, and then Hampton Court, where Henry the Eighth had cavorted in silk bloomers with his Anne and others. All the way to where the Thames wound more, and was less than a third of the river it had been at the start. It also smelled better. The banks on either side were growing green, reedy along the edges, and there were groves of trees, many of them forlorn but lovely willows. Every so often Hazard caught a glimpse of a large private house. The sky had a high haze now, the sunlight softened as though it were coming down through pale blue gauze. It was indeed a nice day, Hazard thought, especially for a nice little picnic. He wondered if there'd be hot dogs.

Just before Lower Holliford the Riva's driver favoured the west bank. He soon came even closer in and stopped alongside a high retaining wall of mortared granite inset with large iron rings for tying up. There were three other speedboats there. Several rope ladders hung down the wall and Hazard climbed the most accessible. The Riva's approach and the height of the wall had blocked a view of what lay above, so when Hazard reached the top he wasn't prepared for what he saw.

First, Catherine's country house. It was at least forty rooms, Queen Anne style, with numerous room peaks and large chimneys. Between the house and the river was an expanse of grass, a gentle slope of green so impeccably kept that it gave the impression of a vast new carpet that had been rolled out for the occasion.

On the lawn were about fifty or sixty people. Not gathered but separated into groups of threes and fours, spotted here and there. Each group had its own spread picnic cloth of pale yellow linen.

As Hazard walked by and around and up to the house, he noticed cut-crystal goblets and fine silver. He felt a bit self-conscious but no one paid any attention to his arrival. They were all too preoccupied with themselves; were sprawled, kneeling, sitting in poses that were like pages of *Harper's* and *Queen* nearly come to life, as though contrived to portray the perfect picnic. Conversation was subdued, punctuated by fragments of forced laughter. They were all young or at least gave that impression, and while each competed for attention there could be no winner, because, in their attempts for originalities, they resorted to merely mimicking one another. Each girl was evidently her own favourite person. They were dressed in long, loose organza or chiffon; floral patterns borrowed from earlier in the century but worn now with nothing underneath. Faces framed by wide-brimmed hats, straws with ribbons that streamed from oversize blossoms of pale silk. Pretty. The young men were hatless. Possibly that was the one sure way of distinguishing gender, because their hair was just as long and their bodies just as thin as the girls', and their gestures not very definitive. They wore sheer shirts with billowing sleeves tight at the wrists, shirtfronts carefully unbuttoned all the way down, not as a matter of comfort. The beautiful androgynous people. They used that description themselves, believing it synonymous with personal liberation.

By the time Hazard got to the house he felt out of place. He found Catherine reclining beside her picnic spread just below the wide steps of the back terrace. It was a position that afforded her a view over all. Flanking her was Peter, the so-called personal secretary Hazard had met at the Pierre, and a young woman named Brett who preferred being boyishly handsome.

123

Catherine didn't notice Hazard immediately, but when she did she jumped up to hug and give him welcoming cheek kisses. How happy she was to see him, she said, keeping hold of his arm. There was some small talk about the boat ride down and how long he planned to be in London, during which a servant came and took his piece of luggage. Hazard figured Catherine would have him sit there with her, but she glanced around and said, 'Now, where shall I put you?'

She settled on two girls and a young man off to the extreme left beneath a large maple. She told Peter, 'Fetch Benedict for me,' and then to Hazard, 'You'll take Benedict's place.'

'Anywhere's all right,' Hazard said, thinking he'd like to escape. 'Don't bother what's his name.'

'No bother,' said Catherine. 'It's your good turn, actually. Benedict couldn't possibly have been very content with those two.'

A servant brought a basket that Catherine passed to Hazard. A large, round wicker one with the necks of two wine bottles protruding from its yellow linen covering. Its handle was tied with a yellow bow, and in the folds of the bow was a white card with the name *Terence* crossed out and replaced by *Haz*.

Catherine sat down and resumed her conversation. Hazard went over to the two girls under the maple.

Their names were Lindy and Laura. They were both extremely pretty, with brown hair and matching wide-set nearly pea-green eyes. They looked and moved very much alike. Lindy was the one with some fresh buttercups twined in her hair. The first thing they wanted to know from Hazard was, 'Do you fancy birds?'

Meaning girls, he assumed. He told them he did.

'Exclusively or also?' asked Laura.

'You guess.'

'Also,' said Lindy.

'Also,' was also Laura's opinion.

'Wrong,' Hazard said, not entirely sure that would be considered a point in his favour.

But they seemed delighted, as though they'd come on something rare. They immediately changed toward him. For example, Lindy reached and intentionally allowed the loose armhole of her dress to fully expose her right breast. And
124

Laura soon contributed a nearly identical manoeuvre to show she was by no means a slouch.

Trying not to be an obvious voyeur, Hazard paid some attention to his picnic basket. There was goose-liver paté, sections of cold roast pheasant, tiny cheddar-coated biscuits, a bunch of huge African grapes, a container of Beluga Colossal, some very thin chocolate-covered cream mints, and an individual round of well-aged Holland cheese. One of the wines was a vintage Burgundy 1966 Romanée-Conti *premier cru*. The other was a chilled champagne, Dom Perignon 1959. Crystal and silver were included, and, as an extra favour, a small vellum envelope contained three marijuana cigarettes bearing Catherine's monogram.

Hazard took a taste of everything. More than a taste of the Burgundy. He commented that it was exceptional.

Laura didn't agree. 'I'd like some Campari. I love Campari.'

Lindy was sitting with one leg crossed under and the other arched. Her white chiffon dress was gathered up. She had on white silk, seamed stockings, and matching garter belt. To flash bare thigh accessorized by the fasteners and tendrils of a garter belt was apparently the newest old rage. 'These grapes are orgasmic,' she said, biting one in half with her front teeth.

Laura flung the wine from her goblet, then took off her hat and sailed it away. Lifting her skirt she manoeuvred around on her knees and then lay back, resting her head face up on Lindy's lap. It was all performed with nonchalance, as though her only purpose was to make herself comfortable. However, now her body was extended offeringly toward Hazard and her legs were relaxed, slightly apart. She tucked her chiffon dress down between her legs, defining herself. Then she held up her hand with only her index finger extended. 'Know what this is?' she asked Hazard.

'Same to you,' Hazard said.

'Not that. I mean, right here is where they can stick an acupuncture needle to tonify your sex life.' She indicated a specific place on the back of the finger between the nail and first joint. 'It's called point cx nine.'

'Tonify?'

'Stimulate,' explained Lindy. 'Don't you think it's a coincidence that it should be *that* finger?'

'Same place both hands?' asked Hazard, going along with it.

'Only the right,' said Lindy.

'Then it's not a coincidence for anyone left-handed,' said Hazard.

That amused Lindy. When she smiled, Hazard noticed one of her upper front teeth was slightly crooked. The imperfection was an asset, adding an incongruous provincial touch.

Hazard accepted their routine for what it was. Seductive choreography. He wondered if they practised regularly. But he had to admit he was flattered. They were very pretty, doubly so together. Which thought brought Keven to mind; however, he also remembered Kersh had prescribed distraction. He looked over and saw Catherine had left her place and was down the slope, mingling.

'You going to drink that?' he asked Laura, indicating her bottle of Burgundy. He'd finished his. She handed her bottle over to him, and he got up and walked away.

He went around the side of the house and off into a grove of oaks, over a falling rock wall, and across a small swale of wild grass. Walking anywhere just for the walk, pausing frequently to swig from the bottle. The sun was on its way down, not yet setting but already its light was a weaker amber. It was the time of day he liked most, from then until dark. The wine was getting to him, not a lot but he felt it some in his legs and head. He knew he ought to be concentrating on the Badr problem, trying to figure out his next move. He also felt guilty that he was feeling so good.

His eyes caught on a structure on the opposite side of another rock wall. He went to it, climbed over, and found it was the remains of a small stone cottage, overgrown with ivy and creepers, roofless and with only three sides.

On the north side some moss had grown a bed.

On it were Laura and Lindy.

They provided a tableau. And for a man who fancied only birds, the rest seemed inevitable.

Hazard had no trouble finding his way in the dark back to Catherine's house. He merely headed in the direction of loud, thumping music.

He was astonished at seeing the inside of the house for the

first time. Its authentic Queen Anne exterior was only a façade. Inside every surface was linear, stark white contradicted by jolting splashes of primary colour, accessorized by mirror and chrome and lucite. It was brightly, evenly lighted, shadowless, enhancing the clean, spatial effect. Neon geometrics, huge mazes of shining wires. Even incidental functional objects such as ashtrays seemed cool and unfamiliar. It was like transcending the present, stepping from the past right into the future.

He felt a hand take his, fingers lacing. 'I was wondering about you.' Catherine smiled.

'It's a big place.'

'You've been exploring?'

'I need a ride back to London.'

'We haven't had a chance to talk.'

He almost told her that wasn't his fault.

She led him away from the crowd, out of the room, and down a long, high passage only wide enough for two. It seemed to go nowhere but as they approached the end of the passage a partition automatically opened to reveal a small elevator. It was entirely mirrored inside, and going up in it Catherine waited for Hazard's eyes to find the view reflected by the floor.

'That's the one disadvantage,' she said.

'Depends on how you look at it.'

They stopped at an upper floor where there was the same sort of décor but in pastels, a softer effect.

'This is my part of the house,' she said. 'There's no way up except the elevator and no way for anyone to call it down. How's that for guaranteed privacy? Here...' she went ahead '... is your room.'

'I can't stay.'

'I'll be hurt if you don't.'

He glanced around the room but didn't see his piece of luggage. Catherine slid a panel back with her finger, revealing a built-in wardrobe. His things had been unpacked, folded and put away. In the top drawer was his Llama in its holster, with the straps wound neatly around it. And his knife. On the wardrobe's mirror-top surface were his three passports and the carton of images. Maybe it was English hospitality, but he resented it.

127

'See, you're all moved in,' Catherine said. 'All three of you.'

He didn't have to explain, he told himself. Anyway, he didn't have to tell her the truth. 'I'm in a hassle with the government,' he said, the first thing that came to mind. 'They don't believe I reported all my income over the past ten years. And they're right. So, before they could put me in I got out. Under an assumed name.'

'Stevens or Beech?'

'Stevens. The other's a spare.'

She seemed to believe him. 'Evidently you were prepared to shoot your way out.'

The gun. 'No,' he told her, 'just an old friend who never goes anywhere without me.' He realized how phony-tough *that* sounded.

She stepped back and looked him down and up. 'You're a wanted man.'

'In some parts,' he said, straining to keep it light.

'Edmund Stevens. Must I call you that?'

'I'd appreciate it.'

'I much prefer Haz.' She added pointedly, 'I always did.'

He thought how right he'd been about her. He remembered telling Carl she needed a kick in the ass. She hadn't cried a drop at the funeral. It was a wonder she'd even showed up. 'Get me a ride back to London,' he told her.

She shrugged. 'I'll have my driver take you.'

He expected her to go to make that arrangement but she stayed there as though entertained by his angry movements as he packed.

Hazard didn't really know her, had never wanted to, had seen her briefly only three or four times over the past five years. Probably he'd never see her again. She was truly nothing to him now that Carl was gone. He'd often wondered about her, though, especially why she'd married Carl. They were such an obvious mismatch. Carl had been way out of her freaky league and she must have realized that from the beginning. So why had she married him? Hazard decided to ask her now.

'Didn't Carl ever tell you?'

'We never talked much about you.'

She thought back a moment, then said, 'I owed it to him.'

128

It sounded as though it had been a debt she'd grudgingly paid. 'We first met in Cairo...'

That Hazard had known, but not the rest of it.

It had been June, 1967, the second day of the Six-Day War. Israeli planes were over the city and nearly everyone had taken shelter. Carl was at the U.S. embassy. Looking out the window during a raid, he saw a pretty girl just walking along the deserted street with incredible nonchalance, as though it were any pleasant, peaceful afternoon. Carl opened the window and shouted down, warning her, but she only looked up, smiled, and waved. Carl hurried down and out to her, urged her to come inside. She first ignored him and then resisted when he forcefully carried her in.

She was not grateful for the rescue, called Carl a meddler, and sat brooding by a window like a child prohibited from going out to play. She'd been well aware of the danger, had been inviting the sky to send down her death, hopefully a direct hit. To die that way was abstract, impersonal, not the same as suicide, which required too much of one's self. It had been an opportunity and Carl had deprived her of it.

When Carl learned that these were her thoughts, he looked on her as a victim of another sort of war. She immediately became his private cause. Dedication made him almost immune to the abusive ingratitudes she put on him. He never wavered, kept her there, tried to reason with her, watched over her. She was literally a prisoner of his concern. Until, on the seventh day, the war was over. She was free to go.

She left on a final, thankless note. But two days later she was back. His optimism was contagious, and she'd caught some of it. He'd given that to her, and she wanted to repay him. No matter that he didn't suit her customary tastes and values. That, at the time, only qualified him all the more. He was good to her, for her. Hadn't she lately been laughing almost genuinely; wasn't she almost content to be only with him; didn't she nearly believe it herself when she said she loved him?

Within a month they were married.

Within another two she was miserable, as miserable as ever. Her sanguine outlook was that quickly corroded by self-doubt, habitual fears, the same old hang-ups. They hadn't really gone away for good, just for a holiday, and with their

129

return came the need for the same old defences. Such as ennui. Life with Carl now bored the hell out of her. His patience and devotedness irritated her. The whole new hope thing had been no more than an illusion. She'd been temporarily deceived into believing she had the ability to love and feel loved. She'd never be fooled again. She wanted out.

Now, with a resigned smile and her eyes set against showing regret, she told Hazard, 'Except for the unsavoury minor details, that's how it went.'

Hazard hadn't expected such openness from her. Maybe he hadn't been fair, had based his opinion of her on superficial things. He remembered what she'd said that afternoon at the Pierre about being the one who wanted to die. Maybe underneath she was less a barracuda, more someone in deep water who had to tread like hell to keep from going under. 'Why didn't you divorce Carl?' he asked.

'He didn't want a divorce.'

'Why didn't you?'

Hazard was asking her to peel off another layer. Reluctantly she told him, 'I suppose I always held a bit of hope for myself. It was something to go on, a sort of life line that might let me find my way back again to that first good feeling I had with him.'

An understanding nod from Hazard. He'd finished his packing. Now he unzipped his bag, flipped it open, and said, 'I'd like a beer. Can you get me a beer?'

Catherine was very happy to oblige.

They sat side by side in another room, more neutral than a bedroom. She called it her gallery. A completely enclosed area where several paintings took the place of windows. One, a Nolde, gave a view of some dark, furious sea, the madness of the waves ridged with luminous gold beneath a vermilion sky. Another was a Leonor Fini, a nude young girl, pearl-skinned chimerical, her head laden with vague flowers, in her hands a large, platter-like leaf serving her breasts to the onlooker. The only lights in the room were those exactly illuminating the paintings, heightening the impressions that those creations existed in an outside world. There was also a portrait of Catherine.

'Shouldn't you be downstairs with your party?' Hazard asked.

'It won't miss me.'

'Wouldn't you rather be with your friends?'

'No.'

Even in that high sanctuary the music from below could be heard. Its pervasive thump was like a pulse throughout the house. It was so much a part of Catherine's usual experience that she no longer really heard it. Conversely, Hazard's hearing at that moment seemed hypersensitive, irritated by the thumps and twangs. 'Don't they ever take an intermission?'

Catherine used a nearby phone, and a few moments later the music cut off abruptly. 'Silence,' she said, 'is something a lot of people can't tolerate.' She obviously included herself.

Hazard pulled his shoulders back to stretch the tension from them. His legs were straight out and crossed. He settled down and took a gulp of beer. Five more bottles were being kept cold in a silver bucket of shaved ice.

Catherine changed her position so she was lying on her side, giving him all her attention. He sensed she was studying his profile. 'This tax trouble you're in, is it just a matter of money?'

'Why?'

'I have much more of that than I need.'

'Money won't settle it now. They want me to pay them some prison time. For evasion. Anyway, thanks.' He was sorry he had to lie to her.

'But now that you're out of the States they can't touch you.'

'I can be extradited.'

'Then we just won't let them know you're here.' She smiled, an accomplice.

A long silent moment, while she decided she was really very attracted to him. She wondered if his being Carl's brother had anything to do with it. Possibly. But Haz was a lot different. Haz would know how to handle her. At least he seemed to promise that. She imagined herself with him and just picturing it aroused her. That wasn't an extraordinary reaction for her and she had no reason to trust or depend on it. But usually much more was required to cause such a response in her. Perhaps, she hoped, as she'd hoped many times before, it was the stir of something substantial, something that wouldn't be so easily discouraged. It might be, just might. She'd never know until she'd put it to the test, and that was impossible at the moment, with Carl and his death between them. She'd have to obscure that, gradually charm and diminish it. 'Let's hear more about you,' she said.

Hazard didn't want to talk about himself, and after a while manoeuvred their conversation back to her.

Her people, as she expressed it, came originally from Northumberland. Probably way back her ancestors had been Nordic but there was no way of tracing that. Sometimes, she told him, when she was feeling especially pagan, she believed it was that ancient bloodline at work.

Her industrious great grandfather had made the family fortune from woollen mills at a time before there was any such thing as an inheritance penalty. So his wealth was passed on intact to her grandfather, who succeeded in expanding the family holdings to such an extent and to organize them in such a clever way that even when he died the Government's bite was a comparative nibble. Her grandfather lived to be eighty. She knew him only as the surly, grunting, patriarchal figure whom she saw and was prompted to curtsy to on special occasions. The entire family, and it was large, was unctuous and spittle-licking (she loved that description) around the old man. Her parents were no exception. She had been too young to care and once in protest at being forced to deliver a dutiful kiss to grandfather's old, dry mouth she had stepped on his old, gouty foot. She claimed it was an accident, but always thought Grandfather knew better. Anyway, she'd never been close to him, not nearly as close as most of the others. That was why she often believed his leaving everything to her was only a matter of chance, as though he'd drawn her name from a hat or made a list and threw a pen like a dart at it.

What about her parents? Where were they?

Gone, in 1958, when she was twelve. Both drowned while sailing under the influence of too much wind and brandy – off Holyhead, of all places.

Grandfather outlived them by a year. At thirteen she inherited, along with his fortune, the family's sycophantic attention. At first she rather enjoyed having aunts, uncles, cousins – even those twice and three times removed – fawn over and oblige her. She was never reprimanded. She always won at

132

games and whatever she asked for would soon appear, sometimes in duplicate or triplicate, depending on the number of
relatives present when she happened to speak her desire. Her
eager benefactors never mentioned that they charged their
gifts to her account at Harrod's and elsewhere.

It wasn't until she was sixteen that she fully realized what
counterfeiters her relatives were. She began to devise little
tests for them, and they all failed. And when they were all
eliminated from her faith, she found an awful loneliness had
set in.

Did she tell them off and send them packing?

No, not then, anyway. She didn't even let them know she
was on to them. That, in fact, was how she got back at them;
by letting them continue their insipid pretence. She toyed with
them, doled out encouragements and then enjoyed dashing
their hopes. It was, she thought, a fitting, excruciating punishment. They nearly had a mass stroke when, at twenty-one, she
married Carl.

After that she was more irritated by their hypocrisy. By
then many of them had come to live here in this very house. It
had been part of her grandfather's estate and belonged to her.
She paid for its upkeep but never liked the place and so had
never made an issue of her relatives moving in to stay. The
place was overrun with them. They were literally waiting in
line for a vacancy. Then one day, apparently on a whim, she
announced she intended to have the house redone. They'd all
have to leave. They could, however, take with them whatever
they wanted.

They correctly understood from her tone that it was the end
of the free ride. They took everything, stripped the house bare
of the many valuable pieces it contained, not overlooking the
doors and boiserie. She didn't care. In one fell swoop she'd
got rid of her sponging relatives and saved herself the trouble
of having to sell off the ugly, traditional junk. Shortly thereafter she had the house gutted and commissioned the best
Italian interior designer a lot of money could buy to do it the
way she wanted, as it was now. No memories.

Hazard was on his fourth beer. Normally he wasn't a good
listener, but he'd been interested in Catherine's ironic account
of her past. Now that he knew her better he felt differently
about her. He even liked her for the first time.

'What are you going to do for money?'

Test question, thought Hazard, and told her, 'I've got some.'

'I just don't want you to go without. By the way, since this seems to be my night for confessions, I've got another to make.'

'What?'

'This afternoon I purposely put you with those boobsy twins.'

'Boobsy?'

'They're notorious for pooling their assets and going to work on a single target. I wanted to see if you'd succumb or not. Did you?'

'No.'

'Actually, it wasn't a fair test now that I think of it. Those two could probably defile the Pope if he granted them an audience.'

Hazard laughed but thought he'd have to keep on his toes with her. He used an honest excuse for cutting the evening short; he'd been up since 4:30 that morning.

At the door to his room Catherine said her good-night with cheek kisses closer to his mouth than before and a bit more lingering. Also, when her lips passed from cheek to cheek they once ever so lightly brushed his lips.

When he got into bed it was ten minutes to twelve. The bed was not set against the wall, but cantilevered by a stubby chrome column, like a giant flat-topped mushroom. Not having a headboard made him feel vulnerable and he hoped it wouldn't keep him from getting some sleep.

The carton of images was on the floor near by. When his watch approached midnight he took out at random one of the small envelopes. He carefully opened it and slid out the image. He saw the one he'd chosen was unlike the drawn, outlined ones he'd worked with before. It was a colour photograph and in that respect more realistic.

A white gull in flight against a blue sky.

Because it was more realistic it might be easier to send, Hazard hoped, and fixed his mind on it. He had trouble. His concentration was diverted by thoughts of Catherine, and also there was that question he'd been asked that afternoon: 'Do you fancy birds?' He had to stop, refocus and remind his

134

mind it was supposed to be communicating with Keven. She seemed so far away.

After several intense efforts he gave up. He was sure he hadn't got through. He wrote the day and date on the reverse side of the image card, along with the understatement: *present surroundings may be a distracting factor.*

Kersh would understand. So would Keven...

10

THE NEXT noon when Hazard went down he found Catherine having brunch on the terrace. He joined her for rarebit, rashers of Irish bacon, a portion of sunny tranquillity, and then told her he definitely should return to London.

Catherine had other plans for him but she nodded and said she'd go into town with him. They'd have dinner. She said it with such enthusiasm that Hazard had to choose between agreeing or greatly disappointing her.

They took her Maserati Ghibli. It only had about fifteen hundred miles on it, even though she'd owned it for over a year. She drove, said she wanted to. She drove too fast but with impressive authority. Hazard's only complaint was she often took her eye off the road. Suicidal lapses? he wondered. He hoped she didn't just conveniently forget to match a curve with a curve. She stopped off for a moment at her town place. It was in a Nash-designed complex on Chester Terrace, Regent's Park. Then they went on to a restaurant in Chelsea, small, expensive, casual. Along with cognac and coffee she gave him his choice: Annabel's or Tramp for dancing and looking, or her place for quiet, privacy, and well, whatever...

Hazard told her he felt lucky.

If he'd been wearing a tie she'd have taken him to Cleremont, but as things were she decided on the Pair of Shoes. Even there, Hazard's open collar was an exception allowed by the proprietor, who knew Catherine and was persuaded mainly by her quick request that he honour her cheque for five thousand pounds worth of chips. Hazard felt a bit small-time buying only three hundred.

First they played blackjack.

Hazard took it slow, betting twenty pounds a hand. Catherine went for a hundred. He saw right off she didn't know the game. She asked for hits when she shouldn't have and stayed when she shouldn't have. However, after three quarters of an hour she was five hundred ahead and he was down fifty. Irritated, he suggested they take a break at the bar.

The Pair of Shoes was more intimate than most London casinos. It offered in the same room two blackjack tables, a craps table, and roulette. The place was deep red – velour on the walls and plush carpet underfoot. So much red would have been garish under normal lights but with the lighting bright only over the playing tables it created an elegantly wicked atmosphere. Standing at the bar permitted a good view of the entire room, but Hazard was turned away, paying attention to the gilt-framed sketch that hung over the bar: a fortunately endowed girl wearing only a pair of shoes. He thought the odds on anyone being that physically ideal were at least a million to one, against. Although he'd known a few who came close. Keven, for instance. Keven...

Catherine claimed him with her hand on his arm, light, not pressuring. She told him 'I read someplace that gamblers are quite pathological.'

'Quite.'

'It said the urge to wager is connected to the childhood need to masturbate.'

No comment.

'It also said gamblers are aggressive and enjoy trouble. Do you?'

At that moment a group of people were entering the room. Five men and four women. Hazard turned and noticed them. He almost dropped his drink. There they were, all three.

Badr and Hatum and Mustafa.

One of the other men in the group was also obviously Middle Eastern. He was huge, as thick-chested as Mustafa and half a head taller. His large nose looked as though it had been broken and rebroken. One of his eyes was half shut, so only a slit of pupil showed – glazed, milky, and useless. The fifth man wasn't an Arab. Hazard didn't get a good look at him but overheard the club proprietor call him by name. Pinchon. The women with them were young, but overstated, brittle looking, apparently paid company.

They all went directly to the crap table, bought chips, took places around the end of the table, and began to play.

As Hazard watched them, the back of his neck flushed hot and his stomach went hard. The same overwhelming hate he'd felt when he'd stood at Carl's grave.

Catherine noticed the change in him and asked if anything was the matter.

He only half heard her but the interruption helped him regain control. It occurred to him then that their showing up here was too much of a coincidence. Were they on to him? They'd hardly make him aware of the fact by putting in a public appearance. Maybe, being typical Arabs, they just enjoyed gambling. And here in the West End there weren't all that many attractive casinos. Maybe. Anyway, right now he'd better decide how he was going to handle this. Only in his wildest fantasies had he imagined getting on to all three of them at once. Now fantasy was reality, but he'd be crazy to try for all of them at the same time. He'd just have to play it as it fell, be ready.

'Let's try some craps,' he told Catherine, hoping his voice sounded calmer to her than it did to him.

'I favour roulette,' she said, but went along with him.

They stood at the end of the table opposite the Arabs. It was Hazard's first good view of them. He studied them casually. He didn't know which was which but he was sure that going up against any one of them would be more dangerous than it had been with Saad.

'New shooter, coming out,' announced the stickman.

Badr took the dice.

Hazard thought Badr had the look of a loser. Against his instinct, Hazard dropped five twenty-pound chips on the pass line, betting with him.

Badr noticed, acknowledged it with a confident grin and let fly. The dice hit the rail just below Hazard and snapped sharply to a stop with a six and a five on top.

'Eleven, a winner.'

Hazard let the two hundred ride, despite his hunch that Badr would next throw a craps, snake eyes probably.

Badr came right back with another eleven.

And the bastard hasn't even got to the sevens yet, Hazard thought as the stickman pushed a pair of hundred-pound stacks his way. Better pull now, Hazard advised himself, and was about to pick up his winnings when Catherine tugged at his arm and said, 'I want you to meet Jean-Claude.'

Hazard turned to face the man who'd arrived with the

138

Arabs, the one the club owner had called Pinchon. He had an arm around Catherine, pressing her side intimately against his. Obviously Catherine and Pinchon weren't strangers.

She introduced them, almost forgetting to use Hazard's assumed name, hesitating for a moment to remember it was Edmund Stevens.

Pinchon offered his hand. His smile revealed teeth so white and even Hazard didn't believe them. The rest of Pinchon was no less indefectible. He had a fashionably gaunt enough face with ideal features, symmetrical and well-balanced. Mouth perfectly right for the nose perfectly right for the eyes perfectly lashed dark and thick. Black hair not over-disciplined, sideburns not a fraction off. A tan that was evidence of much leisure. Pinchon, taller than the average Frenchman, appeared lean in his clothes, which were expensive, meticulous, undoubtedly made for him. The only thing Hazard could find wrong with him was he was too perfect.

Pinchon told Catherine. 'I missed you by a day in Barbados.' His mouth especially expressed disappointment.

'It was dreadfully muggy there,' she said, glancing at Hazard, hoping for some sign of jealousy. She knew Pinchon usually caused that in other men.

But Hazard was wondering what was Pinchon's connection with the Arabs. He was obviously out of his element with them, so what was it? Hazard noticed Pinchon's precisely knotted silk tie and thought he was the sort who'd spend an enjoyable hour clipping the hair from his nostrils.

Pinchon offered cigarettes from a gold case. Catherine accepted and Pinchon was quickly attentive with a tiny gold lighter. He stepped in, closer to Catherine, a tactical move that more or less excluded Hazard.

Hazard let him get away with it. He returned his attention to the table, saw Badr still had the dice. His own bet on the pass line was now four stacks of two hundred. In the interim Badr had made two more passes and was now trying for another.

The point was ten.

Hazard thought in dollars and figured what he now had going was two thousand. Enemy or not he was now for Badr making that ten. For the moment a common cause. Come on ten, big ten. The Arabs urged the dice loudly. Hazard, with

139

the composure of a pro, silently asked the dice to cooperate. After a few rolls up came a five and a five. The hard way.

Badr got a backslap from Mustafa, a hug from Hatum. The one with the broken nose merely grinned. The girls with them received more chips as a bonus.

Hazard picked up his winnings. Badr had made him four thousand dollars richer, and there he was now looking down the length of the table at Hazard, expecting a show of gratitude.

Hazard didn't smile, nodded once. Badr could take it to mean whatever he wanted. Hazard was only thankful that the line of opposition was clear again. For a moment there it hadn't been. At least he knew now which name went with which face, from having overheard them. They'd called the one with the broken nose Gabil.

The dice soon came around to Hazard. Normally he never touched them, preferred to bet and let others do the shooting, but he decided he'd make an exception this time, show the Arabs how the game was meant to be played, show them he was no ordinary pass-line sucker.

He chose a pair of dice from the half dozen the stickman shoved at him. The Arabs, he noticed, were getting their bets down on the pass line. He put two hundred on the won't pass line.

He didn't fist the dice but held them loosely, respectfully, with the ends of his fingers and gave them a nice easy lobbing toss.

Pair of sixes. Crap.

The Arabs moaned their loss. Hazard won two hundred.

Having got that out of his system, he moved the four hundred to the pass line and threw a four. He paused to hand the stickman six hundred and told him, 'Cover the numbers.' The stickman divided the chips with brisk competence and placed a hundred on each of the squares in a row numbered four, five, six, eight, nine, ten. Whenever Hazard threw any of those points he'd get paid. A seven at any time would lose it all for him.

The Arabs were impatient but fascinated by Hazard's method. The stickman knew a real player when he saw one.

Hazard took time to make sure all his bets were correctly placed. Then, hoping for a good long hand, he started rolling.

A six, another six, a five, a nine, a harmless three, an eight, a meaningless eleven, a ten and then a four, his point.

'Coming out again, same shooter.'

His new point was nine. He followed it up with a six, an eight, another six.

All the while he was aware of the Arabs at the other end of the table, pulling for him. They liked him. He was a good shooter. They were winning the comparatively small bets they placed on the pass line. Hazard, meanwhile, had helped himself to over a thousand. Pounds.

There are no sevens on these dice, Hazard told himself. He was only vaguely aware of Catherine and Pinchon off to the side, still talking, missing the action. No matter, Hazard had the audience he wanted, the ones he hated. He was showing them his style.

He doubled up his bets and went on rolling. No sevens, only numbers that multiplied the chips he kept neatly arranged in the concave receptacle of the table rail in front of him. He was having a hot hand, a beautiful hand. Maybe the best of his life.

But then Pinchon appeared at the other end. Pinchon had the attention of the Arabs. He was taking them from the play. They seemed to be leaving. Catherine came to Hazard's side. 'Well, darling,' she said, 'you do very well without me.'

Not now, thought Hazard. Now wasn't the time for the bastards to leave. Angrily he flung the dice down the length of green baize and even then they won for him.

He turned and saw the Arabs were cashing in their chips. The dice were back in his fingers ready to again behave as though he owned them. But the Arabs were going out, with Pinchon leading the way.

Now Hazard had all the more reason to hate them. Reluctantly he handed the dice to Catherine and told her, 'I'll be back.'

Out on the street he saw Pinchon, the Arabs, and the girls had split into two groups and were getting into separate cars, Rolls-Royces, a black and a white. Gabil, the one with the broken nose, was the driver of the black. Badr was behind the wheel of the other.

No telling where the attendant had put Catherine's car. Hazard had to wait for it to be brought around and by that

141

time the two Rolls-Royces were down the block. Hazard kept his eye on them, and as he got into the Maserati he saw them turn left. He went after them, reached where they'd turned just in time to see them down the street taking another left. He came up behind them when they had to wait for traffic at Park Lane. They went south there, past Hyde Park Corner to Knightsbridge, Brompton, Fulham Road.

Hazard had no problem keeping up, although the steering wheel on the right was strange to him. What gave him more trouble was having to drive on the wrong side of the street. At least wrong for him. He had to keep reminding himself to stay on the left, and sometimes when there was oncoming traffic, habit tempted him to meet it head on.

That was no longer a problem when they were on the M4 with its separate double lanes. After a half hour of doing eighty they came to a roundabout and the long underpass Hazard remembered from his arrival. Heathrow Airport. That was okay. Hazard had his things in the Maserati's luggage compartment, but how would he explain his presence on the same plane with them? That would be too much of a coincidence.

The Rolls-Royces pulled up at the terminal area designated for continental departures. Hazard stopped a discreet distance away. He watched Pinchon and Mustafa get out of the white Rolls. Hatum got out of the black one. Both cars pulled away as the three men entered the terminal.

That solved it for Hazard. No need to fly anywhere. He now had Badr isolated from the others. One on one was better.

He got on the tail of the two cars again in the underpass and followed them back into town. On Kensington High Street the black Rolls turned off, the white, containing three of the girls and driven by Badr, continued on to Alexandra Gate, where it cut through Hyde Park to Bayswater. After a few short lefts and rights the white Rolls stopped momentarily to leave off one of the girls. Hazard figured as soon as the other two girls were taken home he'd have Badr the way he wanted him. Alone.

The white Rolls continued on to Edgware Road and then Maida Vale. There it turned off on to a side street and stopped at the kerb near an apartment building, a comparatively new high rise. The two girls got out of the car. Badr also got out and went with them into the apartment building.

Ten minutes passed. Apparently Badr wouldn't be coming out for a while. It was two-thirty. Hazard glanced up at the building and saw a few lighted windows. Badr was up there somewhere, no doubt enjoying a double helping of what had been paid for.

Hazard could use the time. He unlocked the luggage compartment from inside and got his Llama from the suitcase. He strapped it on under his jacket and inserted the knife down into the upper part of his right boot. To help pass the time he switched on the radio, got some Isaac Hayes all the way from Luxembourg. A few raindrops hit the windshield and soon it was coming down hard, obscuring Hazard's view of the Rolls. He wasn't familiar with the complicated instrument panel of the Maserati but he finally found the lever that activated the wipers. He set them on slow and as they swept hypnotically back and forth he thought about how good to him the dice had been that night. If he could have kept rolling he'd have owned that place by now, including the picture behind the bar. He wondered about Catherine. How was she going to take being deserted and her car borrowed without asking? Borrowed? Maybe in anger she'd report the car stolen.

An hour went by. Two.

It was still raining, a steady drizzle.

Hazard got out of the car and went into the apartment building. An intercom panel in the foyer displayed the tenants' names on small black plastic strips. About fifty. Only five names were obviously foreign and none of those were Arabic. It had occurred to Hazard that possibly Badr lived there rather than the girls. But no. He returned to the car, wetter and no better off.

It now appeared Badr had bought himself not only a double header but an all nighter as well. Hazard pictured his adversary bedded between the two girls, while there he was cramped and worried in the Maserati. He thought it wouldn't be so bad if he had someone to talk to. Keven. If she were there he'd be passing the time playing their old smart-ass game or something. Keven. What time was it where she was? The luminous dial of his watch said nearly five.

He was sleepy. He felt as though he could lay his head back

143

and drop right off. How perverse. Now was a time when he wanted to stay awake, had to, and he could hardly keep his eyes open. He fought sleep by trying to ignore the back-and-forths of the wipers and by thinking how convenient it would be if he could go a few laps around the block at 186,001 miles per second, faster than the speed of light, and then, according to Einstein, he'd be able to view in retrospect how all this had turned out. Maybe he wouldn't like what he saw.

Dawn came. But with the rain darkness just changed into a dreary grey. Still, Hazard welcomed the sight of the first early riser on the street and soon there were others, all rather anonymous in raincoats and hunched down beneath standard black umbrellas. He was more alert when people started coming out of the apartment building. But after that early-day activity the street became relatively quiet again.

Hazard had the Maserati parked a way back and opposite the Rolls. However, now the space directly behind it was available so he pulled up into it. With the rain it wasn't likely Badr would notice him when he finally came out. If Badr ever did.

A small boy in a yellow slicker passed by, enjoying the rain and carrying a bag of groceries. Hazard was hungry. He opened the car door and looked back to the main way. There seemed to be a store on the corner. He decided to chance it.

He sprinted to the corner and went into the small neighbourhood grocery. He bought whatever came to sight first. A box of jelly doughnuts, four bananas, and a carton of beer. While paying he noticed a ball of common store string on a spindle. It wasn't for sale but the grocer was glad to take a pound for it.

This time when Hazard got back to the Maserati he was drenched, rain running down the back of his neck and into his eyes. But maybe it was worth it. He tried one of the jelly doughnuts. It looked good, dusted with powdered sugar, but tasted bad, was dry and contained only a smidgen of imitation jelly. He opened one of the beers, which after the doughnut was awfully bitter. The bananas were over-ripe and mealy. He ate all four.

He got out of the car again, taking the string. He tied the end of it to the rear bumper of the Rolls and fed the ball out along the gutter to the Maserati and through its right window.

He got back in and whirred the window up, leaving a crack. He wound the string around his wrist and hand several times and then sprawled across the two bucket seats, his legs up and his head down against the door panel. He closed his eyes. It felt very good to be able to close his eyes. He was doubting he'd sleep at the moment he went off.

Four hours later the string went suddenly taut, cut into Hazard's hand and broke. He sat up quickly to see the white Rolls pulling away. He drove after it and was soon right behind it in the thick rush of London traffic. He wasn't yet fully awake, so everyone and everything along the streets seemed abnormally accelerated to him. He lowered the window, stuck his head out. It helped clear him, the rain on his face. He'd become fairly accustomed to driving on the left side of the street from the right side of the car, but to be sure he fixed on the white Rolls just ahead and played follow the leader.

All the way across the rain-slicked, car-logged heart of the city. To High Holborn, Newgate, Cheapside, down King William Street, over Eastcheap, and on to Trinity Square. There on the right was the Tower of London, hard grey and soft green. Then a sharp left into a maze of shorter narrow streets with such unlikely names as Savage Garden and Crutched Friars.

On one called Seething Lane the Rolls pulled over and stopped. Hazard continued on a short way and stopped. In the side-view mirror he watched Badr cross the street and enter a building.

Hazard got out and walked back to inspect the building from across the street. It was a brick structure about four stories high, and windowless like a warehouse. It occupied nearly half the entire block, was larger and not in keeping with the other buildings in that area of older London. The others were places of business but had the appearance of well-preserved residences.

From the outside there was no way of telling what purpose the building served. The only hint was a painted metal plaque, the seal of the British Commonwealth, bolted to the wall near the entrance, which appeared to be the only way in or out. It had clearance to accommodate a large truck or van. At the moment it was wide open.

Hazard strolled across the street and into the building. He

entered a large, high room where bright overhead lights shone down on rich hues and intricate patterns.

Oriental carpets.

They were arranged in stacks, spread out and layered one on another. Hundreds of such stacks, some reaching as high as six to seven feet. Literally thousands upon thousands of Oriental carpets all in this one place.

It was a clearing depot under the jurisdiction of Her Majesty's Customs and Excise Tax Department. This particular building served as the gathering point, the Mecca for nearly every Oriental carpet destined for sale in the Western world. They came from all parts of the Mideast and Far East. Carpets of every size and quality, ranging in value from thirty to ten thousand pounds, new and antique, some machine-loomed in the factories of Istanbul, Izmir, and Tehran, others made in the large private workshops at Kerman, Nain, Isfahan, and Tabriz. The majority, though, were produced in the remote regions of Persia by individual families. Created by them in the ancient painstaking way of tying knot after knot day after day, month after month, reproducing symbolic patterns that had been handed down through so many generations that their original meanings were by now unknown. Once out of those patient fingers the carpets brought profit after profit for middleman after middleman and, finally, accumulated into large lots, they arrived at this building on Seething Lane. Usually the Arab dealer or his representative accompanied the carpets to London. Hardly ever did a shipment arrive without an Arab escort to keep watch over it.

When Hazard entered the building he felt suddenly outnumbered. Twenty Arabs and no smiles. Silent, practically motionless, the Arabs sat crosslegged on small prayer rugs. Each in front of his stack of carpets.

At that moment Hazard thought it might indeed have been more prudent if he'd waited in the car. He was tempted to retreat but went ahead, between the rows of stacks, trying to ignore all those Arabs who might be comrades of Badr.

Badr? Hazard didn't see him anywhere in that first room, so he went on to the next, which was equally large and contained many more stacks of carpets. And watchful Arabs.

This second room was L-shaped because part of it had been sectioned off for an office area. Inside the office were three

146

uniformed customs officials. One glanced out through the glass partition, saw Hazard, and came out to him. He was British polite. 'May I be of some assistance, sir?'

'I'm looking for a friend.'

'Several visitors were in earlier on, sir. Perhaps you missed him.'

'No, he's probably running a little late.'

'We'll be closing up here in a half hour.'

'Mind if I wait around?'

He didn't mind, went back into the office, and Hazard continued looking for Badr. He didn't find him there but noticed some wide stairs and took them up to the same sort of brightly lighted room, but not as many stacks – or Arabs. In several places carpets were rolled, wrapped with brown paper and piled high like long logs.

Hazard wondered if somehow he'd missed Badr. It was a large place and with all the islandlike stacks he could easily have not seen him. Possibly Badr was already gone. For Hazard that would mean lost. He continued on down the length of the room between two rows of stacks and was about to go back between others when he heard a voice: 'It's you!'

Hazard turned. There was Badr, grinning. 'My friend, the dice player.'

For a moment Hazard pretended not to recognize Badr.

'I won you money,' Badr reminded.

'That's right,' Hazard said. He sensed what Badr was about to ask so he beat him to it. 'What are you doing here?' As though he belonged there and Badr didn't.

'This is my business, carpets. Is it yours?'

'No, I'm only a sort of collector. A friend of mine in New York told me about this place, thought I should see it.' Hazard glanced around as though he found it all interesting.

Badr's smile was contradicted by the suspicion in his eyes. 'Last night, and now here.'

'Lucky for me,' Hazard said amiably. 'I was hoping to learn a few of the finer points about carpets. No doubt you're an expert.'

Badr nodded, apparently satisfied. 'I received a shipment today from Tabriz.' He gestured to the near corner, where an Arab helper was in the process of unwrapping and unrolling carpets to form a stack. Evidently Badr had also been hard at

147

it. He had his jacket off, tie pulled down, and his shirt was splotched wet with perspiration.

Badr went to the corner, obviously intending Hazard should follow. Hazard took the opportunity to survey the immediate area. There was no one close by except the helper, who said something in Arabic to Badr. Badr dismissed him with a backward wave and the man departed, his working day over.

'Look,' said Badr. He removed three carpets from the stack, good-sized, heavy carpets, but he did it easily, a casual display of strength that didn't go unnoticed by Hazard. Now on top was a carpet of beige and ochre hues woven into a graceful, intricate floral pattern. 'This is a rare one,' Badr said proudly, running his hand over the carpet and stepping back to admire.

The carpet was truly beautiful, had a lustrous, silky sheen. Badr bent to it again, turned it over to show its reverse side. 'A half million knots to the yard,' he said and looked up for Hazard's reaction.

Hazard thought how easy it would have been just then to put a bullet into the back of Badr's head.

'Perhaps you really don't appreciate carpets,' Badr said as he stood.

Hazard didn't know much about them, but once in Brentano's in New York he'd thumbed through an illustrated book on the subject. 'That's a really fine Kashan. Best I've ever seen.'

That seemed to reassure Badr. 'I have many even better.'

Actually, the Kashan was the best of the lot, the showpiece. Most of the othes were quite ordinary, and some had been purposely bleached to make them appear older – a common practice.

'Maybe I'll buy one,' Hazard said.

'One?' Badr explained the dealers there only sold by the lot. They'd never consider selling just one carpet.

Hazard, pretending interest, asked why.

Badr explained that each piece of every lot was numbered in sequence, had a bonded customs seal attached to its corner. If a dealer sold a carpet from the middle of his lot the missing number would be noticed. Not by the customs people; they never bothered with one carpet more or less. But a potential
148

buyer would make a point of looking to see if a lot was complete. If a buyer saw even one carpet missing he'd claim that one had been the best of all and use that to bargain down the entire lot. Naturally, the carpets that happened to be the first and last of a lot could be sold off without any problem.

Hazard glanced at his watch. The place would be closing in ten minutes. He had to decide what to do, at least where to do it. He could just leave and keep tailing Badr and hope it led to some suitable, isolated place. But that would be taking the chance of losing him. To hell with that. Besides, Hazard decided, he'd done enough following and waiting.

Looking down the row of stacks, Hazard saw that several of the Arabs had gone by now and the rest were getting ready to leave.

'How much would you spend for a carpet?' Badr asked, no doubt recalling how much he'd seen Hazard win at dice.

'What about this one?' Hazard indicated the Kashan.

'Impossible,' Badr said. 'It's in the middle of the lot. I just told you —'

'But it's not perfect. There's a small hole...' Hazard pointed vaguely.

Distressed at such a possibility, Badr bent over to examine the carpet.

Hazard's right hand moved beneath his jacket and drew the Llama down and out. He pressed the muzzle of its silencer to Badr's head, just behind the ear.

Badr immediately realized what it was. He remained still.

'Over there,' Hazard said.

Badr cautiously straightened up, and Hazard kept the gun on him as they went around the stack to the corner close to the wall.

'Down.'

Badr squatted behind the stack. Hazard was right beside him.

'Why?'

'Quiet,' Hazard said, but decided he wanted to tell Badr why before he killed him.

It was now a matter of waiting there until everyone was gone. Hazard figured they'd lock up the place to prevent anyone from getting in, not out. The few remaining Arabs were

149

leaving now, chatting gutturally as they went down the stairs. Then silence.

Hazard could hear Badr's breaths, short with fear. His own breathing, he realized, wasn't much different. He concentrated on the gun, ready to pull the trigger if Badr made a move.

After a few minutes the silence was broken by someone coming up the stairs. Whoever it was paused momentarily at the top and walked down between the stacks in the direction of the corner. Heavy footsteps came closer, then stopped on the other side of Badr's stack.

Hazard jabbed the gun at Badr, maintaining pressure while he looked around the corner.

Gabil. The big one with the broken nose. Evidently he'd come to meet Badr. He'll assume Badr's gone, Hazard hoped. Gabil scanned the area and then walked away, from the sound of his steps on down the stairs.

Relieved, Hazard took a deep breath.

Cologne and perspiration made him suddenly realize he'd forgotten about Badr's jacket. It was out there somewhere and Gabil might have seen it. Hazard looked over and spotted the jacket lying in plain view on top of an adjacent stack. It seemed incredible that Gabil could have missed it, yet evidently he had or he wouldn't have gone.

It was 5:30 now. Closing time, according to what the customs man had said. Hazard hoped the British reputation for punctuality wasn't an exaggeration. A moment later there was a sliding rumble below. The large entrance door being lowered. Hazard listened for any further sounds from inside the building. It seemed everyone had gone, but he decided to give it a few more minutes to make sure. He looked at Badr and thought the man didn't seem as apprehensive as before. In fact, Badr's face showed no emotion; his eyes were fixed straight ahead. Hazard guessed Badr had fatalistically accepted that he was going to die.

Badr was waiting. But not for death, for darkness.

The lights went out.

Badr jerked his head away, just before Hazard pulled the trigger. Hazard pulled off a second shot in the dark, aiming lower, thinking Badr might have gone to the floor. But the moment the lights went out Badr had moved back and away. Hazard didn't know, couldn't see that Badr was standing flat

150

against the wall no more than eight feet from him.

The two men remained frozen still, each listening for the next move of the other.

Badr made it. He dove on to the partial stack. He landed stomach down, rolled across and on to the floor where he wedged himself against and under the front edge of the stack.

Hazard had no chance to get off another shot. Anyway, it would have been a wild one in that darkness. Hazard figured Badr would head for the stairway, so he went as quickly as possible along the wall, between the wall and the stacks, feeling his way. As he neared the stairs he saw light coming from the floor below, dim but helpful. Probably, he thought, the customs men had routinely left a light on in the office.

He chose the stack that was most strategic, overlooking the stairs. He climbed up on it and lay there, not sure from which direction Badr would come.

Badr had the advantage. He knew the place. When he heard Hazard moving along the wall he went to where he'd left his jacket. He didn't pick it up, took no chance of something dropping accidentally from it. He felt for and found its inside pocket. Carefully he slipped out the revolver, a snub-nosed .38. He would enjoy drinking the blood of this Jew.

Hazard's eyes were beginning to water from trying to find and focus on something in the dark. Once he thought he saw a movement between the stacks opposite and down a way but it could have been his imagination, or his eyes. He cursed the place for not having any windows. It was still daylight outside but almost pitch black in there. Badr must have known about the lights, known they'd be turned off by someone. Who? Everyone had left the building by then. Had the lights gone off automatically? Probably, but what difference did it make anyway?

It could make a big difference, Hazard realized. It was a long shot but might pay off. He thought it out, exactly what he'd do.

He transferred the knife to his pocket and took off his boots. Sliding feet first over the side of the stack he reached the floor and immediately went front down on it. From there the stairway landing was about ten feet away. The light from below defined the top step. That, he knew, was where he'd be most vulnerable. He began crawling slowly across to the top of the stairs. When he was almost there, just a few feet away, he paused in the shadow. The Llama felt slippery in his hand, which was nervous wet. He tightened his grip and told himself what he was about to do wasn't much different from plunging on a horse in the last race, hoping to go home a winner. Sometimes he'd been lucky.

He shoved off with his knees and elbows, squirmed quickly to the top of the stairs. For an instant he was silhouetted there by the light from below, the entire length of him a conspicuous target.

Badr saw him. Badr fired twice.

Hazard felt the first bullet pass in the air just a fraction above his head. The second wasn't that close because by then Hazard had rolled off the edge and down several steps. Once out of range he recovered and took the rest of the steps four at a time to the bottom.

Badr wouldn't come down after him. Hazard was almost certain of that. Badr wouldn't come down those lighted stairs where he could be easily picked off. He'd stay up there in the dark.

Hazard went into the office. He examined the walls hoping to find the switch box for the lights. It wasn't there, but he found a flashlight that he took with him to search elsewhere.

He located the switch box in an enclosed recess under the stairs. He opened it to see an arrangement of high-voltage fuses, and directly below those was the automatic timing device. Off to one side was a separate circuit for the office lights, not connected to the automatic control. The timing device was a flat brass disc like the face of a clock, with white numerals one through twelve for day and the same in black for night. Its perimeter was notched all around at quarter-hour intervals, geared precisely to accommodate a pair of small tripping levers, one for 'on' and the other for 'off'. The on lever was set for white 8:30. The off for black, 5:45.

Hazard looked at his watch. It was twenty after six. He figured ten minutes would be time enough. With extreme care he adjusted the on lever so it would trip automatically at 6:30.

After double-checking the timer and his watch he went back to the office. He shoved the flashlight in his jacket pocket just in case nothing worked. Then he turned off the office light. In total darkness he went to the stairs and up, quietly, all the way to the top.

He'd already decided he would avoid the stacks. For his plan it was better to go straight ahead, slowly, silently, down the space between the rows. In the total black he didn't know if he was keeping on a straight course, worried that he might be veering off, might bump into one of the stacks. Even a noise that slight could give him away.

God, the black was thick. He felt pressed by it, surrounded by its substance. Nothing to go by. The boundaries of his own body seemed inaccurate, his feet on the floor too far below, his hand holding the gun too far away. It would, he thought, be easy to panic.

He had his right forearm over his left wrist, concealing the luminous face of his watch. Keeping his arms in that position, he paused and brought them up to see how much time was left. Only a glimpse but it was a relief to see something, even that little glow. It indicated less than two minutes before 6:30.

How far into the room had he come? He'd counted thirty steps. Where would that put him? Halfway was where he wanted to be, centred where he'd have an equal chance all around. For the Llama's range he'd have to be within fifty feet of Badr, sixty at most. The closer the better. But that part of it was beyond his control. On a hunch he took five more steps and stopped for another look at the time.

Forty seconds to go.

He put his imagination to work. Visualized a bright light. If he could prepare his eyes, mentally precondition them, it would give him an edge. Contrary to the blackness his eyes were experiencing, he pictured bright light. He concentrated intensely on the thought, the image of glaring brightness, willing his pupils to dilate, as though they were looking directly into the sun. Brilliant, blazing light.

It came on.

Badr was no more than twelve feet away, directly in front of his stack of carpets. Badr blinking, squinting from the sudden shock of the light. Badr, tensed, crouched, but he was confused, betrayed by his eyes. Desperately, he fired a shot in the wrong direction.

Hazard went down on one knee so that he had an upward

153

angle of fire. He squeezed the trigger of the Llama.

The bullet struck Badr in the soft spot under his chin, exactly between the jawbones. The bullet spread on impact, peeled apart like a four-petalled blossom, went up through the back of Badr's throat, entered, tore a path through Badr's brain, and lodged in his skull bone. Badr snapped as though hit by an uppercut. The top half of him spun partly around while his legs gave way. He collapsed backward on the stack.

Hazard went over to make sure. Badr's open eyes looked false and glassy and were beginning to turn pink. The bushy growth across the ridge of his brows twitched and then all of him was still. Blood was seeping from him, spoiling the subtle beauty of that precious Kashan carpet.

Hazard put the Llama back into its holster. He wondered whether he should leave Badr there. He was repulsed at the idea of touching him, decided he'd just find his boots and leave. He turned and found...

Gabil.

In that split second no chance to avoid Gabil's arm that came down on him like a telephone pole.

The next Hazard knew he was on the floor looking up, unable to move. It seemed as though he were suspended just below a filmy surface. Gabil loomed above him, a tower with a gun. There was the black little mouth hole of its muzzle and Hazard anticipated the flash that would come from it; the last thing he'd ever see. Gabil reached down to search his pockets. Hazard's DIA identification. Gabil examined the small plastic-coated card front and back and then dropped it on Hazard's chest.

Now his life was supposed to flash before his eyes but he didn't believe his eyes. Gabil stepped over him and out of view. It was merely a postponement, thought Hazard, a brief reprieve for some reason.

He lay there for what seemed a long while. Gradually his senses cleared and he was able to move. He sat up and looked around. It didn't make sense. Gabil was gone.

Badr's body was also gone. And the blood-stained Kashan carpet. Gone. No evidence of any of it.

Why?

Still aching and spinning from the chop he'd taken from Gabil, Hazard found his boots and went downstairs. The way out he found was a side door. He could have locked it shut after him but didn't bother. The place deserved to be robbed.

The Maserati was on Seething Lane where he'd left it. No sign of the white Rolls. Two parking tickets were taped to the Maserati's windshield. Hazard ripped them off and ripped them up. The rain had stopped but the threat of more was hanging overhead. It was early evening. He got into the car and started up, thinking he'd go to his hotel. However, as he made his way across London, using his memory to guide him, he realized how tired he was and how hungry he was, and dirty. He hadn't shaved in a day and a half. His clothes had been soaked, slept in and crawled on. He'd been shot at, knocked down, close to death and he didn't deserve being alone. Besides, he had to return her car.

When he pulled up at her house on Chester Place he doubted she'd be home. But she was. In long pale blue silk and with a nice smile. She didn't even mention being deserted the night before. She made all the right moves, knew what he needed and supplied it. Warm bath, shave, food and a big bed.

When he was relaxed, stretched out between the luxury of the world's finest sheets, Catherine came to him with a red Cartier box.

'It's yours,' she said, tossing it.

He suspected it was an expensive gift that he wouldn't accept. He opened it and saw it contained money. A thick sheaf of fifty-pound notes.

'I couldn't just stand there and do nothing,' she said. 'It was incredible. I'd throw the dice and time after time the croupier would push them back to me along with more chips.'

He'd left about seven thousand dollars worth of chips at the table. He riffled through the banknotes and estimated fifteen thousand. He didn't know whether to believe her or not. Maybe she'd lost everything and was more than making up for it. She was now sitting on the edge of the bed. He wanted to believe her.

'I had no idea what I was doing,' she said convincingly. 'But aren't you pleased?'

'Very.'

Delighted, she let her head fall back on the pillow beside his. Her body was angled away but she was close enough for

Hazard to breathe the promising clean fragrance of her.

His conscience did its best to remind him tonight was one of those every other nights when he was supposed to send to Keven.

11

FIVE HOURS difference.

In London, Keven thought, people were in the middle of their night while hers hadn't yet begun. She was a little disturbed by the idea of anyone, particularly anyone in London, being ahead of her. It seemed they had the advantage of already knowing the immediate future.

Fifteen minutes until exercise time. At exactly seven o'clock she'd be in touch with Hazard. In touch, she thought regretfully, wasn't true. Hearing from? Seeing? Feeling? All those. Maybe a better way of putting it was sensing. Yes, she'd be sensing him. But not in touch, not touching.

All that day and the day before she'd been looking forward to this exercise, her anticipation building as the time drew nearer. No matter that the connection would be tenuous, brief, and one-way. It was, she felt, a privileged form of communion, actually more intimate than a letter or phone call. The intimacy of it was enhanced by the fact that this time she wouldn't be all wired up. Kersh had suggested they forego the computer analysis and monitoring, at least for the first few of these overseas exercises. He had her sit outside on the flagstone steps with a watch, an ordinary sketch pad, and a spectrum of crayons. She welcomed not being responsible to all that complex electronic equipment and, in her opinion, the late-day sun reflecting on the Sound was much more helpful than a black nothing wall. She was on her own – a condition she'd always told herself was best.

He'd been gone four days.

The previous Friday he'd left her in bed at his place, just given her a kiss and picked up his bag and gone to the airport. Good-bye was something they'd never said to one another, so it would have seemed an ill omen to say it then. Earlier he'd asked her if she wanted to see him off at the airport and she'd told him no, keeping her reason to herself. Soon after he left she got up, dressed hurriedly, and took a cab out to Kennedy.

157

She knew which flight he was taking and from a discreet vantage she watched him check in at the counter. Him, outstandingly familiar to her among strangers. It was a sad amusement for her to observe his stance, the various physical ways he alone expressed himself, gestures and facial expression. She recognized signs of his impatience and believed she also saw his anxiety.

He stopped at a concession to buy candy bars and she mentally chastised him for eating such junk. He also bought a couple of magazines she knew he'd be able to read from cover to cover in practically no time. He'd be bored, she thought, but not if she were going with him. If she were going with him she might even let him eat the candy without saying a word.

He headed for his boarding gate. Going up the long red-carpeted tunnel there weren't many people, and if he'd turned to look back then he would have seen her. If that happened she was prepared to run to him and present herself as a surprise. But he didn't turn and she kept her eyes on the back of him, picturing how he looked from the front.

She didn't follow him into the boarding lounge. She waited in the tunnel until she was sure he'd gone aboard and then she went to the vacant lounge to stand by the window and see the silver, red, and white mass of the jet already disconnected and moving slowly away sideways. There were the plane's many windows framing the lighted faces of passengers looking out. She tried to find his face but couldn't definitely and finally had to settle on one she believed was his. She waved for attention with both arms, and she kept on waving until after the jet rolled forward and out of view. For a long while she stood there. It wasn't like her to cry and as usual she didn't have any tissues in her bag. She blamed the damned aeroplane.

Back in the city she went to her own place. She hadn't been there for days and mail had accumulated. Nothing important, just junk mail trying to get her to send money. Among them a solitary handwritten one. A letter from the mother. She knew what it would say and she skimmed the lines for the sum of it. Can you spare a little? Love and kisses and God watch over her. At least this time, thought Keven, the mother wasn't asking for the money to be sent Western Union, not that desperate this time.

158

Better do it now and get it out of the way. She wrote a cheque for a hundred, tore it up and wrote another for a hundred fifty. The cheque alone in an envelope seemed too severe. She enclosed a short note saying all was fine and hope this helps. She stamped it with an air mail and then, as an after-thought, put on enough additional stamps and printed 'Special Delivery' above the mother's current address. If she mailed it that night it would arrive in Salt Lake City the next day. But she undressed completely, let her clothes just drop anywhere and went into the kitchen hoping to find something to eat that suited her mood.

Not much there. Celery and carrot sticks she'd cut a week before had kept fresh in a jar of water; so, some of those and a slightly stale slice of organic whole-grain bread. She poured too much Tupelo honey on the bread and ate it standing there, getting honey on her fingers and the corners of her mouth. As she licked off the stickiness she suddenly became very aware of her tongue, reminded of its various uses. She recognized the thought as a wedging one that might open up serious self-appraisal if she allowed it. She replaced it with the happier prospect of ice cream. In the freezer compartment she found some forgotten rocky road, her second most favourite. Half a quart weeks old with lots of frost crystals on it. She took it and a spoon into the other room.

An everything room. She called it that rather than the renting term 'single'. One space with a section near the entrance that was supposed to be a dining area. Every time she moved she vowed the next place would have a bedroom but she always eventually settled for another similar everything room. Always only partially furnished because she too quickly lost interest in it.

She lay nude and uncovered, with a leg up on the back of the convertible sofa, an immodest alone position, and her thoughts went to him flying away at thirty-five thousand feet. He was way up and she was down. The ice cream had a refrigerator taste but it was better than nothing. He was just away on an ordinary trip he would surely return from, she pretended, thinking positive. She couldn't keep her thoughts from turning over to the negative side. The spoon was too short for the quart container and the ice-cream was frozen hard but she dug in, scraping, not wanting to wait until it

159

softened. He was flying away at hundreds of miles per hour. Why is it, she thought, men are always hurrying away and women always waiting? There was no consolation in his reason for going. Actually, his reason was selfishly masculine, indulgent, careless, and ... admirable. However, he could have stayed to fight insomnia and watch old movies and been safe with her.

Cope, detach, she advised herself. And, trying, she reviewed some of the rules she'd set for survival: Win without sympathy for the loser, never accept defeat, and never even consider surrendering. Abandon, amputate without a wince, hurt instead of be hurt no matter how much it hurt. Avoid the pitfall of the old romantic promises. Don't let your body trap you!

New by-laws of her gender.

Keven wondered if any woman could really live up to them. She knew deep down that she couldn't. As much as she wanted to prevent being victimized, from being unfairly forced into the old abject female role, she had to admit to a natural side of her that found virtues in those very things she resisted. Sometimes, especially lately, she thought it would be marvellous to have the courage to surrender, the confidence to just give in. Maybe she'd already had too much independence, been on her own too long. Somewhere along the line she'd come to realize there was a rock-bottom fact of life that one had to get down to sooner or later.

Aloneness.

Not to be confused with loneliness. There were many clever cures for loneliness, but aloneness was something no one could overcome. Everyone wanted to join and share, share experiences. Trying to do that, trying vainly to make up for not being able to do that, left one feeling so futile. And certainly independence didn't help. If anything, independence left one facing aloneness alone, and who could handle that without crashing?

Maybe, thought Keven, aloneness was not without purpose. Maybe things were intentionally arranged that way to get people to depend on each other all the more, to take comfort from one another. To love. Of all the alternatives it seemed to her that love was the only possible way to offset aloneness. Not a remedy but at least it helped.

If at that moment he'd been there she would have insisted on doing his feet.

She finished the ice cream and turned on her portable television, just picture, no sound. Burt Lancaster was being an incredible pirate. She'd seen that movie three, probably four times. Nevertheless she watched intently as Burt invited danger and miraculously escaped death with chest and teeth bared.

Haz could do it, Keven thought with recharged optimism. He could come back all right.

After the movie she decided against converting the sofa into a bed because a bed would be lonelier. From the bottom drawer of an unpainted chest she got a crocheted wool afghan to cover herself. She was chilled, possibly from the ice cream. The afghan smelled of moth repellent. It had been a gift three Christmases ago from the mother, who claimed months of loving labour spent on it. But the mother had overlooked a little manufacturer's label sewn to one corner that gave away her lie. The mother was always incriminating herself ridiculously like that, often in ways most people would consider unforgivable. Keven had long given up blaming her or hoping she'd change.

Numerous times over the years the mother had voluntarily revealed to Keven who the father was. As though it were an important secret. But each time she'd named someone different and, anyway, to Keven they were only names. Keven was convinced the mother didn't know, hadn't ever really known the father. An impulsive, passionate moment between two first-name-only strangers who immediately afterward had gone separate ways. Keven imagined that was the truth of it. And she was the result, thank you very much. She wasn't bitter about it. Her compensating philosophy was that being 'a child of passion' was something most people couldn't claim. It even sounded more sensitive.

She tucked the afghan around her and lay on her side, legs drawn up, hands pressed between her thighs. She closed her eyes but didn't go to sleep until in her mind she was sure his plane had landed at Heathrow.

She slept exceptionally deeply, longer than usual, and was proud of that. See, she told herself as she drew open the drapes to view an upright rectangle of clear sky between two

161

buildings, see how well you can cope when you have to.

In that mood she spent what remained of the morning cleaning the apartment, and while she straightened, vacuumed, and dusted, her mind kept repeating parts of a Liza Minnelli song:

> It was a good time,
> It was the best time ...

Every so often it came out as a hum or she'd sing the first line, not really conscious of how appropriate the words might be, their past tense.

> It was a good time.

In the early afternoon she went out to mail the money to the mother and take a walk anywhere. Down Lexington, window-shopping along, feeling the urge to buy but saving it. All the way to Bloomingdale's, where she went to a crowded first-floor counter and spent nearly an hour trying on inexpensive summer hats. Various shapes and colours: precocious, head-hugging pink; icy, innocent white; floppy, worldly black. Her face in the mirror responded accordingly. She hardly saw the hats. Look at me looking at me, I'm not apparently unhappy, she thought, and after a final long, contemplative gaze into her own eyes she smiled her best soft, comforting smile to herself, causing two comma-shaped lines to appear at the corners of her mouth.

From the hats she took the escalator up and happened to notice that the bosoms of display dummies were now realistically punctuated. About time. On the fourth floor she watched a man cutting wine bottles into drinking glasses, making it appear easy, and another demonstrating a motorized tumbling rock polisher. She was immediately sold on the polisher. It would be fun to find pretty pebbles and make them shine even prettier. She remembered she already had a few she'd picked up to never forget some of the places she'd been. Charge or cash, she was asked. She paid by cheque. Sensibly she'd cancelled all her charge accounts when she'd quit her last steady job. Take or send? The rock polisher was compact but quite heavy. However, she didn't hesitate to say she'd take. The burden was more endurable than having to wait for something she'd already bought. The sales clerk tied a handle on it for her.

She left Bloomingdale's via one of the Third Avenue exits and strolled down to 58th Street. There was a famous personal landmark. The Off-Track Betting parlour where she and Hazard first met. On impulse she went in to pay sentimental tribute. She wagered ten dollars on the sixth race Exacta at Aqueduct, coupling the horses' designated letters H and K. They were both outside long shots running in a large field but, she thought, anything was possible. She tucked the OTB ticket into the snug rear pocket of her jeans, for luck.

Then back up Third. The 59th Street area was crowded, mostly with people not going anywhere. When she'd first come to the city four years before, the district around 59th had been smartly unconventional, a cleaner uptown version of downtown. But it had seen its day and was now well on its way to sleazy, spoiled dirty by being the place to go, meet, and be seen, by the invasion of too much pizza, tacky boutiques, cheap shoe stores, and even porno film theatres. East 60th was better preserved and Keven headed for it and Serendipity, where she knew she'd be able to get cold fresh-squeezed carrot juice and an organic sandwich.

She was almost there when she was approached head on, her way blocked by two conscentiously tailored Negroes. Their eyes held directly on Keven's as they told her she was a *foxy lady* and advised that she should go with them because she would dig it, coke and all.

She stepped back to go around them, but they casually prevented that. She was considering a groin kick when they gave way to let her pass, their fingers snapping at the wide brims of their hats: *dig it, baby, it's your loss.*

Keven knew what they were. A pair of dudes out looking to recruit another girl to their working string. It made her remember being financially desperate in California at eighteen and someone trying to persuade her to go topless for big tips. Instead, she'd taken a job as a receptionist and gone to UCLA nights. There'd been many such decisive things, but fortunately she'd always chosen the straight, if not the expedient, way to go. She was grateful for her good judgment. She believed she must have got it from the father. Anyway, now she was past the danger point, a survivor.

163

However, the encounter with the two dudes had depressed her, put a chink in her fragile good mood. The whole damned city was a mess, one endless gutter, a summer festival of dog droppings, a combat zone for the greedy insane.

She hurried to Second Avenue, took a cab to Grand Central, and just made the 4:05 Bridgeport express.

When she arrived at the installation Kersh was finishing up for the day. He was, as usual, pleased to see her. She tried to appear buoyant and animated, but Kersh saw through that. He called Julie to tell her Keven would be having dinner with them and staying the night. It was not an offhand, easy gesture, because ordinarily Kersh and Julie enjoyed being alone, spending time on one another as though it were their own precious, personal currency. Respecting that, Keven resisted the hospitality but Kersh wouldn't have it.

He gave her a bright red crash helmet, put on a white one himself, and within minutes they were speeding over the narrow black ribbons of sideroads on the Harley-Davidson with Kersh's hairy sheepdog Baldy chasing after them. The growl and vibrations of the old heavy motorcycle made it seem to be going faster than it really was. Keven couldn't help being a bit apprehensive. She leaned forward against Kersh's broad back, put her arms around him and locked her hands. Then she felt more secure, protected by his husky solidness. When they paused at a crossroad, Keven glanced back but Baldy wasn't in sight. 'What about him?' she asked, having to shout.

'He knows the way,' Kersh assured her, and roared ahead. But at the next crossroad Kersh idled until they saw the dog come over the rise some distance behind, a fluffy grey ball rolling their way. Kersh encouraged the dog with a wave and continued on. After a short way they turned off on to a dirt road and were there.

It was a three-story, wood-frame farmhouse set on enough land for privacy. Painted clean white with shutters of blue. It had a wide porch all around and there were large, old, friendly trees and lilac bushes. Set off to the right was a barn, settled askew and nicely weathered.

Julie came out to greet them. She gave Kersh a kiss on the mouth and then hugged Keven, though it was a bit awkward because she was so pregnant. Seven and a half months now, causing her long cotton skirt to hike up unevenly in front and

164

her blouse to strain and gap from the fullness of her breasts. She was obviously very happy with her condition, glowing with a kind of self-amazement.

Baldy came lumbering in, panting, his pink tongue hanging, exhausted but needing to wag and bound around. Kersh gave a few rewarding pats and led the dog into the house for water.

'Come help me pick some lettuce for the salad,' Julie invited and Keven went with her to the rear of the house, where there was a vegetable garden neatly rowed and fenced.

It was one of Keven's someday wishes to have a garden like that, growing fresh things she knew for certain were uncontaminated. She took the small fruit basket Julie handed her and went down between rows, eager to pick.

'It's early lettuce,' Julie said. 'This will be the first we've had.'

That made Keven feel that her presence was an occasion. She bent over and broke off some of the outer greener leaves of a plant, liking the crisp, healthy snap her fingers experienced. Glancing down the row she saw Julie squatted gracelessly, her reach and mobility restricted by her unborn burden. It occurred to Keven that perhaps pregnancy overcame aloneness. At least during pregnancy one was connected to another person. That could be the joy of it, a temporary relief from aloneness. Reason enough for any woman to feel special.

The thought was interrupted by the clatter of a dull bell. Across the way in a small pasture two cows were munching and swishing. 'You even have your own milk.'

'Not quite yet,' Julie said lightly, and then realized Keven meant the cows. 'Oh, them. They're both old and dry.'

'They're just for atmosphere?'

'Well, they also make valuable contributions to the garden.'

'They don't look very friendly.'

'They'd come in the house if we'd let them.'

Keven thought she'd get acquainted with those cows if she had the chance.

At that moment Julie lost her balance. From her squatting position she toppled over backwards. Keven rushed to her, but Julie was laughing. 'It happens all the time,' she said. 'I'm always overcompensating for being front heavy.'

Keven helped her up. Julie slapped the dirt from her skirt

as though annoyed at herself and immediately squatted to start picking again.

They had dinner out on the side porch. While they ate dusk gave way to dark and with it came the pleasant sounds of all the little night-loving creatures. Moths performed around the kerosene lamp on the table. The conversation went from one trivial subject to another.

After dinner they all helped clear the table and then returned to the porch with mugs of tea and ginger cookies. They sat on the edge with their legs over, facing the night. Below them in the grass Baldy was suddenly alert for no apparent reason. He barked twice and wandered away.

Keven said: 'Animals are very telepathic, aren't they?'

'Some seem to be,' said Kersh.

'Especially dogs,' Julie said.

'And horses,' said Keven, wondering how those two outsiders had done that afternoon at Aqueduct.

'Quite a few telepathic experiments have been done with dogs,' Kersh said. 'The other day I read a paper by a Russian scientist named Bekherev. He put a thousand identical sticks of wood in a room, just scattered them around. Each stick was numbered. From a separate room he telepathically commanded a dog to go in and retrieve a particular, numbered stick. I don't remember the exact results but about ten times out of every hundred tries the dog retrieved the right stick.'

'I'd like to try that with Haz sometime,' Keven said, entertained by the thought.

'You'd be fetching the sticks,' Kersh told her, reminding her of her receiver's role.

'I suppose,' she said vaguely. It was the first time that night Hazard had been mentioned. They'd been avoiding the subject for her sake and now she'd done it to herself, making her feel a sharp longing for him. To pull out of it she told them, 'This afternoon on the train I sat beside a very fat and nosey woman who wanted to know my life history. When she asked what I did for a living I told her I was a telepathist. Just to see what her reaction would be. She told me she had a niece who also works for the telephone company.'

That got a laugh.

'I'm always doing battle with the infidels,' said Julie.

'Infidels?' Keven was amused.

166

'She tries to make a believer out of everyone,' Kersh said. 'Next thing she'll be on the street shaking a tambourine and handing out leaflets.'

'I've converted a few,' Julie said.

'Including me,' Kersh said.

'You were easy. Your mind was wide open.'

'Half open.'

'Well, that's half more than most people.'

'I think people experience telepathy every day and don't realize it,' Keven said.

Julie also thought that. 'They prefer to call it something else like willpower or intuition.'

'Or plain old coincidence, like two people getting the same thought at the same time. That's happened to everyone.'

'Especially to people who are intimately involved,' Kersh said.

'Why is that?' Keven asked.

'I don't know for sure, but it's a piece of recurring evidence. The area of the brain that controls emotional behaviour is the same area that has most to do with telepathic abilities.'

'You mean love might have something to do with telepathy?' Keven asked.

'Let's just say it seems to help.'

'What gripes the hell out of me,' said Julie, 'is the way people claim to be believers just because it's fashionable. Scratch the surface and they're really as sceptical as ever.'

'Can't entirely blame them for that,' Kersh said. 'If anyone's to blame it's the scientists.'

'Not all scientists,' Julie said, and gave Kersh a possessive hug.

'No, but it's their fault for not making people more aware of how far science has gone. The average person sees and judges things according to the so-called laws of nature, disbelieving anything that doesn't apply. Such as telepathy. Actually, compared to some recent developments in the exact sciences, telepathy seems almost ordinary. For instance, we know now about negative mass – particles of anti-matter that correspond to every known particle of matter in the universe. A sort of duplicate of everything.'

Keven imagined another Keven somewhere.

'What do you think happens when an anti-particle meets its counterpart?' Kersh asked.

'They fall in love,' Julie guessed.

'Quite the contrary. They annihilate one another.'

'Figures,' Keven said.

'We also have time flowing backward and things called neutrinos that we know travel faster than the speed of light, which until only a few years ago was *known* to be impossible.'

'What are they called?'

'Neutrinos.'

Keven said it sounded like an Italian restaurant.

Kersh laughed. 'And they're just about as predictable. Neutrinos are particles of matter that come from space and have no respect at all for any of our rules. They pass right through solid mass as though it wasn't there. Right at this moment billions of neutrinos are shooting through our bodies and going on their way into and all the way through the earth. Although the neutrino is matter, obviously it exists in an entirely different dimension.'

'That's really far out,' said Julie.

'But why,' Keven said, 'when scientists are involved with such fantastic things are they so set against telepathy?'

'Some of them are coming around, especially the physicists. They're getting closer to it.'

From somewhere out in the dark, Baldy's bark punctuated the moment.

Kersh asked Julie and Keven if they were chilled. The night air was dewy and cool, but they didn't want to go inside yet. Kersh went in to get sweaters. He also put the London Symphony on the stereo, Vaughan Williams' Number Six in E minor. When he came back to the porch he sat with his back against a post and Julie snuggled into the cave of his arms.

'Someday,' Julie said, 'telepathy will be a regular way of communicating. People will use words only when they want to. The greedy, old telephone company, Western Union, and the post office will all be out of business and movies will be silent again.'

'And a receiver will have to marry a sender,' Kersh said.

'Not necessarily,' Keven said. 'By then probably everyone will be going both ways.'

'That seems to be the tendency,' Julie commented.

168

'Anyway,' said Keven, 'in the future people will look back on now as the blabbering dark age.'

Kersh said he doubted that. 'Chances are people may be even more talkative.'

'You mean with their minds.'

Julie and Keven needed convincing.

'With their mouths,' Kersh said.

'But that's ridiculous,' said Keven. 'Why should they talk even more when they're telepathic?'

'You're assuming – as most people do – that telepathy is a new kind of human ability that will be refined and developed along with interplanetary weekend excursions and humanoid sex partners.'

'Isn't it?'

'I don't think so,' Kersh said.

Julie reacted as though Kersh had committed blasphemy. In all their many discussions she'd never heard him say such a thing.

'Rather than an ability we're developing, telepathy may be something from our evolutionary past.'

'You mean we used to be better at it?' Keven asked.

'Possibly. Anyway, there's quite a bit of evidence in favour of such a theory.'

Julie and Keven needed convincing.

Kersh smiled and asked if they wanted the deluxe or economy lecture.

'You can stop when we start to yawn,' Julie told him.

Kersh took a moment to decide where to begin. 'At best,' he said, 'we can only speculate about how the human brain originated. We've very little to go on besides a record of fossils and there are still a lot of gaps. But by using comparative anatomy, embryology, and a few other related disciplines we can piece together a fairly accurate picture. It's believed that man's earliest ancestors were tiny organisms that lived in the waters of the Cambrian Seas some five hundred million years ago. We call these creatures primordial chordates. They occupied the warm surface areas of the seas, and the sunlight hit on their backs. Apparently, as a reaction, they developed a strip of sensory cells called neurons. Even now in the human embryo the first sign of development of a nervous system is the same such strip of tissue.'

169

Julie patted her stomach and said it was her Cambrian Sea.

'At first this strip of nerve tissue was dangerously exposed. So, for protection it rolled itself into a more rigid, tubular shape and sank into the body of the organism. Then for even more protection it was encased in a bony substance and became the spinal cord and column.'

'What does all this have to do with telepathy?' Julie asked.

'I'm getting to it.'

'Well, get, my love,' she said, snuggling.

'Next in evolutionary order came the forming of the brain. At first it was merely a swelling at the front end of the spinal cord. No more than a tiny nodule, then another and another. These three nodules would eventually be the stem on which the advanced brain would grow. But for a long period in our evolution these three earliest chambers were a sensory unit in themselves. They were our primordial brain.'

'Are we still in the water?' Keven asked.

'Probably in and out,' Kersh told her. 'The question is, what functions did this old brain perform? We can determine that more or less from what we know subsequently developed from its three chambers. The forward chamber gave rise to our reasoning mechanisms, the cerebrum. Over the rear chamber was superimposed the cerebellum, which controls the body's automatic and voluntary physical activities. And from the mid-chamber came what's known as the tectum. For an interim period in our evolution the tectum was a highly developed visual and auditory centre, but now neuroscientists say it apparently has no significant function at all.

'Keeping those evolvements in mind, it's reasonable to suggest that the primordial brain possessed to some extent corresponding or at least related abilities. And during this primordial time there must have been some refinements, changes, evolution within evolution. Before we had eyes, no doubt we had a sense of vision and the same applies to all our other senses as well.'

'I'm beginning to see what you're getting at,' Julie said.

So was Keven.

'Good. Well, these intermediate abilities must have been around throughout the transitional period when the old brain was giving way to the new brain. That transformation, remember, took many millions of years and before it was anywhere near complete we were already comparatively advanced creatures.'

'We didn't have any eyes?' Keven asked incredulously.

'At a certain stage, no, not for a long while.'

'How did we see to get around?'

'We sensed,' replied Kersh. 'Even today blind people learn to depend on a remnant of that ability, especially the congenitally blind who've never experienced sight. In primordial times we also had the advantage of built-in distance receptors that made us extremely sensitive to vibrations.'

'We still do,' said Julie.

'To a very limited degree.'

'Maybe that explains why we get spontaneous good or bad vibes from various people,' Julie said.

'What about talking?' Keven asked. 'I suppose we weren't able to talk yet back in those days.'

'No, a spoken language came much later.'

'But we did communicate.'

'No doubt,' Kersh said. 'At first only the most primary things like hunger and danger.'

'And sex?'

'Maybe' – Kersh grinned – 'although that seems to have always had a language all its own.'

'And no trouble expressing itself,' Julie said.

'So, as early creatures we communicated telepathically?'

'Yes,' Kersh said. 'Of course, there's no way of knowing how complex the messages were that we transmitted to one another, and actually that's not so vital. More important is the long-term exclusive dependency we had on that method of communication. Millions of years. And even after the development of the new brain, when man's reasoning power became more advanced, this telepathic ability didn't just suddenly stop. We must have gone on using it for millions of years more – until it became secondary, gradually gave way to other abilities we learned to rely on.'

After a moment of silent reflection, Julie said, rather forlornly. 'So today what we have of telepathy are only the leftovers.'

Kersh nodded. 'It's still there in our brains, the residual of it. Some people have more than others.'

'All that makes me is a sort of throwback,' said Keven, deflated.

'You're still very special,' Kersh told her fondly.

'And I'm still dubious,' said Julie with renewed determination. 'You said yourself this was only your theory.'

'Not mine alone, darling. Many other scientists have hit on the same premiss. Freud, for one.'

'You sound pretty sure about it,' Keven said.

'Actually, you've been convincing me.'

'Me?'

'You and your overactive tectum.'

'I didn't think it showed,' Keven said.

'But it does,' Kersh told her. 'As much as you've disliked being wired up to the computer during our exercises, it has paid off. The electronic depth probes have indicated a remarkable amount of energy coming from your tectum, that mid-brain area that I told you about. But it's not sustained activity. It comes only at certain peak times during each test. But it happens repeatedly and, according to wave measurements, always in the same pattern of phases. For a brief time just before the peak, the rest of your brain becomes dormant, as though bowing out to the tectum and its function. Afterward, for an equally brief phase there is the usual dormancy. A parenthesis. Evidently it's during the peak, those few intense seconds, that your telepathic perception is at work.'

Baldy interrupted, came like a fluffy ghost out of the night with his legs and underside wet from an adventure in tall grass.

Coincidentally the London Symphony played its last, long note.

'And that, children, is it for tonight,' Kersh said. 'My hip's gone to sleep and the rest of me wants to.'

They went in to bed.

Keven managed to get to sleep with her arms around a big feather pillow.

The next morning she looked out her bedroom window and saw the two cows just below. She tried to will them to look up to her but they wouldn't. At breakfast she found in the sports section of the *New York Times* that the sixth at Aqueduct was won by a head by the letter-H horse. The K-horse had run next to last. She told herself it wasn't significant. Julie invited her to stay for the day, but Keven declined and rode with Kersh to the installation.

First thing, she went down to the beach house. It had a shut-up tight smell so she opened all the windows. She thought about tidying the place but decided she'd leave things as they were – Hazard's deck sneakers caked with dry sand in a corner by the door, his sunglasses on the table and some old racing forms, one of his shirts thrown over the back of a chair, a cup he'd drunk from, the bed unmade from the last time.

She sat on the floor and unpacked the electric rock polisher. After reading the instructions twice she assembled it. Then she changed into shorts cut from an old pair of jeans and a T-shirt. Taking along a shoe box, she went out to the beach to walk along the water's edge, searching for pebbles. She almost succeeded in losing herself in that pleasant diversion and by mid-afternoon she'd walked two miles down coast and collected half a boxful. Back at the beach house she sorted through the pebbles, selected only the best according to symmetry and hue. Like small hopes she'd preserve and make brighter, she thought, and put them into the polisher's metal canister along with the powdered pumice and the right amount of water, according to instructions. When she switched on the polisher the canister rotated and the pebbles tumbling inside made an irritating rattling noise. The complete polishing process was supposed to take seven days. She hoped it wouldn't really take that long.

Shortly before seven o'clock she went up to the main house for the first overseas exercise, and at seven precisely she was ready to receive. After Kersh's talk the night before she was more conscious than ever of what she was doing but also more confident that she could do it. The whole idea of telepathy seemed less vague now – a natural mental function.

But when the exercise was over she believed she'd missed for some reason. Instead of a single clear image, she'd received what appeared to be a sort of composite: a blue background with a white horizontal figure floating in its centre. At first she thought it was an angel, but after studying it a while she wasn't sure. Maybe it was a white bird with womanlike configurations, or maybe a white female with birdlike features. It was, thought Keven, too ambiguous to be correct.

173

For the next two days she was restless, constantly on edge. To keep occupied she helped Kersh in the laboratory and did some typing and filing for him. He invited her home but she preferred to stay alone at the beach house.

The nights were especially bad. She sat out on the steps for hours looking to sea, and all the while the damned rock polisher churned noisily away.

Now, finally, it was time for the second exercise. The watch said exactly seven o'clock. The sketch pad was on her lap, the crayons spread out and ready. She relaxed and let her mind go. It raced and opened, reached its receptive phase. Blank white waiting for impression. Nothing came.

Keven felt herself panic, fearing the worst – that Hazard might not be sending, might never again.

She controlled herself and made another attempt, summoning up all her feeling for him, picturing him, fragmented – his hands nice, eyes nice, ears and hair nice, mouth nice, and all the other nice parts of him, and then him altogether. Him. She tried intensely to visualize where he was that instant, how he was. She had to know.

Moments later, when she glanced down at the sketch pad she saw she'd made a large green angry X. It was not an image he'd sent. It was her protest. Maybe, she thought, she'd let her imagination get out of control. But one thing for certain: She was no longer worried about his safety. She now felt only exasperation and a need to fight.

She went down the slope to the beach house. She quickly gathered up everything of his and threw them into the closet. She kicked the electric rock polisher's cord out of the socket and put fresh sheets on the bed.

12

JEAN-CLAUDE PINCHON sat in a soft, velour-covered chaise, with his head up to the mid-morning sun.

Because his eyes were closed and would have to remain closed for several minutes more he felt somewhat uncomfortable, vulnerable. To offset that he kept alert for any unusual nearby sounds and reassured himself that he was on an upper terrace of his villa, alone and inaccessible. He drew further confidence from knowing exactly what his view would be had his eyes been open: the bougainvillaea vines blobbing purple-red all along the balustrade; the new tops of the old sea pines just below, not tossing as they would when the afternoon breeze came up; the Mediterranean, more grey than blue, countless identical disturbances on its surface, like dabs in a pointillistic painting. Directly ahead in the distance would surely be, as always, the vague but darker definition of land that was the Italian Riviera, and closer, clearer, almost looming on his left, Monaco. To his right, nothing. Only the sky and sea meeting, forming a line that deceptively appeared to be a destination.

Pinchon's thoughts went in that direction. As though looking on familiar pages in an atlas his mind's eye started at Tangier and travelled along the coastal profiles of Morocco and Algeria. He visualized each irregularity – peninsula and harbour. Tunisia, Libya, past Benghazi to the Arab Republic, the delta region of the Nile, and all the way to Port Said. At that point his thoughts held on what lay eastward. A lesion on the face of the earth that thrived on its own festering, that would not be satisfied until the entire world had been brought under its control.

Pinchon was no ordinary anti-Semite. He was one by tradition, the only son of a long line of only sons who had conscientiously handed down their hatred for Jews. His great grandfather had been a contemporary of Gougenot des Mousseaux, who authored the bible of modern anti-Semitism – *Le juif, le judaisme et la judaisation des peuples chrétiens.* A personally inscribed first edition of that infamous prophetic volume was a highly valued part of the Pinchon family legacy, and passages from it were read to Jean-Claude even before he was old enough to comprehend their meaning.

By the time Jean-Claude had reached school age he already had been instilled with the concept of a universal enemy. He was not allowed, however, to go to school until a carefully selected tutor had reinforced him with enough insight to protect his mind from being poisoned. Thus it was with a special sense of superiority that he regarded his instructors and classmates at Rosey, especially those who were openly Jewish. They couldn't fool him. He saw through their friendly façades. He wasn't about to be taken in and taken over. In keeping with his father's advice, never once during all his school years did Jean-Claude trust anyone enough to confide his hatred, and his expression of it was limited to such normal displays as suddenly grabbing one of his elbows and saying, '*Oh, mon petit juif!*' (my little Jew) which, for some archaic reason, was the accepted French term for funny bone. Naturally, it was a relief for Jean to spend holidays at home, where he didn't have to hold back his malice and there was someone to share it with.

As had several preceding Pinchon generations, Jean believed unequivocally that the Jews were conspiring to dominate the world. Every Jew was to some degree secretly involved. They were a clever, vastly organized, diabolical element responsible for all the world's suffering and turmoil. To accept this view one had only to imagine a world without Jews, without their avarice, their fierce competitiveness. Even without the minor everyday irritations *they* caused, life would be so much easier, more pleasant. *N'est-ce pas?* Unfortunately, however, one had to face reality – the Jews and their vicious conspiracy. The latter was revealed in that document called the *Protocols of the Elders of Zion*, which was not meant to be seen by gentiles because it laid bare, step by step, how the Jews planned to bring all other people under their power, preparing the way for the Messianic Age, the coming of the anti-Christ, the Apocalypse, when gold will rule, Judaism will be the only religion and a Jewish sovereign of the House of David will govern the world.

176

In one respect, however, Jean's anti-Semitic beliefs differed from those of the Finchons before him.

It first occurred to him one evening when he was perusing accounts of Christian boys ritualistically murdered by Jews during the fifteenth century. Christianity itself, thought Jean, might be a part of the Jewish conspiracy. Christ had been a Jew, and his disciples. Possibly they had merely played their roles in an elaborately contrived ruse. Certainly it was not beyond the Jews to concoct an entire religion to accommodate their ambitions.

Blessed are the meek, turn the other cheek, do unto others as you would have others do unto you. Kindness, tolerance, forgiveness, humility. All these Christian codes of conduct had originally been conceived by Jews. No one could deny that. Nor could anyone fail to see how such submissive behaviour would facilitate Jewish aggressiveness and greed. Yes, Jean-Claude agreed with himself, how cunning of them.

The more he thought about it, the more it seemed a revelation, and he found substantiation for it wherever he cared to look. The Last Supper had been merely a final briefing for the melodrama. Not Christ but a substitute had died on the Cross, enabling Christ to be seen miraculously alive afterward. The Immaculate Conception? Nothing more than a woman claiming innocence rather than admit her indiscretion. The Father, Son, and Holy Ghost were obviously straight out of a Zionist cabal.

Jean kept these concepts to himself, did not even discuss them with his father. The elder Pinchon had already endured enough and should be spared the disillusionment. It took considerable self-restraint for Jean not to declare that paying devotion to Christ, attending masses and confessions, and fingering rosaries were a waste of time. But he held back right to the end when his father died prematurely in St Francis Hospital at Nice. The cause of death was said to be a perforated ulcer, but Jean suspected the doctors were undeclared Jews who'd taken the opportunity to get rid of a formidable opponent. In any case, Jean had tolerantly arranged for his father to receive final rites.

That had been in 1964. Then, at age thirty, as the sole surviving Pinchon, Jean took charge of the family affairs. He was no longer Jean but Pinchon, *the* Pinchon, head of a vast fortune made primarily through interests in North Africa and the Mideast.

From his great grandfather's days up to when Farouk was deposed, Pinchon et Cie. had been the largest cotton brokers on the Cairo exchange. Egyptian cotton and the Pinchon name were practically synonymous. In March, 1954, when Nasser and the Revolution Command Council took over, Pinchon et Cie., like all other outsiders, was obliged to leave Egypt. It did so reluctantly but on terms that weren't altogether unfavourable. The new Arab government paid Pinchon et Cie. a generous compensation and showed further partiality by granting certain concessions, including some very profitable shipping franchises and the rights to explore for oil in certain areas of Sinai. Jean's father had concentrated on the shipping, but one of Jean's first moves on taking over was to exercise those oil rights.

At the recommendation of several reliable geologists, Pinchon put down three exploratory wells near Asi. As predicted, the oil was there, a sizeable field, and by the end of 1966 negotiations were concluded with the Arab government for a joint-venture pipe line. Within a year full-scale production would begin and it was estimated that by 1969 Pinchon would realize a minimum of a hundred million from the venture.

Of course it never happened. In June, 1967, the Israeli Seventh Armoured Brigade overran Asi. Israel occupied the entire Sinai peninsula, and Pinchon took a major loss, including three and a half million invested. But what made Pinchon suffer most was the thought of Jews enjoying the profits from his enterprise.

He couldn't live with that. It ate at him, fed on his hate. If *they* were chosen, *he* was chosen to stop them. He'd have back that Sinai oil and more; literally pull the ground out from under them. He could already see it happening in his mind's eye ... looking eastward from Port Said.

The sound of driveway gravel crunching under a car's wheels brought Pinchon sharply back to the terrace of his villa in Cap Ferrat. That, he knew, would be Colonel Bayumi arriving. No need to hurry. Mustafa would see that the Colonel waited comfortably.

Pinchon touched his cheek with the tip of a finger, gently.

178

He ran the fingertip lightly over his chin, up the side of his nose, and across his forehead. Time enough, he decided. He sat up on the edge of the chaise and opened his eyes. After adjusting to the brightness he was able to view himself in the three-sided magnifying mirror that stood on the nearby table. A half hour before he'd applied a paste-like substance to his face and it had dried to a blue-tinted glaze, exaggerating his nostrils and eyes, a macabre effect.

Using the thumb and forefinger of each hand he pinched at the edge of the substance just beneath his jawline, got it started there and peeled the facial mask up and off in one filmy piece. He enjoyed the transformation, lifted his chin and turned his head slowly from side to side to appreciate his features from various angles, magnified. Closer to the mirror he scrutinized the texture of his complexion. Fine, he thought.

There were a few tiny remnants of the facial substance on his brows and hairline. He picked them off, pausing several times to rediscover his reflection. From the table he took up a fluffy ball of cotton that he dipped into a Lalique cut-crystal bowl filled with a pale pink lotion, a mild astringent. Ever so lightly, he patted his face with the saturated cotton, taking care not to rub, as though that would be irreverently harsh.

A single brow hair, he noticed, was a bit long and defiantly out of place. He isolated it with a pair of silver tweezers and plucked it. The minor sting he felt was a sacrifice. He soothed that brow with his finger, smoothed both brows with a delicate outward motion. Flicked at his lashes. Examined his teeth. Wet his lips. Then, after another long, approving look into the mirror he got up and went inside.

That entire upper wing of the villa was his private quarters. It consisted of a large bedroom, sitting room, dressing room, and bath. The bedroom and sitting room were furnished with authentic eighteenth-century French pieces, somehow miraculously saved from the burning rage of the Revolution. Especially splendid were a pair of perfectly matched Boule commodes that the Louvre would have been proud to display. The carpets were antique Aubusson, and the silk-damask covered walls were hung with such treasures as two Bonnards, a Velasquez, a good-sized Renoir, a Goya, and a Monet. One painting was particularly prized by Pinchon – a rare Fragonard that had been originally done for Madame Du Barry's

179

salon. Pinchon valued it not so much for its beauty or worth, but becaue he had outbid Wildenstein for it at a Drouot sale several years back. Each time Pinchon looked at that painting he never really saw Fragonard's delicate use of colour or the graceful arrangement of three nude female figures; rather he saw the disappointment on Wildenstein's face.

The adjoining dressing room was completely organized, everything built in and concealed. All surfaces, including the ceiling, were covered with mirror, and the lighting there had a flattering tint of pink. When Pinchon felt depressed, a need to be consoled, he would come here, where the opposing mirrored surfaces multiplied his image. It never failed to reassure him that all men were not created equal.

Now he slid aside part of a long wall and from fifty suits selected one made for him by Valentino. A double-breasted lightweight beige flannel. He inspected it. A speck of lint would be unpardonable, a wrinkle a catastrophe, a loose button cause for a tirade.

The beige received his sanction. He put it on, along with a pale yellow shirt of voile, monogrammed on the right cuff, and a blue figured-silk tie that he ceremoniously looped around with precise tension to slide up into a perfect knot. A shallow velvet-lined drawer held a dozen Piaget watches. He decided on one not so formal, platinum with a blue, numberless face.

Finally he stood straight and presented himself to himself from every point of view. His smile was a benediction.

Only one door connected this part of the villa with the rest. Apparently a regular wooden door. Actually a steel door covered with walnut veneer. It was fitted with four electric bolts. Pinchon pressed a small button inset on the inside door frame and the bolts retracted consecutively.

He went out to a long gallery-hallway that was lined on both sides with portraits of his male ancestors. Centuries of Pinchons sharing such a remarkable resemblance that they almost seemed to be a separate species. Their similar faces were not entirely the result of dominant male genes. Pinchons down through the ages had chosen their wives according to a physical standard that would help preserve the Pinchon look. No matter how attractive a woman might be, if she had a single strong feature, such as a slightly long noble nose or a mouth a bit too voluptuous, she was considered desirable, perhaps, but not a serious candidate for marriage and mating. For a Pinchon, a woman had to possess a pristine sort of beauty, fine, symmetrical features that would contribute rather than impose.

Pinchon knew his responsibility. Since he was twenty-one he'd been on the lookout for such a woman. He'd come on several possibilities but for various reasons had disqualified them. All except one. The one he'd met while skiing during the 1970 season at Gstaad. Perfect, he'd thought at first sight, and had her investigated.

What he learned made her all the more ideal. Her ancestry was British all the way back to William the Conqueror. Both her patrilineal and matrilineal sides had settled in Northumberland. There were strong indications her earlier forebears had been Scandinavian. Not a gap nor even a questionable link in her line, which, of course, precluded the possibility of any Jewish blood. Yes, she was physically and genealogically ideal and also, not unimportant, she was wealthy in her own right.

There was, however, a problem. She was already married. Normally that would have cancelled Pinchon's interest, and for a while he did try to eliminate her from his thoughts. Trying to forget her only made him remember her more. Logic told him to find someone else, but his desire said it preferred not to look any farther, and he gave way to the fixation.

Marbella, Venice, Deauville, the Algarve.

Chance meetings. Or so they seemed. Actually Pinchon had arranged always to know her whereabouts. Each morning he was presented with a blue vellum envelope containing that information – exactly where she was, who she was with. No details about her behaviour. He spared himself that.

From the start it was apparent she spent her time as she pleased, hardly any at all with her husband. Pinchon wondered about this marriage. Deteriorating? Reduced to a mere arrangement? He gathered a divorce was surely imminent.

But a year passed and her situation remained unchanged. This husband of hers, this shadowy obstacle, obviously he had some unnatural hold on her.

Another so-called chance meeting. At a soirée in Paris.

She introduced. 'This is my husband, Carl.'

'*Enchanté, monsieur.*' An understatement. Pinchon was elated to find Carl was even less than he'd expected. In appearance and style the American couldn't compare, couldn't possibly compete. Of course, Pinchon already had ordered and received a preliminary rundown on Carl's social, financial, and business status. It revealed nothing to explain why she should be married to this man. There was one thing, however, that Pinchon did find interesting about Carl. His assignment for the American State Department, the fact that he was involved with disarmament.

Now, descending the wide, gracefully curving main stairs, Pinchon's attention went automatically to a console in the foyer. There on its marble surface, as expected, was the blue envelope. He opened it and read:

> She arrived in Eze
> at 2:00 this morning.
> With the American,
> Edmund Stevens.

He was pleased. With her husband dead he'd wanted to press the advantage but more immediate business demands had prevented it. Now she was making it convenient for him by being in Eze, only five kilometres away. Evidently she'd taken the suggestion he'd made when he'd last seen her (again not by chance) at the gambling club in London. As for her being with this Edmund Stevens, that was really nothing to worry about. No doubt Stevens was only another of her temporary amusements. Pinchon decided that as soon as he'd completed his business with Colonel Bayumi he'd call and invite her to dinner for that evening. If she insisted on bringing Stevens along, well ... he could see to it that the American was suitably distracted.

Pinchon started to put the envelope into his jacket pocket but thought better of it. It might cause an unsightly bulge. He tore it in half and left it there.

He crossed the foyer and went into the study. Colonel Bayumi was seated in a deep chair opposite Mustafa. Hatum and Gabil were also there, but standing. Colonel Bayumi was in civilian clothes. He had a brandy and soda in hand and from the look of its colour it was a strong one. Perhaps the drink was responsible for Bayumi's face being flushed, or it could have been his collar and tie cutting into the corpulent folds of his neck. He was speaking in Arabic but stopped, got up quickly, and stood military straight when Pinchon entered. Bayumi was ready with his right hand but Pinchon extended only a verbal greeting and immediately took his place behind a large *Régence* table that served as a desk.

'You had no difficulty getting away?'

'None at all,' replied the Colonel. 'At this moment I am appreciating the splendours of the Sistine Chapel.'

'And your return flight?'

'Four o'clock.'

'What we have to do here should take no more than an hour. The two o'clock flight will put you back in Rome by three-thirty.'

Bayumi was on a short leave from Cairo, had brought his wife and daughter with him to Rome to help make it appear an ordinary holiday. Its true purpose was this clandestine meeting with Pinchon. Bayumi was not pleased with the prospect of an earlier return flight. He'd anticipated a longer meeting, including a large, leisurely lunch. As a member of the Egyptian officer class he was not accustomed to being hurried.

Pinchon was anxious to get down to business. He dismissed Hatum and Gabil and instructed Mustafa to arrange for a seat on the two o'clock flight from Nice.

When they were alone Bayumi asked, 'You don't trust those three?'

'Mustafa.'

'Not the other two?'

'Hatum is limited, does what he is told and pretends he is a devout Muslim. He knows little and asks nothing except to be paid. The big, unsightly one, Gabil, has been with us only a month. Mustafa brought him in.'

'A Palestinian?'

'His family was killed when the Israelis bombed Es-Salt. He served with Arafat in Jordan and after that was on his own around Mount Hermon.'

'What happened to his face?'

'The Israelis, trying to get information from him when he was a prisoner in Ramleh. He revealed nothing, killed three guards, and escaped.'

'I've never known anyone escaping from Ramleh.'

'We verified it,' Pinchon said. 'What impresses me most about Gabil is his hatred. He has it here, here, and here.' Pinchon indicated his head, heart, and groin.

'It is in our blood,' Bayumi said.

Pinchon's nod included himself.

'I can well understand why you trust Mustafa,' Bayumi said. 'He's a Bedouin with the old look in his eyes. When offended no man is more dangerous.'

Pinchon agreed. Mustafa would go to any extreme to preserve what he considered his honour. On the wedding night of his younger, only sister, when her husband did not publicly declare her to be a virgin, Mustafa had slashed the girl's throat. According to the old way, that was the only honourable way of settling the matter. 'For Mustafa,' Pinchon said, 'the Jewish occupation of Arab lands is a personal disgrace.'

'It is unfortunate we did not have more men of his sort,' Bayumi said, implying past defeats by Israel might then have been avoided.

Pinchon held back his opinion that that would not have made a difference. No need to offend those he needed.

Bayumi took up his attaché case, snapped it open, and took out the most recent issue of *Réalités*. Almost ceremoniously he placed the magazine on the desk before Pinchon.

Enclosed within the magazine's pages, Pinchon found several eight-by-ten glossy photographs printed on lightweight paper. They were in a meaningful sequence. The first was a view of an oblong block of concrete. Others showed the concrete progressively chipped away to reveal a long, cylindrical-shaped object. Then a view of the object entirely free of concrete.

It was a metal canister resembling a regular oxygen or acetylene tank, twice as large around and three times longer. Stencilled lengthwise on its metal surface was a series of numbers and letters.

The final three photographs were closer views of the outlet end of the canister. Showing a fitted cap sealed in place over the neck. Showing the cap removed and a valve inside the throat of the canister. Showing details of that valve.

Pinchon was pleased as he went through the photographs. 'The other is the same?'

'Identical.'

Pinchon gave more attention to the last photograph, trying to comprehend the various components of the valve. He didn't understand how it functioned but he didn't want the colonel to know that.

Bayumi pointed out an arrangement of irregular metal protrusions that were part of the valve. 'This is the problem,' he said.

'Why?'

'It is a unique kind of locking device. To remove the gas from the canister requires a special piece of equipment that serves both as a key and a transfer unit. It threads into the throat here.' Bayumi pointed again. 'When tightened down, it exerts the exact combination of pressures on the lock to release the gas.'

It sounded very complicated to Pinchon. He sighed his impatience and shifted nervously.

'That is how the Americans designed it,' said Bayumi.

'Can't we break the lock or by-pass it in some way?'

'The gas could escape.'

'Perhaps not.'

'We must assume the Americans devised this elaborate locking system as a precautionary measure. I personally shouldn't want to tamper with it.'

Nor would Pinchon, knowing how lethal the gas was. A minuscule drop anywhere on the skin caused death within sixty seconds. The substance affected the nervous system, causing every muscle in the body to go suddenly into an uncontrollable state of activity. The victim would literally be exercised to death. He would die vomiting, sweating, defecating, urinating, and, ironically, with his penis erect. The chemical compound involved was O-alkyl (2-dialkylamino ethyl thio) alkyl phosphine oxide, which the United States Chemical Corps had appropriately dubbed with the acronym 'O-DETH'. Categorically it was a vx type of nerve gas – colourless, odourless, fifty times more toxic than any other and modified to make it ten times heavier by volume. The latter feature was considered an important advance by military scientists because it allowed the gas to be dispersed from the air with greater accuracy over a limited target area. In the United States arsenal of chemical weapons it had been designated vx–10.

Pinchon inwardly shuddered at the thought of being anywhere near such a deadly substance. He quickly reminded himself he'd never have to be.

Bayumi was saying to him, 'We have two alternatives. Either we obtain one of these transfer keys from the United States or we try to produce one ourselves.'

It was up to Pinchon. He looked at the photograph of the valve, indignant that such a small thing should be a major obstacle. Everything had gone so well up to now. He considered the first alternative. It would mean getting a man into one of the United States bases such as Fort Detrick or Edgewood Arsenal, or finding a buyable man who was already in. Either would involve risk and time. Too much of both. 'Are you certain there is no other way we can transfer the gas?'

Colonel Bayumi was positive.

'How long would it take to make this piece of equipment?'

'A week,' replied Bayumi, although he believed it would take longer.

'You have already arranged for it?'

'Of course,' said Bayumi, a lie. He would make arrangements as soon as he returned to Cairo. It would be extremely dangerous working on the valve, a matter of trial and no allowance for error, but Bayumi was sure he would find someone dedicated enough to want to do it.

'Any other problems?' Pinchon asked.

'Perhaps one.'

'Perhaps?'

'It appears Sadat has in mind dismissing Brigadier Fahmi.'

That was unexpected and bad news. 'Why?'

'He suspects Fahmi may have been involved with the attempted coup last October.'

'Was he?'

'Only to the extent that he knew of it and said nothing. Passive disloyalty, Sadat calls it.'

Pinchon slammed his palm down on the desk. 'Damn Sadat!'

'Fahmi may not be the only one to go. Rumours are there will be dismissals all down the line, including several other division commanders ... anyone who has failed to show enthusiasm for Sadat's policies.'

'Sadat may find himself with an army and no officers.

186

When will this purge take place?'

'Only Sadat knows that.'

There was, Pinchon realized, an advantage to these rumours. The high-ranking Egyptian officers who feared dismissal would now be all the more enterprising. Once Fahmi had matters under way the others would take the initiative without waiting for Sadat. They were also disgusted with Sadat's no-war war, eager to erase the reputation for military incompetence that had come with the Six-Day defeat. In about a week they'd have their chance, if in the interim Sadat didn't dismiss them and Brigadier-General Fahmi as well.

Pinchon didn't like thinking about that possibility. Fahmi was vital to the plan. Under his command were the Fourth and Sixth Infantry Divisions. Forty thousand men garrisoned mainly along the Suez. In perfect position. Included were three airborne border battalions and two paratroop brigades. The latter had been trained by the Russians and were reputed to be the sharpest fighting units the Egyptians had.

'If Fahmi should go who do you think will take over his command?'

'I am sure who it will be,' Bayumi beamed.

'You?'

'How else would I know so much about what Sadat has in mind?'

Pinchon did not show his relief, but there was no point in concealing the fact that he now considered Bayumi in a different light. Bayumi expected that, and now was no time to disappoint him.

Pinchon's foot found a signal button on the floor beneath the desk. Mustafa appeared in the doorway and Pinchon told him, 'The colonel and I will have lunch here.'

Mustafa understood.

'Did you see to the reservation?'

'There were no seats available on the two o'clock flight.'

'As it works out, that's just as well. We haven't yet covered everything.'

Bayumi saw through all this, but reacted to it as politeness rather than deceit. He settled back, relaxed.

Pinchon got up and went to a nearby bookcase. He removed several volumes from a shoulder-high shelf and quickly opened a small wall safe. He had a thick sheaf of new five-hundred franc notes in his hand when he returned to his place. 'Your expenses,' he told Bayumi. 'You should have reminded me.' He placed the money on the desk, close to the front edge.

Bayumi estimated that there were at least five hundred five hundreds in the stack. He did not say thank you as he put them in his attaché case.

Pinchon reached under the desk and withdrew a leather-covered portfolio. A large portfolio with flaps that he opened left and right. It contained an elaborate map of the Middle East. There were circles and arrows, numbers and notations scribbled on it. 'I thought we might use the time to go over the details,' he said.

Colonel Bayumi went around to the other side of the desk to share Pinchon's point of view.

The plan.

An intricate, audacious scheme from the mind of a resourceful fanatic. Over the past two years Pinchon had spent most of his time and a great deal of money piecing it together, covertly recruiting those he felt were essential to its success.

Several pieces had already moved nicely into place.

That the United States had developed the nerve gas vx–10 was a fact readily found in numerous recent books on the subject of chemical-biological warfare. It was also public knowledge that the United States had reduced its c–w stockpile by dumping some of it in the Atlantic Ocean. At first Pinchon tried to acquire the formula for vx–10. He found that impossible. It was too highly guarded a secret. He then considered using a common G-type nerve gas known as Sarin. Though Sarin was easily obtainable it lacked the swift, lethal efficiency of vx–10 – for example, it evaporated too quickly in the air and could not be distributed with nearly as much accuracy. Only vx–10 would do. However, there was no way of getting any of it except from the floor of the Atlantic. Pinchon held little optimism for that prospect, until he learned of the special underwater recovery ship, the *Sea Finder*. Fortunately, the *Sea Finder* was planning an expedition to the Mediterranean. Pinchon set about through contacts to influence its itinerary, and shortly thereafter the Egyptian Ministry of Culture courteously invited the *Sea Finder*'s archaeological team to examine its archives in Alexandria. Still to be determined was exactly where in the Atlantic the United States had dumped the vx–10. That knowledge was not so hard to come by. The crews of various U.S. Navy cargo ships knew the location. A mere hundred dollars or an ounce of hashish would have been an adequate price. But, for personal reasons, Pinchon had preferred to deal with Carl.

So, two canisters of vx–10 were now at Pinchon's disposal. They had been stripped of their concrete encasements in Alexandria and taken to a hiding place in Cairo. As soon as the special valve key was made, the gas would be transferred into six aerial atomizing pods. The pods would be transported by truck at Al Burumbul, then east over a remote, seldom used road to Ras Za' Faranah and down the Red Sea coast to a destination twenty miles northwest of Al-Qusayr. A perfect, isolated area.

There the pods would be fitted on to three MIG–21 jet fighters. The planes were already there, waiting. Over the past six months each of these Egyptian Air Force planes had been reported lost while on routine patrol. Brigadier-General Fahmi had seen to that. The three pilots he'd chosen were more than willing to cooperate and had no difficulty putting their planes down on the open, hard-baked edge of the Eastern Desert.

In the dark early-morning hours of the appointed day the three MIGS would take off and proceed in formation on a northeasterly course across the Red Sea to Saudi Arabia and continue north over Jordan. This was the normal air corridor used by Arab planes bound for various bases in Syria.

Just prior to reaching the Syrian border the planes would alter course and head due east. At a speed of fifteen hundred miles per hour they would reach the Jordan–Israel border in less than two minutes. They would approach the border at an altitude of only one hundred feet, thereby avoiding detection by the Israeli radar screen. Maintaining that low level flight, they would pass over the River Jordan and enter Israeli air space at Al Ghwar (32 degrees 15 minutes north).

At that point the three planes would diverge. Plane one would go southwest to Tel Aviv. Plane three would head northwest to Haifa. Plane two would continue straight on to Nabulus. Planes one and three would each have only fifty miles to cover. Within two minutes they would be over their objectives. By half that time, plane two would have surprised the Israeli military base near Nablus, releasing vx–10 over that area. In one pass it would wipe out an entire Israeli infantry division and three armoured brigades, approximately fifteen thousand men. That would serve as an object lesson to the Israeli high command, demonstrating the inescapable, terrible death that would fall upon the seven hundred thousand people of Tel Aviv and Haifa, if the military refused to co-operate.

Timed to precede this phase of the operation, a group of Palestinian infiltrators, who had already established themselves in Tel Aviv as nonbelligerents would seize the Israeli Government radio service, *Kol Yisrael*. They would broadcast a general-surrender ultimatum, and simultaneously an official written ultimatum would be hand-delivered to Israeli high command headquarters and all key political leaders.

Any attempt to shoot down the planes over Tel Aviv and Haifa, even if successful, would be suicidal, bringing a mist of death down on those cities. The two Arab pilots would be honoured to exchange their lives for those of seven hundred thousand Israelis.

While the planes continued to hover above Tel Aviv and Haifa (they would have fuel enough to maintain a holding pattern for five hours), Brigadier-General Fahmi would order his forces into action from the Egyptian military bases of Al-Kabrit, Al-Shallufa, and Deversoir. Motorized units of the Fourth and Sixth Infantry would cross the Suez and take over Israeli positions in Sinai. Within two hours all of Sinai would be retaken. Meanwhile, from the bases at Faid, Abu-Suwayr, and Kasfareet, Fahmi would dispatch his airborne battalions and paratroop brigades. Their objectives would be strategic military installations within Israel itself, particularly those of the Israeli Air Force. The relatively short distances to these objectives (only 200 miles to Tel Aviv) was an important tactical advantage. With no resistance, Brigadier-General Fahmi's troops would, within three hours or at most four have control of Beersheba, Gaza, Al-Khalil, Elat, and, of course, Jerusalem and Tel Aviv.

During this time the word of liberation would have spread quickly to all Palestinians within and around Israel's borders. They would overrun and reclaim their homeland.

Eight hundred thousand would pour across the Jordan from Judea and Samaria. From Gaza would come four hundred thousand. From Lebanon and Syria three hundred thousand more. Altogether about a million and a half Palestinians. Armed with surrendered Israeli weapons, they would serve rightfully as the army of occupation, easily capable of dominating two and a half million Jews. Among the Palestinians would be the various guerrilla factions, especially in the north. Naturally, they would be merciless.

A six-day war? This one would be over in six hours. Over before Sadat could prepare a statement taking credit. Over long before any major power such as the United States could intervene. (The United States Sixth Fleet would probably be vacationing in Cannes, the superstructures of its warships all strung with festive lights.)

World reaction?

The United States would no doubt rush its Sixth Fleet and missile-bearing submarines to the eastern Mediterranean. War would seem imminent. The President of the United States would issue a strong, threatening protest and follow that up with a public statement condemning inhuman Arab aggression. The thirty million Jews in America would press for swift action. Russia would also deplore the attack, but warn the United States against making any overt move. Russia would not tolerate the possibility of the United States taking over the Middle East and gaining control of three-quarters of the world's supply of oil. It would be a stand-off. Neither superpower would risk a direct confrontation. They would flex military muscles, keep an eye on one another, hedge, buy time. A special emergency session of the United Nations Security Council would be called. Each member would express appropriate indignation. Talk.

Meanwhile, the Arab kingdom would be reunited, Arab pride would be restored. There would be blood on the Wailing Wall.

Pinchon flipped the left and right flaps of the portfolio, closing it.

Bayumi's stubby fingers held up a crystal cordial glass filled with Chartreuse. 'You, sir, are a genius,' said Bayumi.

Pinchon saw no reason to deny that.

13

THE STERLING-SILVER dart flashed through the air.

It struck the forehead of the girl, solidly, all of its inch-and-a-half point going in.

For a moment it seemed incredible to Hazard that the girl did not flinch or cry out or bleed.

'*Merde*,' said Pinchon. He had two more tries. With the second, he hit the girl on the nose. '*Voila!*'. he exclaimed.

The girl suddenly receded, became a full figure in a white silk dress that she slowly peeled off, exposing her breasts and on down. When she was entirely nude she pivoted to present an all-around view, assumed a final flaunting pose, and abruptly disappeared.

Hazard thought at least she deserved some applause.

'She wasn't very good,' said Pinchon. 'The next is much better.'

Catherine retrieved the darts. It was her turn and there for her aim was the face of another girl. Catherine appraised the girl a bit competitively and then made a smooth skilful throw. The dart went into the girl's cheek, just slightly off mark.

They were in Pinchon's game room. At the moment they were playing what he called *Voyeur*, an advanced version of darts, involving a film projector connected to an electronic target board. The object of the game was to hit the nose of a girl who was projected. This in turn automatically started the film, presenting the visual reward. Pavlov, Freud, and Hefner all in one.

Catherine's next two throws were also near misses. She went to the board, pulled out one of the darts and jabbed it point blank into the activating area. The girl on the film began undressing.

'Not fair,' said Hazard.

'All's fair,' said Catherine.

Pinchon agreed with her. He'd taken the liberty of pouring

Catherine a cognac. He held it out and she refused by ignoring it, choosing instead to be close beside Hazard, who reached and took the snifter from Pinchon's hand.

That was more or less how the evening had gone for Pinchon up to then. Not at all as he'd expected. To distract this Edmund Stevens he had provided Contessa Pilar Falconetti, a beautiful, young Italian socialite accustomed to getting on her terms whatever and whomever she happened to want. Pinchon had explained the circumstances to Pilar in advance, and they had agreed her favour was worth five thousand francs. Not that Pilar needed the money, really. She had wealth enough to go along with her authentic title. Five thousand would hardly cover what she spent each month on shoes alone. However, as Pinchon knew from past experience, she preferred being paid. Somehow it always enhanced her performance and increased her pleasure.

Over drinks before dinner Pilar had indicated to Pinchon that she approved of the arrangement. The American introduced as Edmund Stevens aroused a most favourable first impression, and she began at once to keep her part of the bargain, putting a little simmer in her eyes whenever her glance met Hazard's. When her attention was elsewhere but she knew his was on her, she embraced her own bare shoulder or ran her fingers over the inner bend of her arm, suggesting how pleasant she was to touch. Hopefully his hands would identify with hers.

During dinner Pilar was more direct. She flattered Hazard with her laughter and gestures, and in between her contributions to the conversation her eyes said other things to him. Frequently she made sure he noticed the wet pink pillow of her tongue.

Pinchon soon realized his strategy was backfiring. He had counted on Catherine being blasé, as usual. He'd thought she'd be amused and join him in observing Pilar perform her speciality. Instead Catherine showed she cared, reacted possessively toward Hazard and tried to outdo Pilar. Pinchon was not receiving even his fair share of the attention. He had to go on the offensive.

'What do you do, Stevens?' he asked.

'Ed,' corrected Hazard. 'I'm a surgeon.' He'd been prepared for the question but the answer he'd had in mind was

193

advertising executive. He hadn't even considered surgeon. It had just come out.

Pinchon glanced distrustfully at Hazard's hands. 'You're good with a knife?'

Hazard was reminded of the one tucked inside his right boot. 'Actually,' he told Pinchon, 'I'm better with a saw.' Having fun with it, Hazard went on, 'Of course, I never use an axe. Never.'

Catherine wondered what the hell Hazard was up to now.

'I assume you specialize in amputations,' Pinchon said.

Hazard shrugged. 'More often than not it's all that can be done. Though I do manage to save a limb now and then.'

'Admirable,' Pinchon commented.

Catherine smiled, catching on.

Pilar clutched her arms, cringing at the thought that she'd been well on the way to intimacy with this butcher.

'Just last month,' Hazard continued, 'I was called in on a very interesting case in Boston. The patient was over two hundred years old and —'

Pinchon's eyes went up.

'That's not so old,' said Hazard. 'I've seen some over four hundred and thriving. Mostly oaks but even a few hardy maples.'

'You're a . . .'

'Tree surgeon.'

Pinchon was annoyed, feeling that this bit of fun had been at his expense. He doubted Stevens was telling the truth. More likely, the man was just another indolent American floater living by his wits. Anyway, tree surgeon or not, he was hardly a serious rival.

'Are you over on a vacation?' Pinchon asked.

Hazard nodded. 'Pursuing my hobby.'

'Me,' Catherine said.

'Egyptian antiquities,' said Hazard.

'How fascinating,' Pilar said. 'Of course you know Jean-Claude has a splendid collection.'

'I'd like to see it.'

'Perhaps later,' Pinchon said, and then to Catherine, 'Do you still have those Egyptian beads I gave you?'

She didn't remember. And then she did. 'Oh, those. No, I gave them to my secretary, Peter.'

'They were twenty-eighth dynasty, authenticated by the curator of the Cairo Museum.'

'Peter adores them; he wears them all the time.'

Pinchon almost concealed his irritation and told her, 'They belonged to Ankhesenamun.' He asked if Hazard knew who that was.

Hazard managed to pull it out of his mental file. 'She was the widow of Nebkheprure-Tutankamen. Married three times. Once before and once after the death of Tut. Her last marriage was to her grandfather, Ay, who was also her great-uncle. The intent of that incestuous union was to protect her throne from an ambitious general named Horemheb. But Horemheb got to be a Pharaoh anyway. Incidentally,' Hazard added for good measure, 'Horemheb married Mutnedjmet, the sister of Nefertiti.'

Pinchon wished he hadn't asked.

Catherine was impressed, said so, and blew a kiss Hazard's way.

Which inspired Pilar to share with Hazard some of her apricot mousse via the little silver spoon that had been in her mouth.

Having one's ego spoonfed by a ravishing contessa was by no means distasteful. However, Hazard reminded himself of his purpose for being there. When he'd killed Badr four days before in London he'd been left with only one connection that might lead him to the whereabouts of Hatum and Mustafa. The last he'd seen of any of them they were at Heathrow catching a flight with Pinchon.

Hazard, pretending mild curiosity, had asked Catherine about the Frenchman. Influenced by her own motives she mistook his interest in Pinchon as a show of jealousy. An encouraging sign, she thought, certainly contrary to the platonic boundaries Hazard had set on their relationship. She couldn't, of course, come right out and accuse him of jealousy but she playfully hinted it. Hazard got the message.

He also recognized the advantage of it and, playing the part, denied he was jealous. Catherine, predictably, enjoyed revealing what she knew about Pinchon. As it turned out, it wasn't all that much. Pinchon was very wealthy, terribly attractive, had been madly in love with her for ages, and still was. Hardly what Hazard wanted to hear. He wanted to know why Pinchon was socializing with Arabs, particularly these Arabs. Catherine had only a vague notion about that. She said she thought Pinchon had some business interests in the Mideast. Hazard tactfully pressed for more but she didn't know.

The only significant fact Hazard got from Catherine was where Pinchon lived.

A day later he was packed and ready to go.

Where? Catherine had wanted to know.

Just somewhere to relax, Hazard had told her – Paris, maybe, for a day or so and then down to the south of France.

Oh? It so happened, she'd told him, she knew an ideal place. She had a charming, small house in Eze.

Eze?

It was a little mediaeval town set on a coastal peak between Monaco and Cap Ferrat.

Hazard hesitated.

Not to worry, she said with some exasperation; her place in Eze wasn't all that small. It had several bedrooms.

A quick revision of his plans. Instead of moving conspicuously about on his own or trying to arrange some plausible way of meeting up with Pinchon again, he decided Catherine would provide an immediate direct entrée. He'd previously considered and rejected the idea, preferring not to use or involve her any further, but her house in Eze was a good enough excuse and he could hardly stop her from going there. Catherine didn't bother to ask if he minded if she went along, nor did she wait for him to accept her Eze invitation. She quickly tossed a few things into a bag and phoned to order the private jet that was always on stand by.

On the flight to Nice she napped against him, most of the while pretending she was asleep and therefore not responsible for being so close, or for her hands. From time to time Hazard glanced to see if her eyes were honestly shut. They seemed to be. He noticed her lashes were long enough to be false, but were true, and a wisp of her fine, clean hair errantly teased his nose and lips.

He forced his mind off her and on to what lay ahead. If Mustafa and Hatum weren't at Cap Ferrat, at least he'd somehow have to find out about them from Pinchon. On the other hand, if Mustafa and Hatum were there, it would simplify matters. Or would it? What about the big, ugly one they called Gabil? He might also be around.

Hazard still hadn't come up with a good enough explanation for Gabil's actions in that rug place. Vivid in his memory were those moments when he'd looked up into the pointing nose of Gabil's gun, when his life hung on a squeeze by Gabil's trigger finger. Thinking about it still made Hazard's stomach grab. Why hadn't Gabil killed him when he'd had both reason and opportunity? And why had Gabil so conscientiously cleaned up everything – Badr's body, bloody rug, everything? Evidently at the time neatness had been essential. Gabil had to make sure there was no evidence, no incriminating trail ... And the killing of a DIA agent would only have caused more of a mess. So Gabil had to pass up the chance – even though the agent had just killed a comrade.

One thing for sure, by now Gabil had told Mustafa and Hatum who he really was and what he'd done, and no doubt they now had him linked to Carl. That meant no more surprises in his favour. If those Arabs were in Cap Ferrat, he'd be walking right into it.

Turbulence.

The jet buffeted, hit a pocket, and dropped sharply, causing Hazard momentarily to feel weightless. Catherine held on more and he held her. And then the going became smooth again. Catherine resettled herself close to continue her nap.

After a while Hazard removed his arm from around her and found a pillow for her head. He got up and went forward. His piece of luggage was there in a storage cubicle. He pulled it out and opened it, pausing to glance back at Catherine to make sure she was asleep. He couldn't know she was observing him through the diffusion of her lashes.

From the carton of images he selected one at random and slipped it into his jacket pocket. After closing the suitcase and shoving it back into the cubicle, he went aft to the lavatory.

The feeling of being pressured was intensified by the small enclosure. It was also rougher there in the rear section of the plane, which wasn't going to help. At least this time, he thought, he'd be able to make a specific meaningful notation on the reverse side of the image card. Those he'd made up to then had been necessarily vague, rather poor excuses. This, however, would be an interesting first. He'd never tried send-

197

ing from five miles up and going like hell. Maybe it couldn't be done.

Three minutes to midnight.

He ripped open the small envelope to get at the image, expecting it would be, as all the others had been, a colour photograph. Instead it was a message, five words from Byron and no doubt intentionally chosen by Kersh.

HAPPINESS WAS BORN A TWIN

Hazard sat on the toilet and stuck the image card between the lower frame and glass of the mirror that faced him. He slouched forward and down to avoid his reflection, centred his thoughts on the message, told himself to disregard its meaning and just send it. That wasn't easy. His mind insisted on taking it personally, and he felt obliged to deny it. Hell, he'd spent a lot of happy times alone. He had been and could be absolutely happy without anyone. He raised his head just enough to look into his own eyes telling him he was a liar.

Come on, get on it, he told himself, and thought Keven. Thought her. The message. His mind saw it and her and as she would see it, all at once. The fusion was very clear, intense, and lasted longer than usual. And when Hazard was again fully aware of being carried swiftly through the night sky somewhere over France, he would have bet anything that this time he'd scored a hit.

Now, a night later, he was in Pinchon's game room.

As yet, not a sign of Hatum or Mustafa, which was both a relief and a disappointment. Apparently Pinchon and the two Arabs had taken separate flights that night at Heathrow. To find out where the Arabs had gone, possibly where they were, he'd first have to do some repairing with Pinchon. No matter how much he instinctively disliked the Frenchman, he had to stop provoking him. For starters, Hazard decided he'd better go along with what Pinchon had so obviously set up for him – the prepossessing Contessa.

At the moment she was off to the side playing a pin-ball machine. Hazard went over to watch. He saw it was a bit more than a regular machine with flippers. Painted on its slanted inner surface were several nude female figures that anatomically corresponded with its many lively bumpers and rewarding holes. The object was to light up all eight bright

198

red letters of the word BORDELLO, which was the name of the game.

Pilar was good at it, Hazard noticed. She showed excellent reflexes in controlling and working the flippers. Time and time again the silver ball zinged noisily from bumper to bumper and tried to gravitate through the bottom opening. But Pilar would mercilessly flip it back up into play. She had all the letters of the required word lighted, except for one of the Ls. She jiggled the machine to get more action out of it and even applied some body English – short little pelvic thrusts, as though that would influence.

Hazard tried not to pay obvious attention to that but then thought she would probably prefer he did. Between plays he offered her a sip of his brandy. Her smile told him she took it for more than it was worth.

'What happens when you get all the lights on?' he asked, meaning BORDELLO.

She didn't know but assumed it would be something appropriate.

'Maybe all you get is a free game,' Hazard said.

'That,' she said, 'would be most disappointing.' She pointed to a large, white, rectangular area on the upright glass partition of the machine. 'Something happens there.'

'An inside look?'

'Let's hope so.'

With that she released the plunger, shooting the next ball out into action. It caromed from one electric bumper to another, tattooing a sound of tiny bells. It dropped helplessly into holes that quickly rejected it. But somehow it avoided the roll-over that would light up that last letter. Pilar kept the ball in play and Hazard found himself going along with it, wanting to see if she was right about the reward.

He'd never know. Because at that moment Catherine intruded, broke Pilar's concentration, and made her miss with the flippers. The ball escaped.

Catherine asked Pilar to show her the way to the nearest loo.

'I'm sure you can find it.'

'I wouldn't want to get lost,' said Catherine, her words really intended for Hazard.

Pilar obliged, reluctantly. The two women went from the

199

room, leaving Hazard alone with Pinchon.

An uncomfortable moment.

Hazard was tempted to just come right out and ask Pinchon about his Arab friends. Instead he told him, 'You have a very unhealthy pair of *Cedrus libani*.'

'Really?' Pinchon almost looked down at himself.

Hazard explained that he was referring to the two large trees that flanked the villa's entrance. Cedars of Lebanon. 'On the way in tonight I noticed they badly need attention.'

'My grandfather planted them,' said Pinchon.

'I just thought you should know.'

'Are they in danger?'

'Possibly.'

'I don't suppose you'd consider taking a professional look at them?'

'I'm on holiday, but as a personal favour to you . . .'

A false, grateful smile from Pinchon. 'Naturally I'd expect to pay. Let's say double your usual fee, considering the circumstances.'

'On one condition.'

'Whatever.'

'You promised to show me your Egyptian collection.'

'I always keep my word.'

Pinchon wanted to reduce Hazard to an inferior position, an employee. Hazard, meanwhile, was trying to put some noncompetitive points on the board, and also set himself up for a look around the grounds. He crossed the room to where French doors were wide open. He stood in front of them, looking out.

'You know,' he said, 'there may come a day when trees are more important to the world than people.'

Pinchon thought that perhaps with this man trees would be more effective than Pilar.

'You should have music outside,' Hazard said. 'You'd be amazed how trees respond to music. It makes them happier and healthier.'

'I'll keep that in mind,' Pinchon said.

Hazard continued looking out. 'Would you mind if I wander around a bit? I'd like to see what else you have besides cedars.'

Pinchon gestured his permission. He was glad to get rid of

him. Let the nature-loving son of a bitch go worship trees. Catherine would be coming back any moment.

Hazard stepped out on to a side terrace. Feeling Pinchon's eyes on him, he paused to look up appreciatively at the sky. It was a clear, warm night with a pleasant sea smell. He strolled along the terrace and, once again for Pinchon's benefit, stopped to inspect a tall palm. Then he continued on leisurely to a corner of the spacious villa where, sure he was out of view, he dropped the act.

The grounds were well kept and subtly lighted. Hazard went down some wide stone stairs to a landing. He was startled from above by a white figure obscured by shadowy foliage, but he quickly determined it was only an armless statue and went on down to the rear of the villa. He scanned the area, not really searching for anything or anyone, he thought, merely satisfying his curiosity. At most just making sure.

Topiary. Hedges trimmed to form obelisks and spheres, and there was a free-standing stone archway. Hazard went through it to enter a long, dark tunnel. It took him a while to realize he was on a paved path between two precisely parallel rows of pear trees, their slender branches bent and trained to create the tunnel effect. The opening at the far end presented a patch of turquoise that turned out to be a large swimming pool with an extensive cabana. Off to the left and set back a ways was a two-story building that Hazard assumed was a guest house. Its ground-floor lights were on and a series of irregular thudding sounds came from there.

Hazard went to investigate. He approached one of the windows and peered in.

Mustafa was lying face up on a gym mat. Dressed only in a pair of boxer-type undershorts, he was doing press-ups with weighted bar bells – up and down from his chest to straight above his head. His face was red and clenched with strain; his shoulder, arm, and chest muscles bulged powerfully.

Near by was Hatum, also in shorts. He was working out on a heavy canvas punching bag, which explained the thuds Hazard had just heard. Hatum had a fighter's build, hard and tight with strong, thick legs. He didn't move around the bag but stood with his feet planted solidly to deliver spurts of sharp, hooking blows.

Hazard realized the opportunity. He had them completely unaware and unarmed. From where he stood they were easy targets, less than twelve feet away. But the closed window was a problem. If he shot through a pane or broke it out he might be able to get only one of them for sure. Better to make certain, go in and get them both. Then he'd have four of a kind – all dead, all done. It would be messy and incriminating, but he doubted he'd ever get another chance at them as easy as this.

He looked left and right. No entrance there. He looked in again and saw that the way in was from the side. Quietly he went around and found the door. He hoped it wasn't locked.

He paused to think ahead. He'd go for Hatum first because Mustafa was on the floor. He'd get Hatum in the back of the head, at the base of the skull. One shot. By then Mustafa would be on the way up. He'd stop Mustafa with a body shot and finish him off with another, more vitally placed.

He unbuttoned his jacket, reached in under, and slipped the Llama down and out. Its grip felt warm to his hand, familiar by now. He took a deep breath and told himself he couldn't lose this one, it was a boat race. He was about to reach for the doorknob when he sensed someone and glanced around.

Gabil was about six paces away, silhouetted by the swimming pool.

Hazard's impulse was to fire. His finger on the trigger automatically took up the slack.

'No!' Gabil whispered sharply, a command.

Ambivalence froze Hazard.

Gabil came slowly to him, loomed a whole head taller. To eliminate the threat of the Llama he took hold of Hazard's forearm, not roughly, and pushed it down as though it were an unwilling pump handle. 'Come with me,' Gabil whispered, then turned and walked off.

Hazard decided to follow, staying in the shadows as Gabil did. The big man led the way into one of the dark canvas-enclosed recesses of the cabana. Hazard kept some distance between them.

Gabil told him, 'Put it away.'

Hazard still had the Llama in hand. The dim, bluish light reflected from the swimming pool made Gabil appear even more formidable, grotesque. He reminded Hazard of a heavy-weight he'd seen in an old fight film, a giant Italian named

Primo Carnera, who'd suffered a terrible beating from a former champion named Max Baer.

'I don't want to hurt you,' Gabil said with some impatience.

That seemed true enough, Hazard thought. Twice now Gabil had had the advantage and not taken it. He could have easily come down from behind on Hazard just moments before. Hazard figured the least he could do was to stop pointing the Llama at him. As a compromise Hazard brought that hand down to his side.

'We need to talk,' said Gabil, 'but not now or here.'

'About what?'

Gabil ignored the question. 'Tomorrow afternoon in Villefranche at a place called l'Aiguille. If I am not there by three, then the next day.'

Hazard was somewhat taken aback by Gabil's crisp, intelligent manner of speaking. It contradicted the big Arab's ugly looks.

A loud splash, and another.

Mustafa and Hatum had dived into the pool, having a swim after their workout. Gabil left Hazard and went out to them. From the dark enclosure of the cabana Hazard watched them as they swam awkwardly, thrashed the water as though they feared it. That, thought Hazard, was the desert in them. After doing a couple of lengths and floating around some they got out and Gabil went with them into the guest house.

Hazard returned the Llama to its holster, thinking how close he'd been to finishing what he'd set out to do. In a way he was glad he hadn't. It would have been impetuous, perhaps even suicidal. There would be other, more discreet chances now that he'd located his targets. But what about Gabil – what the hell was he up to? Why had he again acted so strangely? Maybe he'd find out tomorrow.

He went back to the villa via the pear-tree tunnel. In the game room Pinchon was trying to keep Catherine amused with card tricks. Hazard went straight for the brandy. Pilar came over to him.

'I have a headache.' Her eyes let him know she was lying.

'Tension,' said Hazard.

'A *splitting* headache.'

'Try some aspirin,' Hazard told her and went over to watch

Pinchon. He saw right off that the Frenchman was using a shaved deck and wasn't really good at it. Catherine was bored. She asked Hazard, 'By chance do you play gin rummy?' She knew damn well he did.

'Strictly by chance,' Hazard replied.

'Jean-Claude is one of the best players in all Europe. He's veritably unbeatable.'

'Would you care to play a few hands?' Pinchon asked Hazard.

'For money?'

'Just enough to make it interesting, say five francs a point.'

Hazard quickly converted that – about a dollar a point.

Pinchon obviously was out to hustle him, and the high stakes were intended to embarrass him in front of Catherine.

'Come on, Edmund, be a sport,' Catherine urged.

'Okay, as long as I can quit whenever I feel I've had enough.'

Agreed.

They moved to an appropriate table. Pinchon broke open a new deck and shuffled with style.

Hazard hadn't wagered on anything for nearly a week. He was hungry for action.

They cut for deal.

That was the only thing Pinchon won.

Hazard's mnemonic ability allowed him to remember every discard in the stack, and by mentally combining the discards with the cards in his hand he knew almost exactly what Pinchon was holding.

While Pinchon cursed his luck and became more and more agitated, Hazard piled up points and boxes, blitzed and blitzed again. At the end of two hours it was Pinchon who'd had enough.

'You play well for a tree surgeon,' he said as he paid off in cash. Fifty-five thousand francs.

Hazard almost felt a little guilty.

Catherine told Pinchon he was a very good loser.

Pinchon wasn't sure she meant that as a compliment.

L'Aiguille was a bistro. A neighbourhood place situated on a side street three blocks from the Villefranche waterfront.

Like nearly every bistro in France it was decorated with tasteless total regard for indestructibility. Every possible surface was covered with garish plastic of one sort or another, and all edges were trimmed protectively with metal stripping. As though to avoid being different, it offered no more than the usual drinks and served only *saucisson, jambon,* and *fromage* sandwiches. There was, however one imaginative aspect to the place. A local rumour had it that the bistro's owner had once been active in drug traffic in Marseilles and out of gratitude and memory of his past, murky pursuits had chosen the name l'Aiguille – the Needle. The owner denied the rumour so emphatically everyone believed it. In fact he'd previously been a woollen-mill worker in Lyon and had chosen the name l'Aiguille because most of the money that financed the bistro had come from saving every centime his wife had earned over the years as a seamstress.

There were only five customers in l'Aiguille that Saturday afternoon in June. Three were regulars standing at the bar drinking *vin ordinaire* and agreeing with typical dour French dissatisfaction that Pompidou was doing everything wrong. They paid no attention to the two men seated at a table in the rear.

Hazard and Gabil.

'Killing Badr accomplished nothing,' Gabil was saying.

Hazard silently disagreed. He'd decided in advance to say as little as possible.

'And now apparently you're after Mustafa or Hatum.'

'Both.'

'Those are your orders?'

A nod from Hazard. It was better they believed that.

Gabil appraised the man opposite him and thought he didn't have the look of an official killer. No cold, covered anxiety in the eyes, although some tightness at the corners suggested inner tension. Most disarming was his casual manner. A practised style, no doubt, but convincing. It would encourage one to accept this easy-going American at face value, make the mistake of underestimating him. Gabil recalled how deliberately Hazard had blown Badr's brains out.

'The least I can do is forewarn you,' Gabil said.

'I thought you would.'

'There's no way to talk you out of it?'

'Don't even try.'

'I can appreciate that.' Gabil nodded. 'You're expected to

do your job. However, I hope you'll be equally understanding.'

Hazard waited.

Gabil told him, 'I promise I won't kill you unless it is unavoidable.'

'You avoided it in London,' Hazard said.

'Yes.'

'Better to keep things uncomplicated, right?'

'Better for me if I had killed you,' Gabil said. 'I could use the credit.'

'You make it sound like I was spared out of the goodness of your heart.'

'Not exactly.'

Again it struck Hazard how paradoxical Gabil's manner of speech was. His English was crisp and overprecise, as one would expect from a well-schooled foreigner. It was alarming, actually, that a man who looked so threatening should also be intelligent. With that in mind Hazard told him, 'For what it's worth, you're not on my list.'

'That is reassuring,' Gabil said, and smiled.

They were having coffee. Bitter stuff, cold by now. As he sipped it Hazard thought about what Keven's opinion would be of this black, nerve-grating bile. He felt edgy.

Gabil shifted uncomfortably. The tubular-and-plastic bistro chair was inadequate for his size. 'I'd like another look at your identification,' he said.

Hazard saw no reason to cooperate, but then on second thought he realized it couldn't hurt, might even help, even as much as it had before. Reaching into his shirt pocket he also exposed the Llama for a reminder. He brought out the little plastic-coated card and handed it across.

Gabil studied it carefully front and back before returning it to Hazard. 'Scepticism is a valuable habit,' he said somewhat apologetically.

'You doubt what I am?'

'No.'

Hazard sat back to seem more relaxed and sure of himself. Now that he'd been warned and certified, he hoped for some answers. Gabil was looking thoughtfully at the table top. As though having come to a decision, he brought his eyes up abruptly to Hazard and asked, 'How much do you know about Mosad?'

'Who?'

Gabil's rapid Mideastern pronunciation of the word prevented Hazard from visualizing it. More clearly Gabil repeated, 'Mosad.'

Now it registered. Hazard remembered it as the name for the Israeli Central Bureau of Intelligence and Security. 'What about it?' he asked.

'That is my affiliation.'

'You're saying you're an Israeli agent?'

'Yes.'

'Prove it.'

'I already have.'

'How?'

'By not killing you in London or last night.'

Hazard realized it was a better explanation than any he'd thought of.

'You doubt me?'

'As you said, it's a good habit.'

'How can I convince you?'

'What about your identification?'

'We never carry any.'

'Convenient.'

'Prudent.'

Couldn't argue that, Hazard thought. Especially for an Israeli agent hanging around with Arabs. 'If you're really what you claim, why tell me?'

'I tried my best to avoid it.'

'You also said you'd try to avoid killing me.'

'We can eliminate that possibility if you now accept me at my word.'

'Okay, say I do.'

'Then we work together, exchange information and take care not to get in one another's way.'

Hazard pretended to be considering that while wondering what information Gabil was talking about. He himself had nothing to contribute.

'Our two countries have often shared secrets,' Gabil added.

'I suppose I could have you checked out,' Hazard said, though he had no intention of doing so.

'You could try. It would take time and I doubt it would get us anywhere. A great deal of effort went into creating my cover. Mosad would not want to risk spoiling it. They would deny my existence. I am afraid this will have to be between us, a matter of personal trust.'

Could be all this was an attempt to divert him, Hazard thought, although it seemed unlikely they'd take such an approach or go to such an extent. While he was thinking it over, Gabil got up, went to the bar and came back with two fresh coffees. Hazard let his sit there. Another dose of that straight caffeine would turn his nerve ends into live wires.

'What have you decided?' Gabil asked.

'I'll need more convincing.'

Gabil downed his coffee with one gulp, savouring the bitterness that remained in his mouth. 'I am known by the name Gabil el-Kahled,' he said. 'Actually, I am Abraham Ben-David.' He went on to say that he thought of Al Birah as his home, a small town about fifteen kilometres north of Jerusalem, despite not having lived there since 1956. His father had been a schoolteacher, his mother a refugee from Krakow, and he'd had a sister two years younger.

Hazard noticed the past tense.

The reason was Arab artillery shells. A sudden, senseless barrage on Al Birah, including a direct hit that left him at age sixteen the only survivor in his family. The visible evidence of the catastrophe was his face. After recovering in a Jerusalem hospital he was cared for on a kibbutz near Netanya, where he worked and studied and eventually qualified for the university in Tel Aviv. He specialized in languages, wanted to become a teacher. But then came the war of 1967, in which he served with the 202nd Israeli Infantry. Afterward he decided to stay in the army and was now a captain. In 1969, during a pitched skirmish in the Golan Heights, a Palestinian guerrilla was seriously wounded and taken prisoner by an Israeli patrol. The Arab was identified as one Gabil el-Kahled. He was not particularly notorious, not a well-known leader, merely another of the fanatics who transiently enlisted themselves in the nomadic, dangerous, and anonymous guerrilla life. Mosad took an interest in el-Kahled, decided he could be of use. To help matters, el-Kahled died from his wounds three weeks after capture. His death was kept secret, and Mosad set out to find someone who might assume his identity. It required an unusually large man, as el-Kahled had been.

Mosad's first approach was to search the army files, which led to Captain Abraham Ben-David. Mosad could not have asked for a better double. Not only was he the right size, he was also a language expert who spoke fluent Arabic in the appropriate dialect. And his facial wound from 1956 would help substantiate the cover. Would he volunteer? He did. He submitted to having his old wounds surgically reopened to make them appear recent; his nose was broken and rebroken to compensate for any difference in resemblance. He was then placed in Ramleh Jail, where among the other terrorist prisoners he was at once accepted and soon gained a reputation for his intense hatred for Jews and his obdurate loyalty to the Palestinian cause. After five months in Ramleh, a believable escape was arranged, along with passage to Beirut. He had no specific assignment. Mosad listed him as a floating agent, which meant he was on his own to infiltrate whatever enemy activity came his way and that he considered important. It was two months ago in Beirut that he was brought to Mustafa's attention. Mustafa sought him out, was impressed, checked him over, and recruited him.

Gabil told all this as though he were reciting someone else's history. Hazard heard and used his imagination to fill in the rest.

'Do I call you Abraham?' Hazard asked him.

'No, think of me strictly as Gabil el-Kahled. At least for now.'

Hazard raised his cup and drank to that, acknowledging the trust with this small, bitter sacrifice.

'I must get back to the villa,' Gabil said. 'I would appreciate your telling me what you know.'

'It's a long story,' Hazard said, now regretting his lie and hoping to put off revealing it.

'Then briefly.'

Hazard told the truth, beginning with Carl's death.

And when it was all out Gabil seemed more disappointed than angry. 'You have no idea what Pinchon is up to?'

'Do you?'

'I am not yet trusted to that extent.'

Now Hazard understood what Gabil had meant when he'd said he could use the credit.

Gabil told him, 'You are aware, of course, that Hatum and

209

Mustafa take their orders from Pinchon, as did the other two.'

'You're sure about that?'

'Yes.'

'Who tells Pinchon what to do?'

'My guess is no one.'

'But you're not sure.'

Gabil admitted he wasn't.

Hazard decided that his vendetta had to stop somewhere. If he added Pinchon to his list there would probably be someone else on top of him and who knew how many others. He could end up taking on all the Arabs and Jew-haters in the world. As things were he had two down and only two to go and he was anxious to have it done and over with. No matter that he disliked Pinchon, that in some way Pinchon might be implicated; he would limit himself to those four he knew were directly responsible for Carl's death. He told Gabil his decision.

'I have a better suggestion.'

'What?'

'Stop now while you are ahead. Forget it and go home.'

'Thanks for the advice, but no thanks.'

'You may find yourself involved in something more serious.'

'Are you worried about me or that I might blow your cover?'

Gabil resisted the obvious lie. 'Mainly my cover.'

Honest Abe, thought Hazard. 'Well, that being the case, you've got nothing to worry about.'

14

CATHERINE DECIDED it was time she was properly compensated for all her strategy.

She had, she thought, been extremely patient. They'd been together almost constantly for a week, seldom more than a reach apart. Except, of course, when they were separated by a bedroom wall. Drawing from her knowledge of men, Catherine was reasonably convinced that Hazard wasn't the type to endure abstinence for any length of time, surely not voluntarily, especially not when he was being so artfully provoked by her. Also, the fact that they hadn't spoken about Carl since that first night was a good sign. She took it to mean Hazard was now seeing her as a woman in her own right rather than merely his brother's widow. If, however, when it came down to it he still had guilts about trespassing, she believed she now knew how to handle them. By sharing them.

Once was all it would take, she thought. Once together, once over the wall and freely occupying intimate territories, they would both be relinquished and bound. For her that would be the battle half-won. Then she could begin to put what she felt to the test. Humiliations, hurts, the creating of doubts, the flourishing of jealousies, evident faithlessness, intentional deceit – how far would she push him? And for how long before she had enough proof to feel and sustain faith? She didn't know. No one except Carl had ever cared enough to make a serious try at playing it out. Hopefully, Hazard had as much or even more perseverance.

As Catherine saw it the night ahead was crucial. She spent all afternoon preparing for it. While Hazard was off to Villefranche on the excuse of sightseeing, she sunned nude – just enough for her skin to have a subtle, pink flush, be slightly feverish, and that much more sensitive to any touch. She also swam and was acutely aware of her vigour and suppleness; swam until she was nicely tired, which gave her a prelusive sense of submission.

211

She attended herself. First, her nails. Not that they needed doing. She was only concerned with their sharpness and used a strip of emery to hone them. She wished her nails were retractable, like a cat's, so that baring them would be another sign of arousal.

Every part of her body received such purposeful attention. Her skin was given a coating of clear, pure oil to create a more desirable sort of friction. Not a single tiny crease was overlooked. She shampooed her hair with a special substance that softened and enhanced its fair shade and she treated her lower hair to the same advantage. That private growth, the quality of it, she believed important, having herself responded negatively at certain times to the coarse, wiry resistance offered there by other women. She was more fortunate; hers was a golden floss, fine, relentingly soft and not entirely concealing. She sun dried and brushed the hair of her head and used a different, gentler brush on that below.

Not to interfere with her own natural fragrance, she chose to use only oils, powders, lotions, and cosmetics that were odourless. While applying those she thought out the details. Her bedroom or his? Neither? A more neutral atmosphere would be better. Perhaps the main room on the thickly carpeted floor, with an abundance of helpful pillows. That would be freer and seem more spontaneous. Deciding on that, she thought to remind herself to have her little ruby-crusted Louis Quinze snuffbox placed conveniently nearby. At the right moment she would insist on sharing its contents. She would not drink much and she would see that he didn't either. Only some very good wine and perhaps some Strega. Anything potentially depressing would be avoided. For that reason she had gone all day without a cigarette. Other considerations: What for dinner and where? In or out? And what should she wear? More or less?

Confidently anticipating the prize, the pleasure, Catherine devised the denouement.

Hazard returned at seven.

After his meeting with Gabil he'd wandered around Villefranche and happened on the ancient waterfront chapel known as Saint Pierre's. It was just another nice enough old church, except for the way Jean Cocteau had decorated its

212

interior, made it into a gentle atmosphere of pious pastels.

Hazard recalled the opening lines of his own early childhood prayer: *Our Father who art in heaven, hollow be thy name*. Purely innocent blasphemy. He'd never been one to ask for help from upstairs, although at times, for example when he was looking to draw a card to complete a straight, his requests were in that general direction. Anyway, he hadn't gone into Saint Pierre's to do any praying, but it was a good, quiet place to just sit and think.

The cold, objective fact of the matter was that now he and Gabil were on even terms. Each held the other's life in his hands. What a thing to have in common, thought Hazard, especially when it was probably the *only* thing they had in common.

He compared himself to Gabil, and felt he was coming up short. He wouldn't though, accept full blame. There was quite a difference between being an Israeli and an American these days. If he were an Israeli he'd be willing to put himself on the line, have the ideals and make the sacrifices. An Israeli didn't think of his country as an abstraction. An Israeli had a real sense of involvement with his land, a sort of new love. That was it, a new love. It seemed to Hazard that America had unfortunately grown away from that. Raw, spontaneous American patriotism was a thing of the past. Gone were the days when all it took was a slap in the national face, a President's emergency speech, and a parade to stir a man into volunteering for the long, honourable rest in Arlington Cemetery. Now the President sweated out a speech on television almost every week to sustain his public image, and people complained because he pre-empted Sonny and Cher or Flip Wilson. Now there were longer-than-ever parades every rain-or-shine Saturday and Sunday down Fifth Avenue and playing of the 'Star-Spangled Banner' was something to tolerate impatiently before every sporting event. Oh, sure, there were still plenty of so-called American patriots around ready to place a hand over the heart and sing 'the rockets red glare, the bombs bursting in air' and conscientiously stick decals of the dear old Stars and Stripes on the rear windows of their new Japanese economy cars. But what didn't exist any more was that all-together thing known as the great American people. That solidarity started giving way right after the last big war

213

to end all. And it was still disintegrating.

Now it was everyone for himself first, everyone looking out for his own ass, more or less resigned to the idea that the Government was hopelessly screwed up and the men who ran it were out to get theirs one way or another. All those separate nests getting well feathered, and meanwhile the courts and prisons and mental hospitals were overloaded, the police corrupt, the blacks irreconcilable, the kids shooting hard stuff during recess – and there were Mr and Mrs America up to their asses in false receipts to justify deductions on their income taxes.

That was the state of the nation, and it would take a lot more than even a major incident to provoke the people out of their split levels and into another fight. Even another Pearl Harbor in Miami might not be enough. The foreign-affairs analysts kept cocking their heads and triggering their eyes and declaring the Middle East a hot spot, likely to erupt into another major war involving the United States – but, bullshit. It would be no go.

And that just about explained it, thought Hazard. He wasn't really a cynical exception, just less of a hypocrite.

He sat there in Saint Pierre's a while longer. His eyes found a regiment of candles flickering in perpetual devotion for loved ones lost. He wondered if what he'd just offered himself was an explanation or only an excuse.

When he got back to the house in Eze some of that mood was still with him. He thought being with Catherine might pull him out of it; all he needed were a couple of laughs. However, he found she was secluded in her bedroom and a note to him was taped to her closed door saying she was having a snooze and why didn't he do the same. Meaning join her? No, because there was more (over), telling him they'd be having dinner out at eight-thirty. In case he was ravenous she'd arranged for a little something to tide him over.

Ridiculous, her suggestion that he take a nap, as though that were so easy. It showed how little she knew him. But then, when he went into his room he thought perhaps she did, because there on the side table on an ornate silver tray was caviar and a split of champagne kept very cold by shaved ice. Not just average good caviar and not just a measly portion of it. Huge grey grains of the largest fresh Beluga, a half-pound
214

heap. The champagne was a '59 Dom Perignon.

The sight of it raised Hazard's spirit. He undressed, transferred the tray to the surface of the bed and lay beside it. He'd eaten nothing since breakfast, so sips of the champagne went all the way down into him like lighted arrows. He ate the caviar straight, enjoying the sensation of it bursting under the pressure of his teeth. The fact that each spoonful was worth about five dollars didn't faze him, but it did occur to him that various gourmands had given testimonials on behalf of caviar's aphrodisiac benefits. Could be, he thought, with his mouth full. Not that he needed it.

Promptly at eight thirty he went out and found Catherine was ready, waiting to go.

What she had chosen to wear was neither more nor less but allowed her the best of both possibilities. A long-sleeved caftan by Grés made of that finest weave of cotton called *lawn*. White, opaque, loose – more effective than a tight fit or transparency the way it declared, as she moved, that her body was absolutely uninhibited underneath. From Hazard's reaction at first sight of her she was sure the score was already in her favour.

'My, don't we look marvellous,' she said, complimenting him.

He had on the new dark-blue suit he'd bought in London with some of his winnings.

Her eyes upon him went down, up and down. 'Only one discrepancy.'

'What?' Hazard thought she probably meant no tie.

'Mind you, it's not a complaint, but your front is open.'

He'd forgotten to do up his fly. It had buttons rather than a zipper. 'A Freudian oversight,' he said, while fumbling to match the buttons with their corresponding holes.

Catherine decided that unfortunately it was a little too early for her to help.

To avoid the bother of driving somewhere, she'd reserved for dinner at a local place. They walked arm in arm over the narrow, cobbled ways of the old village, and when the going was steep she used it as an excuse to cling and press more to him. Within minutes they reached the restaurant, which was small and impeccable, with a dim, conducive ambience. Hazard estimated its prices would be in keeping with where it was

215

situated – high on the sheer hillside facing the sea.

Catherine acknowledged the maître d'hôtel by first name. He was suave and overly cordial. He ushered them to their table, isolated from all the others, which had been shifted away and given less space. Catherine and Hazard sat beside rather than opposite one another, their backs to the rest of the room, sharing the night and distant lights, a shimmering panorama from Nice to Monaco. It seemed unreal, at least to Hazard.

Everything had been prearranged by Catherine. Two waiters were assigned to them alone with instructions to be attentive but not to intrude. Hazard's saying he thought he'd have a beer was disregarded. A 1962 Moet and Chandon rosé was served along with the first course. *L'oursin natur* – raw sea urchins plucked that day from the rocky waters and now served in half their spiny shells on beds of blue-tinted ice.

Hazard glanced dubiously at his portion and then summoned his courage. He scooped one out and up and into his mouth. The first he swallowed whole with some difficulty, the second he bravely chewed.

'Try a squeeze of lemon,' Catherine suggested.

'I prefer them plain,' he said, as though this wasn't his initiation.

'They have a very distinctive flavour, don't you think? Sort of ... well, how would you describe it?'

He thought a moment and told her, 'Carnal.'

'Femininely so?'

His shrug said what else.

'By that you mean unpleasant?'

'Not at all.'

She spooned one up, studied its slick, coral-hued flesh and took a nibble. Her tongue passed judgment. She smiled. 'You know, you're absolutely right.'

After the sea urchins came *lapin sauvage*, roast wild rabbit, braised celery, and artichokes sauced with fresh ground Dijon mustard. Not a heavy meal, actually. She didn't want them handicapped later by feeling logy. Catherine had also stipulated that everything be amply seasoned with cracked cayenne and saffron. Each dish she'd chosen had a traditional reputation for its libidinal influence. (True or not, the possibility was worthwhile, she reasoned.) Particularly the fresh, raw Périgord truffles marinated in cognac.

Catherine purposefully led the conversation to such topics as erotic minorities, the advantages for a man in never having to work, and the guilt-ridden sex lives of most American women.

Hazard was between a bit of spicy rabbit and a comment on Tantric Buddhism when he felt it. Like two subtle pressures on the back of his head, a sense of being under the beam of a stare. He glanced around and his attention fell on whoever that was standing to one side of the entrance. The dim lights obscured detail but he could see she was wearing faded denim – jeans and a matching short Western-style jacket. She had on mirror-surfaced sunglasses. Hazard turned back to Catherine, deciding it was only a resemblance or a product of his wishful thinking. But that disturbing sense of being stared at persisted. He had to look again. This time she was coming toward them and he saw it was definitely she.

'Fancy meeting you here and all that,' said Keven.

Introductions weren't necessary. Keven and Catherine had met at Carl's funeral. Hazard was so shaken by Keven's sudden appearance that it was left to her to deliver their hello kiss. Her mouth, however good it felt to him, was a weapon that bit his lip sharply, just short of drawing blood.

'What luck,' said Keven. 'Someone just happened to recommend this place to me.'

Catherine silently vowed her housekeeper would soon be unemployed. She also wished that Keven would evaporate in a puff of steam.

Hazard signalled a waiter, who brought another chair. Keven sat down and settled herself. She removed the Mexican peasant net bag that was slung from her shoulder. 'I'm famished,' she said, and demonstrated her rights by helping herself to a leaf of Hazard's artichoke. The mustard sauce ventilated her larynx and made her eyes water. Regaining her breath she pointed at the truffles half submerged in cognac. 'What are those?'

Catherine told her, as though it were unsophisticated of her not to know.

'I thought they were stewed prunes.'

'Really?'

'I read somewhere that they use virgins to locate truffles.'

217

'Pigs,' Catherine corrected.

Keven nodded. 'No doubt that's why they're virgins.'

Hazard laughed nervously. He thought it better to stay out of it. He had plenty of questions for Keven but not then or there. Just to say something, he asked her why the mirrored sunglasses.

'So certain people can see how they look in my eyes.' She reached down into her net bag and brought out a handful of sunflower and pumpkin seeds. She deposited them on the table cloth, pinched up a few and began crunching away. The maître d' had come to ask if she wished to order something. He eyed the little pile of seeds with disgust.

'Maybe just a salad,' Keven said.

He suggested endive.

'How do you say manure in French?' asked Keven. 'Is it *merde de cheval*?'

'*Engrais,*' said Catherine, accent perfect.

'I thought you'd know,' said Keven.

'Would you like it baked or sautéed?' asked Catherine.

'I never eat anything unless it's organically grown.'

The maître d' suggested *une salade de Pissenlit*.

Sounded like piss in bed, Keven thought.

'Dandelion salad,' the maître d' translated.

That suited Keven fine. She imagined happy children sent out to gather dandelion greens from sunny hillsides.

The salad was brought right away and served with ceremonial flourish. Keven declined the dressing and ate with her fingers, delicately. The plain greens were a little bitter and nippy to her tongue, but she took that as evidence of their natural goodness. Completing a long, healthful chew, she asked Hazard in an offhand manner, 'Where are you staying?'

Her question hung over the table.

Hazard popped a truffle into his mouth. It tasted strong, too much of a good thing. His silence was both an answer and a choice.

Catherine broke the spell by telling a waiter to bring her a double whisky and a pack of Gauloises. She wasn't a good loser but did hope to save some face. 'It was sweet and very thoughtful of you to have dinner with me,' she told Hazard, 'but there's no need to waste your entire evening. My friend...' she said, implying a man and more than a friend, '...will be along soon, so whenever you like, please do feel free to go. Don't be the least concerned about me.'

'I'm ready if you are,' Keven said, pushing her plate away.

Hazard got up.

Catherine extended her hand. A single fifteen-carat diamond issued a taunting flare.

Hazard gave it a platonic shake.

Keven was already headed for the way out.

She had rented a car, dependable Peugeot. It was parked outside Catherine's house. Keven waited while Hazard went in and got his things. They didn't speak until they were well on the way to Cap Ferrat. 'You're my husband and you just came in on a flight from London,' Keven told him.

'What the hell does that mean?'

'They only had one room available at the hotel.'

'Really?'

'Believe me, I would gladly have got two.'

'They'll want to see my passport.'

'No problem.'

'Our names won't match.'

'I registered as Hazard.'

'How could you?'

'That's what's on my passport.'

'Who's idea was that?'

'Kersh's.'

By then they'd arrived at the Hôtel du Cap. As predicted, he had no trouble at the desk; was treated as though expected. For obvious reasons, he wished he'd been registered as 'Stevens', but there wasn't anything he could do about it now. The room, number 307, was third floor and second rate by du Cap standards. It overlooked the drive and parking area rather than the sea, but was otherwise pleasant enough.

Keven kicked off her espadrilles to be barefoot. She also removed the faded-denim jacket under which she wore an ordinary white-cotton tank top. Hazard busied himself with opening his suitcase, watching her peripherally and wondering if she would undress all the way. But she stopped at that and even kept on her sunglasses. She flopped down on the bed, propped a doubled-up pillow underneath her head and crossed her legs.

219

Hazard sat in a chair opposite the foot of the bed, about as far away as he could get, short of retreating into the bathroom. To escape the twin mirrors that hid her eyes and, as well, the twin punctuations of her tank top, he surveyed the room. Among a scatter of other things on the long dresser he noticed a room-service tray with three compote dishes that he guessed had been a triple order of ice cream. There were also a portable tape recorder and several cassettes. Next to that, wrapped in clear plastic, was a six-inch-square chunk of light-grey stuff that looked like modelling clay, the kind he used to take his hostilities out on when he was a school kid.

'What's that?'

'What does it look like?'

He told her.

'I brought it along just in case,' she said.

'Of what?'

'I feel the need to express myself.'

Better she should take it out on that stupid stuff than him.

'How's Kersh?'

'Fine.'

'Julie?'

'They send their love.'

'She had the baby yet?'

'Any second now.'

Another long silence. It was punishing for him because he was really happy to see her; excruciating for him because she was a million miles away across the room. He tried sending her that but apparently her receiver wasn't switched on.

'How did you know where I'd be?'

'It figured.'

'You didn't just know.' He hoped to God she wasn't tapped in on him to that extent.

'The queen told me.'

Meaning Peter, Hazard realized. She'd been to London. He pictured her going to all that trouble to track him down and he liked it, but then his thoughts turned practical. 'You shouldn't have come,' he told her. 'I'll bet Kersh was against it.'

'He suggested it. He thought it would help,' Keven said.

'I don't need help.'

'No one said you did.'

'Besides, what about the exercises?'

'They were a bust.'

'Nothing got through?'

'See for yourself.' She gestured vaguely in the direction of the desk in the corner. Hazard went over to it and found a manila envelope that contained Xerox copies of reports covering the first three of the overseas exercises. They showed the images he'd sent compared to those she'd received. The first, the gull, was a reasonable match. The second, the time he'd failed to send, looked right because her big green X was a sort of graphic cancellation. The third he'd sent had been a photograph of a group of fifty men standing on the steps of a public building. What she'd recorded were five horizontal lines of ovals, but exactly fifty of them in an arrangement that corresponded with the men's faces. So that one was hardly a total miss.

Hazard was pleased. 'I'd say we did damned well considering.'

'Yeah, considering.'

'There was nothing wrong with my sending,' he claimed.

'Okay, so the reception was bad.'

'How come?'

'Too much interference.'

Her tone warned him not to pursue that. He asked her about the night before last, if she'd received the one he'd sent from the plane, the Byron quote.

'No,' she said indifferently.

He was disappointed. He'd been so sure about that one. 'Why not?'

'I forgot to try.'

More silence.

She remained the same, legs crossed.

He'd gone back to the far-away chair. Unable to avoid looking at her, he imagined leaping high at her, floating down in slow motion upon her, softly, his mouth finding her mouth finding his and all of him sinking into her so nicely, together.

'Been getting any?' she asked.

'Any what?'

'Sleep.'

'How about you? You been sleeping?'

'Like a baby. I can drop right off any old time.' She did a

221

big yawn to demonstrate.

That did it. He got up fast and went into the bathroom, closing the door hard. Angry at everything, he pulled off his jacket and ripped off two of the fly buttons while getting out of his trousers. One bounced and clicked happily on the ceramic-tile floor. The other flew mockingly into the bidet.

There was a glass-enclosed shower stall. He stepped in and turned the water control handle halfway between *chaud* and *froid*. Cold came shooting out but before he could swear much it changed to warm. He adjusted it to hotter and let it hit between his shoulderblades, a point he always considered the centre of his tensions.

He didn't hear her enter the bathroom. He didn't know she was there until she opened the shower door.

All she had on were the sunglasses.

'I want in,' she said, contritely.

His smile welcomed her.

They hugged tight as possible, kept their full lengths pressed for a long while.

The water splattered and ran in rivulets down the mirrored surface of her sunglasses. She let him take them off.

He was happy for himself and sorry for her when he saw the little dark circles below her eyes. Gently, he kissed, left and right, that evidence of her lack of sleep.

She reached for the bar of hotel soap and said, 'I'll lather.'

15

CATHERINE.

Ten o'clock the next morning.

She was wrapped in one of Pinchon's silk robes. Sometime after midnight she'd come roaring, swerving in and managed to park her yellow Ferrari half on the drive and half on the lawn. She'd left the lights on and motor running, so Pinchon had personally gone out to turn them off.

In any condition, even that drunk, he was glad to have her there. And despite her drunkenness, she knew clearly why she had come. She wasn't the type to take rejection standing up.

Now she was in the anteroom of Pinchon's bedroom, where he usually took breakfast when the weather wasn't nice enough for the terrace. He was trying as best he could to minister to her hangover. Aspirins, black coffee laced with brandy, and frequent consolations.

She was, however, far from restored as she looked out the near window and thought the day, dull and drizzling, was a suitable accompaniment to her feelings. She placed her cup on the table. The front of her robe slipped carelessly apart. She sat back and closed her eyes. 'The son of a bitch,' she said.

Pinchon knew whom she meant from her mumblings the night before. He gathered, with pleasure, that she'd had a falling out with Stevens over some other woman. It only bothered him that Catherine was reacting so to it. He advised her to forget it.

'You can bet your ass I will.'

'Good.'

She massaged the back of her neck with her fingers. 'He's not much of a man anyway,' she said, thinking aloud.

'A tree surgeon,' said Pinchon disdainfully.

'Remind me, Jean, I owe you fifty some thousand francs.'

'Why?'

She told him, replenishing her ego by reducing Hazard to a

223

level of outright deceit. It showed what a user he was, the way he went around victimizing people, she said.

Pinchon detested that he'd been taken at cards, but he pretended it hadn't been important. Curious, though, and thinking there might be more to it, he calmly, sympathetically, drew her out.

Without realizing the serious harm of it – she didn't know the actual reason Hazard had come to Europe – Catherine eventually revealed who Stevens really was.

Pinchon registered only mild surprise. He appeared to be more concerned for her. She shouldn't waste any more emotion on the matter. Why didn't she soothe herself with a warm bath or a sauna? It was a good day to spend in bed. Not to worry about anything, he would care for her.

She was already feeling somewhat better. What a dear he was, she said.

He agreed.

Moments later he excused himself to attend to what he called a business problem. He thought it out on his way downstairs. Not for a moment did he believe it coincidence that the brother of the late Carl Hazard was now on the scene under an assumed identity. Quite possibly this Hazard was the reason Badr hadn't come in from London as expected four days previous and now couldn't be located anywhere. Badr was very reliable, had always been; it was unlikely he'd disappear without a trace. And Saad was missing in New York.

He summoned Mustafa, Hatum, and Gabil to his study. He told them what he wanted done. They would have no trouble finding Hazard; probably he was at one of the hotels in the vicinity. There might be a girl with him. In that case she would also have to be dealt with.

No further instructions were necessary. No questions. They were on their way out when Pinchon stopped them with an afterthought. Two of them could manage it easily, he said. Mustafa and Gabil. This would be an opportunity for Gabil to prove himself.

Hatum stayed behind, feeling a bit slighted.

Pinchon had something else for him to do. Hatum was to go to Grasse to pick up a flacon of perfume. A fragrance not available elsewhere, one that had been created, blended, bal-

224

anced, perfected generations ago exclusively for the Pinchons. In two and a quarter centuries only four women had been granted the privilege of wearing it.

Now, it seemed Catherine would be the fifth.

16

AT THAT moment Hazard and Keven were less than five hundred feet away.

They were in the Peugeot parked off the Boulevard de Gaulle, opposite the private drive that led to and from Pinchon's villa. The rain handicapped their view to some extent and the car's windows were so fogged inside that Hazard had to keep wiping them with the flat of his hand.

The circumstances, the rain and the car, reminded Hazard of the last time, that miserable long night in London he'd spent waiting for Badr. What made this time better was Keven. She had refused to be left at the hotel, despite Hazard's reasoning that she'd be safer there, that she'd be merely an additional responsibility if she went along, that it was none of her damn business anyway. She didn't argue, but he might as well have been talking to himself.

They'd been parked outside the villa for almost an hour now. Hazard was watching and hoping something advantageous might develop. To help pass the time Keven put his memory through a few calisthenics. Things she'd especially looked up for ammunition.

'Who holds the record for swinging?'

He shrugged. 'All swingers are liars.'

'Not that kind. I mean ordinary old back-and-forth swinging, like at a playground.'

'Oh.' He thought a moment. 'Two guys swung for a hundred hours in Seattle on August 1st, 1971. Jim Anderson and Lyle Hendrickson.'

'Okay, how about the world's record for spitting?'

'For what?'

'Spitting.'

'Snakes or people?'

'People.'

'Altitude or on a line?'

'Quit stalling,' she said, believing that perhaps at last she had him stumped.

'On April 1st, 1971, a guy named Don Snyder reared back, snapped his neck, and let fly for a distance of 31 feet, 6 inches. Of course, that was one of his better days.'

Keven sighed, conceding. As a reward she shoved a shrivelled-up, dried, organic apricot into his mouth.

It was so tough Hazard couldn't bite through it, almost tasteless, more bitter than anything. Finally it softened enough for him to chew and swallow it.

'Apricots are loaded with Vitamin A,' she declared.

'What else have you got in that bag?'

She'd brought along her Mexican-peasant net bag. It was bulging. 'All kinds of goodies,' she said.

'How about something bad for a change?'

She brought out a handful of tablets like dark brown M&M chocolate candies. She put a few in her mouth and mmmed as though they were delicious.

'Give me some,' he said, reaching.

She decided she'd better not trick him that much. 'Desiccated beef liver,' she said.

Hazard jerked his hand back.

Time for a kiss, she thought, and took the initiative, quickly dissolving away his distaste with a short and then a much longer one. When they broke he used the hand that had been under her sweater to wipe the windshield.

Just in time. A dark grey Mercedes sedan was coming out of Pinchon's drive. Mustafa with Gabil behind the wheel.

It might have been an opportunity had Mustafa been alone, but Gabil's presence made it too complicated. No use forcing Gabil into a tight situation, Hazard decided. Watching the Mercedes out of sight, he asked Keven, 'Was there anyone in the back seat?'

'I didn't notice.'

The possibility that both his targets had been in the Mercedes with Gabil made Hazard decide to give it up for now and come back at night. Maybe Mustafa and Hatum would be working out again, and if so, this time he'd take the chance and to hell with the consequences. He was for returning to the hotel and making better use of the afternoon.

'Let's wait a while longer,' Keven said.

'Why?' He thought perhaps her mood didn't match his.

'Give it ten minutes and then if nothing happens – we'll do what you want.'

A few minutes later another Mercedes, a black one, came out of the drive and turned north. It was Hatum, and definitely alone.

Hazard quickly started up the Peugeot and went after him.

It soon became apparent that Hatum wasn't bound for the local *boulangerie*. He drove up the Corniche Moyenne and went east to Nice. He circumvented the more-congested section of that city and got on to the superhighway to Cagnes. There he changed off to a typical French back-country road, black-topped but crumbling along the edges, with no shoulders and allowing only a few inches clearance between cars passing in opposite directions. Traffic was sparse. However, each time a car came from the other way Hazard felt he had no choice but to meet it head-on or run off the side. At ninety kilometres per hour he managed to stay a discreet distance behind the Mercedes. Hatum was driving as though the road were one way, his way, right down the middle, somehow always swerving at the last second to avoid cars coming at him.

After about five kilometres they reached a small place called la Colle sur Loup, where, for no apparent reason, the road improved, at least to the extent that it had paved shoulders.

Where the hell was Hatum going, Hazard wondered. Keven demonstrated how relaxed she was about everything by commenting on the scenery. Rugged, arid country, steep slopes covered with scrubby pine and cork oak and cacti. Hard, beautiful country, the high bony instep of the Alps. Huge fingers of granite shoved upward, gigantic fists of it holding remnants of ancient ramparts; old frightened villages that had been perched defensively against the fierce Germanic invaders and Muslim pirates. All of it now freshly washed and darkened by the rain that had finally stopped.

'Shit,' said Hazard.

Keven disagreed. 'I think it's pretty.'

He meant they were almost out of gas. The fuel indicator was nearly parallel with the red 'empty' line. 'Didn't they fill it up when you rented it?'

'I assumed they did.'

He couldn't really blame her for that. It was a mistake he

himself might have made. But it created a critical problem. The only thing to do was to keep going and hope the Peugeot had enough reserve.

Ten minutes and fifteen kilometres later the black ribbon of road wound huggingly around the side of a sheer rift, then came out suddenly to present a wide, lower-lying plateau with a village set on it. They saw the distant surrounding hillsides largely patched with the red and pink and yellow of flowers. A road sign announced 'Grasse', and Hazard informed Keven that it was the perfume-making centre of France, the world really. She said she knew and quickly rolled her window open all the way and, yes, the air was remarkably fragrant. She inhaled deeply and sighed with pleasure.

Hazard accelerated to get closer behind the Mercedes as the highway descended and became part of the town – a small town, considering its special importance, less than two kilometres from end to end.

They entered from the north on Avenue Victoria, which was the main way. Along both sides were modest houses of pale stucco, most with their shutters closed. Avenue Victoria changed without apparent cause to become Boulevard Thiers, lined with plane trees and small shops that more than anything else offered perfume for sale to tourists who believed they could save by coming to the source and ended up paying double dearly for the fancy bottles made of thick glass that magnified meagre quarter ounces.

Hazard was only a car length behind the Mercedes when they reached the Place de la Foux. It was then that the Peugeot began to jerk and cough. Hazard could do nothing but coast and just barely make it to the sign that said '*essence*' and to the two gas pumps that stood at the kerb. There was no hurrying the wine-faced attendant, who pretended not to understand in order to sell a whole tankful rather than the five gallons Hazard tried to say was all he wanted. It was by no means a fast pit stop. Hatum was long gone. Hazard considered trying to catch up but decided it would be futile. Might as well return to Cap Ferrat.

'As long as we're here let's look around,' Keven suggested.

'You want some perfume?'

'Do I need some?'

'No.'

x

229

They drove down the main boulevard, which again arbitrarily changed its name to du Jeu de Ballon and then reverted to de Gaulle for a single block before becoming Victor Hugo. On reaching the edge of town, Hazard turned the car around and went back.

It was at a square with a fountain that Keven spotted a black Mercedes. Maybe it was the one. It was parked down a divergent one-way sidestreet, and Hazard had to circle around the narrow streets to get to it. As they approached the Mercedes they saw Hatum come out of a building that identified itself with a tasteful black-and-gold plaque as the Parfumerie de Fragonard. Hatum was carrying a pale blue carton about half the size of a shoe box. No chance for Hazard. Hatum got quickly into the car and pulled away.

Hazard followed left and right and on to the boulevard, and it was soon obvious they were headed out of Grasse the same way they'd come. Hatum was now bound for Cap Ferrat. For Hazard it would be nothing but a useless round trip.

'Anyway,' said Keven, 'I enjoyed the ride.'

Hazard promised himself he'd have a more productive evening.

The Mercedes was then about a hundred or so yards ahead, going up the grade beyond the outskirts of town. Suddenly its tail-lights flashed amber as it braked and swung off on to a side road, a dirt road.

Hazard went on past because it would have been too conspicuous to follow. He immediately found a place to make a turn around and go back. He paused and saw the dirt road ran between two vast fields of flowers. The Mercedes was stopped on it about a hundred and fifty feet in. Hatum was out of the car. He had walked a short way from it and was standing faced away.

Hazard stomped down on the accelerator.

Hatum was in the midst of urinating, enjoying relief while preoccupied with the acres of bright pink roses that lay before him. When he heard the car coming he glanced around furtively, at the same time attempting to stop mid-stream. Before he could do much else the car was there and he recognized Hazard. No way for Hatum to make it back to the Mercedes. He jumped down into the roadside ditch, scuttled along the bottom of the ditch, kept on his hands and knees, and saw

230

that his only chance was the rose field. He scrambled over into it and when he was out of sight he stopped. His trousers were wet from himself. He tucked in, zipped up, and took out his gun.

Hazard had quickly got out of the car, his Llama drawn, but had caught only a flash of Hatum disappearing into the roses. Hazard returned to the safe side of the Peugeot and instructed Keven to lock herself in and *stay* in, no matter what.

'What if —?'

'In that case drive away,' he told her. 'Just go like hell.'

She nodded, and he knew she had to be clutched up frightened inside, at least as much as he was. It showed in her eyes, wider than usual. He hoped she didn't panic. He gave her a final reassuring look and left her sitting there, holding her net bag in her lap.

He went around to the rear of the Peugeot, using it as a shield while he appraised the situation. The field was large, about six acres of roses. They were planted in thick rows parallel with the road. He estimated the bushes were four to five feet in height. Heavy foliage. There was perhaps a yard between the rows, and at intervals along each row were narrow unplanted spaces providing passage from one row to the next. Those spaces, however, were located irregularly, and in that respect the field was a kind of maze. From his slightly higher vantage the field resembled a pink sea, so brilliant it appeared to be moving, although the air was still. He decided that if he wanted Hatum, he'd have to go in to get him.

He took a deep breath to steady himself and tried to erase the thought that came to him – it smelled like a funeral.

Keeping low, he went down into the grassy roadside ditch and crawled into the rose field about thirty feet from where Hatum had gone in. No sign of Hatum up that first row. Hazard paused to get acclimated. A different perspective now – the bushes were denser than he'd thought and it was darker because the leaves above reached out and across from row to row. The bare ground was wet, muddy and scattered with pink petals from the rain. The lower stems of the bushes were at least two inches in diameter, armed with half-inch red thorns that curved slightly and reminded Hazard of the spurs on a fighting cock.

Belly down, he made his way slowly forward along that row to an open space. He glanced up and down the next row. No Hatum. He crossed over and went up that row to another space. Cautiously he continued from row to row until he was deep into the field. From rugs to roses, he thought.

He stopped, held his breath, and listened. There was a rustling sound off in a diagonal direction. He was about to start moving toward it when two shots made him press down tight to the ground. The bullets had come close, he knew, because he'd heard them cutting through the nearby stems and leaves. He remained motionless for what seemed a long while before chancing to go farther.

Down that row he crawled, inching along to another open space. Concentrating on where he believed the rustling sounds had originated, he made out a patch of black that had to be Hatum's suit. At the most, twenty-five feet away. Unmissable. Hazard levelled the Llama and squeezed off three sure shots. He saw the black flinch as the bullets hit. He fired another for good measure and then, confidently, up in a crouch, he went quickly around the next two rows to get to it.

It wasn't Hatum. It was Hatum's suit-jacket. Evidently Hatum had got badly hung up on the thorns while trying to get through a small opening. To free himself he'd slipped out of his jacket.

Hazard saw Hatum's shoeprints in the mud, leading off to the right. He followed them, advising himself not to be over-eager, to take it slow. But when he reached the next opening and saw Hatum's tracks again to the right, it occurred to him that Hatum might be circling back toward the road and the cars. The direction of the tracks along the next row convinced Hazard that was it.

He straightened up. His head emerged from the sea of pink.

Hatum. At the edge of the field and headed for the road. Too far away for a shot.

Hazard ran fast as he could – to the next opening, the next row, through and down and around, slipping in the mud from row to row, running the maze.

Hatum was now over the ditch and climbing up to the road.

Hazard saw it was impossible. He'd never get there in time. On a straight line, maybe, but not this long way around and around, not if he continued following the maze. He still had three rows to go.

To hell with it.

He went full speed at the row ahead, threw himself at it, tore right into it and gasped, cried out with the sudden pain. It was as though a hundred furious cats had leaped on him all at once. The thorns snagged, clawed and ripped at his clothes and flesh. He fought his way through and went on into the thick of the next that resisted, almost sprung him back, caught, stuck, and stabbed him.

One more row.

He went headlong into it, thrashing, using his arms and hands to fight aside the network of green and pink that had also become his enemy. It took all his endurance to break through and come stumbling free down into the ditch.

Hatum was getting into the Mercedes.

Hazard started diagonally up the bank, going for the Mercedes, hoping to get into range for a last shot. But then, adding to the confusion of the moment, there was Keven. Out of the car, also running. Right at him.

She didn't grab at Hazard. She threw herself at his legs, clipping them out from under him, sending him sprawling with her into the ditch.

Hatum's fingers were turning the key in the ignition of the Mercedes.

The explosion caused a concussive wave across the sea of roses. A million petals dropped with the shock. Flames burst and a cloud of black smoke rolled up, hung high in the damp air. Chrome and other metal parts of the Mercedes came scattering down.

For a moment Hazard didn't know what had happened, or how. It didn't take long to figure it out.

That grey stuff that had looked so much like modelling clay. She'd brought it along in her net bag. She'd learned to work with it when they'd been at the DIA farm in Maryland. While he was learning how to fight with a knife, she, according to her nature, had favoured a course in explosives.

Mustafa and Gabil were in room 307 of the Hôtel du Cap.

They'd had no trouble finding out where Hazard was staying. Mr and Mrs Hazard, in fact. Actually the du Cap was the obvious place, the first they'd checked. Getting into the room was a simple matter. It had taken Mustafa only some twenty seconds to pick the lock.

The most difficult part was the waiting. They'd already been there over two hours. Mostly to occupy himself, Mustafa had searched the room, all the drawers and luggage. The one thing he'd found that puzzled him was the carton of images. Why, he wondered, would anyone keep those little photographs and sentences in individual sealed envelopes? He guessed it was some sort of collection or a kind of American game.

A more valuable find was the pound bag of Mosouka raisins that were in the drawer of the night table. Mustafa ate them by the handful. With the flavour of the raisins freshening his mouth he smoked more than usual, lighting up a cigarette every few minutes, taking only a few puffs and extinguishing it in the water of the toilet bowl. After about an hour he was on the last in his pack, and when he'd smoked that one down past the holding point he regretted having wasted all the others before. He persevered for a while and then complained aloud.

Gabil volunteered to go down to the lobby and buy him a new pack.

Mustafa decided against that, but soon the habitual urge got the best of him. He told Gabil to go, but hurry.

Within a few minutes Gabil returned with the cigarettes, and Mustafa once again began alternately inhaling strong smoke and chewing sweet raisins.

Mustafa's plans were not complicated. As he saw it, it was just another killing to be done as swiftly and methodically as possible. Gabil would be positioned in the closet with the door slightly ajar. Mustafa would be out of sight in the bathroom. When Hazard came into the room they would simply step out and shoot, catching him in a crossfire. If the girl happened to be with Hazard, she would be Gabil's target while Mustafa took Hazard. It would be over in an instant. No noise. They would use silencers on their Magnums.

Mustafa was now relaxed in a chair. He had Gabil stationed at the window to watch for Hazard in case he drove up. During the last two hours Mustafa hadn't said more than twenty or thirty words, mostly instructions. That was his way – close-mouthed, stoic, he relied on gestures or one emphatic word at a time. During the entire next hour he only grunted a few times, as though silently conversing with himself.

234

Then, from the window, Gabil saw Hazard and Keven drive up in the Peugeot and get out.

Mustafa must have sensed a change in Gabil. He looked questioningly.

Gabil hoped Mustafa didn't come over to the window because he told him no, it was nothing – although Hazard and Keven were now in full view, walking to the hotel's entrance.

Mustafa slumped down, muttering impatiently.

Below, Hazard hesitated before entering the hotel. He had good reason to feel self-conscious. Although he'd managed to clean himself up some, he was really beyond repair, a mess. His suede jacket was nearly in shreds and he couldn't take it off because underneath his shirt was soaked with blood. His trousers were torn all down the legs, and there were gaping rips elsewhere. What little was left of his clothes was caked stiff with mud.

'Walk in front of me and stay close,' he told Keven.

They went in, and in tandem stride quickly crossed the lobby to the elevator, but not without causing several incredulous stares. Once in the elevator and going up, Hazard felt relieved until Keven asked him if he had a key. He didn't as usual, and as usual she'd left hers in the room.

He'd wait for her on the third floor landing while she went back down to the desk.

She returned promptly. Along with a key she also had in hand a small envelope, hotel stationery.

'What's that?' Hazard asked as they headed for the room.

'It was in our box. Probably the bill.'

'Too soon, and too skinny,' he said, and took it from her.

They were rounding a corner of the corridor and approaching 307 when Hazard opened the envelope and read its hastily scrawled note.

> Mustafa upstairs with me
> to kill you. Go to Avignon,
> Auberge de Noves. Will call.

It was initialled ABD.

Seconds later Gabil, glancing down, saw Hazard and Keven hurry to their car, get in, and drive away. He assumed they'd got his message. He wondered what he'd have done if they hadn't.

17

It was a two-hundred-sixty-five-kilometre drive from Cap Ferrat to Avignon.

The Auberge de Noves was situated at the top of a spiralling private road. It was a small inn but by no means prosaic or inexpensive. Through all seasons its dozen suites were usually occupied. One could not just drop by and expect to be accommodated. People who tried that were more often than not turned away even when there was space available.

Hazard and Keven, however, were welcomed as though they'd had a long-standing reservation.

The proprietor personally received them. He was a slender man in his early fifties – kind-eyed, smooth-mannered, a fifth-generation Frenchman and for countless generations a Jew. His name, as he said it, was Monsieur Feldman. He recognized Hazard and Keven immediately from description. He asked no questions nor did he mention Gabil. Considering the circumstances, Hazard assumed Monsieur Feldman was more than emotionally involved with his distant homeland. Probably a link in the network of Mosad.

Because they arrived well after nightfall, neither Hazard nor Keven fully appreciated where they were until the following morning. Wrapped in fresh robes they ate breakfast outside on a balcony that was theirs alone. Then they saw they were surrounded as far as they could see by gentle, amiable earth colours – pointed exclamations of cypress, greener olive, and almond. A blossoming lime tree was right there within touch, the tips of its branches pointing, as though singling out Hazard and Keven to receive its fragrance. And from out of the stillness came the constant harmony of bees.

The heart of Provence.

They were eager to go meet it.

But first Hazard needed something to wear. Keven drove into town and bought him a pair of jeans and a blue chambray shirt. She also stopped in at a pharmacy to get an herbal ointment for his scratches and to replenish her stock of vitamins. Fortunately nothing irreplaceable had been sacrificed in their retreat from the Hôtel du Cap – not their various passports nor Hazard's roll of winnings. Unknown to Hazard at the time, Keven had taken those things along in her net bag, which he now referred to as her bag of tricks.

The rest of that day they lost themselves among the folds of the fields and along the banks of the River Durance. The air was clear, cleansing, and it carried their laughter. They felt they'd suddenly been transported to a place they'd separately imagined. Frequent pauses along the way for kisses seemed only to enhance the unreality.

The mood carried over into the night, when they lay together and experienced more together than ever before. They took turns at worship. Each touch was a tribute. Selfish generosity. So intensely did pleasure reflect and mount between them that their separate roles became obscure. They were both at once in and around, enclosed and enclosing. No words were exchanged, but an identical declaration crowded their mouths and silently exploded, again and again.

Afterward there was not the usual afterward. They held on, remained within the chrysalis they'd spun, and went early, easily to sleep.

The days passed.

Hillside carpets of wild lavender, a flock of sheep to wade through, white-washed houses baking. Gnarled trees as seen by van Gogh. The rotating faces of sunflowers, cold *jus des framboises*, a quixotic windmill, some gypsies stealing along without destination. The three hundred bells of Avignon saying daily good morning. Places heavy with history. Arles, Nîmes, Tarascon, St Remy. Les Alyscamp, where Christ said mass, and there were the stones his knees impressed. Warm bread smeared with local sweet butter. A bouquet of flowering thyme. Roman ruins, a solitary mitred tower to be invaded and its ramparts used for impetuous afternoon passion.

On the eighth night (time was precious and therefore counted) the telephone rang like an alarm. It had to be Gabil. He was calling from a public phone at the air terminal in Nice. In an hour he'd be leaving for Cairo.

'Why?' asked Hazard.

'I will know when I get there.'

237

'Did they find Hatum?'

'Not entirely. Did you know that he was a kinsman of Mustafa?'

'No.'

'A close cousin.'

'So what?'

'Mustafa has pledged his honour against your death. For him it is now a blood thing.'

'It was always a blood thing,' Hazard said. 'Where is he now?'

'In the restaurant having coffee.'

'He's going with you?'

'I am going with him.'

Hazard thought a moment and asked, 'What's a good hotel for me in Cairo?'

'Go home,' advised Gabil.

'Cairo,' Hazard repeated decisively.

'Then stay at the Hilton like a good tourist.'

'How about a place called the Mena House?'

'If you prefer.'

'Tyrone Power stayed there once,' said Hazard, something he'd read. 'Where will you be?'

'I will contact you.'

'For sure?'

Gabil gave his word before clicking off.

The next morning Hazard and Keven expressed farewell gratitudes to Monsieur Feldman and drove south to Marseilles. In that city's better shopping district Hazard, at Keven's insistence, went into a men's shop and a quarter hour later walked out wearing a complete change. The sleeves of his new brown-suede jacket were a bit short and the new velour trousers were a bit tight in the crotch but there was no time for alterations. They also bought one small piece of luggage to carry, mainly for appearance.

At Marseilles airport, they surrendered and paid for the rented Peugeot. There was a flight to Cairo via Rome and Athens at 3 P.M. Keven had already stated and restated all the reasons why she should go with him to Cairo. Hazard didn't say no, just let her go on about it, and she thought maybe she had him convinced until he bought their tickets and handed her a one-way to New York, departing at 3:15 P.M.

Too late to argue.

Their planes were to leave from different ramps, so they stood during the final few minutes in the terminal.

'I'll be sending to you,' he said, the way most people promised they would write or phone.

'When?'

'Every night, say ... around nine or ten.'

'Around?'

'All right, nine, starting tomorrow night.'

'I'll count on it.'

They kissed lightly, then turned from one another. As usual, they didn't say good-bye.

Hazard's flight took off on schedule.

At 3:15 Keven tried to cash in her ticket. Air France said it would mail her a refund. She doubted that and said so. She also had difficulty making the auto-rental clerk understand that for purely sentimental reasons she wanted to re-rent that particular Peugeot.

18

CATHERINE WAS now Madame Pinchon.

Or, as she sardonically referred to herself, Madame J.C.

Pinchon's marriage proposal, in the form of a serious suggestion, couldn't have been more timely. Not that Catherine's ego needed such extreme repair. Actually, as a result of being rejected by Hazard, her self-confidence suffered only a slight abrasion, which healed itself almost overnight. Yes, she was amazingly resilient when it came to that.

What did persist, however, was a resentment that she'd been horribly cheated at her own game. It was as though her partner (opponent?) had suddenly abandoned the match, walked off before a winner could be decided, and there she was, left with no one to test.

Feelings of unlovableness were already starting to take advantage of her. Next would come awful deep depression and total ennui. Unless she did something about it.

She could, of course, resort to a new, half-hearted relationship, as she'd frequently done in the past under similar circumstances. But this time she didn't feel that would suffice, wouldn't supply nearly enough proof. Neither was she in the mood to expend the patience and effort needed to set up another protracted involvement. Especially not after having wasted so much restraint and good behaviour on Hazard.

Conveniently, there was Pinchon. She accepted him as a secondary target.

His idea was to fix a future date for their wedding, say a Sunday in a month or six weeks. He figured by then his scheme would be a *fait accompli*.

Catherine, in a now-or-never tone, insisted the marriage take place at once.

Pinchon misinterpreted her eagerness in his favour. He arranged for a civil ceremony at the local *marie*. Ordinarily a three-day waiting period was required by law.

Catherine did not want to wait.

Pinchon exerted his influence – money – to get the waiting period waived. They could go to the *marie* and be married immediately.

Catherine did not want to go to the *marie*. She preferred to be married there at the villa, outside on the lawn.

Pinchon tried to reason with her.

Catherine wouldn't have it any other way.

Pinchon gave in.

Catherine chose a pleasant, shady spot on the lawn and had a white, double-seated glider swing placed there. She and Pinchon sat opposite the over-starched little town clerk and a fat stranger the clerk had brought along to serve as witness. While the official words were droned, Catherine used one of her bare feet to get the glider going back and forth. Ignoring Pinchon's reproachful glances, she blithely maintained the momentum.

The moment being so crucial, Pinchon decided against ordering her to stop. He thought perhaps she was merely too happy to contain herself.

When the town clerk came to the part of the ceremony that asked Catherine would she take this man, etc., her apathetic response was: 'Why not?' The clerk's pause requested a more conventional reply. She curtly told him to get on with it.

And when the moment called for Pinchon to contribute the family ring, a forty-two carat, oval-cut emerald, Catherine extended only the second finger of her right hand. To offset what seemed a most impertinent gesture, Pinchon quickly slipped the ring on. After the solemn pronouncement he kissed both corners of Catherine's mouth, presumably to seal it from all others for ever. The clerk and the witness departed, complaining of motion sickness.

Catherine had agreed to forego an immediate wedding trip. She was cooperative when Pinchon explained that he had an important business matter pending, one that required his personal attention. There was no reason, however, why their marriage should go uncelebrated.

Catherine said she would enjoy having a few of her friends in.

Pinchon approved. He imagined a brief, informal soirée, with himself the principal attraction. It was only natural, he thought, that Catherine should want to show off.

Her friends began arriving within an hour after the ceremony. Nearly a hundred came down from London.

Pinchon reminded Catherine that she'd said *a few*.

She told him not to worry, she'd pay for everything.

It wasn't a matter of money, he told her.

'Oh?' she said, and made a remark about the French – a nation of string-savers was her description.

Pinchon flared but placed his hand on hers and calmly assured her it really didn't matter how many people she invited.

She smiled contritely, reached up with both hands and brought his face down to her, tenderly, as though it were a precious, fragile bowl. She sipped a long kiss and called him love.

He disliked having his face handled by anyone, so it was not entirely pleasant for him.

Had she known that, it might have been her reason for doing it, but her affection was even more contrived. To effectively mistreat a man one also had to treat him well. As it turned out the hundred from London were merely the nucleus. At least double that number were there by nightfall and double that many again by midnight. They arrived on flights chartered for them by her or via private jets dispatched by her to fetch them.

How insolent and presumptuous they were, thought Pinchon. Taking for granted they would stay, they had literally appropriated the entire villa. *Mon Dieu!* Their amplified guitars were threatening his Baccarat crystal, their heels were torturing his Aubusson carpets, the stench of hemp and hashish was permeating his silk-damask hangings. How dare they shove furnishings aside to make space for their dancing. He never allowed anything to be out of place, not a single thing, never.

'*Arrêtez!*' he shouted. '*Arrêtez!*'

But the music was louder and those near enough to hear him only laughed and nodded. From their induced high points of view he was merely expressing exuberance.

What recourse did he have? Calling the gendarmes was out of the question. There'd be no way of explaining all the drugs that would be found. Trouble, disparaging publicity had to be avoided, *especially now*. Besides, if he disclaimed these people, used the excuse that they were not his but his wife's guests, he would be bringing down the worst sort of ridicule on himself.

Pinchon wandered from room to room, despising such atrocities as cigarettes stubbed out in huge bowls of caviar, a shattered Lalique figurine, a puddle of Dom Perignon eating the finish from a Vernis Martin table, eight people occupying one chaise longue, aboard it as though it were a boat, buckling its delicate legs.

Mass derangement – they were everywhere. In the kitchen, helping themselves to delicacies (the servants had already deserted). Down in the wine cellar, helping themselves to the better vintages. Upstairs in the bedrooms and baths, helping themselves to one another or more than one another.

Additionally unbearable for Pinchon was that except for a few lighthearted swishes who wanted to kiss the groom, no one seemed to realize or care who he was. Conversely, Catherine was basking in constant homage. As she moved about they competed to be near her, as though her mouth, eyes, and hands were distributing blessings.

At various times over the evening she made it a point to seek out Pinchon. To sustain him with an embrace or more intimate show of affection. She realized his exasperation but concealed how much it amused her. Several times she cajoled him into a smile and then quickly rejoined the confusion.

At 4:30 A.M. Pinchon still saw no sign of a let-up. Actually, everyone seemed more stimulated than ever. In nervous reaction he himself had drunk too much cognac. He was in the foyer then, trying to make his way through the jostling and milling, when Catherine again came to him. She kissed him a moist lingering one near his right ear and inserted her hand in under the back of his jacket. Feeling through the silkiness of his shirt, her hand glided and performed possessive little grabs.

'I'm going to lie down for a while,' she told him.

He was also in favour of that.

'No,' she said, and left him abruptly.

He watched her go up the wide marble stairway. She was flanked by two handsome young women dressed in St Laurent, smoking. With arms around, sides locked to sides, up they went together. Pinchon noticed the flash of the oval-cut family emerald. It was on the finger of the extremely short-haired, dark-haired one on Catherine's left.

Not to be obvious, Pinchon waited a moment before following them up. On reaching the upper landing he hesitated and then chose to go to his private quarters. It was the only area of the villa they hadn't been able to violate, thanks to his elaborate precautions.

He closed the door behind him. The multiple electric locks shot back into place.

A sigh expressed how relieved he was to be alone. Under no condition would he let anyone in, perhaps not even her.

He undressed quickly.

Merde. Their interminable music invaded even here. He got two small cubes of malleable pink wax from a bedstand drawer, worked them into proper shape with his fingers and inserted them into his ears. Then he could hear only his inner self. It was a bit alarming.

He went into his dressing room. Standing at its centre he observed his nudity in the opposing mirrored surfaces.

As for her, Madame Pinchon, a slapping around or two would straighten her out.

19

HAZARD HAD been detained at Cairo International Airport because he didn't have a visa.

'The purpose of your visit?'

'Sightseeing,' Hazard told them.

They examined his passport page by page, to make sure he hadn't been to Israel. They also opened his piece of luggage. Seeing it contained only a soiled pair of jeans, shirt, and toilet articles, they asked, 'How much currency are you bringing in?'

Hazard decided it would be beneficial to show them. He flashed it all – a little over eight thousand in dollars, pounds, and francs. He fanned it out so they could do a quick count.

The senior immigration officer's eyes were stealing the money while his hand reached for the visa stamp. He took his frustration out on the passport, slammed a complicated pink impression on a fresh page, and initialled it with a steel-pointed pen that had to be dipped into a well.

For a while Hazard had thought they might search him routinely, find the Llama and give him real trouble. Saved by money. It didn't just talk, it knew all the languages.

A half hour later he was in a taxi in night traffic on Shari El Nahda, also known as Ramses Street. Feeling more displaced then ever, he gazed out at Arab words, chicken scratchings that seemed even more incomprehensible in neon. Just ahead was some Pharaoh's statue presiding over the upward spurts of a public fountain, and a bit farther on, contrasting with blocks of anonymous concrete business buildings, was the fancy minaret of a mosque.

Hazard suddenly realized he was on the edge of the seat, anticipating, behaving like a gawky tourist. He eased back but continued looking out, and it occurred to him that probably Carl had walked along that very street many times. He recalled several letters from Carl, long ones describing Cairo. Letters never answered because Hazard had never been a writer. Carl knew that and hadn't blamed him, Hazard hoped.

The taxi went on past the Egyptian Museum to Shari El Corniche. On the left were such large hotels as the Hilton and Shepherd's. On the right was water that had to be the Nile. It looked no different from any other old river. They crossed over via the El Gama'a Bridge, not far from the spot where Moses was found in the bullrushes.

It seemed too long a ride. Hazard suspected the driver was taking him for one, just running up the meter. He leaned forward and crisply reminded the man, 'Mena House!' The driver glanced around, nodded, displayed bad teeth with a big smile. 'Zoo,' he said, indicating the park-like area they were now passing. Hazard decided he'd know for sure he was being hustled if they recrossed the Nile.

Soon they reached the section called Giza and headed down Shari El Haram. It was an absolutely flat street aimed straight at the Pyramids. Hazard caught sight of them through the dirty windshield. About five miles away, illuminated, geometrically perfect. He'd take time to visit the Pyramids no matter what, he promised himself.

The taxi continued on Shari El Haram. Hazard kept his attention on the Pyramids, which grew larger in view and still larger until they loomed ahead as though they were the only possible destination. Fascinating, thought Hazard, but hell he didn't want the Pyramids tonight, he wanted his hotel. He was about to tell the driver that when the taxi wheeled sharply right and after a brief, gritty skid stopped at the entrance to Mena House.

Hazard was pleased and a little disappointed that the driver had turned out to be an honest Arab. He paid the fare in dollars, ten, which he knew was three times the hundred and fifty piastres that had registered on the meter. The driver said 'hello' for good-bye and made a fast getaway with what he believed was a foreigner's stupid mistake.

From the moment Hazard entered the lobby he was glad he'd decided on Mena House. It was over a century old and all the better for it. Originally built by the Khedive Ismail as a royal hunting lodge, it was later expanded to serve as a royal guest house during the opening festivities of the Suez Canal. Since then, all of its palatial ambience had been conscientiously preserved. Ornamental blue tiles and intricate mosaics, brass-embossed doors, huge hanging Islamic lamps, furnishings inlaid with ivory and mother of pearl, rich Persian carpets and, throughout, an abundance of that highly decorative antique lattice woodwork known as *mushrabiyyeh*, much of it dating back to the fifteenth century.

Royalty had stayed there. Albert Edward, Prince of Wales, Princess Eugénie, King Gustav of Sweden, King Alphonse of Spain, Emperor Haile Selassie. And celebrities such as Churchill, Roosevelt, the Agha Khan, Cecil B. de Mille, and, of course, Tyrone Power.

At the moment, this being summer and not *the* season, there were plenty of accommodations available. Hazard got a deluxe third-floor suite at the incredible rate of seven hundred fifty piastres, about twelve dollars a day. A boy robed in impeccable white and topped with a bright red fez carried Hazard's bag up. The boy lighted the rooms all around, checked to see the bath had an ample supply of linens, and as a final show of service (knowing it nearly always inspired a more generous tip) he folded open the tall louvered windows to present the view.

It was like having the Grand Pyramid in one's own backyard.

Hazard doubled the dollar he'd intended to give. The boy bowed and said seven 'thank yous' on his way out.

Hazard now observed something strange about the lights on the Pyramid. They weren't constant. They brightened and dimmed, went off and on all around the structure. Along with that was a loudspeaker voice in the distance speaking in German. Curious, Hazard asked about that when he called down for a pair of gin-and-tonics. He was told it was *Son et Lumière*, the nightly sound-and-light show that related the history of the Pyramids and Sphinx.

'Why in German?' he asked.

'Tomorrow night English, sir.'

Hazard closed the louvered doors.

First thing off were his new trousers. He'd been suffering the cut of their tight crotch for ten hours, and during the long flight he'd had to take frequent walks up and down the aisle to maintain circulation. Now, getting some revenge, he balled the trousers up and threw them into a corner. He put his money, passports, the Llama, and the special knife under the

247

bed pillow and went into the bathroom. There was something he'd never seen before – a brass bathtub and sink, shiny and luxurious looking. He washed up in the sink with sandalwood-scented hotel soap.

Mindful of the next day's comfort, he filled the tub and tossed in his jeans. He was on his hands and knees plunging and rubbing when the drinks arrived. They were tall and strong enough to be doubles. He downed one and went back to doing his laundry, thinking that if Keven were there she'd be doing it. Maybe. After wringing, he shook and snapped out as many wrinkles as he could and hung the jeans to dry over one of the towel racks.

With the second drink in hand he reopened the louvered windows and saw no lights on the Pyramid now. Evidently the Ministry of Tourism had finished its number for the night. Hazard switched off all the lights in the room, drew over a chair and sat there nude, looking out.

Fronds of tall date palms were silhouetted and being rustled by a slight breeze. The moon was close to full and it had a face. He slid a sliver of ice into his mouth and contemplated the massive funerary monument of Cheops. To accompany his point of view, he thought on some of the things he knew about it.

Statistics: 2,300,000 chunks of granite averaging 5,000 pounds, some weighing as much as 60,000. Covering an area equal to seven midtown blocks of New York City. Two hundred and one stepped tiers arranged in regular all-around courses rising 481 feet, the height of a modern forty-story building. Blunted on top with a level platform because seven of the original uppermost tiers and the capstone were missing. On the north side sixteen courses up was the authentic entrance, and ten courses below that was the gaping scar where the Arab Al Mamum had forced entry in the year 820. Those two passageways converged at a point 100 feet in, and from there the way went down and up to the various chambers. It was said that on August 12, 1799, Napoleon spent three hours alone in the king's chamber and came out noticeably changed, pale and shaken, as though he had witnessed something extraordinary.

Possibly, thought Hazard.

It was also said that for some inexplicable reason the

248

Grand Pyramid possessed a natural power to mummify; that is, a corpse would dehydrate but not decay within its confines. Some scientists theorized that the pyramidal shape was the reason.

Could be.

Then there were those who said that the builders of the Grand Pyramid were of an ancient civilization that had progressed far beyond ours, and had used levitation to raise those gigantic stones into place. Supposedly the structure had served as an earthly reckoning point for space vehicles.

Not very likely.

Nor did Hazard go along with the idea that the Pyramid was an instrument of divine message, cryptically prophesying with all its degrees, measures, crevices, and niches the fate of mankind, like a creator's calendar that timetabled in advance all major occurrences: the revelations of Moses, the birth of Christ, plagues, wars, discoveries, and eventually holocaust and extinction.

For sure, that bewildering arrangement of rocks transmitted an unusual eeriness. If it stood for anything, Hazard concluded, it stood for death.

He was suddenly chilled, shivering.

He blamed that on the ice, the desert night, and his nudity – rather than the fleeting impression that the Pyramid was reminding him how slim were the chances of anyone winning a four-horse parlay.

He closed off the Pyramid and climbed into bed. Lonely goddamned bed. He finally fell asleep while reminiscing about exceptional poker hands he'd held.

At ten the next morning he was awakened by splashes and playful shouts. He got up for the bathroom, on the way back glanced out to see the hotel swimming pool directly below. Centre of attraction were two, three blonde girls in mini-bikinis, showing off what they were sure they had. Frauleins on vacation from Dusseldorf. It was too early for Hazard to appreciate them. It looked hot, blazing bright out there. Maybe later he'd get some trunks and take a dip. Anyway, he'd stay around the hotel not to miss Gabil's call.

He ordered up some breakfast. While waiting for it he put on the jeans that now fitted good and snug, the way jeans did when freshly washed. They were still damp at the waistband

and around the pockets but they'd dry on him.

A knock on the door.

That would be room service. Hazard opened and found himself looking up at Gabil.

Right off it was apparent Gabil hadn't dropped by to bid him welcome to Cairo. The man was grim. He didn't return Hazard's smile. He sat down as though his body were a burden.

'Mustafa expects me back in an hour,' said Gabil.

'Where is he?'

'Not far from here.'

'Where?'

Gabil went to the window. He directed Hazard's attention across the way to the sun-scorched golf course, one of the hotel's facilities. At the distant edge, about a half mile off, was a line of cypress trees and beyond those, mainly obscured, were some white structures.

'The house is there,' Gabil said.

'Whose?'

'It once belonged to the Pinchons.'

That was a piece of luck, thought Hazard, having Mustafa that close by, not having to contend with the problem of unfamiliar (and unfriendly) Cairo.

Breakfast came. There was only one cup on the tray. Hazard filled it with coffee for Gabil. He drank his own from a water glass.

'What's Mustafa doing over there?' asked Hazard.

That opened the way for Gabil to talk about it, let out some of his tension, and perhaps see things even more clearly by hearing it himself. He gave Hazard a detailed rundown on the situation. He'd seen the atomizing pods and the two canisters of vx–10 nerve gas. The special transfer valves were finished and in place. The gas could now be released. The only hold-up was a minor additional attachment, a nozzle, that would fit on to the intake valve of the pods. The nozzle was being made, would be ready in two days. On Sunday, three days from now, the pods would be filled and transported elsewhere by truck.

'Where?'

Gabil didn't know. He'd tried to find out from the workers and guards around the place, but they didn't know either.

They only knew the vx–10 was somehow destined for Israel. That was how the operation had been set up, on various levels, with each limited to knowing about and performing its special phase. Of course, Mustafa and surely a few others higher up had full knowledge.

It seemed incredible to Hazard that anyone would go to such extremes, but then he thought of the Lod Airport massacre, the 1972 Olympics, the murder of diplomats in Sudan ... 'Where did they get the vx–10?'

'From your country.'

'How do you know that?'

'From the markings on the canisters.' Gabil, with difficulty, had memorized the serial numbers. He now wrote them down and gave the slip of paper to Hazard.

USACC–FD–12–70–B2046–ABV–10
USACC–FD–10–71–B2867–ABV–10

The first three and last three digits of each of the series were enough to verify the source. 'How did they manage that?' Hazard asked.

'Pinchon arranged it.'

'How?'

Gabil could easily have said that was something else he didn't know. Just the day before Mustafa had proudly revealed to him the success of the operation thus far, including how Carl had been used. The Arab had especially enjoyed the part about Carl. It was a way of dishonouring a sworn enemy – in this case, Hazard.

Gabil decided omission would be as bad as a lie. He preferred to keep things straight with Hazard. He told him all of it.

Hazard was obviously shaken, but he insisted that Carl didn't give them the information.

'Perhaps he did.'

'No.'

'Perhaps he saw no possible harm in it. Considering where the canisters were, under that much ocean, they doubtless seemed secure enough. I myself would have thought so.'

Hazard wanted to believe that.

'Did you know there was such a ship as the *Sea Finder*?'

'No.'

251

'Nor did I,' Gabil said. 'And I doubt your brother did. Evidently Pinchon disliked your brother personally.'

'What makes you say that?'

'He ordered him killed.'

'For the information?'

'Hardly. It wasn't the kind of secret one would need to kill for. It could have been easily and cheaply purchased from numerous other sources.'

It took a moment for Hazard to rearrange his perspective, but then it all did fall into place. *Carl, Catherine, Pinchon.* That had to be it. Bitterly, Hazard added Pinchon to his list, telling himself that he should have had him there all along, on the top, with an underline.

Gabil noted the time. 'I have to get back.'

'What are you going to do?'

'The only thing I can do.'

'What?'

'Empty the canisters.'

'You mean just open the valves and let it come.'

'It's the one sure way.'

'But—'

Gabil raised his huge hand. It was settled, understood. What Gabil proposed to do was sacrifice himself.

'When?' Hazard asked.

'The day after tomorrow. Before they can transfer the gas to the pods,' Gabil said. 'I have a favour to ask you.'

'I owe you a few.'

'Go to Tel Aviv for me, to the Mosad. Tell them about all this.'

'Don't you have a contact here in Cairo?'

'None that I can trust, not *landsmen*, only opportunists who may be working both sides. Those I could be sure of were recently exposed and arrested.'

'I'm not a *landsman*.'

Gabil grinned. 'You might be, if you looked deep enough.'

'Why not just phone a contact in Paris or Rome and have him relay the information?'

'Telephone service here is under Government control. Every international call is strictly monitored by security people. If they hear one questionable word, they cut you off.'

It made Hazard realize how little he knew about this business. 'Anyway,' he told Gabil, 'what can the Mosad do?'

'If I fail at least they will be alerted.'

Hazard said he would see that the Mosad was informed.

Gabil thanked him. He took a final gulp of the coffee that was cold by now.

'Do me one more favour,' Hazard said, 'It might help if I knew the layout of that house.'

'You still want Mustafa.'

'More than ever.'

After Gabil left, Hazard sat on the edge of the bed for a few minutes. Maybe, he thought, that was the last he'd ever see of the Israeli – the big, ugly son of a bitch. It made Hazard depressed.

He shaved, finished dressing and left the hotel at noon. It was even hotter outside than he'd thought, an arid heat that reminded him of a long ago July in Needles, California, when he was on the road thumbing at cars all day and finally got a ride from a wife on her way to a Tiajuana divorce, so eager for freedom she couldn't wait.

He went up the short, steep rise to the plateau of the Pyramids. Immediately he was set upon by a swarm of *dragomans*, Arab guides with their camels and donkeys in bleached, dusty trappings, wanting to show him around for a price. One in particular was persistent, followed, kept selling and stopped him. Hazard asked him where the Sphinx was and gave him two dollars just for pointing the way.

The heat made it seem a longer walk than it was, and Hazard wished he'd thought to get some dark glasses because everything reflected the sun harshly. He passed by the much smaller satellite pyramids on the eastern side of the Grand one and continued down to the large excavated recess that held the Sphinx.

It didn't appear as impressive as he'd imagined. Not wise as legend had it nor as large and mysterious, really. Baking and biscuit-coloured, it looked like something that had come crumbling unsuccessfully out of an oven. Hazard remembered a sphinx was also an ancient symbol for female lust, but he saw no reason for that, unless it was the preying, ready-to-spring posture. Standing between its extended paws, he realized the reason for his apathy. He was just too distracted to appreciate anything at the moment. His mind was taken up with thoughts of Gabil and those canisters of nerve gas bearing the serial numbers like a trademark, *made in the U.S.A.*

By the time he returned to the hotel and air conditioning, perspiration was dripping from his nose and trickling down his back. He found the bar and ordered another of those generous gin-and-tonics. Except for the bartender and an older foursome at a table, he had the place to himself. Music was coming from somewhere. An old Beatles song. He dug the section of fresh lime from his glass and sucked on it without making a sour face. Those serial numbers came to mind again, kept intruding, the last three digits especially standing out from the others. Serial numbers. He supposed there was one on every bomb, every grenade, every weapon. And somewhere there were clerks who kept an accurate corresponding record, a death-dealer's catalogue.

Just for the hell of it, a small challenge, he started to try to translate the serial numbers of the canisters. USACC was obviously United States Army Chemical Corps.

After twenty minutes and another gin he felt he had most of it deciphered. United States Army Chemical Corps – Fort Detrick (Maryland) – December, 1970 – Batch number 2046.

USACC–FD–12–70–B2046–

But those last five digits:

ABV–10

had him stumped. Assuming v–10 represented the type of gas, why had they left out the x? Was it army shorthand or army oversight? But then, what did the AB stand for? What difference did it make, anyway?

He gave up on it, went up to his suite and decided on a bath in that big brass tub. He was in the water, observing his distorted, yellow image in the curvature of the tub when he got back to it again – because it was taunting, eluding him like a critical word in a *New York Times* crossword puzzle.

ABV–10

Look at it from a different angle, he told himself, a fresh approach. If he'd never heard of vx–10, what would he have thought? Well, b could stand for base, or battle, or booster, or biological. Only the last seemed plausible, although chemical
254

and biological were two distinct categories. CBW were initials he'd seen in articles, short for Chemical-Biological Warfare. A biological v–10 nerve gas didn't make sense. But he felt he was on the right track and should keep on it. He associated biological and got bacteriological, and then it occurred to him there probably wouldn't be an adjective in a serial number. The noun was bacteria. That could be. Assume it, work from that. What could the A stand for, an A-Bacteria? The first, and worst, one that came to him was Anthrax. Anthrax bacteria? Sure, why not?

But if it was anthrax bacteria the v–10 couldn't be a nerve gas. Not both. It had to be one or the other. Was that why the x was missing? If so, what did v–10 signify? The number 10 could be a rating or type designation. That would mean there were other types, a variety of them numbered from one up. A variety. Variety? Variant? Same thing. He settled for variety and put it in sequence:

Anthrax Bacteria Variety 10

He felt as if he'd accomplished something. But was it possible that Pinchon and the Arabs didn't have what they thought they had? When they'd retrieved the canisters from the ocean floor, in their hurry and eagerness, had they been misled by those last three digits? The United States had dumped all kinds of chemical and bacteriological stockpiles into the Canary Basin. The Arabs could have made that logical error.

So what? In many ways anthrax was even more horrible than nerve gas.

Anthrax, also called Black Bain, Charbon, Malignant Postule, Splenic Fever, Woolsorter's Disease. One of the most dreaded of all infectious diseases. Caused by a rod-shaped bacterium or spore, *Bacillus anthracis*. Infects the bloodstream. Can cause death within eighteen to twenty-four hours when inhaled.

Another ugly fact Hazard recalled about Anthrax – its extreme resistance. As a spore it could contaminate the earth, remain alive in the soil, and be capable of causing the disease for as long as a hundred years. The promised land could suddenly become a disappointment – a vast, diseased wasteland.

He felt futile. Nothing had been gained from his mental

efforts. Besides, he was probably wrong about the serial numbers. He had only been playing a game with himself, following a hunch.

At six o'clock a hotel boy delivered an envelope. It was from Gabil – the plan of the house and other useful information. Gabil had drawn, freehand but carefully, a detailed overhead view with everything indicated, including approximate measurements. He had marked Mustafa's room with a red circle. One notation said that no one was allowed in or out of the house from dark to dawn. Hazard examined the plan briefly and then tore it into small pieces that he flushed down the toilet.

At nine o'clock he sent to Keven.

His first message told her to stand by for further messages he would be sending every fifteen minutes exactly on the quarter hour.

For accuracy, he sent only four words at a time. He did it with confidence, drawing assurance from past successes, telling himself it was undoubtedly possible. His mind was lucid, his concentration good. Despite the pressure, or maybe because of it, he was able to superimpose and hold the required images in position for longer than before. It took him an hour and a half to complete the transmission, and not until he was done did he realize how much energy he'd used. It left him thoroughly drained.

He lay on the bed in the dark, his body sapped but his mind racing. He tried to bring his mind to rest, but it was charged with impressions of Mustafa, Pinchon, the canisters, the situation. A stray thought came through. It seemed only another piece of trivia from his mental storehouse. He passed over it but it returned for attention:

The disease anthrax may be contracted through the eating of inadequately cooked meat.

It set him to thinking in a new, possibly more hopeful, direction.

20

AT A FEW minutes to nine that night Keven was on a hillside rock a short distance from the Auberge des Noves.

She had returned to Avignon because she felt it would be easier for her to do her waiting there. Not that any place could really reduce her aloneness or her fear for Hazard, but at least there she had a residual of recent happiness with him that she could draw on.

Now that it was almost the hour they'd set for their nightly communion, she wondered what his message would be. Maybe he'd send her a romantic thought, like the one he'd sent from the plane, which she, out of hurt and pique, denied receiving. *Happiness was born a twin.* She'd liked that. Or maybe he might send something erotic, which wouldn't be at all bad.

It was time. She took a deep breath. The Provençal air offered the fragrance of wild-growing spices. Her mind began its usual race, all sorts of thoughts in rapid succession. She'd come to think of this phase as a sweeping away – a stirring up of old impressions like particles of dust in her mental atmosphere. Suddenly there was the clearing, the opening of the inner envelope to disclose a white whiter than any other white.

She got the message.

Realizing its tone of urgency, she hurried to the Auberge and when it was 9:15 exactly she was in the suite with pen and paper ready to record whatever came to her.

It didn't come with absolute precision, not as though she were a human teletype. It came in various ways and with different degrees of difficulty. Some parts of it graphically, in the form of pictures. Other parts letter for letter, spelling out. And some words came whole.

Altogether it was something like a rebus that she had to interpret. She wasn't sure of a couple of things but used common sense to fill in and construct a continuity.

ALERT ISRAELI INTELLIGENCE
PINCHON ARAB EXTREMISTS PLAN
VX—10 ATTACK GAS NOW CAIRO
TRANSPORT SOMEWHERE SUNDAY
ISRAEL TARGETS UNKNOWN

She printed it out neatly on a sheet of Auberge stationery, folded it once and took it downstairs. She found Monsieur Feldman alone at the reception desk. She said nothing as she handed the piece of paper to him. He read it without reaction.

'Should this mean something to me?' he asked politely.

Keven remembered Hazard's opinion about Monsieur Feldman's affiliation with Mosad. She had to depend on that now. 'Doesn't it?' she said.

He asked where she'd got this strange piece of information.

'From a travel agency in Cairo,' she said, surprised at how she sounded, very much like a regular spy. 'I assume you can make the necessary arrangements.'

Monsieur Feldman scanned the message again. After a thoughtful moment he looked up and told her yes.

Keven went back to her suite. For a while she sat there in the dark gazing out, her thoughts prayerlike, asking for her man's safety. Then, deciding she possibly hadn't done all she could, she placed a trans-Atlantic call to Kersh.

As soon as he finished talking with Keven, Kersh called DIA district headquarters. A secretary told him that Mr Richland wasn't in and wasn't expected until next week.

Was there any way of reaching Mr Richland?

No.

It was very important.

Mr Richland's orders were he was not to be disturbed except in case of extreme emergency. Was this an emergency?

Yes, but never mind, Kersh told her.

He called Washington, the Pentagon.

After several misconnections and long waits he finally got through to Mumford.

Mumford listened for only a few moments before interrupting. 'I'm in an important conference,' he said. 'If what you need is more than a yes or no you'll call back.'

258

'When?'

'Tomorrow.'

'This can't wait. It's vital that —'

'Call back,' Mumford said.

'Is there anyone else I can talk to?'

'I think not.'

'I'm coming down,' Kersh told him.

It was then almost five o'clock. Washington would be gone for the day by the time he got there. He took the shuttle at seven the next morning. He was at the Pentagon at nine. He got in to see Mumford at ten.

Mumford had a different office now, slightly larger than the previous one but no less sterile. Same cheap gold-fringed Stars and Stripes, same framed photographic line-up of Chiefs on a wall, except for Nixon, a new one of Nixon. Mumford himself had changed. He'd had his suits taken in and then gained back all the pounds he'd lost, so that now he couldn't even button up. He didn't stand for a handshake when Kersh entered because he had his trousers undone at the waist.

Kersh got right to the point by showing Mumford a typed out copy of Hazard's message. Mumfort mumbled the words aloud as he read them. 'Where'd you get this?'

Kersh told him.

'You put a man in there?'

'He's there,' Kersh said.

'Who? What's his name?'

'Hazard.'

Mumford cleared his throat. 'One of your telepathy spooks, I suppose.'

Kersh resented that.

Mumford explained that spooks was the normal term for agents. He asked Kersh, 'Is that how he got the message out, using telepathy?'

'Yes.'

Mumford seemed a bit relieved. A secretary came then with a cup of coffee, a heavy white G.I. cup. Asked if he wanted some, Kersh impatiently declined. Mumford took a swallow and placed the cup down on the message.

'You don't believe it,' said Kersh.

'Anything's possible. You know, of course, you were out of

line sending someone in without first getting an okay. Way out of line.'

'I didn't come down here to be chided like a schoolboy.'

'Just so you know.'

'What I want to know is what you're going to do about that.' Kersh indicated the message.

'Our Plans Section will get right on it. They handle this sort of thing.'

That sounded much too routine for Kersh. 'What will they do?'

'Well, seeing it's Middle East, chances are this won't be news to them. For obvious reasons we're tight in on that picture. Anyway, leave it to me.'

'I'm concerned about Hazard.'

'Naturally. He's in over his head. But don't worry, we'll handle it.'

As a final show of reassurance Mumford took a pair of rubber stamps from his middle desk drawer. He inked and slammed them on the paper above the message. One was ROUTE TO PLANS SECTION. The other was PRIORITY ATTENTION.

Kersh thanked him.

After Kersh's departure, Mumfort initialled a thick sheaf of intra-agency memos that his secretary brought in. Then he picked up the Hazard message and went over it again. He reminded himself that just the week before a white directive had come from the Chief regarding *Information Overkill.* Too much information was being collected by the various intelligence agencies, most of it was redundant and/or trivial. With all the new surveillance gadgets at work, such as the Project 674 Satellite and high-spying SR–71 jets, the intelligence community was being inundated with perishable, unsifted information. The Chief wanted less raw stuff and more analysis.

Mumford considered routing the Hazard message to the Information Sifting Unit for routine evaluation, but then ...

... well, for one thing, vx–10. That had to be an error. There was just no way anyone could get vx–10.

Also, there was this telepathy angle. What a crock.

Mumford decided it wasn't even worth feeding into the Possibility Computer. He crumpled the message and dropped it into his wastebasket.

The morning of that same Friday Hazard was up early.

He made out a list of the things he'd need. Then he went down to the lobby. At the desk he changed fifty British pounds into five hundred twenty-six Egyptian pounds and arranged for a car with an English-speaking driver.

A half hour later he was in downtown-Cairo traffic – crush of nervous taxis, impudent, overloaded buses, and pedestrians daring to dodge across for their lives.

At Ezbekyia Garden near the Opera House the driver pulled over. He gave directions to Hazard and said he would wait there, *effendi*.

Up a lane too narrow for cars, then right and left brought Hazard to a section of old Cairo known as El Muski. All along there were stalls and small shops, some no more than yard-wide slits between buildings. Barrow and cart vendors by the hundreds, selling all sorts of second-hand things. Motors, plumbing fixtures, electric fans, odd wheels, cooking pots, shoes, batteries. Hazard thought that even the food being sold there smelled second hand. By no means was it a fashionable bazaar, nor could it be called quaint or colourful. It was dirty, teeming and stinky.

In Shari' el Khiyamiya, Hazard came on to a stall that looked promising. It displayed a great variety of junk, all of it used, most of it stolen. The moment Hazard paused the fat stallkeeper came scurrying over. What had caught Hazard's interest was a strip of metal hanging high up. The stallkeeper got it down, handling it as though it were precious.

Hazard recognized it immediately as a piece of magnesium alloy – an extrusion about five feet long, six inches wide, with slightly raised edges like a shallow trough. It weighed only a few ounces. Despite its thin gauge it was stronger than steel, had no give to it at all. Hazard noticed Russian lettering stamped into the metal at one corner and guessed that the piece was intended for the fuselage of a jet fighter or bomber.

It would do perfectly, Hazard decided. He asked the stallkeeper how much.

The stallkeeper told him, '*Etnen guineh.*'

Hazard didn't understand. The stallkeeper showed him with two fingers. Two Egyptian pounds. Hazard agreed. The stallkeeper glanced upward to Allah and shook his head in disdain of anyone who didn't care enough to bargain. He

261

would have settled for half that, even less.

Now Hazard held up his fingers. He wanted six of these magnesium extrusions.

The stallkeeper understood and was momentarily at a loss. He had only this one. But he knew where he could get others. He rushed off and in a few minutes came back with five more of the same. Not precisely the same. Three were about a half inch less in width.

All the better, Hazard thought.

The stallkeeper bound the extrusions together with cheap string, and Hazard found his way back to the car.

Next stop was Hannoux, the large department store on Shari El-Tahrir, where Hazard bought:

   a long black caftan robe
   a black shirt
   a pair of tennis sneakers
   6 ordinary hot-water bottles
   4 crystal vases packed safely in polystyrene
   a ladies' compact containing black mascara

From there he was taken to a hardware store in the Bulaq district for:

   2 empty gallon cans
   100 feet of quarter-inch nylon line
   15 bolts and nuts
   an electric drill
   a set of metal-working bits
   a galvanized-tin funnel
   several jig-saw blades
   a can of flat black paint
   a paint brush
   a screwdriver
   a pair of pliers
   a toilet plunger

They then went to a used-car lot on the road to Alexandria, where Hazard bought a 1956 British-made Willys enclosed Jeep with four-wheel drive and special traction tyres for desert travel. Hazard took it for a short test drive, and, although considerable black smoke came from its exhaust which meant it was an oil eater – it ran pretty well for a seventeen-year-old.

Anyway, it should still be good for a sprint.

He paid the dealer six hundred dollars, drove the Jeep away and followed the hired car back to Mena House.

A hotel boy came out and carried Hazard's purchases up to the suite. All except the empty cans. Hazard took those to a gasoline station about a half mile down Shari Al Haram. He had the Jeep lubed, gassed, and its oil changed. He also filled the pair of gallon cans with gasoline.

When he got back to the hotel he took the cans up with him. The moment he entered the suite he noticed something new. In his absence the hotel had installed a television set. There was a note begging pardon for the inconvenience Hazard had presumably suffered until now without a TV.

It was quarter after five. He had a lot of work to do and was anxious to get at it. However his stomach was empty and complaining. He'd eaten nothing all day. Instead of ordering from room service he went down to the hotel restaurant for a thick steak and a double order of scrambled eggs. Steak and eggs, the traditional fare of boxers before big fights.

After the meal he stopped in at the gift shop off the lobby to buy a map of Egypt and a Zippo-type cigarette lighter that had the face of the Sphinx crudely painted on it. The woman behind the counter fuelled the lighter for him.

Back up to the suite.

Before starting he got organized, laid everything out on the floor. He selected the proper-sized bit and locked it into the electric drill. Using the arms of a chair for support, he measured, marked, and drilled three holes, left, right, and centre, a half inch from both ends of each of the six magnesium extrusions. He inserted the bolts to make sure they fit.

Next, he unpacked the vases. Placing them to one side, he removed the polystyrene from the cartons and took the chunks of that white, light stuff into the bathroom. Also the funnel, the hot-water bottles, the gasoline, and the toilet plunger. He kneeled down beside the bathtub and closed the drain.

First the polystyrene. He tore it into tiny shreds that he tossed into the tub. It covered the bottom of the tub with a four-inch layer. Then he poured in the gasoline. He used the toilet plunger to mash and stir until the mixture was a sticky

263

viscous substance. Over the tub as he was, the fumes got to him, made him a little dizzy. He had to leave the bathroom for a short breather.

Getting back to it, he inserted the funnel into the neck of one of the hot-water bottles. With a hotel water glass he transferred some of the substance from the tub to the bottle. When the bottle was plumped out full he screwed its cap in good and tight. They were common red-rubber hot-water bottles with a little loop at the bottom for hanging up. He filled all six of the bottles and still had some of the substance left over. He drained the tub and rinsed it, as well as the plunger and the funnel and the glass. An oily film stayed on everything, but he hadn't made too much of a mess.

Bathtub napalm.

He thanked his memory for the formula that he'd seen in one of those CBW articles.

It was now ten to eight.

Plenty of time.

He placed each of the magnesium extrusions diagonally upright against the bathroom wall. He painted their bottom surfaces and outer edges black. He also painted the sneakers. It was a fast-drying paint – dull, flat black. Keeping things neat he put the lid on the paint can and discarded it and the brush in the wastebasket.

It was getting dusky outside. He switched on the bed lamp and took a look at the map. He saw that the entire area west and northwest of the Pyramids was, as he'd thought, nothing but desert – the Sahara. His eyes drew a line directly northwest to the Mediterranean and hit on the coastal village of Sidi Abdel Rahman. Most of the coast along there was uninhabited. Hazard mentally x'd a spot ten miles east of Rahman. The next nearest place, he noticed, was El Alamein, the famous World War II battle site.

At nine o'clock he sent to Keven. Telling her once more to stand by for messages on the quarter hour. Again he sent only four words at a time. He kept the total message to twelve words so it required only three transmissions.

TELL ISRAELIS IMPERATIVE RENDEZVOUS
TOMORROW DAWN MEDITERRANEAN COAST
TEN MILES EAST RAHMAN

That was just in case, a way out for him if his luck held. For sure there'd be a lot of pissed-off Arabs on the lookout for him at the airport and all other usual departure points.

Which was also the reason he'd bought the Jeep. Now, he decided, it was time to attend to it. He went out to the parking area where he'd left it. At the end of the hotel drive he took a right and drove up to the plateau of the Pyramids. No one there now. He parked the Jeep out of sight on the west side of the Grand Pyramid between two of the many large humps of dirt that were the old tombs. He realized then how bright the night was with the moon flooding a silvery light, defining things even at a distance. It wouldn't help.

Returning to the suite he had some time to spare. He ordered up a couple of beers. The hotel offered Schlitz and Pabst but he decided to try an Egyptian brand called *Stella*. It was quite strong and had a strange liquorice flavour. Swigging straight from the bottle, he turned on the television. The show in progress was 'Peyton Place', and he got a laugh watching all those small-town mixed-up American characters emoting in Arabic. When that was over, in place of a commercial a woman commentator came on to extol the benefits of intra-uterine devices. With diagrams. After her came an old 'Bonanza'.

At eleven-thirty he got ready.

He put on the black shirt and the painted black sneakers. Then he cut several short lengths of nylon line and knotted them together to create a harness that went over both shoulders and around his chest and back. He tied the six hot-water bottles to it, so that he had one on each side, three behind, and one right front. That left room for the Llama and its holster.

He checked the Llama. It had a full clip. He took it off safety.

Six pockets: His jeans had four and the shirt two. Into them he put the bolts and nuts, jig-saw blades, pliers, screwdriver, mascara compact, Zippo lighter, his passports, money, and the key to the Jeep. He reserved the right front pocket for his special knife.

He tied the magnesium extrusions together and wrapped them in some of the store paper from his shopping. What remained of the nylon line, about eighty feet, he gathered into a

265

neat series of loops and hung from his belt. He rechecked to make sure the hot-water bottles were secure. Then he put on the black caftan robe. It was floor length and plenty loose all around. He felt bulgy but didn't look it.

He switched off the television, paused to guzzle the last of the beer, picked up the package of extrusions and went out.

He felt conspicuous going through the lobby but no one paid him any special notice. As far as they were concerned he was just another tourist gone native. As he left the hotel it occurred to him that he was beating them for the tab.

Down the road a short way, he crossed over to the golf course. No need to hurry, except to escape that part of himself telling him it was foolish to risk everything on little more than a hunch. He countered that with *there are no sure things* and other times when he'd gone against the form and won. Like that afternoon two years ago at Belmont when he'd bet it all on a maiden filly just because he'd liked the way she held her head, and she'd got out in front and gone wire to wire for him. He also thought maybe he wouldn't be doing this if he'd had some action lately. None for two weeks. Hell, how long can a boozer go without a drink?

He passed between two cypresses and there was the house, less than a hundred feet away. As shown on Gabil's plans it was large and enclosed all around by a fifteen foot wall. The wall was two feet thick. Set six inches above its top surface was an infra-red alarm system with small relay units spaced at regular intervals. Anyone trying to climb over would unknowingly break the invisible beam and activate the alarm, a wowing siren. There were also floodlights along the top of the wall, directed in and down. The house was situated well within the perimeter like an island within an island.

One thing at a time, Hazard told himself. He paced off forty yards along the west side and looked up. There was where he'd try to go over. He took off the robe.

Then he got out the mascara compact. His mouth was so dry he had to tongue his palate and gums to work up saliva. He spat on his fingers, rubbed them on the little black cake and then on his face, repeating that until his face, neck, ears, and hands were covered.

Kneeling, he unwrapped, untied, and separated the extrusions according to width. He connected one of each size with

266

the bolts and nuts, using the screwdriver and pliers to tighten as much as possible. Alternately adding a narrow and a wide, he soon had them all joined. He picked up the thirty-foot length they now created. It was light, but unwieldy.

He leaned it against the wall, so that one end hit about two thirds of the way up. Gauging from that, he lifted slowly until that end was where he wanted it, precisely on the upper outer edge of the wall. For a test he reached up where he could along the length of extrusions and hung all his weight from it. It was rigid. The lower end dug in and held in the sandy soil.

What he had was a ramp six inches wide going up at about a thirty-degree angle.

It turned out to be more difficult than he'd thought. He went up slowly, hesitating after each step to make sure he had balance before taking the next. He couldn't have done it in regular shoes, but the sneakers really grabbed.

As he climbed, more and more of the house came into view beyond the wall and then the compound around the house, brightly lighted. At the rear corner of the house, about seventy feet to his left, he saw an armed guard. A clutch inside cost him concentration. He wavered but managed to regain his balance.

A few more steps and he'd reached the top of the wall. He placed one foot on its outer edge, then the other foot. The advantage he had was knowing the infra-red beam was there, knowing exactly where it was. It gave him a clearance of six inches below to work with and nearly twelve inches on each side. He told himself to imagine the beam was a visible high-voltage wire, and stepped high over it to gain the inside surface of the top. Keeping in place, he turned to face out.

The next part was going to be tough. He couldn't squat because of the beam. He had to bend from the waist to reach the end of his makeshift ramp. Using both hands, he got a good grip on it and pulled it to him and up, more and more of it, hand over hand until he had enough to bring it up horizontally over his head. He executed another slow turn in place, to again be facing the house.

Gabil's plans had indicated a distance of at least forty feet all around from the wall to the house. Except here where the servant's quarters winged out some and were built lower, about equal in height with the wall. It was, according to

Gabil's plans, twenty-five feet from the wall to the flat roof of the servant's quarters.

Hazard fed out the length of extrusions, black side down, until it reached. Carefully he allowed the far end to rest on the roof. Then he placed his end on the inner top surface of the wall, between his feet.

In addition to the man on guard at the rear corner of the house there were two others at the front corner. All had automatic rifles slung to their shoulders. They were leaning, slouched, restless, smoking, apparently feeling secure – at least they weren't very alert. The compound was bright as day from all the lights along the wall. That, as Hazard had hoped, was in his favour. The lights mostly eclipsed anything above their downward glare. Hazard's painting the underside of the extrusions black and making himself as obscure as possible were extra precautions. The house, Hazard saw, was three tall stories with various levels and balconies, about thirty rooms.

He placed a sneakered foot on the narrow ramp and took the first step. Then another. He told himself to take it slow and sure, just keep going, but when he was halfway across he was pounding so hard inside he wanted to stop. He tried not to think about the consequences of falling; bullets from their automatic rifles chopping and burning into him. What was happening to his legs? He felt as though he didn't have legs, numb from the hips down. Still, his feet kept moving, short step after short step until he reached the roof.

He let out a long, quiet exhale. Had he held his breath all that time?

He decided there was less danger in leaving the ramp where it was. For his return trip. Stepping lightly, he went across the roof and over a railing to be on a wide exterior balcony. From that balcony he went up to another level and from there climbed on to the main roof. It was also flat.

Again from Gabil's plans, Hazard knew all he had to do was cross over and go down one level to reach Mustafa's room. Mustafa might be sleeping. With a window open. It would be easy. One silenced shot and it would be all over.

The notion tempted Hazard but he pushed it out of mind and went to the far rear edge to look down.

About six feet below was a spacious horizontal roof of glass, countless individual panes framed by wood. In most other parts of the world the frames would have been metal and the panes sealed tightly in; however, here where rain was a miracle there was no need for that.

Considerable dust had gathered and caked on the panes but Hazard could make out the lighted room beneath. No one there. It was, as Gabil had said, a swimming-pool area, all blue-and-white mosaic tiles. No water in the pool, instead thick planks forming a platform.

Resting on the platform ... the canisters.

Hazard swung his legs over and got a foothold on a small architectural outcropping. He gently lowered himself on to the glass roof, not sure it would take his weight. He felt it give a little, but staying on the edge where it was likely to be stronger he made his way to the corner. Just around the corner, he noticed, was an upright balcony column that might serve his purpose.

He took out the screwdriver, squatted and got to work. The putty around the panes was sun baked and old and under the blade of the screwdriver it came off in chunks. When he had removed all the putty from around the first frame he inserted the blade of the screwdriver between the glass and its frame and pried the glass up so his fingers could lift it out completely. He repeated that process until the six corner panes were removed.

He used a saw blade to cut through the frames. They were soft enough wood and the saw didn't make much noise, but it was tedious work. Hazard's impatience made him want to just break the frames out. However, he kept sawing and he'd soon created a large-enough opening. He removed the nylon line from his belt. A helpful idea occurred to him at that moment. He let the line go free and then regathered it in layers of equal-sized reverse loops. He inserted the end of the line through the loops and as he pulled it through and out it automatically formed knots every three feet. He'd learned that one night in a Lackawanna boxcar from a black ex-sailor whom he now thanked.

He tied the line securely around the balcony column before dropping it down through the opening.

Knot by knot he went down the line, about thirty feet to the tiled floor. He saw there was only one entrance to the room – large double doors that connected to the rest of the house.

The doors were closed now. Gabil had told him two guards were constantly posted outside the room. He had to be quiet. No mistakes.

The atomizing pods were off to one side. The canisters lay no more than a yard apart on the platform, their business ends pointed toward the shallow part of the pool nearest the door. Noiselessly, Hazard stepped on to the platform. He saw the serial numbers on the canisters, and hoped he was right. He took a quick look at the unlocking valves the Arabs had made. They were threaded into place. A simple lever on the valve would release the contents of the canisters. The thought of it gave Hazard a chill.

He untied one of the hot-water bottles, unscrewed its cap, and poured napalm over one of the canisters. The substance was thicker, more gluey now. It ran slowly down and around and under the cylindrical shape, adhering to the metal. He distributed the rest of his supply of napalm equally over the two canisters.

Anthrax bacteria cannot survive under conditions of extreme heat. That was what Hazard was counting on. That thought he'd had about inadequately cooked meat and anthrax had given him the idea.

The napalm would heat the canisters and their contents to a high degree. Because the canisters were made of metal they would be very conductive. The anthrax bacteria would be dead in minutes. Pinchon and his Arabs would have nothing. *If* the canisters contained anthrax. Heat would not affect vx–10.

He lit the Zippo, held it at arm's length.

The napalm burst into flame, immediately producing a heat so intense that Hazard had to back off. That canister ignited the other and then both were aflame along their entire lengths, underneath and all around. The flames went up, six, eight, ten feet. Black smoke spiralled.

A few minutes and the flames subsided, but Hazard could still see the heat simmering and swirling the air above the canisters.

A tinkling sound.

And another, louder.

Hazard looked up and realized what was happening. The extreme heat was causing the glass above to crack. Sections of

270

the panes were falling and shattering on the tiles. More and more glass came raining down.

The Arab guards had to hear it.

Hazard was in the shallow end of the pool. He'd never get up and out of the room in time. He crouched down close to the side of the pool, out of sight.

The double doors opened.

The two Arab guards saw the smouldering canisters. What was it, an accident? They took a couple of steps forward, their automatic rifles levelled and ready. Actually, they doubted anyone was there. They were more afraid of the canisters.

Hazard's first thought was to go for his Llama. The two Arabs were only a dozen feet from him. If he suddenly stood up he might get one. Might.

He glanced up at the canisters. Their valves were just out of reach. It was, he decided, a chance. At least it was a more useful way to go.

In a single swift motion he reached up with both hands; left and right he pulled down the levers on the valves.

Hiiiss . . .

The two Arabs knew what vx–10 could do. The sure agonizing death of it. They quickly retreated from the room, slamming the door shut behind them.

Hazard stood up. He was right in the stream of the expelling canisters. Their invisible pressurized contents struck and flowed around him.

He'd know in a minute if he'd been right or wrong, won or lost.

Be there, baby.

It was the longest minute of his life. He waited for the symptoms. His hands were trembling. He noticed the air smelled sour, stale.

More than a minute went by.

He felt all right. He felt fine, great to be alive.

The canisters were still harmlessly hissing away when he went hand over hand up the line and out on to the roof.

Below in the lighted compound there was now plenty of activity. Arabs running about, shouting. One voice stood out from the rest, issuing crisp, angry orders. Mustafa.

Hazard climbed up to the main roof. He went across and

looked over the edge. They'd discovered his ramp, were pulling it down, eliminating his only means of escape. They had him trapped, stranded on an island within an island.

He drew his Llama and went around the perimeter of the roof, looking down for any possible way. He saw the front gate to the compound, a formidable iron gate. It would be locked until dawn, as Gabil had said. Parked off to the right, well away from the wall, was a large vanlike truck. No doubt the one they'd intended to use to transport the pods. Two cars were parked directly in front of the house.

A muffled sound from the opposite edge. Hazard turned and immediately went stomach down on the roof. Two of them were climbing up the side from the balcony just below. They were about thirty feet from him, easily distinguishable in their light khaki clothes, outlined against the darker sky. Hazard, less visible, had the advantage. He aimed and squeezed. A heart shot to the one on the left. The other one managed to spray off some wild shots before Hazard put two into him.

All the lights went out.

Apparently it wasn't strategy by the Arabs because there was confusion below and guttural cursing. Hazard also heard the truck being started and put into gear. Its headlights went on as it moved swiftly across the front compound. When Hazard saw it deliberately bear down on two Arabs and send them sprawling he knew it had to be Gabil behind the steering wheel.

Full speed, the truck went around the corner of the house and down its longer side, hitting anyone who got in its way.

In the dark, Hazard crossed over the roof and swung down to the balcony. That offered access to another lower roof and another balcony, and finally he was on the roof of the servants' quarters. From there he saw Gabil jam the truck into the corner of the compound. There was the screaming of metal against concrete as he wedged the truck close up to the wall. The impact smashed out the headlights.

Hazard jumped and began running. He had about a hundred feet to go.

The Arabs were shooting in the direction of the truck. Hazard could hear their bullets plunking into its metal and ricocheting off the wall. He expected to be hit, but he reached the truck, climbed up on its hood, to its cab, to the top of its van. He pulled himself up to the top of the wall, bellied over and dropped to the outside ground.

Gabil came down hard beside him.

On the run Hazard told Gabil about the Jeep, and they headed for it. They were by no means in the clear. The Arabs were after them, coming over the wall and out the front.

Gabil led the way through the cypresses to the sandstone depression below the sheer ledge of the pyramidal plateau. A traversing path got them to that higher ground. Running full out over sandy rubble they reached the Grand Pyramid, the east base. The Jeep was stashed on the side opposite. They had to go around.

When they were part way along the north base, two cars pulled up sharply at the northwest corner. Gabil and Hazard reversed their direction, but by then the Arabs on foot were at the northeast corner.

Only one way for Gabil and Hazard to go.

Climbing the pyramid, Hazard discovered, was not nearly as easy as it looked, not a matter of merely stepping up from one level to the next. The stones were about waist high and he had to negotiate them childlike, alternately kneeing up and standing. By the time he'd clambered up twenty of the courses his shins were bruised and his knees skinned. Gabil, taller, had a somewhat easier time of it. On the twenty-fifth course he waited for Hazard to catch up.

'How many?' Hazard asked, meaning the men still after them.

'Eight, maybe nine.' Gabil had his revolver in hand.

They agreed to separate to improve their chances, go up another thirty or so courses, and then try to work their way around and down to the Jeep.

A bullet chinged off a rock a ways below. Another above. And only seconds after Hazard and Gabil resumed climbing, a barrage of bullets struck and sparked on the granite around the spot they'd just vacated. At least it meant the Arabs knew only approximately where they were, couldn't be certain because the moon was now to the south and down some and the north face of the pyramid was completely shadowed.

On the twenty-ninth course Hazard slipped, scraped his ankle at the bone so painfully it made his eyes water. Stopping a moment to rub away the hurt, he noticed movement off to his left a few courses down. One of them, but how far away? A hundred feet? Possibly double that. With the dark and only the pyramid's massive dimensions for comparison it was difficult to estimate.

He glanced to his right.

Another one. They were coming up on both sides. Out of range for the Llama. If they spotted him they could pick him off easily with their automatic rifles.

He slid up on to the next course and lay still, listening. The scuffing of their shoes on the rocks, climbing sounds. Suddenly, nothing. They'd stopped, were waiting, watching for him to make a move.

A volley of shots farther up the face and then two more different cracking ones followed by a short gasping cry and a tumbling sound. Had they hit Gabil? Hazard decided no, it hadn't been the kind of sound that would come from Gabil. Anyway, now it seemed no direction offered an advantage, and there was certainly no place to hide on this organized pile of rocks.

That thought caused Hazard to visualize more objectively where he was. On the north face, close to the original entrance, he decided. Was the entrance to his left or right?

Left was his hunch. But he figured luck had already been too good to him that night. Don't press it, he advised himself, and chose right. He squirmed along, not even lifting his head, feeling his way until he came to an edge, an abrupt drop-off.

He'd found the entranceway, located about fifteen feet in from the sloped face. Long ago, in removing the outer stones, a kind of topless landing had been formed, which served as an approach to the entrance. It was about a dozen feet wide, with walls on each side created by the ascending courses.

Hazard changed his mind, decided not to use that indentation for cover. It was too vulnerable, especially from above. No matter that it was dark and concealing; once he'd committed himself to it he would be trapped. They could just spray it with bullets. Besides, hiding there was too obvious an idea. They would surely think of it.

He would make sure they did.

Slowly he went up two more courses and over a short distance. Now he was directly above the entranceway. He still

274

had the pair of pliers in his back pocket. He took them out, held them over the edge and let them drop. They hit sharply on the stones of the entrance landing twenty-five feet below. Then he took out the Zippo lighter and waited.

He saw the two Arabs approaching, moving toward the entrance. They reached it and took positions left and right of the landing. Crouched there, they listened for another sound.

Hazard accommodated them, tossed the Zippo over the edge. Its loud clank on the stones below was like a cue for the Arabs to begin their performance. Simultaneously they stood and fired their automatic rifles from the hip in sweeping bursts, the bullets ricocheting within the hard confines of the dark entranceway.

The brief compressed sound of the silencer on the Llama was lost in all the noise. The range was only about twenty-five feet. Again Hazard went for the heart. First, the Arab on the left, then the one on the right, who was too caught up in his firing to notice the other man's death or prevent his own.

No time to count blessings. Hazard continued quickly up the north face, less cautious now. When he reached the forty-eighth course he was startled to see someone no more than ten feet from him, sitting in a slouch with legs over the edge. Just sitting there in the shadow as though relaxed, enjoying the view. Hazard thought it might be Gabil, because whoever it was had had an easy chance at him and not taken it.

'Gabil?'

No reply. The figure remained motionless. Hazard moved closer, was relieved to see it was one of the Arabs. Dead from a bullet that had gone in at the corner of the right eye.

A few courses farther up, Hazard came on another dead example of Gabil's marksmanship.

The odds were improving.

It was time to work his way around. He headed for the west face but stopped momentarily when he heard shots. They sounded far away. He recognized the staccato bursts of automatic rifles punctuated with individual, sharper reports. The firing seemed to last a long while. No doubt, Gabil was in the middle of it. Hazard plugged for him and, when the firing stopped, it occurred to Hazard that the silence afterward was death, one way or the other.

He continued along that course to the corner, where he

275

took a look around. The west face was raked bright with moonlight, and there, about a hundred feet away in clear view, was another of the Arabs. On a higher course, twenty or so above. He was headed for the north face.

Another decision for Hazard: Confront him or try to evade him? He chose the latter, thinking he might be able to do it if he timed it right.

He waited, concealed in shadow, until the Arab had reached the corner. Hazard's idea was to stay close to the vertical rock and go around at the exact moment the Arab's concentration was focused on safely managing the same thing in the opposite direction. They would, in effect, exchange places.

The moment came.

Hazard made his move.

Not quickly enough.

The Arab opened up on him, the bullets chinged close. All Hazard had succeeded in doing was to trade advantage for disadvantage. Now he was in the moonlight and his adversary had the dark. For cover, Hazard pressed full length into the inner angle of the course. The bullets chipped the edge no more than a foot above him. He couldn't stay there. His only chance was to get back to the dark side. Making things worse, he was also now headed in the wrong direction.

Keeping tight against the inner angle of the course, he used his hands to push and his toes to pull. It required all his strength to retreat inch by inch. Finally his feet felt the vertical edge of the corner, and then the edge was at his thighs, at his waist, and half of him went around and drew the rest of him around into the dark.

The Arab had been firing all the while, and was still firing sporadically at where Hazard had been. Which meant he hadn't noticed Hazard's reverse move. From the flames that spat from the muzzle of the automatic rifle, Hazard guessed the Arab was fifty to sixty feet away. Just barely within the Llama's range.

He waited until the Arab fired again and using that to gauge his target, he squeezed off two, three shots. Had he missed? Underestimated the range? He moved quickly up two more courses and squeezed off another round, another, and then he heard the Arab feel the pain and fall.

Hazard went up to him, saw he wasn't dead but doubtless would be soon. In any case, he was unconscious, out of it.

To hell with the west face, Hazard thought. He'd try the unexpected. He'd go all the way up and, according to how the situation appeared from there, choose the best way down. At the moment it seemed a good idea.

But not so good later on, after Hazard had climbed another fifty courses. He stopped, only halfway up, to catch his breath and convince himself he was doing the smart thing. His shins and knees didn't agree, but he resumed climbing. Instinctively, the farther up he went the less he felt in danger. And by the time he reached the one hundred fiftieth course he was almost taking the rocks like a regular any-day tourist.

He stopped again for a rest. It was then that it occurred to him that he had an empty clip in the Llama. Stupid. He released the empty and reached to the holster strap for his last remaining spare.

It wasn't there.

Somewhere along the way, probably during the belly-down crawling, it had worked itself loose and out.

Nothing to do about it now except curse the Pyramid. In the last hour he'd learned to hate this wonder of the world. It was punishing him.

Up he went, with his new problem of no ammunition. Now it was vital that he reach the top to determine which of the three moon-lighted faces offered a safer trip down. Keeping in mind that Gabil had said there were eight or nine Arabs at the start, the most there should be now was five – counting, possibly, Mustafa. At least one, perhaps two, would be at the base of the dark side because it was the obvious way. That left three for the other faces, one each. Unless during that lengthy volley of shots he'd heard earlier Gabil had managed to get another one or two. Maybe not, thought Hazard, maybe none, maybe Gabil had been subtracted.

On the hundred ninety-ninth course, just two from the top, Hazard paused again. He was tired, breathing hard and feeling the climb in his legs, which were rubbery and aching. He sat for five minutes, then went to the top.

It was a fairly level platform about forty feet square. Nothing of interest there, just more rocks dull and worn from exposure and the tramplings of millions of sight-seers. He went

277

first to the east edge, looked down and saw no one. He crossed over for a look down the west face, which also appeared empty of any sign of life. That made him all the more uneasy about the south face. He cautiously approached that edge. Coming right up the middle, now only about twenty courses from the top, was Mustafa. Alone. On the hunt with an automatic rifle. He hadn't seen Hazard.

The best Hazard could do was to try to hide. He quickly went to the dark side and down one course. Again he stretched out and wedged his body along the inner angle formed by the step of the rocks.

He soon heard Mustafa climb up on to the platform, breathing heavily. After a moment he heard Mustafa's footsteps, and judging from them, knew he'd gone over to survey the west face. Then across to the east.

The north, the dark face would be next. Hazard wedged even tighter into the shadowed angle as the footsteps headed his way, drawing closer. Suddenly, there was Mustafa standing on the edge above. Hazard took shallow, short, noiseless breaths.

All Mustafa had to do was look directly below. Even dark as it was there, chances were he'd notice Hazard. Mustafa's eyes scanned and strained to make out the courses farther down. Literally overlooking Hazard, he turned and walked from that edge.

What Hazard next heard was the familiar scratch and flaring of a match. Supporting himself with one arm, he slowly raised up, kept his head horizontal and brought one eye just above the level of the platform.

Mustafa was faced two-thirds away, having a smoke, the first in over an hour. For the moment the need for nicotine took precedence; he would also take the opportunity to reload the rifle. It had to be near empty by now. He altered his hold on it, pressed the release and jerked the thirty-shot magazine free. He shoved it into his left jacket pocket. He had two spare magazines in the right.

Hazard had no time to consider his next move. Almost as a reflex he leaped up and went for Mustafa.

For that second or two the rifle was useless. Mustafa managed to get the full magazine from his pocket but he was only close to snapping it into place when Hazard hit him.

278

He hit him with a head thrust, came at him fast, lowering his head at the last moment to catch Mustafa exactly front centre between the curves of the ribs. The impact drove Mustafa back and down. The rifle flew from his grasp.

Mustafa didn't try to retrieve it. He also didn't give Hazard a chance to push his advantage. In a single, swift motion he recovered and came up. With a knife.

The sight of it backed Hazard off. He dug quickly into his pocket for his special knife. The blade flicked out. He'd wanted a confrontation, but not this.

Mustafa had good reason to be confident. He'd learned to fight with a knife almost before he'd learned to eat with his left hand. He took his stance – a crouch with knees bent slightly for spring, feet apart and flat so that he could shuffle and more surely feel the surface beneath them, arms at chest level, extended to about half their reach. He circled Hazard, who stayed in place, merely turning defensively to keep Mustafa in front of him.

Hazard's mouth was dry and his stomach felt as though it were cringing into a hard ball. He tried to recall his instructions, theories, hours of serious but not so deadly practice at knife fighting. This was different.

Mustafa stalked around, gripping his knife lightly, like an artist would a brush. He dabbed the air with it, painted the air with little intricate, distracting designs.

Don't look at his knife, Hazard warned himself, watch his eyes.

A sudden move by Mustafa, a sort of zig-zagging lunge with a swipe to it.

Hazard went up on his toes, arched, pulled his midsection in.

Not soon enough. It felt like a fine, white-hot wire had been drawn across his chest.

'*Weld l-qáhba!*' – son of a whore – Mustafa said, adding insult to injury.

Hazard didn't know how badly he'd been cut but he could feel the blood running down. Desperation made him go on the offensive. He lunged forward, slashed, but Mustafa easily avoided his pass. Hazard realized then he couldn't win on these terms. No way.

Mustafa continued his circling stalk. '*L-ihûdi hallûf!*' – Jew pig. He would, he thought, toy with Hazard, prolong it, carve Hazard into submission, weaken him with loss of blood, and then, when Hazard was down, helpless, and asking for his life, he'd end it. Bedouin style. By severing Hazard's spinal cord.

Hazard concentrated on Mustafa's eyes. He saw them tighten just slightly, perhaps telegraphing the start of another lunge. He'd have one chance.

He straightened and kept one leg perpendicular while he swung the other out in a swift semicircle. The side of his foot connected with Mustafa's thrusting forearm, parrying Mustafa's knife hand, sending it upward and away. In almost the same motion Hazard snapped that foot down and shifted his weight forward on it. He came in low, bringing his knife up. A diagonal stab.

The point went into Mustafa just below the right rib cage. The moment it met resistance the six-inch blade activated, rotated, spun in through skin and fat, bored in through muscle and vital organs, blood vessels and arteries. To the hilt.

Mustafa's neck stiffened and his chin went up. Hazard caught a glimpse of Mustafa's disbelieving expression. A protesting grunt came from the oval of Mustafa's mouth just before he collapsed backward over the edge of the south face and tumbled deadweight down about forty courses.

Hazard controlled the urge to throw away the knife. He retracted its blade and put it back in his pocket. His wound was burning. He tried to determine how bad it was but really couldn't. From the pain and his shirt sopped sticky with blood, he knew it was more than a scratch. He picked up Mustafa's automatic rifle, found the magazine, snapped it into place, and started down the west face.

No trouble on the way down, maybe they were all dead or gone. The Jeep was where he'd left it. Gabil was in the passenger seat.

'Mustafa?' Gabil said.

Hazard nodded decisively as he got behind the steering wheel. He was relieved to see Gabil, genuinely pleased. It now looked as though they both might make it. The moment called for some show of camaraderie and, soon after they were under way, Hazard extended his hand, palm up. Gabil wasn't familiar with the new American custom of a palm slap
280

for well done. His huge hand enclosed Hazard's and gave it a couple of shakes.

Landsmen, thought Hazard. It was a good feeling. He told Gabil about the rendezvous near Rahman.

Gabil wanted to know how he'd managed that.

Hazard explained as briefly as possible, self-conscious about how farfetched it must have sounded to him. He expected Gabil to be incredulous but all the Israeli said was, 'Keep the moon over your left shoulder.'

By then they were well out on the desert, with the headlights finding nothing but the endless beige of sand. Seldom a flat stretch, mostly dunes and hollows, one after another. The grind of the Jeep's transmission and the repetition of its rather unhealthy engine added to the monotony.

'What will you do when you get home?' Hazard asked.

Gabil didn't reply.

Hazard glanced over and saw Gabil was slouched down, chin to chest, apparently dozing.

Hazard thought of the answer to his own question. Gabil's days as an agent for Mosad were over. Now that his cover was blown he'd no longer be of any use to that organization; he'd be too easily recognizable. Would Gabil go back to the army, or to his original ambition and be a teacher? Probably both. Fighter and teacher. Yes, in Israel he would be both. Hazard decided he wanted to keep in touch with Gabil; maybe even write letters.

Crest of a dune ahead. And then there was an unexpectedly steep drop off. Hazard braced himself for it and noticed Gabil didn't try to hang on. Gabil lurched forward and stayed slouched against the dashboard.

Hazard asked was anything wrong.

No answer. No movement.

Gabil was dead, shot twice in the lower part of his back. He hadn't complained, not even mentioned it. Maybe he'd thought he could last the trip or more likely, he'd known he couldn't and at least wanted to be headed toward home.

Hazard decided he'd try to take Gabil home, not leave him in this enemy land if he could help it. He pulled Gabil back to the seat so that he appeared more comfortable.

It was half past four. Dawn was only an hour or so off. No way of making it to the coast by then – the rendezvous time he'd sent to Keven. The eastern horizon was already hinting orange.

He still had fifty miles to go when the sun came up. And it was much higher, creating a bright, hot morning when Hazard saw a vast field of white military crosses in the distance. El Alamein. Sown with the lives of thousands, but barren ground, bleached and deathly dry.

A short way farther on was the coastal road, a black, incongruous ribbon. Hazard crossed over it and after five miles more there was the Mediterranean. He concealed the Jeep in the dunes.

Getting out, standing for the first time in hours, his head felt light, his legs heavy. Everything seemed to be tilting and he was suddenly nauseated, had to use the fender of the Jeep to steady himself. Blood had seeped down and saturated the waistband of his jeans. He was very thirsty.

He surveyed the beach. It was deserted, no sign of anyone having been there recently. He'd have to negotiate a fairly high embankment to get down to the water.

Every movement required extreme effort. He assumed that was from loss of blood and delayed shock. He got the automatic rifle from the back and placed it on the hood. Then he went around, opened the door and squatted to pull Gabil over and out. He got his shoulders and back under Gabil's body, but it seemed he'd never be able to rise with all that additional weight on him. He thought of having to leave Gabil there and, determined not to, he slowly straightened up. One hand helped balance Gabil. The other took up the rifle. Hunched over, wobbly, hardly able to lift his feet, he went down the crumbling incline and across the wide beach to a large, jutting rock at the water's edge. He dropped Gabil in the shade of it and fell to the wet-packed sand.

He closed his eyes, but when he felt himself slipping away into a deep, red vortex he opened them, forced them wide open, blinked and shook his head sharply to try to clear it. The day had seemed stark clear to him before, but now there was a haze. Caused by the sea?

Five minutes past nine.

Maybe the Israelis would come back for another look. A final onceover before giving up. Ten miles east of Rahman. Hell, Hazard realized, he could be twenty miles east for all he knew, way off the mark. Probably the rendezvous message hadn't even got through. Stupid of him to have put that much faith in it. Telepathy. A mental game, that's all it was. Unpredictable, tenuous. Who could seriously believe in it, count on it? He had and he was going to die alone here on a desolate North African beach. Sure as hell.

And for what?

He gazed over at the late Abraham Ben-David.

The tide was coming in. Hazard felt it reach his feet, cold. It lapped up. Was that how it would be? A cold sort of drifting away?

Thought of his father and Carl. Ironic that his father would never know how and why he'd died, would never get to enjoy the pride of knowing. As for Carl, maybe somehow Carl had been with him all the way.

Saving best for last, his thoughts went to Keven. Times with her crowded up. Now he knew they were his only true times. Only with her had he ever, ever been touched and reached.

He raised his head and shoulders, his body went rigid, and his hands at his sides fisted in protest.

No use. He lay back.

Keven. How much she'd meant to him, really. Much more than he'd ever told her. She must have known. But ...

Keven, if you were here now I would tell you. I would hold me to you. I would say it over and over into your mouth until I was out of breath. I would.

He felt the same sense of futility he'd known when Carl had died. The same impotence from not being able to say what had been left unsaid. Was there a way to say it now?

He fixed his mind on the words, making them the image that he desperately wanted to send. Detaching his awareness of everything else – the pain of his wound, the beach, the water, oncoming death – he visualized Keven's eyes, their special blue with slivers of silver.

Her eyes.

The image.

As he saw it.

As she would see it.

With her eyes.

The image.

It was not difficult for him to bring the two together. No strain to keep them simultaneous in his concentration. They seemed eager to merge and remain one.

Keven and *I love you.*

He prolonged the experience, finding it pleasant. But a sound interrupted.

Incredible sound.

A camouflaged helicopter was coming in low over the water.

21

AFTER TEN days in Tel Aviv.

Having been sutured, transfused, fed and rested back into excellent condition, Hazard was now on the way to reunion.

A sign said only sixty-five kilometres to Avignon.

To hell with the rain that had just started coming down hard. Hazard floored the accelerator pedal of the rented car. He was going to surprise Keven. She wasn't expecting him until the day after tomorrow.

Earlier that afternoon at Cap Ferrat the sun had been out. He'd gone to the villa to settle with Pinchon, found the Frenchman and Catherine out by the pool, just the two of them. Pinchon sitting on the edge, with his feet in the false-blue water and a mirror up to his face, applying an estrogenic-placenta cream to ward off smile lines and crows' feet. Catherine, nearby, sunning nude on a soft-cushioned lounger. Pinchon, despite his tan, went white, sure that he was seeing his death when he saw Hazard.

Except for Hazard, Pinchon was in the clear. The useless canisters had been thrown back into the sea. There was no evidence, and no one to implicate him. Mustafa was dead. Colonel Bayumi, Brigadier-General Fahmi, and the others involved would not make trouble for themselves. Of course, Israeli Intelligence, Mosad, would keep a close eye on him, but Pinchon doubted it would order its anti-terrorist agents to take action against him. Hazard was the only real threat.

Pinchon got up and was calling for help when Hazard hit him the first time. Catherine said nothing, did nothing. While Pinchon cried out and tried to protect his face by covering it with his hands, Catherine turned over to bake evenly.

When it was over, when Pinchon's nose was fractured, split open and laid like a flap on his cheek, when Pinchon's jawbone was broken and out of line, when Pinchon's eyes were beaten shut and the ridges of his brows gashed deep enough to scar, Catherine still remained unmoved.

Blubbering, bloody Pinchon. Hazard looked down on him

and told him, 'Get a plastic surgeon, have him fix it. I'll be around to mess it up again.'

That had caused Catherine to smile.

Now, only twenty-five kilometres to Avignon and dark enough for headlights.

Hazard wondered what Keven would be doing when he got there. He pictured her looking out at the rain, munching on pumpkin seeds and raisins and wishing time would hurry.

His own eagerness made him glance frequently at the kilometre indicator. The last ten seemed like a thousand, but finally the turn-off was just ahead. He slowed to take it.

And there she was.

Just standing there, waiting, under a dripping tree at the foot of the hill. She was drenched, her wet blouse adhering, her hair soaked flat to her head.

'Nasty night,' she said, getting in.

No surprise. No big hello, or big hello kiss, or anything, as though he hadn't even been away. She couldn't possibly have known he was coming. He still didn't want to believe she was *that* tapped in on his mind, although . . .

He drove up to the Auberge.

'My timing was slightly off,' she said.

. . . although, if she was, thought Hazard, at least he'd never have to ask for certain things.

Up in the suite she went immediately into the bathroom to take off her wet clothes. He sat in a chair, waiting.

'Julie had the baby,' she said from in there.

'You heard from Kersh?'

'This afternoon. They had a girl.'

She came out towelling her hair. 'We've got real rain on the roof tonight. How about that?' She stood before the dresser, her back to him, seemingly preoccupied with getting her hair dry.

He wanted her to come to him, deliver herself, bring her soft, lean body to him. He sat still, then without a word got up and went to her, put his arms gently around her from behind.

Now was the time to tell her.

'By the way,' she said, smiling, turning within his embrace so they were pressed front to front. 'I got your last message.'

286

All-action Fiction from Panther

THE IPCRESS FILE	Len Deighton	50p	☐
AN EXPENSIVE PLACE TO DIE	Len Deighton	50p	☐
DECLARATIONS OF WAR	Len Deighton	35p	☐
A GAME FOR HEROES	James Graham*	40p	☐
THE WRATH OF GOD	James Graham*	40p	☐
THE KHUFRA RUN	James Graham*	40p	☐
THE SCARLATTI INHERITANCE			
	Robert Ludlum	60p	☐
THE OSTERMAN WEEKEND	Robert Ludlum	50p	☐
THE MATLOCK PAPER	Robert Ludlam	60p	☐
THE BERIA PAPERS	Alan Williams†	50p	☐
THE TALE OF THE LAZY DOG	Alan Williams†	50p	☐
THE PURITY LEAGUE	Alan Williams†	50p	☐
SNAKE WATER	Alan Williams†	50p	☐
LONG RUN SOUTH	Alan Williams†	50p	☐
BARBOUZE	Alan Williams†	50p	☐
FIGURES IN A LANDSCAPE	Barry England	50p	☐
THE TOUR	David Ely	40p	☐
THEIR MAN IN THE WHITE HOUSE	Tom Ardies	35p	☐
COLD WAR IN A COUNTRY GARDEN			
	Lindsay Gutteridge	30p	☐
KILLER PINE	Lindsay Gutteridge	50p	☐
LORD TYGER	Philip José Farmer	50p	☐

*The author who 'makes Alistair Maclean look like a beginner' (*Sunday Express*)

†'The natural successor to Ian Fleming' (*Books & Bookmen*)

All these books are available at your local bookshop or newsagent; or can be ordered direct from the publisher. Just tick the titles you want and fill in the form below.

Name ....

Address ....

....

Write to Panther Cash Sales, PO Box 11, Falmouth, Cornwall TR10 9EN
Please enclose remittance to the value of the cover price plus 15p postage and packing for one book plus 5p for each additional copy. Overseas customers please send 20p for first book and 10p for each additional book.
Granada Publishing reserve the right to show new retail prices on covers, which may differ from those previously advertised in the text or elsewhere.